ALSO BY ESMERALDA SANTIAGO

Nonfiction

The Turkish Lover

*Las Mamis: Favorite Latino Authors Remember
Their Mothers* (coeditor)

Almost a Woman

*Las Christmas: Favorite Latino Authors Share
Their Holiday Memories* (coeditor)

When I Was Puerto Rican

Fiction

América's Dream

CONQUISTADORA

CONQUISTADORA

A novel

ESMERALDA SANTIAGO

Alfred A. Knopf   New York   2011

THIS IS A BORZOI BOOK
PUBLISHED BY ALFRED A. KNOPF

Knopf, Borzoi Books, and the colophon are registered trademarks of
Random House, Inc.

Grateful acknowledgment is made to New Directions Publishing Corp.
for permission to reprint an excerpt from "Adam" by William Carlos
Williams from *The Collected Poems: Volume I: 1909–1939*,
copyright © 1938 by New Directions Publishing Corp.
Reprinted by permission of New Directions Publishing Corp.

Library of Congress Cataloging-in-Publication Data
Santiago, Esmeralda.
Conquistadora : a novel / Esmeralda Santiago. — 1st ed.
p.   cm.
ISBN 978-0-307-26832-7
1. Women plantation owners—Fiction. 2. Sugar plantations—
Fiction. 3. Plantation life—Fiction. 4. Spanish—Puerto Rico—
Fiction. 5. Puerto Rico—History—19th century—Fiction. I. Title.
PS3569.A5452C66 2011
813'.54—dc22
2010051324

Jacket art: *Fuensanta* by Julio Romero de Torres Córdoba. Courtesy of
Sotheby's Picture Library, private collection, Madrid
Jacket design by Carol Devine Carson

Manufactured in the United States of America
First Edition

For Lucas and Ila

Underneath the whisperings
of tropic nights
there is a darker whispering
that death invents especially
for northern men
whom the tropics
have come to hold.

—William Carlos Williams, "Adam"

Conquistadora

EL ENCUENTRO/THE ENCOUNTER: NOVEMBER 19, 1493

———◆◆◆———

They came from the sea, their battered sails and black hull menacing the indigo horizon. The vessel was many times taller and longer than the people's canoes and from them came the stench of unwashed bodies and pine tar. The men who dropped from the ship were monstrous creatures with shiny carapaces on their chests, upon their heads, and around their arms and shins. They carried spears, flags, and crosses.

The people of Borínquen were afraid to reveal themselves because their villages had been ravaged so many times that they knew nothing good ever came to their shores unbidden from the sea. The mighty goddess Guabancex often unleashed *huracán* winds and heavy rains from the ocean to sweep away their *bohíos,* flood their cassava plots, and change the course of rivers. Fearsome *caribe* warriors paddled their long canoes to raid their land, steal their food, kidnap their women, and slaughter their men.

Although they were frightened, *borinqueños* were a brave, hospitable, and hopeful people. They called to Yucahú, the mighty god of the seas, to protect them from horrors delivered from the ocean. Then they emerged from the forests.

"Taíno," the *cacique* greeted the men from the ship with the word meaning "peace," even though armored men who carried weapons seemed anything but peaceful.

The sailors looked at the *borinqueños* as if they'd never seen humans. They gaped at the tattooed and pierced bodies, and swept their eyes over the women with an especial hunger. They stared at the *cacique*'s feather headdress, at the golden disk he wore on his breast, at his gold bracelets, and at the small nuggets knotted with cotton thread around the warriors' necks and arms. The *cacique* was a shrewd leader and noticed the covetous glances. He told his *borinqueños* to give the men the adornments given to them by Atabey, the goddess of sweet waters and of rivers. The *cacique* also gave away hammocks woven by the most gifted weavers in the village, baskets full of cassava bread, sweet potatoes, peanuts, guavas, and pineapples. The *borinqueños* filled barrels with clean drinking water. With these gifts, the *borinqueños* thought, these men encased in metal who rattled every time they moved would climb into their enormous sailed canoe and disappear into the same horizon that had delivered them, hopefully never to return.

They did leave on that November day, but waves of them came back, their vessels slicing across the horizon. Wherever they landed, they demanded tribute from the *caciques* and the *cacicas,* who offered more clear water, ever-larger baskets filled with food, the best hammocks, and more nuggets. The ships would leave. And more would return.

Because the first sound from the mouths of the *borinqueños* was the word *taíno,* the men from the sea thought the people were describing themselves and renamed them for the word "peace." The men from the sea also renamed Borínquen, meaning Great Land of the Valiant and Noble Lord, as San Juan Bautista, meaning Saint John the Baptist. They came with weapons that severed a man's head in one stroke. They brought animals that *borinqueños* had never seen: horses, pigs, hounds, goats, cattle. They trampled through the yuca fields, smoked the people's tobacco, and raped the women.

The *caciques* and *cacicas* rallied the people. They charged their warriors to poison their arrows so that when the tips entered the men's unarmored flesh their blood would flame and boil inside their bodies. When a warrior dropped his heavy club over an unhelmeted head, the *macana* crushed his opponent's skull as easily as if it were a calabash. They held the newcomers' faces down in the clear, fresh water of Borínquen's rivers until their bodies went limp. The women fed them unprocessed cassava to churn their guts into mush.

The men from the sea were too strong, their weapons lethal. They brought enormous dogs to chase and herd the people from their villages, and after a man in heavy robes sprinkled the *borinqueños* with water and made perplexing gestures over them, they changed the *borinqueño* ancestral and clan names to their own language. They forced the women to cover their breasts, their bellies, the hallowed parts from which their children reached into the sun. They called themselves *católicos;* they called themselves *españoles;* their chiefs called themselves *caciques,* even though none were born in Borín-quen from *borinqueñas.*

Their most famous chieftain was Juan Ponce de León, who lined up the *borinqueños* and pointed at this one, at that one, at the other. He separated men from women, mothers from children, elders from their families. He formed them into groups. Then his men led the *borinqueños* from their villages to other parts of the island. They enslaved the *borinqueños* to labor in waist-deep water in the island's rivers, and forced them to rip from Atabey's pebbled, sandy veins the shiny nuggets she'd so willingly gifted before the men came from the sea.

The *borinqueños* began to die from diseases they'd never known and from infected wounds opened on their backs and arms and legs from whips they'd never experienced. They died in rebellions, their numbers easily overwhelmed by men on horses carrying sharp swords. They died from exhaustion in the mines processing the shiny nuggets into blocks. They died from terror. They threw themselves into the chasms above the highest peaks of the mountains. They drowned in the sea. Sharks attacked them when rafts broke up as they paddled, searching for another island where they could rebuild their vegetable plots and their communities. They fled into the mountains, where they were chased and captured by hounds. They died of humiliation after hot irons branded their foreheads. They died in such numbers that their language began to die, too, and the names of their ancestors and most of their gods were silenced from tongues. The *borinqueño* culture, traditions, and history were chronicled by the conquerors who called them savages, who misinterpreted their customs and rituals, who told them that if they didn't renounce their own gods, they would live in flames in the next life.

Borinqueñas were made to lie with the newcomers because the men from the sea didn't bring their own women, and another race grew from their children. The last full-blooded *borinqueño* saw another kind of people walking upon Borínquen's ground—men, women, and children kidnapped, chained, and transported on groaning ships across the ocean from lands beyond the dawn. Like the *borinque-ños,* they knew the ways of the forest, but they were darker skinned and spoke different languages. They, too, were branded, dragged, pushed, and whipped to work in the rivers, and when the goddess Atabey refused to give up more gold, the black men were made to cut down trees, to build dwellings made from wood and from stone for their masters. The sacred yuca fields were razed so that other crops more amenable to the conquerors could grow, because even though there was no more gold in Borínquen, men, and even women, kept coming from the sea.

I

CONQUISTADORES
1826–1849

DE MÚSICO, POETA Y LOCO,
TODOS TENEMOS
UN POCO . . .

———◆———

We're all a bit of a poet,
a bit of a musician,
a bit mad . . .

CONQUISTADORES

———◆———

Ana was a descendant of one of the first men to sail with the Grand Admiral of the Ocean Sea himself, don Cristóbal Colón. Three men on her father's side were among the first conquistadores, Basque sailors with intimate knowledge of the sea and fearless curiosity about what lay beyond the sunset. Two of her Larragoiti ancestors died at the hands of fierce *caribes* on Hispaniola. The third, Agustín, distinguished himself as a bold civilizer and Christianizer and in 1509 was rewarded with an entire village of natives on the island of San Juan Bautista.

The *taínos* collected enough gold to allow Agustín to return to Spain, where, for reasons the family never learned, he chose to retire in Sevilla rather than in his ancestral village. He also changed the spelling of his surname, dropping the final *i* and substituting it with a *y,* a letter that didn't exist in the Basque language. Ana surmised that for Agustín, the homely *i* at the end of Larragoiti was not quite as grand as the looped, curlicued *y* that bespoke affluence and masculine aggression. Subsequent generations of Larragoity sons and nephews sailed down the Río Guadalquivir from Sevilla, hoping to repeat Agustín's success. According to Ana's father, Gustavo, there were Larragoity descendants in Mexico, Peru, and Venezuela, all said to be rich beyond imagining.

On the Cubillas side, her mother, Jesusa, boasted three soldiers, two Franciscan friars, and three merchants whose journals and letters describing the rigors and rewards of settling in the West Indies were passed down the generations, read and discussed at solemn gatherings. Cubillas descendants, too, were scattered all over the New World, their fortunes secure, and said to be among the leading families of the Antilles.

The feats over man and nature that brought such pride, however, were speculation. Neither the Larragoity nor Cubillas families in Spain knew for certain what happened to the conquistadores, merchants, and *religiosos* after 1757, when letters from the last correspondent in the colonies, a tobacco grower in Cuba, stopped. Their written exploits, by then mythologized and exaggerated so that they bore little resemblance to the firsthand accounts, were kept in safe boxes in the homes of the current patriarchs of the Larragoity and Cubillas clans.

Their wealth, pride, and honor depended on male heirs, but Gustavo and Jesusa buried three consecutive sons within weeks of their birth. In the seventh year of their marriage, and after a day and a half of labor, Jesusa delivered a healthy girl on July 26, 1826, who looked nothing like her living relatives, all of whom were tall, sturdy, light-haired, light-eyed, long-nosed men and women whose supercilious lips curled in disdain at the smallest provocation. If Jesusa hadn't suffered for twenty-nine hours to deliver her into the world, she wouldn't have claimed the small-boned, black-haired, black-eyed girl who looked like no one but the portrait of don Agustín dominating the gallery. Jesusa named her Gloriosa Ana María de los Ángeles Larragoity Cubillas Nieves de Donostia, called Ana in praise of the Saint protectress of pregnant women, on whose Day Ana was born. A sturdy Gypsy was hired to nurse her, since it was unbefitting for elite women to offer their own breasts to their children. Ana thrived and survived beyond a few days, then three months, then six, then nine, and by her first year was wobbling and lurching from her nurse's arms to those of her maid.

Jesusa doubled her prayers and charity work, hoping that Santa Ana would intercede on her behalf so that she'd conceive again, this time a boy. But her prayers faded into the quivering air before her candles, and her womb remained fallow. Jesusa blamed Ana as the reason she was barren, and whenever she looked at the girl, she saw her vanished hopes and her own failure to deliver an heir. With no male issue, Gustavo Larragoity Nieves's homes, furnishings, and inherited wealth would, upon his death, pass to his younger brother, whose fertile wife had brought forth three healthy sons.

From infancy, her parents consigned Ana to North African maids. Almost as soon as Ana was used to one, Jesusa dismissed her and replaced her with another. She often complained to her friends that it was impossible to find reliable servants.

"We should have never freed the slaves in Spain," she said, and her friends agreed.

Spanish slaves had been captured in wars or kidnapped from Africa and Spanish America. The practice was abolished in Spain in 1811, although not in its colonies. Nearly two decades later, Jesusa was still angry that her personal maid, Almudena, who had been with her family three generations, disappeared as soon as news arrived that slaves were free, never to be seen nor heard from again. Jesusa was imperious and demanding, and by the time Ana was five years old, she understood why Almudena had left as soon as she could.

Ana's earliest memories were of being summoned to Jesusa's parlor, where she had to impress her mother's visitors with pretty curtsies and good manners. She was allowed a few minutes with the ladies, nearly smothered by their ruffles and tiers of shushing skirts. They ignored her almost as soon as she curtsied, and talked over her head until Jesusa remembered she was still there and ordered the maid to take Ana away.

At ten, Ana was sent to the same convent school in Huelva where Jesusa was educated near the Cubillas estate. Some of the nuns in the Convento de las Buenas Madres remembered Jesusa as a girl and unfavorably compared Ana to her mother, who, according to them, was everything Ana was not—devout, obedient, humble, and demure. Unlike Ana, Jesusa was never forced to chew a hot pepper because she stumbled over *"ora pro nobis peccatoribus"* during the Ave Maria. Her mother was never made to kneel in a corner bare-legged on rice grains to cure her of unladylike constant fidgeting. Jesusa never skipped Mass so she could lie on the new grass of a dazzling spring morning, watching the floating redness where there was usually blackness with her eyes closed. For that infraction, Ana had to lie an entire day and night facedown on the stone floor of the chapel, with no food or water, praying loud enough for the nuns who took turns during the vigil to hear her.

Ana spent her Christmas vacation and Holy Week with her parents in Sevilla, where she was allowed to take the air in the court-yard, but not permitted to go into the teeming city without her mother and a footman. Like many *sevillanas,* Jesusa veiled her face when she went out, as if she were too beautiful to be seen. Ana was happy that she was still a girl and could look around as they walked through the city.

The streets were crowded with vendors, pickpockets, nuns and monks, sailors and merchants, Gypsies, vagrants. Ana and Jesusa heard daily Mass in one of the chapels at the magnificent Catedral de Santa María de la Sede, built in the fifteenth century, its construction and decoration paid for by the riches streaming into Sevilla from the Spanish Empire. The vast Gothic arches, the gold-encrusted saints and virgins, the elaborate altar and numerous niches manifested the wealth of the city and Spain's glorious history. Ana felt small and insignificant under the vault. Its towering columns were like fingers reaching toward purgatory, where she was heading, the nuns assured her, if she continued to be so defiant.

Ana and Jesusa lit candles before the gilded saints, and dropped a coin or two to the beggars on the steps. They walked to the cemetery to leave posies over the graves of the three dead boys for whom Ana was no substitute. They delivered remedies to housebound neighbors. They exchanged gossip with women and girls who visited and must be visited in return, and evenings, when she was old enough, they attended balls meant to display Ana to prospective suitors. In between religious obligations and social engagements, Ana was confined indoors, sewing or embroidering alongside Jesusa while two fat pugs grunted and snored in a cushioned basket at her feet.

"Keep your eyes on your work," her mother snapped when Ana's gaze strayed to the sliver of sky through the richly draped, narrow window. "That's why your seams are so crooked. You don't pay attention."

Her mother criticized Ana for never sitting still, for speaking as if her opinion mattered, for not dressing her hair properly, for not having friends in Sevilla.

"How can I have friends here? You've banished me to a convent."

"Swallow your sharp tongue," Jesusa warned. "No one talks to you because you're so disagreeable."

She wondered if other girls felt as she did, that she was of no consequence and unwanted by her parents. She resented Jesusa's obvious disenchantment at the same time as she tried, unsuccessfully, to earn her love. She avoided her father, who scowled whenever she was near, as if she offended him by being female.

She reached puberty at the same time Jesusa entered menopause. When least expected, Ana caught her mother's gaze, a combination of envy and disgust that confused them both. Were it not for Iris, her maid, Ana would have believed she was dying the first time blood appeared on her pantalets. She was embarrassed by the changes in her body and her heightened emotions, mirrored by Jesusa. But she was discouraged from discussing or even thinking about any of her bewildering, disjointed feelings. She explored the new sensations in her body, but envisioned God frowning whenever she brushed her fingers against her budding breasts to feel the pleasure at the touch, so even her thoughts were forbidden.

Her schoolmates talked about the increased closeness to their mothers as they became young women, and Ana wished that Jesusa could be like them—loving, warm, attentive, encouraging, and willing to answer her questions. But Jesusa had buried maternal love with her three dead boys.

"I love you, Mamá," Ana had once said to Jesusa.

"Of course you do," Jesusa responded. Every time she remembered that day, Ana felt even more abandoned because Jesusa didn't say "I love you" back.

While there was no affection at home, Ana knew that at least there was concern about her future. So that she wouldn't be dependent on her haughty uncle upon Gustavo's death, her parents expected her to marry a rich man. Ana didn't think that freedom from dependency could come through marriage—rather the opposite. Her life would be like Jesusa's, closeted behind thick drapes within stone walls, trapped in duty and daily repentance for her trespasses. Whenever she imagined that life, Ana was overcome with rage at the thought that she wasn't in control of her own destiny. It made her want to run away.

Ana would come with a dowry, but not a fortune, so it was unlikely that any of the most eligible bachelors haunting salons and ballrooms would look her way first when there was richer prey. She was also aware that she wasn't a typical *señorita*. She was moderately pretty, especially when she smiled, but she wasn't a good dancer, played no instrument, abhorred chitchat, refused to flatter the young men paraded before her, and couldn't abide the intrusions of *dueñas* and possible mothers-in-law who appraised her narrow hips even through the seven petticoats Jesusa insisted she wear to make her small, thin figure more shapely.

She counted the days until her summer vacation in her maternal grandfather's farm in Huelva, near her school. The old widower wasn't more affectionate than her parents, but Abuelo Cubillas didn't consistently point out that she was a disappointment. He hired a *dueña* to keep her company when Ana lived at the farm. Doña Cristina was a local widow of modest means, impeccable character, and no imagination. As soon as Ana could, she ran from doña Cristina's religious tracts and embroidery hoops.

Abuelo let Ana do as she pleased so long as she didn't interfere with his rituals of eating, sipping wine, smoking his pipe, and reading on a cushioned leather chair, his legs on a footstool, his lap and thighs covered by a quilt hand-stitched by his mother. Abuelo was born during an earthquake in 1755, and spent as much of his life thereafter in stillness, as if waiting for the aftershocks to subside.

After prayers, Ana had breakfast with Abuelo and doña Cristina, then went outdoors. She learned to ride horses astride like a Gypsy from Fonso, the groom, chaperoned by his sturdy, widowed daughter, Beba.

"A woman should know how to defend herself," Beba told her, and gave Ana a small folding knife to keep in a pocket. "Don't be afraid to use it if you have to."

Fonso set up targets beyond the pasture, where Ana learned to shoot a rifle. She once shot a boar. She went on exhilarating rides through the countryside, the wind whizzing around her ears, her face flushed, her heart pounding. She was free and strong and capable, everything she never felt in Sevilla.

Every morning Beba fed the chickens, ducks, and geese, and found the fattest, meatiest ones for the cook. She collected eggs and showed Ana that she must always leave enough for the hens to hatch into chicks. Beba also taught Ana how to slaughter fowl (break their necks) and how to pluck and save the down from ducks and geese for pillows and quilts, and the feathers for beds.

She demonstrated as she pulled tail feathers from peacocks and pheasants. "Let the shaft dry. You can use them to make fans and to decorate your bonnets."

Ana learned to milk cows, sheep, and goats from the milkmaids, and the gardener's wife taught her to make cheese. She loved the cool, damp cave where the cheese was aged, the first whiff of the musky curds, the sharp scent of whey. She learned to wield a sharp knife when she helped graft fruit trees with the ancient gardener. She churned butter with his wife. She was happier in the gardens, fields, and orchards around the farm than in the parqueted salons of Sevilla.

Doña Cristina was scandalized by Ana's attachment to the lower classes, but Abuelo was delighted with his granddaughter's democratic impulses.

"I hate nothing more than a prejudiced, narrow-minded woman," he said.

"Why, *señor,* if you think I'm either of those things . . ."

"I accuse you of nothing," he said.

"I'm not criticizing your beloved granddaughter, *señor.* I simply point out that it's—well, she's a *señorita de buena familia* and she consorts with—"

"You exhaust me," he said. "Leave me, and let her be."

But perhaps because of doña Cristina's concerns, Abuelo insisted that Ana make time for other pursuits.

"Fonso and Beba and the servants will teach you the practical and natural sciences," he said, "the nuns will nourish your spirit, and your mother and your *dueñas* will teach you how to become a wife and mother and train you in the duties to manage a household. But I have the key to the greatest gift: an agile and creative mind." He allowed her at will in his library, where she could read any book that interested her. It was there that she found the journals of her ancestor don Hernán Cubillas Cienfuegos. The ragged, yellowing pages scratched in his hurried cursive in fading, splotchy ink fired Ana's hunger for adventure.

Don Hernán was among the conquistadores in the service of Juan Ponce de León during his first official expedition to San Juan Bautista in 1508. Don Hernán was there when most of the pioneers died in the insalubrious swamp Ponce de León first chose for his settlement in Caparra, and he was among the men to persuade the conquistador to move the colony to the breezy, healthful islet across the harbor. By 1521, when Ponce de León died, Borínquen was being renamed again by the *españoles.* The island was now called Puerto Rico and its fortress capital San Juan.

Don Hernán's journals and letters were illustrated with land-scapes, colorful birds and flowers, strangely shaped vegetables, bare-foot men and women with feathers and shells in their hair. Most of the women were naked, but some wore a short apron that don Hernán labeled *nagua*. The men appeared to wear nothing at all, al-though it was hard to tell, since don Hernán always portrayed them in modest three-quarter profile, or from the side, or holding a stick, bow, or other prop that covered what Ana most wished to see.

Don Hernán wrote of a harsh existence punctuated by deadly raids by *caribe* warriors, by earthquakes, by fevers, by violent storms that destroyed everything in their path. But he also described gold nuggets gleaming in the sands along pristine rivers, unusual fruits that dangled from climbing vines, impassable forests, and tree trunks wider than the arm span of five men standing around them finger to finger. He saw endless possibilities in that mysterious land, he wrote. Like all the conquistadores, he was there to enrich himself, but to earn his bounty he first had to tame a wilderness.

Don Hernán's letters stopped in 1526. A chest containing his jour-nals and papers was delivered a year later by a soldier charged with letting his family know that he died of cholera, but he still lived in Ana's imagination. As a girl, she spent hours reading his accounts, studying his drawings, trying to imagine what it was like for a pale, blue-eyed Spaniard to encounter the brown, black-eyed natives of the New World for the first time, and what it was like for the *taí-nos* to see men dropping from sailed vessels, rowing ashore wear-ing metal helmets and bright pantaloons, carrying gleaming Toledo swords, accompanied by hounds and a man in robes holding aloft a crucifix.

Late into the night, hunched over the tremulous candlelight that illuminated don Hernán's journals, Ana despaired that she was born female and centuries too late to be an explorer and adventurer like her ancestors. She read every account she could find about the wondrous enterprise that Spain undertook to discover new lands, to pacify the natives and harness the riches of a hemisphere.

She learned that most of the conquistadores were impoverished men, second sons, and soldiers with many battles behind them but little future before them. She was none of those things, but she felt don Hernán's hand reaching across the centuries toward her. She was a girl, cloistered and swaddled in the expectations of her class, but she identified with the audacity of the conquistadores, with the confidence that, if they turned their backs on country, family, and custom, they could make fortunes and more exciting lives through the work of their hands, the might of their swords. The more she read, the more Ana longed for a world beyond her balcony, far from the echoing halls of her convent school, home, and disappointed parents.

HER FIRST LOVE

━━━━◆━━━━

Ana and her schoolmate Elena Alegría Feliz had rooms next to each other in the Convento de las Buenas Madres. Elena's face was a perfect, pale oval surrounded by thick, chestnut hair. Her blue eyes were large and innocent. Her lips were shaped like a V, so she always wore a beatific smile. In school the other girls nicknamed Elena La Madona, because she looked as beautiful and pure as the paintings of the Holy Mother. They called Ana Bastoncito, because she was so short that, next to Elena, Ana looked like her walking stick.

After candles off, and against rules, they curled on one or the other's cot in their cell-like rooms, sharing the secrets and fantasies of schoolgirls with lively imaginations. One night, while Ana was telling her about don Hernán's exploits, the ribbon that closed Elena's nightgown loosened, revealing one perfectly formed breast. Elena stared at it as if she'd never seen it, then looked at Ana, who was just as mesmerized. Ana's uncertain fingers reached to stroke Elena's breast, and the nipple hardened. Elena gasped. Ana recoiled. Elena pressed Ana's hand to her breast and unfastened the ribbons so that the gown dropped off her shoulders. Tentatively, Ana caressed, and as Elena responded, she kissed, then used her tongue. They explored each other with furtive, fluttery fingers, hot mouths on cool flesh, wet tongues in salty crevices. So much sensation left her weak. Embarrassed, she pressed her bony back against Elena's belly. Elena slid her middle and ring fingers into Ana's mouth to suck until they both fell asleep.

They confessed once a week to fusty, nearly deaf Padre Buenaventura, who was sometimes heard to snore from behind the screen of the confessional.

"Forgive me, Father, for I have sinned." In the list of schoolgirl transgressions ("I'm guilty of vanity, Padre. I looked in the mirror three times yesterday"), buried within the urges that beset adolescent girls ("I'm guilty of envy, Padre. I wished my hair were as long and shiny as María's"), there was always mention of carnal thoughts, but never of carnal acts. In the stale, airless confessional, Ana and Elena risked the eternal fires of hell, crossed themselves, and sinned by omission, their fingers still stained with the other's pudendum.

Elena was an *hija de crianza,* raised in the same household as twin boys. Orphaned at four years old, Elena was raised by don Eugenio Argoso Marín and his wife, doña Leonor Mendoza Sánchez, relations so distant that Elena was unsure whether they were related at all. In any case, she grew up as niece to don Eugenio and doña Leonor, and cousin to their sons, Ramón and Inocente.

Ramón, as the eldest by twelve minutes, was expected to marry an heiress to increase the family's fortune and status. His younger brother, Inocente, would marry Elena, who was then penniless but was due an inheritance from doña Leonor's parents on her eighteenth birthday. While the engagement was not formal, it was understood that Elena was meant for Inocente.

"But you should marry Ramón," Elena suggested. "We'll be sisters then, and we'll always be together. Ramón and Inocente are rich and handsome," she added, "and the Argosos are from a distinguished family. Their father is a colonel in the cavalry. . . ."

"Is Ramón a soldier?"

"He was, but now both brothers work in an office," Elena explained. "They're learning how to take over their uncle's business."

No *caballero* of Ana's acquaintance, including her father and grandfathers, worked, or at least, not in the sense that they went to an office. "I don't know. . . ."

"They're not boring or dull," Elena said. "They only go there in the mornings. I know you'll like them. They're charming and like to have fun."

"How would I meet them?" Ana was still a bit doubtful.

"Come for my fifteenth birthday and stay for a while. Doña Leonor will surely allow me to have my best friend with me on my birthday. Yes, please do, come to Cádiz. . . ." Elena squeezed Ana's hands so tightly they hurt.

———

Ana had never met identical twins. Two days after Elena introduced them, Ana was still unsure which one was Ramón, which Inocente.

"You look so much alike," she said one morning, as they waited for Elena to come downstairs. "How can I know the difference between you when you also dress the same?"

"If you can tell us apart, we'll marry you," one joked.

"Can Elena tell you apart?"

"No one can," the other answered.

"So you'll both marry the one girl who can distinguish Ramón from Inocente?"

"We will," they said in unison.

"You can't do that!"

"Of course we can. Who would know?"

Until her visit to Elena, Ana had never been alone with a man, including her father and grandfather, but doña Leonor was not as vigilant as doña Cristina or her mother. In spite of her youth and inexperience, Ana was certain that Ramón and Inocente played tricks on her. If one offered to walk her in the garden after breakfast, she thought it was the other who appeared. Or one offered to fetch her shawl inside the house, and the other brought it. That they thought it would be so easy to fool her made her determined to learn to distinguish Ramón from Inocente.

Their pale eyes held the mystery of their identity. Ramón's were playful and seemed to always seek amusement. Inocente's were solemn and critical, and his jokes sometimes had a cruel edge. She didn't understand how no one else saw this, but she realized that the brothers were experts at being the other.

Once she was certain of their different gazes, Ana noticed that they moved unalike, too. Ramón's playful nature was revealed in a looseness of limb and grace that seemed studied in the more serious Inocente. Ramón also talked more, was usually the one to start a joke, the most likely to tell an amusing story. Ana teased them about it, but neither admitted to pretending to be the other. It was as if in their own minds they were interchangeable, one twenty-three-year-old man in two bodies.

Four mornings a week the twins walked to an office over a warehouse by the wharf and were usually back for the midday meal followed by a siesta, awakened by the sweet airs of harp music as doña Leonor practiced her instrument.

"They don't work very hard," Ana told Elena.

"They're gentlemen; they shouldn't be at an office all day long."

"But how can they run a business if they're just there a couple of hours a day?"

"Clerks and managers and people like that take care of the details. Ramón and Inocente check on what the employees do."

It occurred to Ana that none of the Argosos had any idea of the intricacies of commerce. Neither did she, if it came down to it, but her practical nature guessed that a business needed the active engagement of its owners, not just the appearance of ownership.

At dusk, Ramón and Inocente joined other young people on promenade around the Plaza de la Catedral or Plaza de San Antonio. They went out every evening, and Ana heard them stumbling over the furniture in the early hours.

One day the brothers hired a carriage and drove Ana and Elena to the beach. Once they settled the girls, Ramón and Inocente ran back and forth, laughing, lifting a kite into the air, their childlike joy enhanced by Ana's and Elena's enthusiastic applause.

Their mother, doña Leonor, like doña Jesusa, visited and was visited by friends and neighbors to share the local gossip. Ana and Elena smiled demurely as doña Leonor and her friends discussed who was engaged to whom, which officer was promoted, and who failed to impress their superiors. The girls sat straitlaced during these visits, their hands on their laps, their eyes modestly lowered, knowing that they must make a good impression on the *dueñas,* who would, in turn, talk about them the minute they left the sitting rooms.

Several evenings, doña Leonor and don Eugenio escorted Ana and Elena to high-ceilinged, mirrored halls where military orchestras played into the wee hours. The girls danced with dapper officers in full regalia and with civilians who wore crisp cravats, silk waistbands, ribbons around their knee breeches, and shiny kid shoes.

The Argosos had no guest room, so Ana and Elena shared a bed and slept wrapped in each other's arms. Elena always heard the maid coming in the morning to draw the drapes open. She pushed Ana to her side and they settled back-to-back with plenty of space between them. It was the loneliest moment of Ana's day.

Doña Leonor was hospitable and polite, but she looked worried as Ramón and Inocente increasingly turned to Ana for amusement and conversation. She appeared befuddled about which of the twins was wooing Ana, and Ana added to her perplexity by being equally agreeable to both men. She liked their attention, and enjoyed the envious looks of other *señoritas* whose fluttering lashes and powdered bosoms vibrated at the approach of the two handsome young men. Ana was elated as the denied *señoritas* and their *dueñas* practically collapsed when Ramón and Inocente went past them, toward her.

Next to the other girls, and especially beside the willowy Elena, Ana was at a disadvantage. She was petite, just barely five feet tall, but with none of the vulnerability expected from a small woman. She was healthy, tanned and freckled from exposure to the outdoors. Neither dance masters, nuns, nor Jesusa's lessons in deportment could refine her brisk, efficient movements into grace. Ana's own scrutiny showed that she was pretty enough but no beauty. She thought her black eyes were just a little too close together and her lips not full enough. She had the habit of staring at something or someone who interested her with too much intensity, according to the nuns and *dueñas*. She was awkward in society. In spite of her prodigious reading, or because of it, she avoided chitchat. It was an act of will to pretend to be interested in gossip, fashion, and home decor. She disliked little dogs and ignored children. She learned the artifices of the salon but disdained its constraints and pettiness. Women sensed her snobbishness and shunned her. Other than Elena, she had no friends.

Ana knew, however, that whether or not she fulfilled the expectations of her equals, her family names and ancestry held an important place in Spain's vertical society. To people like the Argosos, wealthier but lower down the slope, her pedigree made her more attractive than the coiffed, accomplished, fan-flickering *señoritas* paraded before every bachelor with more money but less dazzling lineage. She also noticed that don Eugenio encouraged Ramón's attentions toward her. She and Elena congratulated each other that their plan might work.

Ana liked Ramón enough to enjoy his company. But when he told her that the Argosos owned land in Puerto Rico, she decided to marry him.

———

Don Eugenio was the younger brother of two in a family of merchants and military men. Two months before Ana's visit, a message arrived in Cádiz to let him know that his childless, widowed brother, Rodrigo, had died in Puerto Rico. Eugenio, who'd spent his adult life in the cavalry, was now the main shareholder in a huge—and hugely profitable—shipping business with offices in St. Thomas, San Juan, Cádiz, and Madrid. In addition to his share of the business, Marítima Argoso Marín, he now owned a house in San Juan, a farm in the outskirts, and a two-hundred-*cuerda* sugar hacienda with twenty-five slaves on the southwestern side of the island.

He had little knowledge of Rodrigo's businesses. Twice a year Eugenio received a statement and a notice that his share of profits and interest had been transferred into his bank account in Cádiz. The amounts differed from year to year, depending on the vagaries of trade and harvests, taxes, duties, insurance payments, investments in materials and labor, rents, docking, wharfage, losses, and loans. Eugenio trusted his brother implicitly and was grateful for the income that Rodrigo's investments made possible. From their birth, and on each subsequent birthday, Rodrigo gifted Ramón and Inocente shares in Marítima Argoso Marín, so after their twentieth year the brothers received incomes of their own.

Unlike his brother, Eugenio didn't have a good head for commerce, but the military had trained him to delegate, motivate, and make others accountable. He knew his sons were as unenthusiastic as he was about trade, but still, after Rodrigo's death, he pushed his sons toward the managers and clerks of Marítima Argoso Marín, hoping that more involvement in the operations might excite and inspire Ramón and Inocente.

After discussions with his sons and with Leonor, Eugenio decided to keep his shares of the shipping business but planned to sell the house, farm, land, and slaves in Puerto Rico. It was a slow process, however. He could do nothing until a complete audit of Rodrigo's estate was filed and taxed by the Crown. He expected that he and his sons would manage the shipping business, but once the house and land were sold, he'd buy a *finca* where he could spend the last years of his life breeding race horses and fighting bulls. He was still relatively young at fifty-two, and Leonor was a sprightly forty-seven. After decades of soldiering, living in tents and rented houses like the one in Cádiz, Eugenio could finally give Leonor a real home.

But the day before Ana was to return to Sevilla, Ramón approached Eugenio.

"Papá, I respectfully request your permission to make an offer of marriage to *señorita* Larragoity Cubillas."

Eugenio thought that Ramón, almost twenty-four, should be settling down to start a family and he thought Ana was a splendid choice for his older son. She was from a good family, well educated, smart, and not silly, like the girls flitting around his good-looking sons. He knew that because don Gustavo lacked a male heir his wealth would go to Ana's uncle, but he guessed that she might come with a handsome dowry and gifts of cash from the Cubillas side.

Eugenio gave his blessing before consulting his wife.

"They hardly know each other," she complained.

"They've spent many hours together in the month since she arrived."

"We know nothing about her."

"We know she's from an illustrious, wealthy family. . . ."

"There's something about her . . . ," Leonor said. "I have a bad feeling."

Eugenio and Leonor had been married for twenty-nine years, and he was used to her fancies and premonitions, but nothing ever came of her forebodings. She argued that it was because they paid attention to her warnings that Ramón and Inocente suffered only the typical misadventures of active boys and spirited young men.

"He's made his choice, *mi amor,* and I believe he's chosen well," Eugenio said. "I encouraged the courtship, but perhaps there's something I missed. Do you have a specific concern about her?"

"No, it's a feeling."

"You're a mother seeing your boy falling in love with another woman."

"I'm not jealous," she snapped. "I think they should be settling down, and yes, I want grandchildren. But why her?"

Ana's parents were not at all pleased with the match either. First there was Leonor. She was a Mendoza and a Sánchez, from families of conversos whose Jewish ancestors had accepted the Catholic faith over two hundred years earlier. Eight generations, however, weren't enough to erase the stigma of having been Jewish in Spain, especially to a family of conservative Catholics. They were also ill disposed toward Eugenio because of his political views.

Before his death in 1833 with no male heir, King Fernando VII convinced the Spanish Cortes to amend the laws defining succession only through the male line to allow his eldest daughter, Isabel, still a child, to inherit the throne. His brother, don Carlos, was favored by conservative elements, chief among them, the Catholic Church. After Fernando's death, Carlos challenged the then three-year-old Infanta's claim and civil war ensued. For six long years the two factions fought for control, until, in 1839, with support from England, France, and Portugal, Isabeline forces were victorious.

Eugenio had distinguished himself on the side of the Isabelinos. But the Larragoity Cubillas families were staunch Carlists loyal to Isabel's uncle don Carlos.

Eugenio traveled from Cádiz to Sevilla to present his son's proposal. Gustavo listened politely, but firmly rejected the request for his daughter's hand. Jesusa then reminded Ana that her impetuous nature sometimes caused her to make hasty decisions.

"Remember when you wanted to be a nun because you so admired your teacher Sor Magdalena? Two weeks later you changed your mind. . . ."

"I was ten, Mamá. What ten-year-old doesn't want to be a nun?"

"You're insolent to your mother," her father said. He threatened to exile Ana to a Carmelite convent in Extremadura if she didn't give up her foolish obsession.

Neither reminders of close calls nor threats of a fate she considered for herself (albeit briefly) succeeded in changing Ana's mind. This was the man she wanted to marry. And now.

A well-raised *señorita* in mid-nineteenth-century Spain didn't challenge her parents. Ana was a good daughter, even if willful and stubborn. She knew it was impudent to argue with Mamá and Papá, so she did what young women of her place and station did when they couldn't get their way: she developed a debilitating and mysterious illness that no physician could diagnose or cure. Chills so severe that her bed shook followed high fevers. Shallow breathing that kept her from sleep on consecutive nights evolved into slumber from which she couldn't be roused. A poor appetite caused such rapid weight loss that Jesusa feared Ana would waste away.

The alternating symptoms kept Ana in bed for nearly two months. During her illness, Ramón (at least that's who Jesusa thought it was) visited to inquire after Ana's health, begging to be allowed to speak to her. The distance between Sevilla and Cádiz was over one hundred kilometers, and the still unstable political situation made travel unsafe. Even Gustavo was impressed with Ramón's devotion and willingness to endanger his own life in order to woo his daughter.

While Ana's dowry seemed generous to Eugenio, it was to be half what Gustavo had received upon marrying Jesusa, not including jewelry she inherited from her grandmothers. Gustavo looked at his daughter critically. At seventeen, she appeared older and—in spite of fashionable clothes, colorful shawls, and hairdressing—common.

Gustavo had studied her in society, where her tart tongue caused other women, and some men, to turn away. Sevilla was a big city, but Gustavo and Jesusa knew everyone worth knowing. No other young man of their acquaintance was interested in Ana. If she never married, she'd be dependent on him the rest of his life and, after his death, on her uncle's charity. Ana lacked altruism and Gustavo couldn't imagine her as the soft-voiced, sickbed auntie in his brother's rambunctious household, or as one of the charitable spinsters who ministered to the poor, or as a companion to the elderly and infirm. She was an intelligent girl, and he was sure that she, too, had considered the same scenarios.

Gustavo ordered his lawyers to inquire discreetly into Marítima Argoso Marín. Reports were encouraging. The company was healthy and the colonel's experience leading men might translate into business acumen. Gustavo was less impressed with Ramón. He was a popinjay, and Gustavo imagined his plain daughter thought she was lucky to have caught such a peacock. She, at least, had some sense, and he imagined Ana would peck Ramón into submission as soon as they were married.

So, eight months after Ana declared who her husband was to be, her father agreed to the engagement.

Ana's recovery was swift once Ramón was allowed to visit. He stayed a few minutes, chaperoned by the tight-faced Jesusa. His good humor and gentle manners, however, won her approval. Over the next month his visits became longer until they stretched into mealtimes, when Jesusa and Gustavo elicited information about the

Argoso and Mendoza families that they could later use to justify their daughter's marriage to a liberal with Jewish ancestors. As soon as Ana could sit upright without exertion, a date was fixed for days after her eighteenth birthday.

The Larragoity Cubillas home in Plaza de Pilatos was impressive if one was dazzled by portraits of men with starched ruffs and shapely calves and women encased in lace and velvet trimmed with ermine. Swords, harquebuses, and daggers were displayed along the walls as if to remind the viewer that the Larragoity men were not to be trifled with. At the bottom of the stairs was a knight's suit of armor, complete with a shield emblazoned with a heraldic emblem featuring an enormous cross capped with a halo of thorns. According to Gustavo, he was a direct descendant of the knight who wore that particular chain mail and plate in the Crusades. But Ana suspected that, like so much of the Larragoity and Cubillas family lore, this was an exaggeration. She didn't believe that either side of her family had risen above village life until centuries later, when the *conquista* made it possible for penniless boys to go to sea in search of fortune. She noticed, however, that Gustavo's and Jesusa's stories impressed the twins.

Sometimes Ramón came alone, sometimes Inocente came as if he were Ramón, and a few times they came together, dressed unalike so that her parents could tell them apart. As she spent more time with them, she discerned that, in spite of the Argosos' plan to make sober businessmen out of them, Ramón and Inocente were romantics, and the bravado of the Larragoity and Cubillas men, especially as presented by Ana's hyperbolic parents, inspired them to imagine that they, too, could have an adventurous life.

"What a magnificent horse." Ramón stopped before a portrait of Ana's great-granduncle, the tobacco planter from Cuba, solid on a chestnut stallion, acres of fields around him and, in the background, a columned mansion and barns.

"He owned three hundred horses," Gustavo said, "and so much land that it took him a day to ride from one end of his plantation to the other."

"He must have needed that many horses," Ana said.

Jesusa ignored her daughter's remark. "It was called Nonpareil. No other could compare."

"Yes, that's what it means," Ana said, but neither her parents nor the twins acknowledged her sarcasm.

She couldn't help herself. Her parents irritated her, but at the same time, she understood that their boasts about glamorous ancestors aroused Ramón's and Inocente's imaginations and confirmed her stories that adventure was waiting across the ocean.

Ramón and Inocente missed the independence they enjoyed before they were apprenticed in their uncle's business. They dreaded that Eugenio's plan to retire to the country and turn over the business to them would mean a staid, conventional life. They didn't want to spend their daylight hours in an office. They wanted to be outdoors amid horses and men.

"I imagine you both on stallions as beautiful as this one," Ana said, sweetening her voice, "riding these vast fields, masters of your own world."

Ana encouraged and flattered them, and Ramón and Inocente began to see themselves through her eyes. Yes, they were young, brave, strong, imaginative. They had learned much about how to manage a business. Why couldn't they go to Puerto Rico and develop the land their uncle left their family? The sugar hacienda already had a workforce in place that knew what to do. Ramón and Inocente could be the saddled *señores* who oversaw the operation and reaped the profits.

"In a few years," she said, "we can return to Spain with a fortune. And stories enough for a lifetime."

She nurtured their swashbuckling fantasies, and they were as eager as she for a life of adventure. To them, she represented their independence. To her, they were the agents of her freedom.

A COMPROMISE

Leonor and Elena were upstairs being fitted for new frocks and Eugenio had just settled in his study with the morning papers, coffee, and a cigar when his sons walked in.

"We need a word, Papá," Inocente said.

Eugenio folded his newspaper, set it aside, and gestured for them to sit.

"We'd like to take over the farm and plantation in Puerto Rico that Tío Rodrigo left in the inheritance," Ramón began.

"I plan to sell those properties."

"But there's greater potential in the hacienda," Inocente started, "than realizing a small profit in the short term," Ramón finished.

"We looked into the accounts." Inocente spread some pages in front of his father. "Tío Rodrigo has owned the farm in Caguas for five years. It's closer to the capital than the plantation, and he used it as a retreat from the city."

"Fruits, vegetables, chickens, and pork from the farm provisioned his ships," Ramón said. "A husband and wife do the entire planting and harvesting with three grown sons who live on the property in exchange for a small plot where they grow their own food. They cared for Tío Rodrigo's house when he was away, and when he was there, the wife and daughter cleaned and cooked. There are expenses here for day laborers when the manager and his family can't keep up with the bounty."

"We've studied the options," Inocente said. "Colonel George Flinter's book has helped us understand the possibilities."

"Colonel Flinter?" Eugenio raised his eyebrows. He tasted his coffee. Cold.

"Do you know him?" Ramón asked eagerly.

"If it's the same man . . . a red-faced, squinty-eyed, bellicose Irishman. He fought for Spain against Bolívar in Spanish America, then distinguished himself here against the Carlists."

"His book was published in 1832," Ramón said.

"—charged to report on the conditions of Puerto Rico—," Inocente broke in.

"—with emphasis on agriculture," Ramón added.

"I never would've guessed he was a writer." Eugenio scratched his whiskers. "Although he could talk until your ears ached. . . ."

"In any case"—Inocente brought his father back to their discussion—"his report is quite informative. The yields per acre in Puerto Rico are superior to any in the West Indies." He pointed to a column of figures. "Here, for example, you can see that rice produces three crops per annum, compared to nearby islands, like Hispaniola, which only harvest two a year."

"Are you proposing to become rice farmers?" Eugenio was still trying to conjure Colonel Flinter beyond his braggadocio and impressive ability to drink anyone under the table.

"No, Papá," Ramón said. "This is an example of how fertile the land is known to be. Look, yams, plantains, and oranges in Puerto Rico yield four times as much as anywhere in the West Indies."

"We propose to develop the sugar hacienda, however," Inocente continued. "The farm in Caguas works well, but the plantation on the other side of the island has been untended and the possibilities unexploited."

"And the figures we looked at"—Ramón riffled through the papers—"indicate that sugar yields in Puerto Rico are five times as much as on other islands. Five times, Papá!"

"All this from Flinter's report?" Eugenio was unable to let go of the image of the swaggering colonel masquerading as an expert on agriculture.

"It was a comprehensive study," Inocente said. "His recommendations to Europeans looking to settle in Puerto Rico are clear and well examined."

"We expect to turn a profit in five years," Ramón explained.

"But neither of you has ever planted so much as a daisy."

Ramón smiled. "We'll be managing the people who do the work."

Eugenio looked at his sons. Their faces were bright, open, and eager. He hadn't seen them so enthusiastic about anything in years.

"You do know that the hacienda is worked by slaves?"

"Yes, Papá, we're aware of that," Inocente said. "But it's not like Cuba or Jamaica, where the *entire* operation is done by slaves. In Puerto Rico they're supplemented by day laborers."

"But there will still be slaves working for you."

"We plan to free them as soon as possible. Perhaps even after the first harvest," Inocente said.

Eugenio could tell that the thought had only just occurred to his son. Ramón exchanged a grateful look with his brother.

"And you," Eugenio turned to Ramón, "you're soon to be married to a *señorita* who grew up with every possible comfort. Not all women are as adaptable as your mother."

"Ana is not only completely in agreement," Ramón said, "she's as enthusiastic about Puerto Rico as we are."

"She's the one who found the Flinter report," Inocente said.

"She studied the history," Ramón added. "Her ancestors—"

"She has family there?"

"Well, not anymore. Years ago."

"Most of her family's fortune," Inocente broke in, "was made in the West Indies."

"They were traders and plantation owners who returned as rich men. Ana knows what to expect," Ramón said, with a hint of pride.

"We'll come back to Spain with practical experience for running a business—," Inocente continued.

"—and we'll be much better able to manage Marítima Argoso Marín," Ramón concluded.

"Who will run the business in the meantime?"

"You can continue to work with the managers and agents," Inocente said.

"You've had a full, accomplished life," Ramón said. "We're young and strong but haven't done much with our lives. Haven't you told us so yourself? We wish to make our own way, Papá."

"And Papá," added Inocente, "we wish to make you proud."

———

Leonor wouldn't hear of her sons leaving Spain. "We'll die alone," she cried when Eugenio presented her with the proposal. "I wish to be near our sons, to be a grandmother to their children. I don't want another outpost. I'd like a proper home. Is that too much to ask, after years of living in tents and cottages?"

A compromise was reached; they'd all go to Puerto Rico. Eugenio postponed his dream of a ranch for horses and fighting bulls in Spain. He, Leonor, and Elena would move to the house in San Juan. Eugenio would manage the shipping business from the capital and spend holidays at the *finca* in a nearby town, like Rodrigo used to do. Ramón and Inocente would take over the sugar plantation on the other side of the island. After five years, they could all return to Spain to enjoy the income with occasional visits to the island or, better yet, sell the much-improved properties. That Ramón would marry Ana, and Inocente Elena (when she came into her inheritance) meant that a potential source of strife would be avoided, since the future sisters-in-law were best friends. Eugenio congratulated his sons for their foresight.

The plans were made without looking at a detailed map. They knew that Puerto Rico was 180 kilometers long by 65 kilometers wide, and the distances seemed short in comparison with Europe. In spite of the fact that, as a soldier, Eugenio knew that even one kilometer on poor roads could take hours to traverse, he wanted to please his wife. He wanted to be near his sons. He'd always been a military man, but he agreed to retire from the cavalry to become a landowner and businessman.

He burnished his sword and saber and slid them into their polished scabbards. He pinned his medals and ribbons on a velvet cloth Leonor made for him. With the ceremony their rank deserved, he folded his uniforms, brushed his plumed hats, rolled his sashes, and stored them in a cedar chest. With a last look before he closed and locked a lifetime of memories within, Eugenio said good-bye to his career and prepared to begin a new life for himself and his family in Puerto Rico.

VICE VERSA

———— ◆ ————

Over the next six months, Leonor often reminded her husband and sons that sailing to the Indies was their idea and that she agreed only because she couldn't change their minds. To emphasize her opposition, she insisted that Eugenio accompany her to lay wreaths on their parents' graves, and to say good-bye to living relatives in Villamartín, the village where they grew up. She had a premonition, she said, that she'd never see Spain again.

Ramón and Inocente went in the opposite direction. In mid-June 1844 they escorted Elena by steamship up the Río Guadalquivir to Sevilla, where she'd help Ana prepare her trousseau for the wedding six weeks hence.

Ana, Elena, Jesusa, and a gaggle of *comadres,* cousins, and neighbors sewed, embroidered, and packed crates, chests, and boxes for hours on the uppermost floor of the house. Ana and Elena were in a constant frenzy. Ramón and Inocente didn't want to interrupt important business, so they left the ladies to their chores and took advantage of their leisure.

Until they moved to Sevilla to be near Ana, Ramón and Inocente hadn't lived on their own or far from Leonor's eye. When they were boys, she prepared them for the indoor life of gentlemen, but they grew up among soldiers, on the periphery of battles, tented along dusty roads, amid the splendid Spanish cavalry. They were educated haphazardly by tutors and by their mother, who refused to send them to boarding school while they followed Eugenio's career. She drilled them in etiquette, dancing, and repartee while their father taught them the manly arts of chivalry, riding, fighting, drinking, and swordsmanship. They saw battles against the Carlists, led by their father, who could kill an enemy on a bloody field but could also step lightly and gracefully to violin music around a polished floor. The ladies who danced with Ramón and Inocente at a candlelit ball the night before wouldn't recognize them the next day, muddy and sweaty, tramping across a pasture, cursing or singing bawdy *coplas*.

Friends and relatives who'd known them since childhood had never seen Ramón without Inocente. They looked so much alike that people didn't even try to tell them apart. Inocente said that people were lazy and it was easier to find the twins' similarities than their differences. It had become a perverse game to test whether others saw them as individuals by deliberately confusing them.

They'd confounded Elena for years. She lived in the school most of the time because Leonor thought it was inappropriate to have a beautiful young woman among so many soldiers. Whenever Elena came home for vacation, Ramón and Inocente took pains to groom and dress alike. *Señoritas* at social events had trouble distinguishing one from the other, but the brothers wanted to know whether one who lived with them would, too. They were sure that Elena couldn't tell them apart. Even their mother frequently confused Ramón with Inocente and vice versa.

From childhood, the brothers had slept entwined until Leonor announced they were big boys and should have their own beds. Still, they set up their cots inches from each other's and often woke up holding hands. They'd compared their penises when they pissed outdoors, arguing over whose stream went the farthest. In early adolescence, they masturbated side by side, competing over which would orgasm first. One morning, however, Ramón woke up to Inocente's hand on his exposed belly, centimeters from his swollen penis. He wasn't sure if Inocente was awake or asleep, so he waited, curious whether the hand would move closer, willing it to do so. It did. Face up, his eyes closed, his hand crept slowly up Inocente's right hip to discover that he, too, was naked and erect. It was much more exciting to have Inocente's fingers on his penis than his own, and he knew that his brother was feeling the same thing.

Long before their father brought them to a brothel to be initiated into sex, they'd already found pleasure in each other without talking about it, aware that the minute they discussed it, all the injunctions against touching each other that way would inhibit them.

They were stunned to learn that their father frequented prostitutes.

"But if you love Mamá," Inocente asked, "why do you visit whorehouses?"

"Men's urges are different from women's," he said. "I love and admire your mother too much to ask from her what I expect from *putas*. Marriage is holy, designed for procreation, yes, but also to elevate us from savagery. A man honors his wife by protecting her from his baser instincts. That's what *putas* are for."

The explanation gave them license to indulge their most ignoble impulses so long as they safeguarded their future wives from them. They'd never, for example, admit to their wives that they liked to watch each other take the same woman.

It's like watching myself in the mirror, Ramón thought.

The only times they didn't share their sexual adventures was when Inocente began to experiment with bizarre contraptions in underlit rooms that spooked Ramón.

"It's . . . exquisite. An exquisite kind of pain," Inocente explained, "not at all what you're imagining."

Ramón tried it, naked and manacled, his eyes covered while a woman barked orders and whipped him. It wasn't as pleasurable as he'd hoped.

The brothers were handsome and sought after in society, but they preferred ladies of dubious reputation. One of their favorites was doña Cándida, Marquesa de Lirios, whose much older husband had died from apoplexy upon discovering her in flagrante with his favorite torero. The Marquesa de Lirios suggested a ménage à trois with Ramón and Inocente. For six months the Marquesa de Lirios guided their fingers, tongues, and penises in fantastic explorations of every orifice, male and female, with such abandon that Ramón and Inocente were never the same.

Four months after the Marquesa de Lirios suddenly and inexplicably entered a convent, Ramón and Inocente met Ana. The competitive spark in her eyes told them that this was no ordinary girl. They were drawn to Ana because she treated them as separate people, looked beyond their identical clothes and accessories to find out who was Ramón, who Inocente. They were also grateful that she didn't give away their deceptions and seemed, in fact, to enjoy being part of their game outwitting others. As they spent more time with her, the twins believed that they'd found a kindred spirit. She wasn't appalled when Ramón said they'd marry the same woman. They'd shared everything with each other; why not share a wife?

Days before the wedding, Jesusa invited Ana into her boudoir and, nearly paralyzed by ahs, ahems, trembling lips, and crimson blushes, told Ana how babies were made.

"Lie on your back as still as you can, and let him do what he has to do," she instructed. "While it's happening, pray two Our Fathers and as many Hail Marys as necessary until it's over."

Ana waited, but no more details were forthcoming. Ana, however, had had free rein in Abuelo Cubillas's library. Hidden in a compartment behind the satirical poems of the Conde de Villamediana, she'd found manuals that left no doubt about how babies were made. The illustrations and, moreover, her lovemaking with Elena, disputed Jesusa's instructions wonderfully.

For a minute, Ana considered adding to Jesusa's embarrassment by asking for details, but rejected the idea. It was rare for Jesusa to impart motherly advice.

"How do I know when I'm pregnant?"

Jesusa seemed grateful to talk about something less prurient. "Well," she said, "with your problem of irregular periods, the only way to know for sure is to look for changes in your body."

"Like my belly growing?"

"Yes, but there will be signs long before that. You might be nauseous in the morning and crave certain foods. With you, I wanted lemons, couldn't get enough of them, and the midwife said it was because you were so sweet. With my first three pregnancies, I had no cravings." She dropped her gaze, yielding to grief, deserting Ana.

"You've always told me the opposite; that I have a sour disposition. Maybe you had too many lemons."

Her words weighed between them as three ghosts floated in the air: the sons Jesusa wanted and lost, the ones who wouldn't talk back or challenge her.

"You'd better finish packing," Jesusa dismissed her.

Ana was both relieved and depressed as she climbed the stairs to the room where she'd left Elena folding linen. It had been her nursery once, but it was now lined with crates, chests, and boxes.

"I still can't believe we're going," Elena said as she counted napkins, towels, blankets, tablecloths, then noted the amounts on Ana's household book. "You look so serious. Did you get into an argument with your mother?"

"Not an argument." Ana knelt before the linens and began to separate them into stacks. "We annoy each other."

"You'll miss her when you're across the ocean, and your father, and your home."

"I won't miss them as much as you or they think. I'd miss more if I didn't go."

"Ana!"

"Why are you so shocked? You know we've never been close."

"They're your parents."

"They're shallow. All they care about is that their neighbors be impressed by their names and position in society."

"Of course they're proud of their good names and their ancestors' achievements."

"But they've done nothing," Ana said. "They have no achievements of their own. They've made nothing, created nothing, worked at nothing. They will leave no trace that they ever existed. They have no legacy except for their names, which they did nothing to earn."

"That's so harsh."

Ana folded and placed an embroidered pillowcase over a stack of napkins. "I don't want to be like them. I'm more like our Larragoity and Cubillas relatives on the walls, the ones who turned their faces toward the future, not the ones who only look to the past."

Elena moved the pillowcase to its proper place with the others. "Not everyone is comfortable with the uncertainties of the future, Ana."

"How can you know what you're capable of if you don't embrace the unknown?"

"Some people, like your parents, like me, don't want to be tested. We're happy living as quietly and comfortably as possible."

"Not me." Ana closed the chest. "I don't expect comfort, or even happiness when it comes down to it."

"How can you not want to be happy?"

"I didn't say I don't want it. I don't expect it. That day and night the nuns made me lie facedown on the cold stone floor, I learned that you pay for your happiness. That's why I don't expect to be happy all the time. I'd rather be surprised by one moment every so often to remind me that joy is possible, even if I have to pay for it later."

"You're more realistic, I suppose, than me."

Ana leaned over and kissed Elena. "I'm happy when I'm with you."

"That makes us both happy, then."

Ana married Ramón on Saturday, August 3, 1844, one week after her eighteenth birthday, in a ceremony attended only by family, with Elena as bridesmaid and Inocente as best man. When she saw her daughter as a wife, Jesusa became the mother she'd never been. She cried through the Mass in the Catedral de Sevilla and at the subsequent reception in their home as Gustavo begged her to restrain herself.

"You're making us both look ridiculous," he said.

"Our darling Anita, our sweet, our cherished only child, and she's leaving us," Jesusa sobbed.

Ana was jealous of the Anita her mother was now creating as she, the real, living, adult Ana, was about to leave home. She couldn't wait to escape Jesusa's emotions. It was too much, too late. Were it possible, she would've sailed for San Juan that minute.

As soon as the wedding luncheon was over, Ramón and Ana, Eugenio, Leonor, Elena, and Inocente boarded the ship to Cádiz. The newlyweds would stay in a suite at a seaside inn until they would all sail for San Juan in one of the Marítima Argoso Marín vessels later that week.

Ana and Elena had talked about her wedding night, and had agreed that Ana should play the innocent virgin so that Ramón would believe that she'd had no experience with sexual intimacy. It was, after all, what a man expected.

That night, Ramón came into the bedroom after Ana had climbed into bed.

"You must be tired, *querida,*" he said, lying next to her but not touching her.

"It was a long day," she said.

"Our life together has begun, and I plan to be worthy of you."

"You already are, *mi amor,*" she said.

"You looked lovely in your wedding gown."

"Thank you. It was my great-great-grandmother Larragoity's. It's now been worn by six generations of brides."

It puzzled her that he made no move toward her, but for the next half hour at least, Ramón continued to make small talk as Ana responded in as few words as possible. She was sure he was trying to be a gentleman, to get her to relax before the inevitable ravishing, but the longer he talked, the tenser she became, which made him more voluble.

When he'd exhausted every possible theme of conversation, Ramón finally turned to Ana and placed his hand on her belly. "I'm sorry, *querida,*" he said. "This might be uncomfortable at first, but you will soon get used to it."

He climbed on top of her, kissed her a few times, told her how much he loved her, fumbled with her nightgown until it was at her waist, pushed her pantalets down, separated her legs with his knees, and entered her with violent thrusts. When he was done, he kissed her forehead, thanked her, rolled over onto his back, and within moments, fell asleep.

She lay in bed stunned, pressing her thighs together against the pain. It wasn't possible—this couldn't be marital life. It had been a long day. The next night would be different. Her handsome, charming husband would make love to her, would make her feel like Elena did, every sense alive, every nerve tingling. She knew it would be different with a man, but she'd expected pleasure, not this utter desolation.

The next day, Ramón was as cheerful and lighthearted as usual, and Ana was sure that this night would be different. They joined the Argosos, Inocente, and Elena at evening Mass, then shared a leisurely dinner at a restaurant overlooking the harbor. When they went to bed, however, there were no caresses, no long delicious kisses, no hands roaming across hot skin. This time, he didn't talk. As soon as he came into the room he extinguished the lamp, rolled on top of her, opened her legs with his knees, and pushed himself into her. Just as on the night before, he thanked her, turned to his side of the bed, and slept.

In the morning, they received a message from don Eugenio.

There was a complication with their travel plans. Word had come that their vessel had met with bad weather on the crossing back to Spain and required more repairs than anticipated. They could be transported to Puerto Rico on one of the Marítima Argoso Marín cargo ships, but it could accommodate only three passengers and a couple of their trunks.

"What are we supposed to do?" Leonor fretted. "They can't take us all. I've already sent most of the furniture. I can't leave my harp."

"You, Papá, and Elena go as scheduled. Ramón, Ana, and I will stay for now," Inocente suggested. "We'll send your harp and the things you can't take. We'll follow as soon as they have room for us."

"A good solution," Eugenio said.

"But that's exactly what I didn't want, with us across the ocean from each other!"

"It will only be a couple of months at most, Mamá," Ramón said.

"I'll make the arrangements," Inocente said. "Don't worry."

Neither Ana nor Elena was consulted about the plan. On August 8, 1844, Elena, don Eugenio, and doña Leonor sailed to Puerto Rico. The same afternoon, Ramón told Ana that they'd move in with Inocente to keep him company until another ship could take the three of them across the sea. The harp, furniture, and chests were sent on different vessels, and every few days either Ramón or Inocente inquired at the Marítima Argoso Marín office when they would be able to leave, but each time Ana was disappointed by another delay.

"It's hurricane season in those waters," Inocente reminded her. "Shipping is often disrupted by the weather."

Over the next six weeks, Ana, Ramón, and Inocente explored Cádiz province. The twins always put Ana between them when they walked along the beach, promenaded around the plazas, or rode into the villages in the foothills. The peasants were rebuilding their cottages and villages following the devastation of the Carlist War five years earlier. Ana saw mostly old men, women, and children. The peasants received Ramón and Inocente with smiles and welcome gestures, happy to see young men again, or with angry, resentful glances if they'd lost husbands, sons, and brothers. With fewer men in their prime years to work in the farms, groves, and vineyards, the forlorn countryside had vast stretches of uncultivated land that had reverted to weeds and grasses.

After their walks around the city or following their rides outside its gates, Ramón, Inocente, and Ana returned to the nearly empty house to bathe and rest. A local woman delivered meals, served, and cleaned, then left them alone as candles sputtered into translucent puddles. When church bells rang eleven, Ana went into the bedroom and changed into her nightgown. At quarter past the hour Ramón walked in. Or Inocente.

She hadn't thought she was really marrying Ramón *and* Inocente after their first teasing conversation when they met. The subject didn't come up again, but within a few days of her wedding, Ana realized that she was wife to both men. At first, in the dark, one twin felt much like the other, spoke like the other, made love with the same impatience as the other. Neither man liked to be touched more than necessary, as if her wandering fingers were an invasion. They were courteous, called her sweet names, but neither man seemed to be entirely present when he made love, as if he were thinking of someone else the whole time. Within a week, she could tell who was Ramón, who Inocente. Ramón talked during the entire sex act as if he needed to hear his own voice in order to get aroused. Inocente was silent, stretched her arms over her head, pressed them against the pillows so that she couldn't move them, opened her thighs with his knees, and rocked back and forth above her. They resisted her attempts to change the man-on-top, woman-on-bottom position. Both assumed that she would not, should not, enjoy lovemaking. They both grunted as they peaked, then dropped to the side and were insensible until the next morning. She often lay in bed after they'd fallen asleep, missing Elena.

When she first realized that the twins were sharing her, Ana was furious. Who did they think they were? Who did they think she was? Other than in their selfishness in bed, however, Ramón and Inocente behaved like men in love. They were attentive, made sure that she was comfortable and safe, complimented her lavishly, brought her flowers and presents, and were in every other way devoted. She'd worked hard to win them, and wanted to believe that they loved her. Why wouldn't they both fall in love with her at the same time, and why wouldn't they find a way for both of them to have her?

She had to be patient. She'd persuaded them that conventional lives were for other people and they embraced her ideas to the fullest. But no one must ever know. Not Elena, who expected to marry Inocente. Not doña Leonor, who always addressed her sons as if they were one person. Not don Eugenio, who was so impressed by Ana's forebears that he encouraged Ramón to marry her. And certainly not Padre Cipriano, who heard her breathless, abridged confessions every Saturday at three in the sweltering confessional of the gold-domed Catedral de Cádiz.

Ramón, Inocente, and Ana sailed first to the Canary Islands, where their Marítima Argoso Marín schooner, *Antares,* had to pick up cargo and more passengers. Ana watched impatiently from the deck as stevedores loaded barrels and canvas-wrapped bundles. On the fourth day, three horses were led up the ramp and, with much effort, persuaded into the hold. That afternoon, soldiers in full regalia embarked, and their commander had each man call out his name and rank to ascertain that everyone was accounted for. Once he was satisfied, the captain ordered that the *Antares* push off the dock, raise the sails, and begin its journey across the Atlantic. Ana had a moment of terror when land disappeared from sight, even though she'd imagined this voyage for years. The ship was a speck in the immeasurable sea beneath an infinite sky, with no beacons to indicate how far they'd come or how much farther they had to go. She felt between time and space, floating between lives.

The *Antares* was one of the older schooners owned by Marítima Argoso Marín. The decks and timbers were mottled with mysterious stains, and the boards were nicked, scratched, and haphazardly patched. In spite of the relatively calm seas, Ramón and Inocente were seasick the first two days, and Ana ran from one cabin to the other soothing and comforting as she controlled her own nausea. The cramped passenger cabins emitted the smells of moisture, human effluvia, and animal musk. As they sailed toward the equator, the cabins became insufferably hot. Ana spent as much time as she could on deck, gulping the fresh air, reading, and trying to forget that she was confined on a creaking vessel in the middle of a vast ocean. One day she looked up from her book and noticed something that she hadn't thought about before. The horizon was at eye level. To change her perspective, she stood along the rail looking toward

Spain, and later peeked through the narrow porthole of their cabin belowdecks toward their destination in Puerto Rico, expecting the horizon to be lower or higher depending on where she was standing. But no matter what position she took, her past and future coalesced at eye level, immutable, unavoidable, but at the same time ever changing as her past folded into her future and the *Antares* sailed toward her destiny.

HER SMALL PERSON

———◆———

The horizon was smudged, like a bruise, but as the *Antares* approached land, a veiled green pyramid emerged from the haze. Ana grabbed Ramón's arm and bounced on her toes, unable to contain her excitement.

"Is that it?"

Ramón wove her left hand through his elbow, and brought her gloved fingers to his lips. "We'll soon be inside the harbor."

"You can make out San Felipe del Morro." Inocente pointed to a mustard-colored headland over the frothing surf.

"It's huge!"

"Impregnable," Inocente added. "Spanish military engineering at its best."

Other passengers pushed closer to the rail, craned their necks, adjusted their hats and bonnets to shade their eyes from the blinding sun. Crewmen hopped around the deck in a dance of sail lowering, rope loosening, latch securing, and the tying down of canvas-wrapped bundles. As the vessel glided through the protected passage into the broad harbor, Ana's breath quickened. This is it, she thought, Puerto Rico. A sense of déjà vu made her dizzy.

"Now I know what my ancestors must have felt," she said, "seeing land after weeks at sea. . . ."

"Let's hope we have the luck of those who became rich and not the luck of those eaten by the Caribs," muttered Inocente.

Ramón and Ana laughed. Some passengers standing nearby glanced at them nervously and gave them a bit more room. The brothers exchanged an amused look over Ana's head. She put her other arm through Inocente's so that they were linked to each other through her. She sighed happily as the walled city came into view.

"At last," she said softly. "We're here at last."

She closed her eyes and mentally etched the date into memory: Wednesday, October 16, 1844.

It was early morning, and the harbor was thick with two- and three-masted schooners, barges, sloops, and fishing boats vying for lanes, most of them flying the red-and-gold Spanish flag. San Juan rose from the waterfront behind the thick walls that protected it from invasions and enemy attacks from the Atlantic Ocean. Wide swatches of green peppered the hill, gardens, or pastures—Ana couldn't tell—but closely packed buildings intersected by roads and alleys defined most of the land. Several towers topped by crucifixes were scattered across the citadel, their bells echoing over the water. To Ana, San Juan looked like Cádiz, the city they'd left three thousand miles behind in Spain.

She freed her arms from Ramón and Inocente and turned to where verdant hills stretched east to west, the vegetation nearly unbroken by man-made structures. Low white clouds formed over the green, blackening the land below. She turned again to the light and sunny city. As the schooner approached the dock, passengers oohed and aahed at the painted houses, the balconies adorned with flowers and foliage on the upper stories. On the flat roofs, women's skirts and fringed shawls fluttered in the breeze in a panoply of color and movement. Some of them waved, and passengers returned their greetings. Other women dressed in black stood as immobile as the sentry boxes over the rock walls of the fort. They were too far from shore for Ana to distinguish features, but so many women in mourning over the gay city palled her humor. She threaded her arms again through Ramón's, then Inocente's, arm and pulled them closer, focusing their attention on the movement on the wharf, away from the widows.

"There he is!" Ramón pointed at don Eugenio standing by an open carriage near the dock, amid the bustle and hubbub around the waterfront. Next to him stood a younger man, somewhat taller, powerfully built, his face shaded by a wide-brimmed straw hat. Eugenio waved when he spotted them, nodded at the younger man, and walked toward the wharf.

The dock was narrower than Ana expected, the boards slippery, set wide apart, and she worried her foot might get caught between them. Crowds made her nervous because she was so short that she couldn't see over people's heads or around the wide feminine silhouette that was the fashion of the day. Ramón and Inocente formed a barrier between her and the multitude. They steered her to avoid women's skirts, a man carrying a heavy valise, an old man being led by a much younger woman. Five impeccably dressed children walked slowly hand in hand, taking up the width of the dock, while behind them, a toddler screeched at the top of his lungs in spite of his nurse's efforts to comfort him. After the fresh ocean breeze on the open seas, the waterfront smelled of dead fish and pine tar, of sweat, urine, rotting wood. Ana was faint.

"Almost there," Ramón said as he led her forward. She finally stepped on solid ground.

"*Bienvenidos,* welcome!" don Eugenio said, kissing Ana on both cheeks. His whiskers were damp. "What a joy to have you near again!"

While he hugged and kissed his sons, she discreetly wiped the moisture from her cheeks with the back of her glove. From the corner of her eye she caught the bemused smile of the man don Eugenio had been talking to. She turned her back on him.

"This way. Your trunks will be delivered to the house."

Don Eugenio helped her into the open carriage, and Ramón climbed in beside her. Inocente and don Eugenio took the facing seats. The driver, a round-faced man with the blackest skin Ana had ever seen, sat on one of the two horses, clucked his tongue, tugged and loosened the reins as he skillfully guided them through the crowd. As Ana opened her parasol, she noticed that the man who smiled at her was still standing in the same spot. He lifted his hand in a wave, and she wondered that he'd be so brazen, but then realized he was waving at don Eugenio, who acknowledged him with a nod.

"Who is that?" asked Inocente.

"His name is Severo Fuentes. He worked for Rodrigo and has been recommended as manager for the plantation. You'll meet him later."

Ana wanted to get a better look, but when she turned around, he'd vanished.

The street was so congested that they made little progress and beggars took advantage.

"Por favor, señora, una limosna," implored a boy whose left arm ended in a stump just above the wrist.

"Por amor a Dios," begged another, his narrow face peeling in strips as thin and transparent as discarded snakeskin.

On the other side of the carriage a woman pressed along, silently, hands cupped, huge eyes imploring.

Don Eugenio scattered them with his walking stick, but they followed, clamoring, while Ramón, Inocente, and Ana tried to ignore them. It was impossible, however. There were so many, and so persistent.

Ana reached into her reticule, and thinking she was about to hand out alms, the beggars changed their outcries. *"Que Dios la bendiga, señora,"* they blessed her. *"Que la Santísima Virgen se lo pague, señora."* Their grateful voices brought more pleas and outstretched hands, bringing the carriage to a stop.

"If you give to one, they won't leave us alone," Inocente warned.

"I know that," she said irritably. She was born in a city where dodging beggars was a skill learned from childhood. She pulled a handkerchief from the reticule and blotted her cheeks and forehead. The beggars' cries of disappointment were followed by curses.

"Go away. There's nothing for you here." Inocente's walking stick struck a boy on the chest, another on the shoulders. A small boy tried to climb onto the carriage.

Don Eugenio pushed him off. "Where are you going?"

A mounted soldier pressed his horse through the crowd and, in between curses and threats, moved the beggars along. They didn't go far, though, just to the carriage behind, already mobbed.

"Everything all right, Colonel?" the soldier asked, saluting don Eugenio.

"Thank you. We're fine now." Don Eugenio saluted back. "Just trying to get home."

The soldier cleared the road in front of them, and soon they entered the gate and were heading uphill. Don Eugenio brushed the sleeves and lapels of his white suit, even though none of the beggars had touched him. "Disgraceful! Something must be done about these people."

"Every city has beggars, Papá," said Ramón, "and orphans and lunatics. San Juan wouldn't be a proper city without them."

"You might think it's funny, but your mother and cousin can't leave the house without being harassed. It's outrageous."

"Why are there so many children?" asked Ana.

"No orphanage," answered don Eugenio, "and for that matter, no lunatic asylum. There's no place to put them. And the city has grown rapidly. The authorities can't keep up."

Don Eugenio continued his harangue, but Ana couldn't concentrate. She couldn't bear the hot, humid air. Her clothes were heavy; the seven ruffled petticoats under her fine cambric skirt weighed against her thighs. Her scalp was on fire even under her parasol and bonnet. Droplets of sweat slid down her neck and back, dampening her chemise, soaking into her corset, the stays digging into her ribs.

"Are you all right, *querida*?" asked Ramón. "You look flushed."

"It's the heat. It will take getting used to."

"We'll be home soon," don Eugenio promised.

She'd never seen such bright sun, nor shadows with such finely defined edges. The contrast between light and dark was so great that her eyes watered and strained, trying to make out the shapes inside buildings and beyond alleys.

Even away from the harbor, pedestrians vied for space with carts, carriages, and soldiers on horseback and on foot, with servants carrying baskets full of produce or stacks of kindling on their heads. Barefoot stevedores in tattered pants and shirts moved sacks and bundles from the wharves into the wooden buildings lining the waterfront and the streets leading to it. In Sevilla there were people from all over the world, but Ana had never seen so many black men, women, and children. And even along the busy waterfronts in Sevilla and Cádiz, human beings didn't carry such huge loads.

Ana had expected San Juan to be pretty. It was the capital of the island, after all, settled three hundred years earlier. It surprised her that it was so unfinished. The road they were traveling on was deeply rutted. Trenches along one side or the other ran with streams of foul-smelling black water. Ana had read that the government decreed that all houses in San Juan should be masonry, but along the city walls, an amalgam of shacks and *ranchos* leaned against one another, most of them built from scraps and roofed with straw or layers of palm fronds. Dogs, pigs, and goats wandered unattended, eating whatever they could scavenge from the mounds of garbage. Hens squawked, flailing their wings into short, ungainly flight to avoid the wheels of slow-moving carriages or the hooves of horses and beasts of burden. The people in the shacks were dressed in tatters, the children naked, the women in thin cotton skirts and blouses cut low on the shoulder, their unkempt hair tied up loosely or wrapped in turbans.

"This section of the city," don Eugenio said, "is less well maintained, as you can see. Most of the people here are *libertos.* They were slaves who fought on the royalist side in the wars for independence in Spanish America, so the government allowed them to find asylum, and liberty, in Puerto Rico."

"But there are whites here, too," Ana said. "So they can't all be *libertos.*"

"Doubtless you've read that this island was a penal colony for centuries. Some of the men here are *desterrados,* exiles who chose not to or couldn't return to Spain after serving their sentences. Others came here as soldiers and established families. Some," don Eugenio sighed, "came to make their fortune but were seduced by the bottle, by cards, by fighting cocks."

As the carriage wheeled west, the dwellings were more what Ana expected: closely set masonry houses two or three stories high with overhanging balconies and terra-cotta roof tiles. Most had businesses on the ground floor with residences upstairs, evidenced by lace curtains waving in the breeze. The only women on the streets were servants and hawkers, most of them dark complexioned.

The higher they climbed, the newer the houses, and the fewer the businesses on the ground floors. Just as they turned the corner from a small plaza, they stopped in front of a solid, new two-story house with carved doors. A painted tile was embedded in the masonry: Calle Paloma 9.

"Here we are." Don Eugenio helped Ana from the carriage. "Take care, my dear, the stones are slippery." This street was narrower, paved with cobblestones and raised flagstone sidewalks on either side.

As they entered the foyer, Ana's eyes adjusted to the dim, cool interior. The hall led to an open courtyard shaded by blooming plants and bushes. A gurgling fountain in the center masked the street sounds. Doña Leonor was waiting at the bottom of a wide set of stairs to the left, and behind her, Elena. When their eyes met, Ana read in them Elena's happiness and her longing.

A flurry of hugs, kisses, and blessings. A young, barefoot maid appeared to take their hats, gloves, Ana's parasol, and the men's walking sticks. Ana noticed Elena's envious accounting of her fashionable pale green dress and lace pelerine.

"Take this, too," she said to the maid, slipping the pelerine from her shoulders. She was immediately cooler. "My goodness, is it always this hot here?"

"The end of October marks the beginning of the dry season," don Eugenio explained. "San Juan is known for its healthful breezes, and it's unusual for the air to be so still this time of year."

"It's a disaster in the countryside," doña Leonor said, snapping her fan open and leading them upstairs. "We've had no rain in weeks. The crops are suffering, and the cattle . . ."

"Come, my dear, no bad news. They've just arrived," don Eugenio chided his wife.

"You've grown taller, I'm certain of it," doña Leonor addressed her two sons as one. "And you, Ana, have filled out a bit. Your face is rounder. It's most becoming."

She led them into a parlor with tall louvered doors facing a balcony choked with potted geraniums and gardenias. The louvers were half open to cut down the sun, but fragrance weighted the air, and Ana again was assaulted by too much light, color, perfume, heat. Ramón led her to a chair away from the balcony in the cooler part of the room. She found comfort in the furnishings she recognized from the Argoso home in Cádiz by their heavy, carved wooden backs and armrests, their solid Spanishness.

"Your harp!" Ana exclaimed when she saw it in a corner.

"Yes, isn't it lovely!" Doña Leonor looked fondly toward the instrument. "It arrived without a scratch, in spite of my fears. You can imagine how much I missed it."

"She fussed and worried about it more than she worried about me!" Don Eugenio smiled.

Ana noticed that Elena seemed confused about where to place herself, as if the arrival of so many people had thrown off the natural balance. She settled in the chair don Eugenio held for her, next to his own. Elena kept glancing from Ramón to Inocente, bypassing Ana's gaze between them. Finally, she looked at Ana, blushed, lowered her lids, and pressed her lips together.

"Will you play for us later, Mamá?" Ramón asked.

"Of course, *hijo*. I'm so happy that we're together again." Doña Leonor wiped her eyes. "It's been a most difficult adjustment—"

"Let's have some coffee," don Eugenio interrupted, and Elena jumped to ring for the maid.

"We missed you, too, Mamá." Ramón held his mother's hand. "We came as soon as we could."

"But you'll be leaving again." She looked accusingly at Ana.

She avoided her mother-in-law's eyes and sought those of Elena, whose expression was noncommittal. How infuriating she is, Ana thought suddenly, so humble and unassuming. She longed to upset her composure, to reveal the true, passionate Elena.

"We must go to the hacienda, of course," Inocente said. "But we'll spend a couple of months with you in San Juan. You must show us the city. I'm sure you've already met everyone worth knowing."

"She's unstoppable, son," don Eugenio said. "Your mother and Elena have made many friends. They're always visiting someone or other."

"We mostly see to the sick and housebound, don't we, Elena?"

"There is much charity work."

"Surely you saw the beggars on your way here."

The maid entered with an ornate silver tray that Ana remembered from Cádiz. She served with the alert submissiveness of a woman who'd been a servant all her life.

"Would you prefer something cool?" Elena asked softly when Ana hesitated before the offered coffee. Her beautiful blue eyes wouldn't meet Ana's.

"Yes," Ana said. "Yes, I would. Water for me, please." She knows, Ana thought, about me and Ramón and Inocente. She knows.

They spent just over two months in San Juan. Afternoons, Ana accompanied Elena and doña Leonor on their visits, most of them to the wives, sisters, and daughters of the officers in charge of the garrison in El Morro. News from Spain took weeks to arrive on the island, and the local women were eager to hear about the latest developments on the Continent, and to admire Ana's trousseau. They attended Mass in the unostentatious Catedral de San Juan Bautista that smelled of moisture, candle wax, and prayers. They visited convents, stitched shifts for the Dominican nuns, attended a gala celebrating the opening of Puerto Rico's first poorhouse, the Casa de Beneficiencia.

San Juan was Spanish enough to be familiar, but Ana was anxious in the city. She was aware of the capital as a way station, a necessary stop on the road to the real adventure on the other side of the mountain range.

Elena's confusion over Inocente's polite, distant behavior raised an invisible wall between her and Ana. Unlike in their schoolgirl days, they couldn't hide under the covers of the other's cot, whispering, giggling, touching forbidden places. There was nothing Ana could say or do to relieve Elena's unhappiness. She certainly could not tell Elena about her unusual arrangement with the brothers, even though Elena seemed to have already guessed that Ramón and Inocente were both in love with Ana.

Elena wouldn't forgive Ana for altering the scheme they'd devised to always be together. They'd be sisters-in-law, married to twins. No one would suspect their true relationship. They could live in the same house, or nearby, and no one would question it because identical twins would naturally want to live near each other. They'd fulfill their duties as wives to Ramón and Inocente, they'd make homes for them, have their children. Love for their husbands was not a part of the plan. On those nights when Ramón and Inocente went to their mistresses, as married men eventually did, Ana and Elena wouldn't pace their rooms wringing handkerchiefs, begging their patron saints to return their husbands' love, lighting candles, offering Masses and novenas at the cathedral. On those nights when they should be alone cursing their husbands' perfidy, they'd have each other.

Ana, who was sixteen, and Elena, who was fourteen when they first came up with the idea that each should marry one of the brothers, had congratulated themselves on their cleverness. They would avoid the fate of women of their class, of marriage as a business arrangement. Ana and Elena found a way to conform and to rebel at the same time, and no one would be the wiser. When they'd dreamed up the plan, Ana loved Elena with a passion, and her ardor had not cooled over the last ten weeks since her marriage. But Ana had decided that her sexual life with Ramón and Inocente, lackluster or even at times brutal as it was, was the price she had to pay for the world on the other side of the island. Ana's gaze had turned toward her future and her attachment to Elena, though once powerful and satisfying, had already begun to recede like a ship sailing inexorably into the horizon.

If they didn't have to escort the ladies in the evening, don Eugenio, Ramón, and Inocente went to the officers' club or to one of the gambling houses. As in Spain, upper-class women were virtually cloistered in their homes. In a fortress city like San Juan, it was unusual to see them in the streets unless a servant or a relative escorted them. With the men away, Leonor took the opportunity to practice her instrument, but Ana and Elena did what other *sanjuaneras* did to get fresh air. They climbed to the flat roof that afforded a magical view of the city, the harbor, the gray Atlantic Ocean and the shadowed mountain range bisecting the island east to west.

As the day cooled, they walked in circles, elbows linked, their voices rising and falling in the moist breeze as the sweet thrums from doña Leonor's harp rose into the night. Ana and Elena spoke of everything except what lay beneath their seeming closeness. Since her marriage to Ramón, Ana hadn't come to Elena in the night. She'd married Ramón, but contrary to their plan, Inocente hadn't proposed to Elena.

A few days before Ana and Ramón were scheduled to sail for the hacienda, Elena knocked on Ana's door. She peeked into the room, her cheeks flushed, as if expecting to find Ramón and Ana in a marital position. Ana was with the maid, who was clearing her breakfast tray.

"Has he left already?" Elena asked.

"Oh, yes, they both went to meet with their lawyer." The maid pulled up a chair for Elena next to the bed, where Ana laid several stiff petticoats, silk bodices with matching skirts, dainty kid shoes, and delicate lace gloves and mantillas. "I should've left these things in Sevilla. I certainly won't need them where I'm going."

Elena fingered a pale blue taffeta bodice. "Everything is so tiny. They look like doll's clothes."

"If you weren't so much taller, I'd give them to you."

"You talk as if you're not coming back."

"Well, it is unlikely we'll travel to the city as much as we'd like. Ramón has learned that the roads between here and Hacienda los Gemelos are impassable half the year."

"Hacienda los Gemelos?"

"They've decided to name the plantation after their twinship."

"I see," Elena said, the two words brimming with hurt.

Ana waved the maid toward the door, and she left the room on silent bare feet.

Elena stood and grabbed the chairback as if to keep from falling. Her eyes were moist, and her breath was shallow within her corset as she fought for control. "Inocente told doña Leonor—" She choked on her tears.

Ana wrapped her arms around Elena's waist and let her cry on her shoulder.

"I know, I'm so sorry. . . ." Ana moved to kiss her cheek.

Elena jerked back. "You know?" She stood at least a head taller than Ana, and she now looked down at her like a mother who'd just discovered her child's mischief.

"What I mean is, I know it hurts," Ana said, feeling like the child found out.

"What hurts?" Elena flicked tears from her cheeks as if the gesture gave her courage, but Ana heard the rustle of her petticoats within the narrow, corseted frame.

"Elena," Ana said, trying to soften her words. "Inocente doesn't want to marry you."

"Did he tell you that?"

"Yes," Bastoncito said, looking up at La Madona.

Elena fixed her eyes on Ana's. Oh, yes, she knows, Ana thought. She's afraid to say it, to think it, even. What we did with each other is not half so bad in her mind as what I'm doing with Ramón and Inocente. The dread in Elena's face reflected her terror that loving a woman might send them both to purgatory, but loving two men consigned Ana forever to the fires of hell.

Ana felt warmth between her legs, a pulsing desire to kiss that beautiful face, to unlace the tight corset and suck Elena's pink nip-

ples, as she used to do under the covers at the Convento de las Buenas Madres. As Elena did to her.

Elena blushed and turned away. "I came in here," she said, her
back to Ana, "to tell you that I'm not angry. It's not your fault." She
pulled a handkerchief from her sleeve and pressed it to her nose.

She's splendid, Ana thought, so lovely, so good, so candid. Ana
wrapped her arms around Elena's waist again, from the back this
time, and leaned her face against Elena's shoulder blades. She
smelled of lemon and verbena. Elena stiffened inside her corset,
but after a second she placed her hands over Ana's and raised them,
slowly, toward her bosom.

"We were supposed to always be together," she murmured.

"I'm here," Ana said, turning her around and kissing the top of
her breasts.

That afternoon, Ana and Elena joined doña Leonor in her sitting
room. "I separated what's essential from what can be sent later," Ana
told her. "Elena helped. Ramón's and Inocente's clothes as well as
mine fit nicely in the trunk you so kindly gave me."

"We'll send them as soon as possible," doña Leonor said.

"Thank you." After a moment, Ana jumped up, startling doña
Leonor and Elena.

"¿Qué pasó?"

"I almost forgot! I'll be right back." Ana ran from the room.

"She gave me such a start," doña Leonor said.

Elena smiled. "She has such energy."

"Is there much to send later?"

"The trunk is full. She's only taking one formal frock and slippers, two plain cotton dresses specially made, two skirts and bodices
to match, and two pairs of leather shoes. She's also taking her riding
costume and boots." Elena picked up an unfinished shirt from the
pile and began stitching. "It's impressive how well she's thought it
out. It's as if she'd prepared for this trip her whole life."

The older woman grunted. "Her whole life . . . *Está loca.*"

She was interrupted by Ana's return.

"Please keep these for me." Ana handed Elena a black velvet
pouch. Inside were a pearl necklace with a diamond pendant, and
pearl and diamond drop earrings.

"These are lovely," she stuttered as she caressed the jewelry. "Why wouldn't you want to take them?"

"They're from my great-grandmothers," Ana said. "I don't want to risk losing them. Promise me you'll wear them."

"Ana, I can't, they're too—"

"They look good on you." Ana held the necklace close to Elena's face. "Don't you think pearls are perfect for Elena?" she asked doña Leonor. "Her complexion is . . . well, they look much better on her than on me."

Elena was blushing so much that the pearls acquired a whiter brightness. Ana smiled, kissed Elena's cheek. "Keep them safe until I come back." Elena put on the earrings in front of a small mirror between the windows. Ana fastened the necklace and admired how the pearls glimmered against Elena's skin. "Beautiful," she said. Elena blushed deeper. Ana pushed the curls from her own face to show doña Leonor her earlobes, bedecked with ruby earrings. "I'm only bringing these with me because they were Ramón's engagement gift. And of course"—she waved her left hand—"I'll never take off my wedding ring."

"I should hope not."

Leonor looked at both girls standing next to each other, one tall and slender, the other smaller, wiry, freckled as a peasant. She didn't understand what Ramón saw in Ana. Maybe it was her restlessness, so unbecoming in a proper *señorita*. Ana, though not classically beautiful like Elena, had turned Ramón's head, and because Inocente did whatever his brother did, she turned his as well.

Leonor hadn't imagined that she'd lose her sons to someone who looked so inconsequential. Until Ramón met Ana, her boys had been devoted sons, seeking her approval for their plans and dreams. Now Ana's small person dictated every move; her eccentric notion to replicate her ancestor's exploits determined all their futures. Leonor pleaded, cajoled, cried, even threatened to withhold their inheritance, but Ramón and Inocente wouldn't budge once they'd decided to come to Puerto Rico. It irked her that the only way to keep her family together was through this girl, this spirited, stubborn, willful girl. And now, after she'd given in, after the long trip across the ocean, after leaving their friends and family in Spain and settling in this outpost, Ana was making her sons go farther, to a godforsaken plantation that even its owner never visited because it was too far from the capital, too inaccessible. And the only way to keep from losing her sons to an uncertain fate in the jungled interior of this island was to be on this girl's good side.

"I wish you'd stay here," Leonor entreated, hiding her resentment behind a pleading smile. "Ramón can come back for you in a couple of months. No one has lived in that house for years. Who knows what condition it's in."

"I promised to follow my husband wherever our lives led, doña Leonor, just as you did when you married don Eugenio."

"I was a soldier's daughter and knew what it was to move from place to place, following my father's fortunes. You've known nothing but luxury your whole life."

"I'm aware of the hardships waiting for us," Ana said. Leonor heard her unsuccessful struggle not to sound condescending. "I've read much about the settling of the New World."

"Your illustrious ancestor was a man, and he, too, was a soldier accustomed to adversity. You're still a girl."

"I may be only eighteen, doña Leonor, but I'm stronger than I look." Ana stood to her full height. "And I'm determined to make a success of the hacienda." She knelt at Leonor's feet, covered her hands with hers. "I know you're worried that I'll be a burden. . . ." Leonor tried to pull her hands back, but Ana squeezed them and kissed her fingers. "I promise that I won't be, that I'll support them in every way. It's not mere chance that Ramón and I met, you see." Ana exchanged a look with Elena, who still stood by the mirror, bedecked in Ana's jewels. "My destiny was to come to this island, to finish the work my ancestor, don Hernán Cubillas Cienfuegos, started."

"Ana, that man lived over three hundred years ago!"

"But when I read his letters and journals, it was as if he were speaking to me."

"It's madness." Leonor stood abruptly, leaving Ana kneeling at her feet. "It may be your destiny, but it is not my sons'. They were raised for a different life." She stood over Ana, looking down at her with such loathing that Ana lowered her gaze. "I'm not afraid to tell you, just as I've told my husband and my sons." Leonor paced, twisting her wedding ring around her finger in quick, nervous movements. "I don't want you, Ramón, and Inocente to go to the plantation. Everyone tells us that area is dangerous, that pirates still come ashore, that runaway slaves come from their hideouts in the mountains to plunder. And to kill whites."

She covered her eyes and seemed to collapse. Elena jumped to her side and helped her to the sofa. She looked at Ana, who shrugged in a "what am I supposed to do?" gesture. Elena nodded toward Leonor, and Ana sat at her other side, waving her hands before her and rubbing her shoulders, as Elena was doing.

"Tía Leonor, I'm sure don Eugenio wouldn't let Ramón and Inocente go if he thought it was dangerous," Elena said. "Don't you agree?"

Leonor's breath came in short, forced gasps, and she pressed one hand to her heart while, with the other, she fluttered her handkerchief before her face.

"Shall I loosen your stays?" Ana asked calmly.

Leonor turned to Ana as if she'd asked her to get naked in the Plaza de Armas.

"Some water, from the pitcher over there." Elena motioned with her eyes toward the small, lace-covered table by the door.

Ana poured a glassful and Leonor gulped it down. She grabbed Ana's hand. "What will you do if one of you is sick or injured? There are no doctors for miles."

"Inocente has already talked to your doctor, and he's given us some unguents and taught us how to dress wounds, and I brought a book of home remedies. I'm confident—"

"*¡Egoísta!*" Leonor exploded. She stood again and leaned over Ana, who still sat on the sofa. "You only think of yourself. My sons were going to be businessmen until you came along. They were going to an office almost every day. But you'd have them be peons—in a place they've never seen. A wild place. You'd have them abandon their family, their future, their country even, all for a fantasy of yours. A fantasy fed by that *maldito* ancestor."

"Ramón and Inocente want to do this, doña Leonor. It's not just my idea." Ana didn't shrink into the sofa, as Leonor expected. She didn't bend or give or avoid looking into her eyes. She sat stiffly, challenging Leonor with her posture, but on her face was a bland expression that revealed nothing about what she might be feeling.

"Perhaps once they're settled, we can go there," Elena suggested quietly. Ana and Leonor turned to her as if she shouldn't have been there but were grateful not to be alone in the room.

"Yes, you must!" Ana said after a while with what sounded to both Elena and doña Leonor like false enthusiasm.

"Of course," the older woman said with a tired, defeated sigh. "We'll do that. We'll come visit you at . . . at, what are you calling it again?"

HACIENDA LOS GEMELOS

—◆◆◆—

They left San Juan on a blistering January morning from the same wharf that had received them over two months earlier. Doña Leonor and Elena insisted on seeing them off, and the last time Ana saw them, they were crying uncontrollably as don Eugenio herded them into a carriage. Ramón and Inocente waved from the deck of the *Dafne* long after it was possible for doña Leonor or Elena to see them. Their anxiety for their mother was touching, but Ana was glad to get away from her disapproval and animosity. It galled her, too, how her mother-in-law caressed and kissed her sons as if they were babies, and wept whenever Hacienda los Gemelos was mentioned.

"Who knows when I'll see you again," she kept saying, as if they were going to the end of the world, not to the other side of the island. Ana was glad to leave the citadel and the Argosos' stone and stucco house with the cloying flowering pots in the balconies and Leonor's brooding glances. Even placid Elena reached a level of hysteria. Ana couldn't understand it. The departure from Spain hadn't led to such displays or to so much reproach and constant need for reassurance.

The *Dafne* was a cargo vessel, and other than the crew, Ramón, Inocente, and Ana were the only passengers. The ship smelled of salted *bacalao* and of men too long at sea. They sailed along the northern coast of the island, its sinuous shape to port the whole time. Around midafternoon an ominous cloud raced from the eastern horizon and made straight for them. It engulfed them in heavy rain and strong winds that made the timbers moan like live creatures. This time it was Ana who spent most of the trip in the cramped cabin she shared with Ramón, alternately retching into a bucket and praying that the ship wouldn't sink to the bottom of the ocean and prematurely end their adventure. She was dimly aware of Ramón or Inocente applying cold compresses to her forehead, of a cabin boy removing the bucket and replacing it with another, of darkness so complete she thought she'd died, of a sharp ray of sunlight through the porthole that stabbed through her closed eyelids and made her sneeze.

"How do you feel, *querida*?" Ramón asked as soon as she could adjust to the light. After the bouncing and pounding on the waves subsided, she was aware of still being at sea, and her stomach pitched. Ramón jumped for the bucket, but there was nothing to bring up, just the sour, bitter taste of bile in her mouth.

The tempest followed them for a day and a half, then faded into the horizon as swiftly as it had come just as they entered the Mona Passage. They had clear sailing again, but Ana was glad when they tacked toward land and above the thatch roofs she saw a steeple and heard church bells. The *Dafne* didn't make for port, however; it followed a southeasterly course. Just after dawn the next morning, they sailed into a protected cove with no visible dwellings. Thick vegetation grew to the narrow sandy beach lined with coconut palms.

Ana, Ramón, and Inocente were helped down a rope ladder to a dinghy that bobbed and bounced next to the vessel. When she looked down, she saw the rippling, sandy sea bottom through the clear water. Fish in surprisingly bright colors darted this way and that as the oars hit the waves and the dinghy plied to the beach. There was something furtive about the approach, but one of the oarsmen told them that it was common for travelers to reach littoral destinations this way because of the island's few deep-water harbors and notoriously poor roads. She peered into the vegetation along the shore, imagining astonished natives watching from behind the overgrowth as they did when don Hernán landed along a similar pristine beach more than three hundred years before her. When she looked toward Ramón and Inocente they were smiling, guessing where her thoughts had strayed.

Four men and two hounds waited on the sand. Ana recognized Severo Fuentes, whom she'd seen on the dock with Eugenio that first day in San Juan. His hat shaded his face, but she remembered his powerful build. Two black men splashed into the water to pull the dinghy to the beach. They were tall, broad, and naked to the waist but had rolled their pants legs to the knees. When they turned around to pull the boat to shore, the scars on their backs, shoulders, and calves glistened accusingly. Ana averted her face.

As they neared the beach, the two dogs bounded toward them. The terrified men pressed against the dinghy, pushing it toward the larger boat, almost upending it as the hounds swam in their direction. Severo Fuentes whistled. Reluctantly, the dogs backed up, growling and showing their teeth. The other man, who was shorter, caramel-skinned, barefoot, pulled the dogs to shore by their rope collars. Once on the beach, he tied them to a tree. Severo patted their heads, scratched the undersides of their muzzles, said a few words, and turned his back on them as he moved toward the tide line. The dogs paced restlessly, their eager eyes following his figure as he signaled to the men to pull the dinghy to the beach.

Ramón jumped into the giving sand, followed by Inocente's more cautious step. The black men were about to help Ana, but Inocente motioned them aside. "We'll help her."

"Let me carry you"—Ramón reached his arms to Ana—"so that you won't get your feet wet."

Severo Fuentes watched with the attitude of someone about to spring into action if needed. Ana was self-conscious about being the only woman among all those men, but she was especially aware of Severo's expectant posture. She sensed that he was evaluating her, that he'd judge what kind of woman she was by whether or not she'd be carried to the shore.

"Don't be ridiculous. I can manage." She stepped quickly to the bow of the dinghy and leaped to the sand. In a few quick steps she was on dry land.

"*¡Olé!*" Ramón clapped.

"Well done!" Inocente said.

Ana couldn't see Severo's eyes but was sure he would have caught her if she fell, and noticed his slight, admiring smile when she didn't.

With one hand, Ana held down her skirts against the breeze, while with the other, she pressed her hat against her head and mock curtsied.

"Very impressive." Inocente laughed. "Come, meet the *mayordomo*."

Severo Fuentes removed his flat-brimmed *cordobés* hat and bowed ceremoniously, unused to such gestures. His hair was a startling golden color. Ana saw his eyes for the first time, flinty green, behind long, feminine lashes and arched eyebrows the same color as his hair. He had full lips and a clean-shaven face. He was centimeters shorter than Ramón or Inocente, but more sturdily built, with long arms and legs, a muscular torso. He'd obviously taken care to dress for the occasion with a starched white shirt, a light blue sash, a blue *chaquetilla* and pants, and cordovan leather riding boots. He could almost pass for a gentleman, Ana thought, were it not for his hands. They were coarse and tanned, making the hair on them, and on his wrists, shimmer like gold thread in the sun.

Their saddles had been sent ahead with their trunks, but the horses on the beach looked old and shabby. Ana's resplendent new saddle, a wedding gift from Abuelo Cubillas, now graced the back of a tawny mare with a dull, placid face. It looked as gaudy on the old horse as a tiara on a wrinkled *dueña*.

"*Lamentablemente, señores y señora,* your plantation does not yet boast horses like what I am sure you are used to," Severo said with a pained expression. Ana pulled down her veil to hide her smile against Severo's forced effort to erase his peasant's accent.

"How long is the ride to the house?" asked Inocente, briskly adjusting the cinch on one of the horses.

"A couple of hours," Severo said. "The paths are overgrown. We've cleared some, but now that we've begun the *zafra* it's necessary to keep the workers in the cane."

As they talked, Pepe, the foreman, directed the slaves to unload the valises and deliver two bunches of plantains and one of bananas, a crate full of fruit, and a couple of casks to the dinghy. The sailors rowed away.

Before Ramón could help her, Ana was on her mount. He shook his head at her agility.

"A woman who rides astride like a man," Ramón laughed, "is a woman not to be trifled with."

Again she was drawn to Severo's reaction, but he'd just turned to mount.

He led them into a trail invisible until they were under its high canopy of thick-trunked, broad-leaved trees. Ana was grateful for her veil; as they entered the path, insects unable to fly on the windy beach began attacking in swarms. Ramón and Inocente flailed and slapped at their necks, their faces, at the naked skin between cuffs and gloves. But Severo seemed impervious, as secure on his horse as on the ground.

Farther in, the trail widened, but brambles and vines choked the vegetation along both sides. Ana had read that Puerto Rico didn't have the large four-legged predators one would expect in a jungle. But that was hard to believe given the thick forest and the rustling, screeching, grunting sounds that came from it. When they made a turn, a bright green parrot, the undersides of its wings a startling turquoise, flew across the path, shrieking wildly, spooking the horses and causing the hounds to bark angrily. Farther along, Ana saw a huge snake coiled on a hummock of red dirt, its diamond-shaped head draped daintily over its body.

They rode single file through portions of the trail, Ramón and Inocente managing to keep Ana between them. The dogs stayed on either side of Severo's horse, their eyes scanning the vegetation, barking at unseen threats. Every once in a while one of them started into the bush, but a whistle from Severo brought him back, as docile, Ana thought, as Jesusa's pugs.

Pepe and the two slaves, Alejo and Curro, brought up the rear. Pepe rode a mule, but the men carrying the valises and parcels walked on bare feet over the pebbly, uneven terrain. Within a few minutes of entering the forest, the three were far behind. Pepe urged Alejo and Curro to walk faster, his voice growing fainter until eventually it was swallowed into the rustling of leaves and the screech of parrots.

One minute they were in the forest and the next they emerged into an open valley in many shades of green, from pale, almost yellow to olive. Grayish lavender tassels rippled over some fields.

"That's the *guajana*," Severo said, "the cane flower that indicates when the stalks are ready for harvest."

In the far distance, soft-edged mountains stretched west to east. What land wasn't under cultivation was forested. Scattered over the valley, smokestacks pointed to the sky from the surrounding green.

"Why is there smoke over some and not over others?"

"On those plantations the cane is not ready, or there aren't enough workers to bring it in, or owners have given up, and left the land and everything on it."

"They just abandon it?" Inocente asked.

"Some do," Severo said. "A stack with no smoke during the *zafra* means bad news for the owners."

"That won't happen to us," Ramón said. "Our chimneys will be smoking day and night. . . ."

They laughed, but the tension didn't lift until Severo pointed toward a group of buildings to their left. "The windmill over there crushes your cane, and as you can see, your chimney is working."

"That's it?" Ramón asked. Severo nodded.

"Hacienda los Gemelos," Inocente said.

Ana's throat tightened. On a rise, there was the windmill, and next to it, a chimney spouting thick smoke into the azure sky. To the left of the windmill, a fenced pasture held cattle. Beyond it, there were roofs and the living center of the plantation, still some leagues away.

She'd been moving toward this destination not knowing exactly where it was, what it looked like, but now Hacienda los Gemelos was spread below her, calling to her. She wanted to be on the ground, to feel its rich earth, to smell it, taste it even. Long before she reached it, she knew she'd love this land, would love it as long as she lived. She was eighteen years old, had arrived at the end of a journey that was also a beginning, one that she'd already decided was final. I'm here, she said to herself. I'm here, she told the breeze that rippled the *guajana*. I'm here, she said, to the clear and vast sky, to the winking water on puddles along the path, to the birds in formation overhead. I'm here, she said to herself again and again and was overcome by dread at what lay before her. She shook her head to banish fear, crossed herself, and mouthed a prayer of thanks and a request for courage and strength as she followed Ramón, Inocente, and Severo down the hill into the canebrakes.

The mature sugarcane stalks were over two meters high, so once they dropped into the valley, they couldn't see over the *guajana*.

"This field," Severo called back, "is ready to cut. Less than half the potential fields were planted, but we're still shorthanded. The *macheteros* should reach here by tomorrow afternoon."

It was midmorning, but the air in the valley was already hot and humid, giving off ripples of heat into the clear sky. Wind whistled through the sharp leaves of the cane, followed by a clacking sound. Every so often scurrying creatures, like giant rats, crossed the path and frightened the horses. The air smelled of green, wet earth, smoke, and a pervading sweetness.

Swish, thwack, thwack, thump. Swish, thwack, thwack, thump.

Ana heard the rhythm of the cutters before they reached them.

Swish, thwack, thwack, thump.

They came to a field where men severed the long stalks close to the ground with one slice of the machete. They removed the long leaves, then stacked the stem nearby. Women and older children bundled and carried the stalks onto the wood-planked beds of cattle-driven carts, the thuds diminishing as the cane grew higher. Bells jangled every time the bullocks moved their heads. Workers grunted. An overseer yelled. Wheels squeaked. But it was the *swish* and *thwack* of the machete against the cane that got under Ana's skin, the rhythmic cutting as the *macheteros* moved through the fields.

"You can see that several acres are already cleared," Severo said. "The *macheteros* leave a couple of inches of the stalk from which another crop grows."

As they passed, the mounted foremen tipped their hats, but if a worker slowed to take a look, a curse, a threat, a shove, and sharp words kept the rhythm going.

Ramón and Severo rode ahead, with Ana and Inocente behind. Severo was explaining things to Ramón, and though Ana could hear only part of what he said, she gleaned the rest. It impressed her how much land was required not only for the cultivation of cane but also for the operations to turn it into sugar.

She'd read chronicles by travelers in the West Indies like George Flinter, whose book so impressed Ramón, Inocente, and don Eugenio. She'd taken notes along the margins of accounts by plantation owners in the Spanish and British isles. She studied their methods and how they managed their land. But looking around the great expanse from her saddle, she realized that little of it had prepared her for her new life. Every one of her senses was alive, and she now understood how abstract her reading had been in Spain. The actual experience was at once familiar but utterly, overwhelmingly foreign.

They reached the main yard before noon. The *batey* was hectic with the comings and goings of women, men, carts, cattle, mules, children, horses, dogs, stray pigs, goats, and chickens. Leaves and chunks of cane littered the ground. Swarms of flies followed the carts loaded with stalks, and buzzed in bothersome clouds around humans and animals alike. The air was infused with the cloyingly sweet aroma of boiling syrup. Fine gray ash from the chimney covered everything, including the busy workers, the equipment, and the animals, and formed a gray scum over the pond that fed the cattle troughs and provided drinking water for the slaves.

The activity in the *batey* seemed chaotic, but Ana recalled from her reading that there was a strict order to how things were done, and that there was urgency in crushing the cane and boiling its juice as soon as possible after it was cut because the stalks decayed quickly.

"That must be the *trapiche,*" Ramón said as they neared the windmill.

"*Sí, señor,* that's where the stalks are pressed, with wind power supplemented by cattle. Those big wooden rollers extract the juice."

"And that's the bagasse, is that right?" Ana said.

Severo looked back at her. "*Sí, señora.* The by-product is the bagasse. We feed it to the cattle, and also use it for mulch."

Now that he knew she was listening, he spoke louder and turned his head to make sure that Ana and Inocente could hear him. "Next to the *trapiche* is the boiling house where the juice is reduced into crystals in that series of copper kettles." He stopped, as if he'd forgotten something. "I'm sorry. Perhaps this is too much now, after your long journey?"

"No, it's fascinating, isn't it, Inocente?"

"Very interesting," Inocente said. "Please go on."

Severo nodded and continued. "Next to the boiling house is the purgery. Those long trays cool the crystals and allow the syrup to drain into barrels. When the sugar is dry enough, it's formed and packed into one-thousand-pound hogsheads for market."

"As I understand it," Ramón said, "the molasses is used for the production of spirits."

"Yes. Most *hacendados* keep some to make liquor for their own consumption, but most of it's sold to distilleries with the equipment to process quantities for market."

The plantation had been neglected for years; its machinery was ancient. The windmill was on a low rise, its enormous blades in need of repair. The boiling house, purgery, barns, and outbuildings were patched haphazardly, with huge gaps where the boards were either not long enough or rotted. They rode past the *cuarteles* of the unmarried slaves, two rectangular buildings separated by a dusty courtyard where hens picked at the ground. Behind the barracks, several small, thatch-roofed shacks housed married couples and their children. Behind and around the quarters, random gardens were tended by children too young to work in the *campo,* and by old men and women too feeble to do much else.

Ana forced herself to inhale deeply and to let her unsettled nerves subside. Most of the slaves were old and bent over at the waist, as if the loads they'd carried over the years still pressed upon their backs. Several were missing ears, fingers, hands, or arms below their elbows. Some were hobbled, their ankles and feet turned into unnatural shapes. The adults were dressed in rags; the small children were completely naked, their bellies puffed over stick-thin legs.

As they approached the living quarters, Ana was further dismayed that the grand house was in no better condition than the work buildings or the people. The *casona* was two stories high, with an exposed porch around the second floor accessible by two sets of rough-hewn stairs, one in front and another in back, near the ground-floor kitchen shack.

"Most of the lower story," Severo explained, "is for storage. There's also a room for the house servants."

Ana blinked in the midday sun. She was stunned at the rustic house, built from unfinished boards nailed to exposed timbers. The interior dividing walls didn't reach to the ceiling or to the wide plank floor. The ceiling was lined with narrow slats below the corrugated metal roof. A bright green lizard the size of one of her shoes clung upside down to one of the boards, defying gravity. The doors and windows were tall shutters that opened to the porch and were kept closed by sliding a thick pole through iron hooks. Furnishings in the rooms were sparse: a small rectangular table with benches in the dining room, another two benches in the living room, and a table and stool in the study. The walls were recently painted, and the smell of resin hung in the air. Every room was a pale, sad-looking green.

Ramón, Inocente, and Severo watched Ana's face as they walked through the house.

"Well, it certainly needs a woman's touch." She put on a brave smile and turned to drop her hat and gloves on one of the benches. In her fantasies of life in the big, wide-open New World it hadn't occurred to her that she wouldn't live in a masonry house with tiled floors and the dark, heavy Spanish furniture of her comfortable childhood. When she turned around, the men's anxious eyes were on her. Severo Fuentes, especially, watched her, with nervous expectancy. "Don't look so worried," she said, meeting first Ramón's then Inocente's eyes and trying to convince herself more than anyone. "It's going to be fine."

The brothers sighed in relief.

Severo nodded as if she'd answered a question correctly on an exam, and again closed-lipped, briefly, surreptitiously, smiled. She sensed that he knew exactly what she was feeling and had noticed her efforts to dissimulate. Annoyed at herself for her foolishness, it irked her even more that Severo could see what Ramón and Inocente didn't. There was a sharp intelligence beneath his dutiful, obsequious veneer. Just as on the beach, he appeared to be both present and one step ahead of everyone else.

He opened the door to the first bedroom and bowed them in. Facing the window was a mahogany four-poster bed with banana-flower motifs on the finials. The footboard and headboard were deeply carved with broad leaves curving toward each other and bunches of bananas dangling from each trunk.

"You're fortunate to have a skilled carpenter working on the premises," Severo said. "José can make anything. As you can see, he also carves well."

"Surprisingly good," Inocente said. "Don't you think so, Ana?"

"Oh, yes," she responded, not trusting her voice to say more. The bed was elaborately made but looked incongruous in the small room with its single window and wide plank floor. The thin mattress was covered with the linens she had sent ahead. In the corner by the window a shelf held her porcelain washbasin and pitcher, her painstakingly embroidered towels folded neatly over a dry branch nailed to the wall. They looked absurd here. Under the shelf was a chipped chamber pot.

The two trunks that held her and Ramón's clothes, shoes, and intimates were pressed against the wall, next to the linen chest. She'd begun assembling the bride's chest when she was old enough to know she'd be married someday. In the six weeks before her wedding, Elena, Jesusa, and her friends and relatives added to its contents. The chest was filled with lace-edged napkins and tablecloths, embroidered towels, sheets. An ancient crucifix in her family for generations was wrapped inside a fine silk cloth, to be used for the household altar. Ana swallowed hard again.

Severo led them to the next room. It was nearly bare, with a shelf for the washbasin, the towel draped over a hook.

"Unfortunately, José had time to finish only one bed," Severo said. "Don Inocente will have to sleep in a hammock for now."

The *hamaca* hung diagonally across the room. Inocente gently pushed at the heavy, homespun cotton. Ana could tell he was eager to jump into the *hamaca,* but dignity wouldn't allow it in front of the *mayordomo.*

"They're surprisingly comfortable," Severo said. "Some people prefer them to beds."

"I've slept on them," Inocente said. "No need to apologize."

Severo led them back to the living room.

"José is working on chairs and a dining table. I'm sure the *señora* has ideas for the furnishings," he continued. "I'll send him whenever you're ready. But please be aware that during the *zafra* we need every able body. Even the skilled slaves work in the fields."

"I understand," Ana said, without giving away her disappointment: it was obvious that it would be years before they'd have a proper home.

Two women and a man were waiting on the porch. Burrs and small twigs clung to the women's skirts; the man's pants and shirt were torn and stained. They'd been working in the fields but had washed their faces and hands, and the women had rewrapped their head coverings.

"If you permit me, *señora,* the house servants . . ." Severo gestured them to come in. One of the women was a head shorter than Ana but older, with large, alert eyes and a smile that she had trouble keeping in check. There was about her such a cheerful air that Ana felt lighter. Severo introduced her as Flora, her personal maid. The taller, fleshier, younger woman with the buckteeth and suspicious air was Marta, the cook, and the diffident gray-haired man was Teo, the houseman who would attend Ramón and Inocente.

"I'll leave you to rest now," Severo said. "Marta will prepare *el almuerzo.* You'll hear the bell. Here's the key to the pantry," he said, with a jangle from his pocket. "And the key to the liquor closet." He handed them to Ana and looked at Marta, who curtsied heavily and left.

Flora and Teo waited for instructions from Ana.

"Put those things away." Ana gestured toward their hats and gloves, dropped on benches when they came in. "And unpack the valises when they arrive." The servants seemed eager to be given orders that excused them from the grueling work outdoors.

"Señores"—Severo turned to Ramón and Inocente—"I'm at your service when you'd like to review the ledgers."

"Yes, of course," said Ramón. "This afternoon."

"We can ride the fields tomorrow," Severo said.

"That will be fine," said Inocente.

Severo bowed and left them standing in the middle of the living room. Ana sat on one of the rickety benches that squealed threateningly when she moved.

"I'm sorry, *querida,* about the accommodations," Ramón said. "If I'd had any idea   "

"Mamá was right," Inocente added. "You should've stayed in San Juan until we were settled."

"Please don't worry about me," Ana interrupted. "You have enough to think about. Our home will be my project."

"The *casona,*" Inocente said, "isn't ordinarily so close to the work buildings. In a proper plantation, this would be the *mayordomo*'s house."

"Have we displaced Severo, then? Is this his house?"

"Probably," Ramón said.

"Where does he live, then?"

"Maybe in one of the cottages on the property," Inocente said. "He did take some trouble to make this one habitable."

"Green walls," Ana said. "As if there weren't enough green out there." She stepped to the porch facing away from the *batey.* As far as she could see, forested lands rose into the hills. Ramón and Inocente followed her.

"We'll use this house," Ramón added, "and as soon as possible, we'll build a proper one."

"After the harvest," Inocente said.

A breeze rippled across the verdure, like a whisper.

"*Sí.*" Ana once again hooked her arms into their elbows, bringing them closer. "*Sí,* after the harvest."

Within a month, they were settled into a routine. The work began at dawn, with the call of the morning Angelus bell from amid the cane. Ramón and Inocente spent most of their days on horseback with Severo, returning when the bell tolled noon for the *almuerzo* and a short siesta before riding again until dusk, when the bell signaled the evening Angelus. After supper, the bell clanged once more to indicate that all lights should be extinguished in the *bohíos* and *cuarteles,* and everyone should be indoors. During the harvest, the grinders and boiling house ran twenty-four hours a day, but the bell still tolled at the same times.

Ramón and Inocente's itinerant life had taught them to adjust to changes quickly. In spite of Leonor's plans for them to work in offices, the brothers were most comfortable outdoors, among sweating men and beasts. Their boyish features darkened in the sun; their bodies grew muscular. Their voices deepened from speaking louder than allowed in Leonor's fragrant *sala,* but as necessary in the canebrakes and trails.

They sought, trusted, and followed Severo's advice on every aspect of the plantation. The *mayordomo* was six months younger than the twins, but he'd lived harder and had accumulated experience that continually impressed the brothers and Ana. He was also eccentric in surprising ways. His dogs, for example, were Tres, Cuatro, and Cinco.

"Why do you give your dogs numbers and not names?" Ana asked.

"I don't give animals Christian names."

Once a week, he joined them for supper, and when asked, Severo told stories of his travels within Spain and across the sea before he finally landed in Puerto Rico. He began life as a cobbler's son and rose by his wits, skills, and ambition to his current position at Los Gemelos. Ramón, Inocente, and Ana understood that his work here was preparing him for someday owning his own plantation.

"'If you are ambitious of climbing up to the difficult, and in a manner inaccessible, summit of the Temple of Fame,'" Severo once recited after a bit too much brandy, "'your surest way is to leave on one hand the narrow path of Poetry, and follow the narrower track of Knight-Errantry, which in a trice may raise you to an imperial throne.' The great Cervantes, *señores y señora,* never visited the New World, but he knew what was required to become a success in these lands."

"You see yourself as a *caballero andante.*" Ramón smirked.

"If you insist, *señor.* Yes, a knight-errant in search of fame and fortune, *sí, señor,* that's me."

"But," Inocente added, with an ironic smile, "the passage you've just quoted is followed by 'With these words, Don Quixote seemed to have summed up the whole evidence of his madness.'"

Severo wiped his mouth with the back of his hand and laughed. "Yes, but don't forget, that *'de músico, poeta y loco, todos tenemos un poco,'*" he concluded, and they laughed.

That night Ana lay in bed long after Ramón had fallen asleep, thinking about the phrase. We are all a bit of a poet, a bit of a musician, a bit mad, she agreed. But she thought that Severo Fuentes, who could quote Cervantes with uncanny precision, was perhaps the maddest of them all.

A VOICE IN HIS HEAD

Back in Boca de Gato, one of the neglected hamlets north of Madrid, his parents had wanted Severo Fuentes Arosemeno to be a priest. He was the third and youngest boy in his family, and it was unlikely that their meager earnings would be enough for three cobblers in their small shop in their village. His father brought him to the parish padre, who taught Severo to read and write, and taught him Latin, the language of the learned. But while Padre Antonio doted on Severo's quickness and intelligence, everyone else in the village ridiculed him for having ambitions greater than to sit at the cobbling bench for the rest of his life as his brothers and father were doing, as his grandfather and uncle did, as who knew how many generations before them.

In spite of Padre Antonio's efforts to make a priest of him, Severo showed no vocation. He wanted a life away from the craggy streets and narrow alleys of Boca de Gato, and longed for a life outdoors, far from the cramped house with attached workshop where day after day his father and brothers carved hard leather into thick-soled boots and shaped pliant kidskin into ladies' slippers.

One morning shortly after his ninth birthday, as he was getting ready to go to the parish house, Severo heard a voice inside his head. "Leave Boca de Gato," it said. He'd heard voices before, but they were usually his own, berating him for doing something stupid or urging him to jump into what frightened him. He'd never heard a voice different from his own, or one with such specific instructions. "Madrid. Go to Madrid."

That very day he kept walking past the parish house and beyond the boundaries of Boca de Gato. The capital was thirteen leagues away on the other side of a mountain range. He scrabbled his way toward the city by working odd jobs in exchange for a place to sleep and a meal. It was 1829, toward the end of a relatively stable period after the depredations of the Napoleonic era and before the First Carlist War. He was modest and hardworking, and the peasants who took him in were mostly kind. All he remembered years later, however, was not the people, but the names of the rough mountain terrain he traversed—Cerro Matallera, El Pedregal, Miraflores de la Sierra.

It took him six months to reach the capital. From the top of a hill, he saw a confusion of roofs and steeples long before he entered the gates. The closer he came to the city, the more people walked with him on the Camino Real, many of them like himself, young boys and men with no other place to go but the road before them.

In the capital, Severo slept in dreary alleys in the shadow of the cathedral. He stole food when he couldn't find work, fought other boys who, like him, had abandoned their homes or were abandoned by their families. Stronger, smarter, and braver than many of the forgotten children of the streets, he soon became their leader and organized a gang of thieves and pickpockets that terrorized the capital for almost two years.

He was caught, beaten, and thrown into a prison with men who'd committed far worse crimes. Murderers, traitors, and political prisoners were hanged, but drunks, thieves, adulterers, and debtors were locked up. Many of these desperate men longed to start their lives over. They filled Severo's head with stories about the New World, territory settled over three centuries earlier by Spain. Those mysterious lands, including Peru, Mexico, and Argentina, were no longer colonies, but it was still possible to become a great *señor* in Spanish America. Severo spent four months in prison dreaming of boarding a swift ship with fluttering white sails that would take him to Spanish America. There he'd make his fortune in gold and silver, which his elders assured him would be revealed if he kicked the ground hard enough.

Severo was eleven years old, child enough to imagine his return to Boca de Gato dressed in splendid silk breeches and brocaded *chalecos* like the ones worn by the dandies who walked the streets of Madrid—the men he so adeptly pickpocketed and whose pretty ladies he admired. He'd build a house for his mother and retire his father from the cobbler's bench, and he'd become a *caballero,* riding splendid Andalusian steeds on a silver-studded saddle.

One day Severo heard the voice inside telling him to confess, so he lined up during the weekly visit of the prison curate.

Padre Gregorio was impressed with Severo's knowledge of Latin and the liturgy. "You're an intelligent boy," he scolded. He fluttered his scented fingers toward the grim, foul-smelling cell Severo shared with nine other men. "How did you allow this to happen to you, *hijo mío?*"

"I was hungry, Padre."

"Thousands of people are hungry in this city, son, and they don't become criminals."

"But many do, Padre," Severo said. The priest gazed at him, looking for contempt in Severo's tone or movements. He saw nothing but regret. Severo's face softened. "I'm not a bad boy."

"No, son, I don't believe you are." Padre Gregorio placed his hand on Severo's bristly head, murmured a prayer over him, and then asked, in Latin, "Do you repent fully and completely?"

"Yes, I do, Padre," Severo responded in the same language, fully aware that the padre's question could be answered in only one way.

"Do you promise to uphold the Ten Commandments, especially the ones you broke in your troubles?"

"Yes, Padre, I promise." His voice thickened, and Padre Gregorio appreciated Severo's restraint, how he pressed the fingers of his left hand around his right wrist as if to keep from slapping his own face. He looked up at the priest with such a pitiable, contrite expression that the old man was moved.

"I'll see what I can do," he said in Spanish, squeezing Severo's shoulder.

Padre Gregorio vouched for the boy after he'd served only half his sentence. He found Severo a job as a runner and floor sweeper for Marítima Argoso Marín. Padre Gregorio also convinced his brother and sister-in-law to allow Severo to sleep in a shack in their backyard. Severo repaid *señor* and *señora* Delgado's kindness with his labor. He was good with his hands and soon fixed hinges on doors, replaced and raised the sagging clothesline in the courtyard, nailed down squeaky boards on the stairs, and straightened wayward balusters. The Delgados were delighted with his industry.

Their cook, Noela, was a tall, bony woman whose husband managed the Delgado farm near Allariz, in Galicia. Noela went home for Christmas, for Holy Week, and for a month in August with her employers, but the rest of the year she lived in a room behind the kitchen. One night, she noticed that Severo brought home discarded newspapers every day and sat with them at the kitchen table after dinner.

"What do you read?" She was hard to understand because she spoke Galician and assumed everyone understood it.

"The newspapers tell about the world," Severo said.

"You're lucky you can read. I never learned my letters."

"I can read aloud, if you like."

After she put the dishes away, Severo read to Noela as she sewed. If he looked up from the papers, however, her bright eyes were on him, not her work, as if she believed that he'd created the contents of the newspapers for her amusement. Once a month, she dictated letters to her husband and parents, which Severo wrote and posted. None of her relatives could read either, but the correspondence was brought to the parish priest, or to a learned villager who charged two pennies to read them, five pennies to write a response.

"Do you write to your parents?"

Severo lied, but that night he wrote to his mother, letting her know that he was safe and had a job, with no mention of his reasons for leaving, the journey to Madrid, the years on the streets, the time in prison.

He worked six days a week at Marítima Argoso Marín's offices. When making a delivery, he was sometimes given a penny or two as a tip, which he saved because he still had the idea that someday he'd sail to the New World to become a rich man. He was known to the thugs and urchins on the streets, who sneered and taunted him for pretending he was better than they were.

Paquito, an older boy who'd become the leader of a gang after Severo was imprisoned, wanted to prove that he was in charge after Severo was seen around town again. He followed Severo as he made his deliveries, jeering and teasing him, goaded by the other boys.

"*No me jodas,*" Severo said. He was carrying a dossier from Marítima Argoso Marín to a waiting customer at a bank.

"Don't fuck with me," Paquito repeated in a falsetto, swishing an invisible skirt to indicate Severo was a sissy.

Severo quickened his pace, but the boys followed and surrounded him, pushing and shoving. He was three doors from the bank and intended to make his delivery, but he didn't want the boys to think he was running away from them. He faced Paquito.

"I don't want to fight, but if you provoke me, you'll be sorry."

"Ay, *la señorita* don't want to be provoke, ay, ay, my smelling salts," Paquito said, pretending to go into a swoon.

Severo took the chance and ran into the bank, caught his breath, delivered his documents, received his tip. He took a moment to talk to himself. I know how to defend myself, he thought, but if I don't put an end to this *jodienda,* I'll have to fight every boy in Madrid. He meant to avoid prison again, and he needed a different kind of respect so that the boys would leave him alone. He was strong, but the streets and prison had taught him that mental toughness was more effective than fists. When he emerged, Paquito and his boys were waiting, as Severo expected.

"Chicken!" they called. *"¡Cobarde!"*

Severo stepped right up to Paquito. The other boys surrounded him, but he knew they were waiting for Paquito's first move. "What did you say?" Severo asked, nonchalant. It was the way he said it, his cool tone and relaxed stance, Severo noticed, that changed something in Paquito. He's scared, Severo thought. "I heard you say something," he said, turning his head toward where they'd surrounded him before. "Over there. What did you say?"

Paquito puffed his chest and his face turned red, his bravado returning. "You're a fucking coward," he said, and to prove it he lunged at Severo as the other boys circled them. Paquito wrestled Severo to the ground, kicking and punching, spitting, calling him a *pendejo* and a sissy and a *mariquita.* Severo warded off the blows as best he could while Paquito flailed wildly. A crowd gathered, and Severo knew that the police would be coming to break things up. He stood and pulled Paquito upright by his breeches, then punched him under his ribs, left, right, left. As Paquito bent over to protect his belly, Severo elbowed the top of his head. The boy crumpled to the ground, his limbs jerking. From the corner of his eye, Severo saw a policeman running in their direction. The other boys scattered as Severo melted into the crowd, rubbing his elbow, working to control his hard breathing. He turned the corner and slowed to a normal pace, as if he'd just come from a good meal. Paquito lay unconscious on the ground as passersby stepped around him. He was just another of the discarded of the city, and no one cared what would happen to him now that all the excitement was over. Severo never saw him again, and the other boys stayed out of his way.

Every so often Severo stole something too temptingly available, like the day he took a copy of *La vida es sueño* from a used-book stall on the street while the vendor argued politics with another customer. And it gave him a thrill from time to time to pick a coin or two from a distracted or drunken *señorito*. But mostly, he delivered dossiers, swept the floors at Marítima Argoso Marín, read as much as he could, helped around the Delgados' house, and tried to stay out of trouble.

His days folded into each other and his boyish squeak changed into a man's voice. Noela teased him about the stubble growing on his chin and upper lip, and how his sleeves were too short for his arms and his breeches too tight. A few days later Padre Gregorio delivered a new change of clothes for Severo, collected from parishioners.

The shirt, pants, vest, and jacket were too big, but Noela took in the seams as he read to her. He buffed the shoes until the leather gleamed, and packed rags into the front to be removed as his feet grew. He wore the entire ensemble to church the next Sunday and noticed the admiring glances from girls and women.

"You already look like a man," Noela said, and Severo realized that she was seeing him differently. Lately, he'd noticed that she sat closer to him than she used to, and while measuring him, and later making sure the clothes fit, she seemed to use her hands more than necessary for the tasks. But he wasn't sure, and he didn't want to get in trouble. One night, when the Delgados were out for the evening, Noela served his supper but instead of staying in the kitchen while Severo read to her, she said she was going to bed early. He was disappointed, because he had a battered copy of *El conde Lucanor*, purchased at the same stall where weeks earlier he'd stolen *La vida es sueño*. She left, her hips swaying in a way that made him wonder. She was probably as old as his mother, although Mamá would never shake her hips like that, nor had Noela done it before. He was confused and decided it was probably time for him not to spend so much time with Noela in the kitchen because he liked living in the Delgados' house, and his job at Marítima Argoso Marín, and saving his money so that he could sail to América where he'd kick the ground to loosen gold nuggets. He finished his dinner, washed and put the dishes away, and took his usual bench at the kitchen table.

It was hard to concentrate on the first story in the book—"What happened to a Moor who was king of Córdoba"—when Noela shuffled in wearing a nightgown and an elaborately embroidered shawl that looked out of place among the blackened pots and pans, the smoking fireplace, the rough table and bench, the stone floor.

"When a woman tells you she wants to go to bed early, and moves away from you shaking her hips like this"—she showed him, with a coquettish smile that was as incongruous as her shawl—"she means she wants you to follow her."

Severo was thirteen years old. He had urges and imagined what it would be like to be with a woman, but he had no idea what women meant or didn't mean. "Did you want me to come to bed with you?" he asked Noela, making sure that what he was hearing was what she was saying.

"You're kind to me and a very good boy, but now you're an *hombrecito.* It's the only gift I can give you."

She was bony and long-legged, and smelled of ashes and garlic. But she didn't laugh when his excitement was greater than his skill. She was as eager as he was but also patient. While he subsequently had many women over the course of his life, Severo never learned as much from any one of them as he did from Noela, whose greatest gift was to teach him that women don't have to be pretty to be desirable.

Severo's supervisors at Marítima Argoso Marín were impressed with his disciplined habits and his ability to read and write. In his thirteenth year he won a promotion from floor sweeper and message boy to assistant clerk. After two years, he was moved to apprentice *escríbano,* scrivener. From time to time Padre Gregorio came around to the Delgados' to see how Severo was doing. The priest died happy that he had extended his protection and friendship to the sort of young man who not only needed it, but who would surely succeed in life only because of timely pastoral intervention.

However, a cobbler's son, even a moderately educated one; a convict, even for petty crimes committed in his youth; a poor man, albeit one with a job could only go so far in Spain's capital. One morning, just as he received his wages, Severo heard an internal voice telling him that, once again, it was time to go. He cleaned his pen nibs, stoppered the inkwells, stacked his papers neatly in their appropriate archives, and walked out of the office where he was tied to a desk from early morning to late evening transferring figures from one ledger to another. He collected his only other change of clothes, the purse where he hid his money under a stone in the floor in his shed, and the five books he owned, two purchased, three stolen. Noela was at the market, the Delgados were in their rooms, the street was congested with servants, vendors, children walking to school. Three *señoritas* selecting ribbons from a dry goods counter turned to watch him go by, and the coachman of the Delgados' neighbor waved hello but asked himself why Severo was on the street at this time of day when he would ordinarily be at work. He noted the bundle he was carrying, and the coachman later told Noela that she should make sure that nothing was missing in the house. "I didn't trust that boy," he said, even though in the five years he'd seen him coming in and out of the Delgado house he hadn't voiced his concerns about their boarder.

Six weeks after he left Madrid, Severo arrived at the port of Cádiz and shipped out as cabin boy, landing in the New World weak from seasickness and the physical and mental abuse heaped upon him by the captain and every seaman on board. The minute he stepped on terra firma in the steamy capital of the smallest of the Greater Antilles, Severo Fuentes swore never to set foot on a ship again.

Directly in front of the dock where the transfer boat dropped him there was a warehouse, and above its massive doors in delicate gold lettering was the legend MARÍTIMA ARGOSO MARÍN. Severo knew, of course, that the firm had offices in Spanish America, but never imagined he'd land almost literally on the doorstep of one of them.

Until then, listening to the voices in his head had worked well for Severo. He knew enough not to appear in the Argoso Marín office to ask for a job until after he'd regained his health and washed and put on the suit of clothes wrapped in canvas brought across the ocean. The alleys leading from the docks up the hill to the residential district and beyond to the forts were packed with cheerless rooming houses just a few steps from disconsolate brothels. A doctor who treated mostly venereal diseases and who set bones broken in fights by men just off the ships attended to Severo's ailments, which were no more nor less than what he saw day in and day out. After paying the doctor, Severo spent what he'd earned aboard ship on whores and liquor. A week later, he appeared at the door of Marítima Argoso Marín.

Rodrigo Argoso Marín took one look at Severo and saw what no one else had, or what perhaps only emerged after two years on the streets, four months in prison, two years sweeping floors and delivering dossiers, another three years hunched over boring ledgers, and seven cruel weeks at sea: Severo was a young man others would fear. The education that made it possible for him to advance far beyond his prospects hadn't tamed him.

It was 1837, and while two years earlier the Spanish Crown had signed a treaty with Great Britain forbidding the trafficking of slaves from Africa, officials looked the other way if chattel first arrived on Martinique, for instance, or Guadeloupe, and were then shipped to Cuba, Puerto Rico, or the United States, where they were necessary for the labor-intensive cultivation of tobacco, cotton, and sugar. To avoid legal complexities, Rodrigo made sure that human cargo in vessels owned by Marítima Argoso Marín arrived in inconspicuous shallow harbors. He needed someone to transport the Africans from wherever he managed to land them near their destinations in sugarcane plantations, the main markets for the trade on the island. The right man for the job must be able to read and write so that he could handle the necessary paperwork. He must be fearless, because the slaves' efforts to escape usually involved killing the boss. In addition, he must be ruthless, because slaves who attempted escape could be punished by death. The most important requirements, Rodrigo thought, were the man's ability to instill fear and respect in another human being and his willingness to kill, if necessary, without thinking too much about it. Severo got the job.

BRAZOS FOR THE FIELDS

———◆◆◆———

Ana's days were long and arduous. She was responsible for the slaves' clothing, health, and weekly food allotment. She oversaw the *casona*'s cleaning and cooking, designed the kitchen gardens, and organized the care of the animals raised for food. With all *brazos*—"arms" as Severo referred to the workers—needed in the fields, she wasn't above collecting eggs in the henhouse, picking a chayote for dinner or a grapefruit for dessert. Their clothes and linen were washed in a nearby river and soon showed the stress of being beaten against rocks and draped over bushes under the sun. Her mending basket was always full and she spent hours sewing, her mother's complaints about her uneven stitches and careless seams a constant echo over three thousand miles of ocean from Sevilla.

After a week at Hacienda los Gemelos, Ana wrote to her parents admitting that her life was more austere than she'd expected, but that she was getting used to the privations.

"Cubillas and Larragoity blood course through my veins. I feel the spirit of our ancestors in this land and am mindful that they met their challenges with courage and curiosity. I'm fulfilled by the rewards of hard work. At the end of each day, I'm proud of how much I have accomplished."

Ramón and Inocente weren't good correspondents, so Ana wrote cheery reports to their parents. She let doña Leonor know that her sons were well and described the hacienda in sufficient detail to give her a sense of how they lived, without undue particulars about the hardships. Don Eugenio, Ana knew, was more interested in whether the inflated numbers of hogsheads of sugar and puncheons of molasses and rum that his sons promised before they left Spain were being realized. Since they were short of workers and less than half the potential fields were cultivated, she explained, their first harvest would yield less than they'd hoped. However, from her cash dowry, she wrote, they'd purchased ten more strong men, each costing three hundred pesos each. Two more fields would be cleared and planted, expected to mature within twelve to eighteen months, to increase their harvest from thirty to forty *cuerdas* of cane cut and processed.

It was harder to write to Elena because there was much Ana wished she could say but couldn't. Over the six months since her marriage, lovemaking had become the least satisfying of her chores. Other than being scrupulous about whose turn it was to have her, Ramón and Inocente had no interest in improving their sex lives. She didn't know how to talk about it with them, and attempts to show them what she liked seemed to embarrass them more than they did her. Intercourse had become as unpleasant and unavoidable a task as mending.

But she couldn't dwell on her yearning for romance and tenderness. Her longing felt like a weakness, vestiges of the unwanted girl who could never do right. She turned to her work instead, and wrote letters to the Argosos, to her parents, and to Elena about what she did but not about what she felt.

The correspondence was stashed in a pouch by the door to be taken if Severo, Ramón, or Inocente rode to Guares, the nearest town, a rough half day's journey on horseback, or if a merchant ship like the one that brought them anchored off the beach to the south of the plantation. Ana only knew for sure if the letters were received when a response arrived, weeks later.

She drew up plans for a house far from the noise of the *batey* and the ash and smoke of the chimney over the boilers. It was a near replica of her grandfather's rambling farmhouse in Huelva, but with bigger windows and doors and a covered gallery to provide shade. She abandoned the plans when she felt nostalgic for Abuelo Cubillas. She was sure she wouldn't see him again, slowly puffing on his pipe, nor his gardens, orchards, and vineyards. He'd blessed her venture, and she now had to create her own place in the world.

She put away her city clothes and most of her fine linens and china in a locked *rancho,* to be brought out when they built a new house. Their table was now set with the crockery found in the kitchen. To supplement it, José made wooden plates. For drinking, he polished coconut shells to a high sheen and made bowls from dried calabashes of all sizes. The gourd cups and bowls, called *ditas,* were the same as the ones given to the workers for their meals, except that José decorated the ones for the *casona* with fanciful birds, animals, and butterflies.

As a mostly neglected only child in Spain, Ana had staved off loneliness and isolation by keeping busy alongside the servants. They welcomed her company, were willing to teach her their skills, and imbued her with the courage that comes from practical knowledge. She didn't mind getting her hands dirty. At Hacienda los Gemelos, she looked at her more unpleasant duties, like what to do about the foul-smelling coops and sties too close to the *casona,* as problems to be solved rather than avoided. At the same time, she was fully aware that the men and women who now worked alongside her weren't paid servants but chattel. They were property, necessary to accomplish her goal to tame a wilderness, just as her ancestor had envisioned.

Ana had read that within a generation of the arrival of the con-quistadores in Puerto Rico during the early sixteenth century, most of the *taínos* don Hernán had observed had escaped to other islands or were annihilated. To provide an alternative labor force, colonists kidnapped Africans. The survivors among the enslaved *taínos* were absorbed into the European and African populations.

The Crown forbade direct commerce between the island, a Span-ish colony, and other countries. The *subsidio,* the Crown's annual subsidy used to pay the thousands of soldiers and functionaries, was often late due to bad weather, piracy, and corruption. Unable to trade legally, the residents evolved a subsistence economy. With the exception of those living on grand cattle ranches that provided meat and skins, the vast majority of the island's farmers were scat-tered among small plots, many of them on untitled lands. Travelers, commentators, and priests examined and reported on the conditions of Puerto Rican peasants—known as *jíbaros*—noting the appalling poverty and the rampant mixing of races.

Field Marshal Alejandro O'Reilly, Friar Íñigo Abad y Lasierra, the naturalist André Pierre Ledrú, and the mercenary George Flinter, among others, also noted the extraordinary fertility of the land but regarded the *campesinos* as shiftless. The *jíbaros,* they complained, moved frequently, squatted on Crown-owned lands, and with a few whacks of the machete cut down palm branches and trunks for their cottages roofed with fronds and straw. The European travelers concluded that Puerto Rican *jíbaros* were content to grow just enough to feed their families so that they could spend the rest of the day swinging in a hammock or raising fighting cocks, drinking homemade *aguardiente,* and gambling. Why, the commentators asked, would *campesinos* want to work harder when they could dig a few *batatas* from the ground, pick a few mangos and avocados, collect a few eggs—enough for their simple needs? A survival economy, they warned the king, doesn't grow and doesn't generate revenue.

In the late eighteenth century, observers and officials recommended that the Spanish Crown increase the size and number of sugar plantations and import more Africans to provide a controllable alternative to the intractable local labor force. A cap was imposed so that slaves wouldn't comprise more than 12 percent of the population.

As the number of slaves on the island increased, so did their maltreatment. In order to regulate the behavior of slaves and owners, the Spanish government issued slave codes, the most recent in 1842. Owners were to "diligently make [slaves] understand that they owed obedience to the authorities, that they were obliged to revere priests, to respect white persons, to behave courteously toward colored people, and to live in good harmony with fellow workers." The code defined how much food slaves should be allotted, how many items of clothing should be given every year, and how many hours made up a workday (ten, but sixteen during harvests). Slaves were "obliged to obey and respect their owners, *mayordomos, mayorales* and other supervisors as if they are their fathers, and [they are obliged to] perform their chores and jobs they are assigned and if they do not fulfill any of their obligations, they are to be correctively punished by the person charged as boss according to the defect or excess, with prison, fetters, chains, stocks or clamps, which will be placed at the feet and never on the head, or with whips not to exceed twenty-five lashes."

Owners were supposed to abide by the forty-eight articles of the code, but abuses were rampant, and if an owner was reported for mistreatment, he was rarely prosecuted.

In 1845, the same year that Ana, Ramón, and Inocente established Los Gemelos, the Spanish government banned the importation of captured Africans into Puerto Rico. By then eighteen slaves—more than half the adult workforce at the hacienda—were *bozales:* men and women abducted from Africa. Most of them had worked on Danish St. Thomas or St. Croix, or on the sugar plantations of the French colonies of Martinique and Guadeloupe. In efforts to escape, they took to the sea, where ships trawling the horizon for runaways picked them up. Rather than return them to their original plantations, the captains sold the runaways at clandestine auctions on hidden coves and beaches on other islands. By buying them in covert sales, the new owners avoided the twenty-five-peso tax the Spanish government imposed for each. Ten of the thirty-five slaves owned by Hacienda los Gemelos were acquired in unauthorized sales by Severo Fuentes.

Severo, who leased them to the hacienda, owned the most-skilled slaves. José the carpenter, his wife, Inés, and their children belonged to Severo. So did Flora, Marta the cook, Teo the houseman, his wife, Paula, and a timid little girl called Nena, who carried water, cleaned the house, and washed clothes by the river.

Criollos made up the rest of the workforce. Born into slavery in Puerto Rico, they had no more rights or license than those captured from other places.

Severo kept a close watch on the *bozales* because they were more likely than *criollos* to attempt escape. They were forbidden to speak their own languages. No matter where they came from, once in the Spanish colonies, they were baptized and given new names. Those from Martinique and Guadeloupe, from St. Croix or St. Thomas, spoke French, Dutch, or English. They, too, were made to learn Spanish.

In spite of efforts to Hispanicize them, however, *bozales* retained the practices and prejudices of their native cultures. Some were natural enemies, their antipathies surviving beyond the grueling transport across the ocean. Liberal use of the whip forced them to work together, but in at least one case, a *bozal* murdered another within a month of arriving in Los Gemelos, because in Africa their clans were enemies. Severo Fuentes whipped him to within a breath of his life, but slaves were so expensive and difficult to train that he was allowed to recover and was put to work in the cane as soon as he could stand.

The Creole slaves were both afraid of and in awe of the *bozales,* who brought traditions with them that the native-born had either forgotten or never knew. Efforts to make them accept Catholicism as the one true faith were only partly successful. Neither *bozales* nor *criollos* saw any reason why they shouldn't worship their ancestral orishas alongside Papá Dios, la Purísima Virgen, and Jesucristo. The *españoles* renamed everything into their language anyway, so Africans called their orishas by Spanish names: Yemayá, the Yoruba goddess of the seas and fertility, was the Virgin de Regla; Babalú Ayé, the god of healing, functioned the same as Saint Lazarus; Obatalá, who created human beings from clay and was the protector of the physically deformed, was the same as Our Lady of Mercy.

Three of the *bozales* were followers of Islam. They refused to eat pork, the principal meat for their sustenance. They traded their ration of fatback to others for vegetables and corn flour. They wanted to pray five times a day, but when they tried, they were lashed and made to return to their labors.

Whether *bozales, criollos,* or slaves from one of the nearby islands, the majority of blacks in Puerto Rico were Yoruba, Igbo, and Mandinka people from sub-Saharan and central Africa.

Flora was a Pygmy from the Congo, captured as a girl along with her mother, who died before they reached the Indies. She'd worked as the personal maid of a merchant's wife.

"She liked I am so small," said Flora, who stood just over four feet tall. Her former mistress wanted a maid below her sight line.

Flora had scars along her shoulders and down her arms, put there she said, "before my first blood." Many of the *bozales* had elaborate designs on their faces and arms created by scarring and mortifying the skin with charcoal and hot-pepper juice. Others were tattooed. Teo had different-size dots around his eyes and across his forehead and cheeks. Paula, his wife, had faint vertical lines across her jaw, and intricate circles on the backs of her hands and arms. A couple of the older men and women had oddly shaped earlobes and lips where they once wore disks, bones, and other decorations. At first, their scars and markings repelled Ana, but the longer she lived at Los Gemelos, the more she looked past what she'd rather not see.

Severo told Ana, Ramón, and Inocente that most sugar plantations in Puerto Rico averaged seventy-five *cuerdas*. That meant that Hacienda los Gemelos, with two hundred *cuerdas,* was huge, although most of the land was woods, pasture, and forest.

"We have thirty *cuerdas* ready for harvest and four trained *macheteros.* Each cutter is expected to harvest a minimum of a *cuerda* of sugarcane per day," Severo told them, "but due to weather, injuries, broken tools, and any number of other disruptions, they don't always achieve their daily goal."

"How about some of the others?" Ana asked.

"Half of them are too young, too old, or too maimed to work in the *cañaveral,*" Severo explained. "When I found the ledgers that the previous *mayordomo* kept, I discovered that three men listed in the account books had run away and were never captured."

Ana computed mentally. There were now forty-eight slaves on the hacienda: thirty-two owned by Ramón and Inocente and the sixteen Severo leased to them. According to him, only twenty were capable of the backbreaking work of cutting, stacking, transporting, and processing cane. They were expected to do the work of twice that many.

As they gained experience of the operations, Ramón and Inocente realized that the work on the hacienda was more challenging than they'd imagined, or Ana had promised. One evening, Ana and the brothers were having dinner. Ana had underestimated how much food to bring from San Juan, and their meals were now only slightly better than what was given to the workers: mostly tubers and plantains, *bacalao,* whatever fruit was in season.

"Do you remember those reports by Colonel Flinter and others?" Ramón asked as he speared a chunk of boiled malanga on his fork.

"Yes." Ana heard the edge in his tone.

"Well, they vastly exaggerated the potential while blatantly understating actual conditions," Inocente completed his brother's thought.

"Of course they would," Ana said. "They were employed by the Crown to encourage Europeans to immigrate to Puerto Rico."

"You didn't say that then."

The resentment in his voice was new.

"I didn't know it then."

"Do you remember, Inocente," Ramón continued, "the accounts told of blacks and whites working side by side in the cane to collectively reap the enormous rewards?"

Inocente made much of pulling a spine from a chunk of stewed *bacalao*. "It's not quite that way, is it?"

"Not exactly," Ana said. "But we've just started. Severo said that by the time he arrived most of the white laborers had already been hired."

That was true, but Ana had noticed that white men, especially, refused to work in jobs traditionally identified as slave labor. When she visited the *trapiche* where the stalks were crushed, and the boiling house where the juice was reduced to syrup, she was nearly overcome by the noise, the heat, the flies, the smoke and ash, the cloying smell, the frantic pace. During the harvest, the *trapiche* and boiling house ran twenty-four hours a day in eighteen-hour shifts with only a couple of breaks for meals. While the work required a high degree of skill and knowledge, few men with other options were willing to work under such conditions, and only slaves processed the sugar.

Like many of their contemporaries, Ana and the twins were ambivalent about the institution of slavery. But living among slaves now, they were confronted with every aspect of its reality. At the same time, what humanitarian feelings pricked at the edge of their conscience were tempered by the urgent need to realize a gain on their investment in *brazos* for the fields.

As their first *zafra* came to an end, Ramón, Inocente, and Ana pored over the ledgers, trying to make sense of the figures. They produced 110 hogsheads of sugar and 40 puncheons of molasses—less than half what they'd hoped for their first crop.

Hacienda los Gemelos belonged to Eugenio, but Ramón and Inocente would inherit the estate jointly. The two brothers wanted to impress their father, and to silence their mother's worries. They knew that the profits from sugar could be impressive, but that it was also a costly enterprise relative to net gains. The biggest expense was the land, but they already owned two hundred *cuerdas*. Money, however, was needed for buying, housing, feeding, and clothing workers and keeping them healthy. As she went through the accounts, Ana prepared numerous lists of what they needed in order to keep the hacienda viable. They had to maintain horses for themselves and Ana, as well as pack mules and cattle for hauling the cane from the fields to the *ingenio* and transporting the hogsheads of sugar and puncheons of molasses to the nearest town, from where the product could be sent to buyers. They needed carts, harnesses, barrels, ropes, copper pans for the boiling house, trays in the purgery. They needed machetes, hoes, pickaxes, wheelbarrows, and shovels. They had to pay foremen and Severo Fuentes.

Ana, Ramón, and Inocente had left the management of the workers to Severo and didn't interfere with his job as boss and enforcer. He found and trained them; he assigned their jobs and organized their work supervised by the foremen, both of them recent *libertos*. He also whipped them when necessary.

Every adult *bozal* at Hacienda los Gemelos had attempted escape, and a couple of the native-born, too. Generally, slave owners didn't buy known runaways, because once they'd tried to escape, they would try again. "What can we do to prevent that?" Ramón asked Severo.

"They have to believe that there are consequences, and that we mean it when we tell them what they are."

A few days before Ramón, Inocente, and Ana arrived, Severo said, he had lined up the slaves in the *batey* and warned them that if they tried to run away, he'd find them.

"And when I do, I told them, the law gives me the right to punish you, and believe me, I will."

His quiet, dispassionate tone was chilling. While he gave no specific example of what punishment he'd deliver, Ana heard the threat as if it applied even to her. "No wonder they're scared of you."

"It's them, or us, *señora*. They will challenge their masters at every opportunity. No one wants to be a slave. They had the bad fortune of being born in Africa."

"You sound like you're sorry for them," Ramón said.

"Maybe, sometimes. But that doesn't keep me from doing my job."

As if to spare her that aspect of the operation, the first time Severo was going to punish a slave he suggested that Ana stay indoors the next morning. Whippings took place in a field behind the barns, and even if she wanted to, she couldn't see from the *casona*. The screams, however, reached her, and echoed in her mind after the sentence was dispensed and the rest of the workers returned to their labors.

"Is there another way to discipline them?" she asked Ramón and Inocente over supper that night. "I couldn't bear the screaming."

"The whip is the only way to train and teach them," Inocente said. "They have to be punished. . . ."

"Who was it? What did he do?"

"Jacobo," Ramón said, "tried to steal a machete."

"Why?"

"Why do you think?" Inocente said.

"He was planning to run away," Ramón said.

"And who knows what else," his brother added.

"Don't scare her, Inocente."

Inocente patted Ana's hand. "Severo knows what he's doing."

"I know," she said, remembering Severo's matter-of-fact demeanor when talking about the slaves. With Severo Fuentes in charge of their workforce, Ana knew they need not worry about whether or how things would get done. He was completely in charge, and sometimes, when reviewing the complex ledgers, she wished that Ramón and Inocente would be as competent on the business side.

She soon confirmed that, as she noticed in Cádiz, Ramón and Inocente hadn't devoted enough time in the Marítima Argoso Marín offices to have a clear understanding of income relative to expenses. They spent much time shaking their heads over the ledgers, never quite figuring out how to balance them.

Her mother and the nuns had drilled Ana on the vagaries of household economy and domestic finance. At first the brothers didn't want Ana involved in day-to-day operations, but they agreed that Ana had a better grasp of bookkeeping than they did, and soon she was managing the accounting as efficiently as Severo Fuentes oversaw the workers. Once she demonstrated that she could maneuver around their financial predicaments, on paper at least, the twins consulted her more often.

"It makes no sense," she said to Ramón and Inocente, "to keep slaves who can't be put to work."

"What are we supposed to do with them?"

"We can enlarge the vegetable gardens and orchards. Children too young for the fields and the crippled or elderly can plant and maintain them. The more food we can raise here, the less we'll have to buy from local farms."

"That alone could save us hundreds of pesos a year," Inocente acknowledged.

"We can raise more animals and fowl for meat and eggs. We can have goats, sheep, and cows for milk and cheese. Whatever we don't use, we sell."

"We'll have to hire another foreman," Ramón said.

"Why?"

"Severo and the two bosses are out in the fields all day long. Ramón and I are also busy. Someone has to train and supervise them," Inocente said.

"I'll do that," Ana said. There was a silence. "Why do you both look so shocked?"

"It's inappropriate," Ramón said. "You'd have to be out with them, organizing them—"

"—training them, giving orders," Inocente continued.

"I don't see how that's different from what I do now, except that there will be more of them."

"Right now you deal with the household slaves like Flora, Teo, and Marta. They know what to do. The field workers aren't used to orders from a lady."

"Are you worried that I'll be calling for smelling salts if they say or do something vulgar?"

The brothers now talked so fast that it was hard for Ana to distinguish which one said what.

"You're already doing enough with the household and ledgers."

"That's the kind of thing women do well."

"It's not right for you to be out in the *campo* ordering slaves."

"What will you do if you have to punish one of them?"

She hadn't thought about that. Would she discipline the old, the crippled, the children she was taking on as her responsibility? She remembered Jesusa slapping her servants, then being shocked that they quit their jobs. "Spain should have never abolished slavery," she complained, and Ana hated that about her mother, that longing to dominate others. Ana cheered when the servants left, and wished she could also run from her parents' overweening sense of entitlement. But she now wondered if it was in her blood. Subjugating the native people was the first thing the conquistadores did, always by force, always by violence.

She was now in the position Jesusa had wished for: one of undisputed power over others. So far, none of her workers had challenged

Ana, but of course, they could. They should, Ana thought. She would, if she were one of them. And that made all the difference.

"So long as they're slaves," Ana said to Ramón and Inocente, "they have to do what I say. I'll train them, and if they refuse their work, yes, I'll punish them. That's what it means to be an *hacendada,* doesn't it?"

A SONG FOR MOTHER FOREST

Flora thought there were too many *patrones*. The slaves who had lived for years at Hacienda los Gemelos believed don Severo was the *patrón*. He'd visited the hacienda a few times, but one morning he appeared and soon the previous *mayordomo* left on his swaybacked mule without so much as a backward glance. Don Severo lined up the slaves in the *batey* and introduced two *libertos* as foremen. He'd bought Flora, José the carpenter, his wife, Inés, and their two boys, led them to the plantation, and set them to work, so they, too, thought he was the boss. It was a surprise to everyone when one afternoon weeks later don Severo assembled the slaves in the *batey* again and told them that the owners were coming. He told Flora, Teo, and Marta to follow him to the *casona*. Marta was ordered to clean and prepare the downstairs kitchen, and Flora and Teo were sent upstairs to smoke wasp nests from the eaves, brush away spider webs, scrub the walls and floors, and, finally, paint the entire inside of the house green. José carved a bed and nailed together a few benches and tables. He also built shelves in the kitchen so that Marta could stack the dishes sent ahead of the lady and the two gentlemen.

Flora observed these changes because it was important to notice everything. A new master meant that she must pay close attention so that she could learn what kind of people they were. Would the masters bother the women? Would the lady spend only a few days a year at the hacienda and live the rest of the time in the city? Would they have much company, or would they prefer to visit others? Would the lady sit against cushions whining that she was bored while ordering maids and complaining that things were not clean or neat enough? Flora had lived among *blancos* for years, and she knew that they were an indolent but violent race. To survive among them, she watched them, and could read them as well as they read their books and letters.

Flora was a Mbuti, and her clan lived in dense forests, hunting, fishing, and gathering, moving from place to place along the Congo River, following the availability of fruits, vegetables, and game. Their low stature and highly developed senses made them agile and stealthy. Children were taught to revere their environment because taking the forest for granted could be deadly. As they moved through the bush, the Mbuti sang to the gods in gratitude and exultation for the gifts of food and shelter.

Among her people she was named Balekimito. When she was blessed with the blood, her clanswomen and friends celebrated Balekimito's first menstrual period in the *elima* ceremony. They built a house from supple branches and broad leaves, and the women and pubescent girls moved in. The elder women taught the girls how to keep embers alive so that they could revive the fire in their next camp. They taught them the adult women's songs and sang about the responsibilities of womanhood and motherhood. Boys congregated around the yard of the *elima* house and sang to the girls, hoping that one would choose him to be allowed inside. The days in the *elima* house were the happiest time of Balekimito's life.

Three moons later, Portuguese slavers captured her and her mother. They raped them, then made them walk to a village where they were thrown into a shack and roped to other captives for two nights. The group was made to trudge over many days through the forest to the sea. There they put the women in airless rooms separated from the men, who couldn't protect them when the hairy white men assaulted them. When the rooms were filled with so many people that it was impossible to sit or lie down, the jailers took them from the cells and threw the people into the moaning, damp hold of a ship. It was there that Balekimito birthed her first child, born dead and flung over the side. When she sang to usher his soul back to the forest, the other chained men and women hummed softly, because none of them were Mbuti and couldn't speak her language, but they all knew her grief. Balekimito's mother, who began shivering the moment they were stuffed into the hold of the ship, stopped trembling after the baby died and she, too, was flung overboard, and again Balekimito sang and the others hummed and cried with her.

The slaver disembarked Balekimito and the others on a long, wide dock. Along the shore, a platform rose steps from the sand. The black men, women, and children who survived the crossing were auctioned off to a throng of white men wearing much fabric around their bodies so that very little of their pale skins showed. Balekimito, who grew up wearing only beads, grass, and body paint, was given a sack to wear. In spite of the hot sun overhead and the itchy fabric covering her body down to her ankles, Balekimito shivered as uncontrollably as her mother had, and was sure she, too, would die from terror.

A man pushed her up to the platform and lifted her chin so that the *blancos* on the ground could get a look at her. Far beyond the roofs along the shore, Balekimito saw the deep green of trees and plants. She thanked mother forest for bringing her to solid ground. The next moment, she was pushed off the platform and a tall, fat *blanco* grabbed her by the arm and pulled her along upon the rocky earth through paths lined with high buildings made from stone.

She lived in a room with solid walls and cried for the dwellings her people built from supple twigs and rippling leaves. She missed singing to the trees and vines, to the sky and clouds, to the rivers and lakes, to birds and snakes and monkeys, to leaves. In the house with the rigid walls, Balekimito was forced by Mistress to clean pots and dishes and tables and the staircase and Master's boots and the rock-hard floors. A man wearing black robes wet her head and made strange signs around her forehead and lips and said her name was now Flora.

She was not allowed out of the house. The windows faced the street or other houses and paved courtyards, so Flora couldn't touch bare earth. Everything she touched was hard, including Master. He climbed on top of her and pushed himself into her, pressing his heavy body until she felt that her backbone would crack against the tile floor. When Mistress realized that Flora was pregnant, she beat her with a broom, then pushed her down the stairs, and Flora lost her second child. For the first time since her mother's death, she sang again, for her lost baby, but quietly, because Master and Mistress forbade singing, even in sorrow.

Master sold her to another man, who took her to his farm, and the forest on the boundaries of that *finca* sang to Flora. There were many slaves in the *finca,* none of them Mbuti, but by now Flora spoke a little of her previous master's language. She hardly knew this master, but the others showed scars and missing ears and fingers and toes that he'd chopped off. An elder who spoke the same babble as Flora's previous master told her that a group were planning to run away. With many gestures and the few words they had in common, the elder was able to explain to Flora that they would hide for a few days in the forest and then walk over the mountains toward the setting sun, to a place called Haiti where there were no masters. Flora had no idea where she was and hadn't heard about Haiti, but she knew that if she went into the forest, it would protect her. She was afraid that she'd be raped again or a part of her body might be cut off, so she agreed to escape with the others.

One moonless night, the men went into the house and the women and children ran into the nearby woods. Flames hissed into the night. Flora heard the bell clanging, hounds barking, and shots. Dogs bit into her calves, her buttocks. She kept running. This forest was different from the one back home, but she sang silently as she ran. She climbed a tree to its highest branch. Mbuti believed that the forest would let her see into her secrets if she were patient, so Flora waited quietly until she could see. Men and dogs ran around below, caught the others, and dragged them to the yard.

Flora slept on the branch, and the next morning she climbed down and found fruit, then walked farther into the woods and scaled high up another tree. There were white men and dogs all over the forest, but she knew how to walk from branch to branch, and when she was on the ground, she walked in brooks and rivers so that she left no scent. She spent many days walking toward the sinking sun each time, eating whatever she could find. She didn't know where she was going, but she knew that she could live in the forest the rest of her life if she had to. She was lonely, but she was not afraid of the forest, only of men.

One day she was trying to catch a fish in a shallow river when two black men dressed like *blancos* leaped from the bushes and captured her again. They knotted her wrists together behind her back and pushed and dragged her to the same camp where they'd tied up the three men who'd planned the escape. They were returned to the charred remains of the farm. The three leaders were whipped, then hanged in front of the others, and Flora was lashed until her back and legs bled. The same elder who told her about Haiti restored her to health. The master was dead and they'd all be sold to different masters.

Don Felipe bought Flora, and again Flora was on a boat, not as dirty and dank as the first one. She slept for two nights on top of crates filled with *bacalao.* When they landed, the forest sang again to Flora. She didn't know where she was before or where she was now. This master spoke the same tongue as the second one. He locked her inside a storeroom and the next morning took Flora to his wife. Doña Benigna gave Flora a dress, an apron, a head wrapping and taught her how to bathe and dress her, how to brush her fine golden hair, to put on her stockings and fasten them with ribbons above her knees, to wash and press her frocks and bodices, to sew and mend. If Flora made mistakes, or couldn't understand, or dropped something or broke it, doña Benigna slapped Flora or shoved her across the room.

So that she wouldn't be beaten, Flora did what she was told, was careful not to drop or break anything, and learned Spanish. The longer she lived with don Felipe and doña Benigna, the fewer beatings she received.

At least, Flora thought, don Felipe didn't trouble the female servants. He kept an office in town, but he and doña Benigna lived on a farm one league away. Flora was allowed to sing but couldn't go into the woods alone or she'd be whipped.

She often accompanied doña Benigna to town, or to visit her friends on other farms. The other ladies were impressed by how well trained Flora was. They didn't say it to her, of course. *Blancos* didn't praise slaves. She heard them talking about her through open doors, or when the ladies gossiped among themselves as Flora served.

"Giving them compliments gives them airs, and you know where that leads to," one of the ladies said to doña Benigna. "No, my dear, don't tell her she's doing well, quite the opposite! Slap her, beat her, make sure she knows you're in command. As soon as a slave thinks he's superior to others, he thinks he's equal to *blancos* and expects the same rights. Look at what happened in Haiti."

By then Flora had learned from others "what happened in Haiti" and that she had been days from reaching it by following the sun. Haiti was on the western end of the island she'd lived before, Hispaniola. Rather than try to escape by sea, slaves in Haiti turned against their masters and won their freedom. After Flora was taken to Puerto Rico, the slaves on the other side of Hispaniola's mountains were also freed, but not before *blancos* escaped with their chattel. Many of the slaves built bamboo rafts and drifted from Puerto Rico toward the setting sun and freedom. No one knew whether they reached land or not, whether they died, were captured, or returned.

Over the twenty years that Flora lived with don Felipe and doña Benigna, she saw people stream into Puerto Rico from Venezuela, from Santo Domingo, Colombia, Peru. These new immigrants were loyal to the Spanish Crown and felt safe in Puerto Rico. Every time word came of another war for independence or about uprisings on other islands or in other parts of Puerto Rico, soldiers marched in large numbers. They settled right in the center of town and practiced battles, their plumed hats waving, their sabers rattling, their horses high-stepping and neighing. They organized local militias: every free man was expected to appear weekly at the practice grounds, where they were trained to repel attacks from those who wanted to make Puerto Rico an independent nation, like the countries in Spanish America. The local militias and the soldiers also practiced how to suppress rebellions because independence and abolition were spoken in the same whispering breath.

If a slave reported on others preparing to escape or to take arms, he or she received a reward and freedom. Leaders were seized and killed, and the others were punished by whippings or by having their limbs crippled or severed. The new elites and veterans from the revolutions on Hispaniola and in South America were determined to keep Puerto Rico Spanish. Rigorous suppression and censorship regulated the written word and even spoken language. Advocating independence for Puerto Rico, even in conversation, was cause for exile.

By the time the Argosos arrived on the island in 1844, there were only two Spanish colonies left in what had been a vast empire. Every other former colony was independent and had abolished slavery. The exceptions were Cuba—and Puerto Rico.

Flora nursed doña Benigna through four pregnancies and helped to raise the surviving three children into adulthood. By then their town, Ponce, on the Caribbean side of Puerto Rico, had expanded into a city right to the steps of don Felipe's house. Don Felipe and doña Benigna were now rich, their children were grown and settled, and as their hair grayed, their conversations turned to nostalgia and Spain. They sold their home, and the morning they left, their human chattel were marched to town. Severo bought Flora, now forty years old, at the auction in the plaza.

Within days of their arrival at Hacienda los Gemelos, Flora was certain that don Ramón and don Inocente would pester the women. She was old now, so she was grateful that they'd have no interest in her. But she noticed how they looked at the women and girls with hunger in their eyes, even though *la patrona* was young and fervent. The floor of the *casona*'s upstairs was one layer of planks, and the undersides were the ceiling where Marta and Flora slept downstairs. Almost every night Flora heard the *pah-thump, pah-thump, pah-thump* of a man pushing himself into a woman, and the groan at the end. Flora's hearing was as acute as her vision. Even though don Ramón and don Inocente sounded and looked alike, she caught the higher timbre of one and the lower pitch of the other. She'd noticed how one was loose of limb and the other held himself tighter. She'd seen don Inocente coming out of the marital bedroom, and she'd caught a look here, a look there, in his exchanges with his brother. At first, Flora wasn't sure whether *la señora* knew the difference between them, and whether the two brothers were playing a trick on her. But after a few days she was certain that doña Ana was complicit.

Flora watched don Ramón, don Inocente, and doña Ana, and she watched don Severo watching the other three and she learned. She'd worried at the beginning when she first met them that there were too many *patrones*. But within weeks she was sure that there was really one boss, and that the other three were working for her.

"WHOM THE TROPICS HAS COME TO HOLD . . ."

———— ⋆◆⋆ ————

Ana worked harder than ever, but four months after their arrival at Hacienda los Gemelos, she still had no complaints and few requests for Papá Dios when she said her evening prayers. She was grateful for the day that was ending, and for what she accomplished in her busy waking hours. Her lonely childhood and passionate adolescence seemed like a long-ago dream, the hours in her grandfather's farm and library like preparation for the rest of her life. She welcomed and was challenged by the privations of her days, the compromises of a life bereft of the luxury she once took for granted. But the more adversity she faced, the more certain she was that Hacienda los Gemelos was her destiny. Doña Leonor's warnings, her mother's terrors of what might lie across the sea, her own misgivings when she first set foot in the house too close to the *ingenio*, seemed as alien now as don Hernán's journals were at first reading.

Days after Easter Sunday, Ana was in the kitchen storeroom with Marta inventorying the foodstuffs.

"*Señora*." Flora ran in. "*¡Visita!*"

"I'm not expecting anyone," Ana said, peering around the door toward the *batey*. Jacobo was leading two huge, well-fed horses to the stables.

"I help you, *señora*," Flora said as she untied Ana's apron. "I wipe face." She flicked a spot of flour from Ana's cheek and folded a few wayward strands into her hair. She patted and brushed the dust from Ana's skirts.

Ramón was in the yard with a man and a woman, both a head taller than Ramón and at least twice as wide. The man was shaped like an egg on stilts. A tiny head sprouted from his oval-shaped body, from which protruded short, chubby arms and incongruously long, skinny legs. As if to aid in maintaining his balance, his feet were enormous. He didn't walk so much as waddle; his feet turned diagonally from his body while his huge belly propelled him forward. The woman was equally round and ungainly, her voluminous skirts sweeping the ground.

Ramón introduced them as their closest neighbors, Luis Manuel Morales Font and his wife Faustina Moreau de Morales. They owned Finca San Bernabé, where they grew vegetables and fruits destined for town markets and supplied neighboring plantations with the staples of the slave diet: cassava, breadfruit, plantains, *batatas,* and cornmeal.

"It's such a pleasure to meet you," Faustina said, her voice a gurgle, as if she couldn't contain her laughter. "Forgive us that we didn't come sooner, but we know how busy it is during the *zafra.* . . ."

"Thank you. It was considerate of you to wait until things slowed a bit."

Ana led their guests to the *casona*'s living room. She was mortified at their undisguised appraisal, taking in every detail of the scanty furnishings, the simple benches and lone table. Faustina noted the rough walls and floor, the lizard-green walls, the absence of the slightest attempt at decoration.

"As you can see," Ana said, "we live humbly." She was annoyed at herself for apologizing.

"Please, don't fret," Faustina said. "We're all pioneers in this wilderness and must adjust to circumstances."

"When we first came," Luis added, "we lived in a palm-frond and dirt-floor *bohío,* like the cottages of the *jíbaros.*"

"You've been here about ten years, is that so?" Ramón asked.

"Longer," Faustina said. "Almost thirteen—"

"You've accomplished much in that time." Ramón turned to Ana. "Their farm is a model of efficiency and beauty—"

"You're kind," Luis said. "But it's taken years."

"Don Luis knew my uncle," Ramón said, "and told him about this land—"

"I would've bought it myself," Luis said, "but we weren't in a position—"

Faustina cleared her throat. Just then, Flora brought lemonade, followed by Marta carrying a tray of crackers, cheese, and sliced papaya. Both women had smoothed their aprons and tucked their blouses into their skirts. Flora wore a new, bright yellow head wrap tied into a jaunty bow. Ana was grateful to Flora, who was often one step ahead of her and didn't require as much direction as the others. She'd even placed a festive bouquet of hibiscus blossoms in the center of the tray.

Faustina looked askance at the polished coconut shell cups for drinking, at the bamboo and woven palm frond trays, at the heavy clay pitcher. Ana's response was to handle them with the delicacy and grace of fine porcelain and crystal.

They chatted as they sipped their drinks, half of Ana's mind on her mental list of chores. Did she lock the pantry and liquor closet before she went outside? It was midmorning. That meant that the guests would stay for *el almuerzo* and a short siesta. They'd have to rest in hammocks in Inocente's room, then a snack before they rode home. There went her day.

"We'll leave you ladies to get acquainted," Ramón broke into her reverie. "I want to show don Luis around the *ingenio*. We'll be back for lunch."

The men left, and Faustina seemed delighted to be alone with Ana.

"We have some interesting families hereabouts," she said, "but it's hard to get to know them. The distances aren't great, but the roads, as you've surely noticed, are terrible or nonexistent."

"I don't know. I've not left the hacienda since we arrived."

"Yes, the *zafra* is all-consuming for sugar planters. We farmers are on a more leisurely rhythm. Do you mind, dear, if I work as we chat?" Faustina pulled a bag from a pocket and began working finely chained crochet as she talked.

Ana found her mending basket. "You knew don Rodrigo?"

"A fine man, and we'll always be grateful to him, may he rest in peace, and be a friend to his family."

"Thank you."

"Our parents fled to Puerto Rico from Santo Domingo, nearly destitute, after Haiti invaded our country in 1822." She looked up to see if Ana had any idea what she was talking about. Ana nodded, but Faustina had to tell her stories in a strict order, regardless of whether her interlocutor knew the details or not.

"When the occupying Haitian government freed our slaves, they also seized our farms and plantations, to nationalize them. Our parents were lucky to escape with enough to start over. Luis and I met in Mayagüez, where most of our family now lives." She set her work down and looked over the canopy of trees, and farther, to the hills north of Hacienda los Gemelos. "Like you," she continued, "we came here with a bit of money and much energy. Of course, at the beginning one never has enough." She sought confirmation from Ana, who was engrossed in her mending. "Don Rodrigo extended credit as we built San Bernabé, and understood when we needed a bit more time," she continued. "He asked Luis to keep an eye for land around here." She turned her work without looking at it. "He was fond of his nephews and hoped they'd live here someday."

"Is that true?"

"Yes, certainly. Luis visited him in that grand new house he built. . . ." She sighed. "Life is capricious. Such a young man when he died, not even fifty years old . . ."

"It was a great blow to his family," Ana said.

"May he rest in peace," Faustina repeated, making the cross.

"Don Luis knew him well, then," Ana said.

"Yes," Faustina resumed her story. "He looked out for opportunities in the area. The fifteen *cuerdas* we're on now was the first purchase. The previous owner built the *casona,* the *trapiche,* and the chimneys. He had six sons."

"All of them in this house?"

"Well, they weren't like you and me," Faustina said. "He lived with one of his slaves but didn't free her. Or for that matter, his own sons." She turned her work. "Things are different here in the *campo.*"

Ana wondered what Faustina would say about her arrangement with Ramón and Inocente.

"Unfortunately," Faustina continued, "they were all partial to drink. The joke around here was that they drank more of their rum than made it to market." She laughed. "When the woman died, he lost his reason. He drank more and couldn't manage the work. He gambled. When he needed money, he sold his slaves and, eventually, his sons. He scattered them all over the island to the best buyer." She locked eyes with Ana for a moment, then dropped them. "Appalling . . ."

"Impossible to imagine." Ana hadn't heard the story of the beginnings of the hacienda. "But when we came here there were slaves. . . ."

"Don Rodrigo wanted to keep it going, but he couldn't leave his business, so he hired Luis to manage it. We sold him some of our slaves and installed one of our foremen as *mayordomo*. Luis did as much as he could, but it was hard to manage this place and ours. We thought the property would be sold after don Rodrigo's death, but we were happy that his nephews were coming. . . ."

As Faustina talked, Ana's temper grew, but she controlled her breathing and loosened the grip on the fabric she was mending. Ana figured that their old, maimed slaves were sold to the absent don Rodrigo by don Luis, who kept the younger, healthy ones for his own farm. She couldn't prove it, but she believed it as if Faustina had said it aloud.

"We're so glad that Ramón came with a wife. Families do better here than single men. . . ."

"Is that so?" Ana asked, to keep Faustina talking.

"Men need women to keep them civilized. A white man without a wife has too many temptations." She arched her eyebrows until they nearly reached her hairline.

Ana had seen several light-skinned, light-eyed babies on the hacienda. When she mentioned it to the brothers, they joked that Severo was increasing their stock. She thought that was impossible because enough time hadn't elapsed. It now occurred to her that their father might be don Luis. She had a hard time conjuring the enormous man ravishing the women she knew on the hacienda. Her anger rose.

"Men alone succumb to drink," Faustina said quickly, embarrassed by her own innuendo. "They play cards and spend days at the cockfights. Most of the property around here was transferred not through the usual channels, but because owners signed them over to creditors, much of it due to gambling losses."

"Is that how don Rodrigo added to the original fifteen *cuerdas* to its current size?"

Faustina was flustered, as if Ana's direct question had broken one of the rules of conversation. "Well, no . . . yes . . . I don't know. . . . My goodness, what a question!"

"I meant no offense."

"Not at all, it's just . . . well, it's true, I suppose. Most of the people around here . . . that's all they own, you see . . . slaves and land . . . and, well, land is the only thing that *doesn't* grow on this island." She laughed at her wit, a jolly sound that made Ana smile because she understood that Faustina laughed often, although not always because she was happy.

"I understand."

"But I've done all the talking!" Faustina waited for Ana to speak. "Our husbands have already become friends," she continued, uncomfortable with Ana's silence. "Severo brought your husband and brother-in-law to meet us at San Bernabé just a few days after you arrived."

"Did you know him, too, before we came?"

"Yes. Don Rodrigo sent him out here to check on the hacienda. He came to introduce himself a couple of years ago. He knows everyone around here."

"He does?"

"Well, yes. He's . . . quite entrepreneurial."

"What do you mean?"

"Oh, goodness, you must think I'm such a gossip!" Faustina laughed again.

"Not at all," she assured her. "I appreciate what you've told me about don Rodrigo. We had no idea that he imagined Ramón and Inocente living here. Certainly their parents hadn't heard about that. It'll make Ramón and Inocente happy to know that their uncle had plans for this place for them."

"He told Luis several times," Faustina said.

"And Severo Fuentes?" Ana prompted, her eyes on the frayed cuff she was repairing.

"Well, he *is* your employee," Faustina said, and waited for Ana, who focused her eyes on her uneven stitches, to say something. "He's very good at securing workers," Faustina continued. "And he has an excellent rapport with the sea captains. . . ."

"Yes, we know," Ana said. Severo had already saved Los Gemelos hundreds of pesos in customs fees and charges for the purchase of slaves and other items from ships on the cove south of the plantation.

"If not for his good contacts"—Faustina laughed merrily—"I couldn't get such fine thread for my crochet." She raised the intricate lace she was working.

Ana was only mildly surprised to hear that Severo was providing goods for San Bernabé as well, and was sure that silk thread wasn't the only item he sold to Faustina and Luis. In addition to finding slaves when no one else could, Severo often delivered goods that were scarce even in San Juan. José couldn't achieve half as much of his carpentry and carving if Severo didn't provide North American tools for the shop. He delivered a cask of the finest Spanish olive oil, another of *jerez,* several cast-iron pans for the kitchen, and a new plow, all sold to Los Gemelos at competitive prices.

In addition to the necessities for hacienda operations, Ana's shopping lists included personal items, like bottles of Agua Florida for her bath and for the men's aftershave, as well as linen, muslin, and stationery. The first time she gave Severo her list, she told him that she didn't expect he'd be able to get everything.

"Don't worry, *señora,*" he said, "I'll do my best to get it all." He did, and from then on she added articles she'd thought she would never use again, like rose-scented talcum and tooth powder. She enjoyed challenging his ability. To the list of the easily available rice, dry beans, tinned sardines, and salted cod, she always added luxuries: hairpins, flat abalone buttons, books and newspapers from Spain. Severo always delivered.

A week after Luis and Faustina's visit—and probably alerted by them—a Franciscan priest rode into the *batey* on a donkey. He was young, with strong Galician features and a regal bearing. Ramón invited him to spend the night.

"You're certainly aware of the slave code of 1842," Padre Xavier said after dinner. "And your obligation to provide religious instruction in the Roman Catholic faith."

"They're all baptized," Inocente said.

"But the nearest church is in Guares," Ana pointed out. "It's impossible to get them there for Mass."

"The code allows for a layperson such as yourself"—Padre Xavier bowed to Ramón and then Inocente—"to teach them their prayers and the rosary."

"Our understanding is, however," Inocente added, "that devotions are to take place after they fulfill their duties."

"That goes without saying. The code also requires that you separate the sick from the healthy."

"One of the cottages is an infirmary," Ana said. "I depend on the elders experienced with herbs and remedies."

"Yes, I understand. You can only do so much," Padre Xavier said.

"When we first came here they were dressed in rags," Ramón said. "Ana has made sure that each received his or her annual allotment of clothes. . . ."

"They look presentable. Your women, especially, are decently clothed. I hope you've taken care to segregate the single women from the men and discourage improper relations. . . ."

Ana felt Severo's gaze and she was glad that the candle flame didn't reach her reddening face. In her previous life, women retired after dinner to let the men smoke, drink, and discuss important matters. But she made no effort to leave, was active in the conversation, and didn't make a fuss when an indelicate subject came up. She thought he was embarrassed for her, and his presumption irked her.

"We have separate quarters for men and women," Ana said, to emphasize her right to be part of the discussion. "The married couples with children have their own *bohíos*."

"Forgive me if I repeat what you already know, but part of my visit is to make sure that owners and *mayordomos*"—he turned to Severo—"understand what's expected."

"We do the utmost to fulfill our obligations to our people," Ana said.

"You're also aware, then, that the code provides their right to purchase their freedom. They may rent themselves to others during off-hours. Or they can apply a particular skill—to grow vegetables for sale, for example, or to make things they can sell toward the cost of their own manumission."

"At least one," Severo said, "is working toward that goal by making items for sale."

Ana turned to Severo with a questioning look.

"José," Severo said to the priest. "During his free time he carves little animals and *santos*. I bring them to town for him."

"God bless you, son," Padre Xavier said, "bless all of you." He made the cross in front of them. "They're God's children, too."

"Amen," they all said. "Amen."

Ana was gratified by Padre Xavier's approval of the way the hacienda's workers were treated. He celebrated Mass under the breadfruit tree near the house and afterward gave Ana a flask of holy water and instructed her on how to baptize children born to the slaves.

"It is their salvation," he added.

To further impress him, Ana began weekly, compulsory attendance at prayers every Sunday morning after chores but before the workers' afternoon off. An open-walled shed roofed with palm fronds was designated for services. Ramón and Inocente took turns reading passages Ana chose for them from prayer books and telling stories of the saints that illustrated the value of sacrifice and faith in a better world after the hardships in this one. Severo Fuentes never attended.

Ana's one luxury, indulged every evening, was for Flora to bathe her. After supper, Ramón and Inocente had a smoke and a drink, sometimes accompanied by Severo. She retired to the bedroom and undressed with Flora's help. In the candlelit room, Flora poured fresh water and a few drops of lemon verbena–scented Agua Florida into a cloth inside a gourd bowl. Ana held on to the bedpost as Flora gently rubbed the damp rag around her face and ears, under her arms, around her breasts, down her belly and back, along the inside of her thighs. After she finished each section with the damp cloth, Flora gently massaged it with a dry one. She knew how to touch the most intimate parts of her naked mistress without making her feel exposed.

Flora hummed a melody in rhythms unlike any Ana had ever heard.

"What's that song?" Ana asked one night.

Flora cowered. Every time she made a mistake or was criticized she expected a slap, or a punch, or something to be thrown at her. "I so sorry, *señora*."

"You did nothing wrong, Flora. But you were singing."

"I forget," Flora said, still nervous. *"Disculpe, señora."*

"I like your singing," Ana said. "You have my permission."

"Yes, *señora*?"

"The song is in your language. What does it say?"

"It is a full moon tonight and I sing about it."

"Sing it again, Flora."

Her voice was high but raspy and rose and fell in mesmerizing waves of sound. Ana sensed that Flora was embarrassed to be performing for her, and that perhaps the act of singing was more meaningful than the words.

"Were you a singer among your people?"

"Everybody sing, *señora*. Men, women, children. We sing all the time. Even when sad."

"You can sing anytime, Flora, even when you're sad."

"You mean this?"

She finished bathing her, resuming her song. Ana was almost certain that whatever the words, if Ana asked for a translation, Flora would tell her the song was about the moon or flowers or something pleasant, and not divulge her true feelings. The rising and falling of the voice carried the meaning: right now, under the mournful melody, Ana thought she heard relief.

Flora powdered Ana under her arms, around her breasts, down her back, with a puff dipped in rose talcum.

"*¿Señora?*"

"*Sí*, Flora." Ana lifted her arms for Flora to arrange her nightgown. When Flora didn't answer, or dress her, Ana opened her eyes. "What is it?"

Flora shook her head and drew the nightgown over Ana's head. "*Nada, señora*, is not my place."

"What is not your place?"

Flora stared at Ana's feet. "Please no hit Flora."

"I will be angry if you don't tell me."

"Are you pregnant, *señora*?"

Ana undid the ribbons around her neckline and looked down at her body. Her breasts did look just a little bigger, and where her belly had been flat, almost concave, it was now round enough that she couldn't see her pubic hair. "Pregnant?"

She was glad Ramón and Inocente weren't there to see her expression, for she knew, from Flora's reaction, that it betrayed distress.

"You not happy, *señora*?" Flora asked.

"Of course I'm happy," Ana snapped. "What woman wouldn't be?" She sounded unconvincing even to herself.

Flora's eyes betrayed nothing.

———

When she told Ramón and Inocente, their reaction was as Ana expected: joy followed by caution.

"You must return to San Juan," said Ramón, "until the baby is born."

No. The mere thought of another sea voyage made her ill, Ana said. "Besides, it's not safe for me to travel in my condition."

Once her belly began to show, a woman was expected to disappear into her chambers until six weeks after the child was born. It was indecent to parade an expanding girth in public, but the thought of months inside the Argoso home in a city enclosed by stone walls on a small island was asphyxiating to Ana.

In Spain, she endured conventions that chafed against her instincts for freedom and movement for the sake of her parents' standing in society. Ana was thin as a girl, with negligible breasts and boyish hips, so Jesusa imposed corsets and numerous petticoats to enhance her bosom and add width to her frame. Ana felt trapped inside the garments, and within weeks of arriving in Los Gemelos, the corset and all but one petticoat were put away. The idea of wrapping herself in yards of fabric again was suffocating. She also dreaded Leonor's intrusive attentions, her worries and premonitions, her constant harping about what Ramón and Inocente should or shouldn't do.

Beyond these concerns, there was also a deeper unease, one that she barely understood but was the true reason she wouldn't leave. Over the past four months, as she discarded the outer layers to reveal her true self to herself, she had also repudiated the world beyond the hacienda's borders. Los Gemelos, nestled in a sea of sugarcane, held her.

"I'm sorry, *señores y señora,*" Severo said the next night after supper. "I'll look into it, of course, but it's unlikely that a doctor with his own practice—forgive me if I can be honest—"

"Yes, of course," Ramón said. "We respect your opinion."

"I don't believe such a doctor would leave his practice for months to take care of, *disculpe, señora,* one woman in an out-of-the-way plantation."

"Isn't there a doctor in the closest town?" Ana asked.

"Dr. Vieira," Severo said. "He was a ship's doctor and recently established in Guares."

"Hours away on horseback," Inocente muttered.

"And he's more experienced with fractures, that sort of thing. . . ."

"There must be a midwife to attend women around here ready to give birth," Ana said.

"There is Siña Damita, Lucho's wife," Severo said. "She's a *partera* and *curandera*. She hasn't lost a baby yet," he said with an air of pride and a long drag on his cigar, as if he'd trained the midwife himself.

Obviously, Ana thought, she was one of his. He bought only skilled slaves. "I wish to meet her."

Ramón protested, "She delivers the slaves and *campesinas*. That's hardly appropriate for—"

"I have no other choice," Ana declared, and the men fell silent. Once she went inside the house, however, she heard Ramón and Inocente questioning Severo about the midwife's capabilities.

Flora, too, was shocked that Ana would allow Damita to be her midwife. "Siña Damita delivers the *jíbaras* and black babies, *señora,*" she said as she powdered Ana's back and underarms.

"My experience has been that we all look and function pretty much the same down there."

"Ay, *señora,* how you speak such things!" Flora reddened and dropped Ana's nightgown over her head.

"You'll be with me, won't you?" Ana pressed Flora's shoulder.

"Of course, *señora. Sí,* if you want me, I will be there."

Siña Damita was a brisk, large woman with big hands and feet that seemed perfectly designed to hold up her wide-hipped broad-shouldered body. Like Flora, she was born in Africa, but from a Mandinka clan, and spoke Spanish with a strong accent in a low, masculine voice. Unlike the other Africans, who were trained not to look at whites directly, Damita had an unwavering gaze. Her first owner had freed her three years earlier, but not her husband and three sons. When Severo bought them, Damita came to live in a *bohío* on the boundary of the plantation so that she could be closer to her husband and sons.

"I deliver black babies, white babies, spotted babies if they come that way," the *partera* said. "Your *enana* thinks I don't deliver *blancos,* but I do. In the *finca* where I work before, no doctor. All the women send for me. *Blancos, negros, pardos,* they send for me." She poked herself in the chest for emphasis.

Ana was surprised to hear Flora referred to as her dwarf, but by now she was used to the prejudices of the slaves who constantly sought ways to distinguish themselves from one another. The lighter skinned were chosen as *esclavos domésticos* and lorded it over the *esclavos de tala,* darker and destined for the fields. Skilled workers like José, the carpenter, and Marta, the cook, cost more, and therefore had higher status. Ana once heard Flora and Marta discussing the price of each of six workers Severo led into the *batey* a day earlier. Slaves knew their financial worth and compared themselves to others based on what the owners were willing to pay for them.

Siña Damita wiped her hands on her sun-bleached, starched apron. "I deliver twins, like your husband and his brother," she said. "Healthy born both, but one died at four. Drowned," she added. "Not my fault. The other, he drive the carts. Strong kid."

Her confidence reassured Ana, and four months later, just after midnight on September 29, 1845, it was Siña Damita's strong hands that held up the wrinkled, red creature that had kept Ana in painful labor for thirty-six hours. "A boy," Siña Damita announced with a grin. "A boy."

When Ramón first held the infant and said, *"Dios te bendiga, Miguel, hijo mío,"* Inocente, who was standing on the other side of the bed, scowled. When his turn came to hold the child, Inocente examined every wrinkle and fold, every hair, every paper-thin nail, and his frown grew deeper. He returned Miguel to Ana's arms and shuffled out, his shoulders hunched, his head bowed. Ramón followed him, and seconds later Ana heard them in the next room, speaking in low, urgent voices. In the morning, she asked Ramón if Inocente was all right.

"He's fine," Ramón said, too quickly.

A newly delivered woman had to observe the *cuarentena,* the forty days and forty nights during which she was to rest and get to know her baby. Sexual relations were forbidden during her quarantine.

The day Ana's labor pains began, a second *hamaca* was strung next to Inocente's, so now the brothers shared a room.

Ana heard them talking late into the night, their voices rising and falling in pleading, sometimes angry cadences. When she asked what they were discussing, however, they said it was business. They were about to buy a *finca* contiguous to Los Gemelos.

"It has a river along its northern boundary," Ramón said.

"We rode the land. We can build irrigation canals," Inocente explained, "from the river into the fields."

"There's also another *finca* with ten slaves for sale, east of us," Ramón added. "The boundary abuts the new road to Guares, the closest town with a deep port. That will make it easier for us to get our product to market."

Ana might be in quarantine, but she was not insensible.

"Spending money to buy land seems reckless when we're twenty slaves short for the *cuerdas* already planted and need at least another five bullocks and carts."

"We're aware of that," Ramón said, "but land is the only thing that doesn't grow on this island." He grinned, pleased with his cleverness, but Ana remembered the same phrase used by her neighbor Faustina de Morales.

She didn't smile back. She turned to Inocente, hoping that he'd see her side of the argument. "Buying land will be costly. Don't forget that we have to repair the boiling house and purgery—"

"If we don't buy what's available along the borders of Los Gemelos," Inocente said, "it will cost more later. People hold on to their land, but these sellers absolutely need the money, and each property can be bought at an attractive price."

"We don't have endless resources," Ana insisted. "We've spent most of the cash we brought with us, including my dowry."

"Don't worry," Ramón said. "Inocente and I know what we're doing. It will all turn out well at the end." A week later, they bought both parcels, adding another hundred *cuerdas* to the hacienda as well as four women and six children.

"We need strong men," Ana complained, "not more women and children."

"The owner had already sold the four husbands away," Ramón said.

Ramón took Miguel into his arms. "Hacienda los Gemelos is for you," he said to the infant. "It is for you that your *mamá* and your uncle and I work so hard. It is for you, *hijo mío.*"

As she watched him kiss and caress the child, Ana asked herself why Ramón assumed Miguel was his son. She had no way of knowing when Miguel was conceived because the brothers were diligent about whose turn it was to sleep with her. Maybe it didn't matter to them so long as there was an Argoso son to carry their name into the next generation. Ramón had registered the baby at the Guares church using both their names and the name of the saint on whose feast day he was born: Ramón Miguel Inocente Argoso Larragoity Mendoza Cubillas.

Doña Leonor wrote asking about every aspect of Miguel's development. "We'd like to come for a visit. We're anxious to hold him in our arms," her first, excited letter read after the news.

"Absolutely not." Inocente slapped the pages on the table.

"But he's their first grandson," Ramón argued. "Of course they'd want to see him."

"They shouldn't come here until—" Inocente paused, wrestling for a good reason. "Until we live more comfortably," he finally said.

Ramón and Inocente looked at each other, communicating silently. Ramón seemed about to disagree. "Maybe you're right," he said, giving in.

As ever, Ana drafted their responses, but she found it harder each time to come up with another excuse the more doña Leonor insisted that nothing else mattered; all she cared about was seeing her grandson.

After Miguel was born, Ramón and Inocente talked as they always did—finishing each other's sentences, drawing plans in the air with their fingers—but Ana could tell something was different. Before the baby was born, no matter whom they were addressing, Ramón and Inocente looked at each other when they talked, as if the other twin were the only person in the room who mattered. Now the tension between them was visible, yet they smiled and joked and talked like always. If she looked them too long in the eyes, however, they shifted their gazes, as if hiding something.

During Ana's quarantine, Flora slept in a hammock next to her bed so that she could help with the baby. Miguel rooted at her breast, but Ana couldn't make enough milk. He howled constantly from hunger and frustration. Inés, the carpenter's wife, was weaning their youngest son, so she was brought in to nurse Miguel. The house that Ana used to have to herself most of the day while the men were away was now a hive of comings and goings, with Flora, Inés, and Damita constantly around her and the infant. She was rarely alone with Ramón or Inocente, and Severo Fuentes never came around, as if her quarantine meant she was infectious.

A couple of weeks after the beginning of her *cuarentena,* Inocente moved from the *casona.* There was a good enough house for him at the recently purchased *finca,* he said. He took his clothes and toiletries, and there were days when Ana didn't see him, although Ramón said that they were together all day long. In order to free a room for Miguel and the wet nurse, Ramón said he'd take the hacienda books and ledgers from the study to the *finca.*

"But it's so far from the house," she complained. "It's easier for me to do the work here."

"Inocente and I feel competent to do that now," he said, "and Severo will help us."

"Severo? Is it wise for the *mayordomo* to know the intimate details of our business?"

"He knows our situation better than we do," he answered.

"Only his side of it, Ramón. Why should he know, for example, how much money we have or don't have?"

"It's his job as the manager, Ana. Let him do it. You have enough to do with the baby."

"I have plenty of help. . . ."

"This is what Inocente and I decided," he said, hardening his jaw. "This is a man's job. . . ."

"Since when—" She bit her tongue, about to tell him that she'd done the work with no complaints or mistakes for months.

"We will manage it now," he repeated.

His new assertiveness made her wonder whether she'd underestimated him. Maybe now that he was a father, he might focus on his responsibilities. But it worried her that he didn't consult her about hacienda business.

Over the next weeks, Ramón, Inocente, and Severo worked late into the night, and sometimes Ramón didn't return to the *casona* until the next morning to change his clothes.

Ana looked forward to resuming sex, not so much because it was satisfying for her, but because Ramón and Inocente had taken her *cuarentena* too seriously and spent entire days away from her.

On the forty-first night, Flora bathed her with warm water scented with crushed geranium petals. She seemed to be as excited about the coming night as Ana. She kept smiling, as if titillated by what Ana and Ramón were about to do.

When he came to bed, Ana noticed a difference in his lovemaking. She expected him to be as impatient as usual. He was, but he was even more distracted and determined to get things over with as quickly as possible. As usual, he rolled over and fell asleep, leaving her raging.

Ramón and Inocente no longer took turns with Ana. Inocente came for some meals and sat on the porch smoking and talking about hacienda business, sometimes with Severo, sometimes not. After the lights-out bell for the slaves, Flora bathed Ana. Ramón knew Ana was ready when Flora asked if there was anything else she could do for him. He had no other request. He joined Ana in bed and sometimes made love to her, sometimes not. But Inocente no longer walked through her bedroom door, and she thought he was avoiding her.

Miguel spent most of his day with Inés, hungrily sucking at her breasts. When he was brought to Ana, Inés and Flora stood nearby as if afraid she'd drop the infant. Siña Damita came to see him whenever she was with her family in Los Gemelos.

"Hold him like this, *señora,*" Damita instructed. "Cradle little head so not hang in the air."

Ana held her son, enjoying the warmth of his body against hers, but she soon returned him to Damita, Inés, or Flora. He was tiny and helpless, and she didn't know what to do with him.

"He likes if you sing, *señora,*" Flora suggested. She and Inés sang constantly to the child. They also cooed, smiled, made clicking noises with their tongues to make him laugh. Ana couldn't bring herself to do that, and felt undignified twisting her features for Miguel's benefit. His big eyes sought hers, but she was uncomfortable staring back, as if he knew something about her that she didn't know about herself.

"I haven't spent much time around babies," she said as she returned Miguel to Flora's arms. Ana was sure the maid thought she was a bad mother.

Her pregnancy hadn't been particularly difficult, but she thought she was unlike other mothers, at least the ones around her. The women of the hacienda, even knowing that their children would be slaves, frequently caressed their growing bellies as if engirdling treasure. They carried their babies in cloth slings close to their chests or, as they were older, on their backs, as if unwilling to let them go into the world. Watching them, Ana expected that she, too, would love her child wholeheartedly, that his presence would nourish the hunger for affection she'd carried from childhood. But Miguel didn't fill that emptiness. She told herself that her own unaffectionate parents impaired her, had cursed her with the inability to love, even toward flesh of her flesh. But it seemed too easy to blame her parents. Holding him in her arms, his little arms flailing toward her, she felt not pangs of love but qualms of doubt. Who—Ramón or Inocente—was his father?

Flora, Inés, and Siña Damita took over caring for Miguel, except for the few minutes she spent with him a couple of times a day. Sometimes Ana felt guilty for not paying more attention to him, but she could see that he was thriving. I was raised by maids and servants, she thought, and I turned out fine. It was true that she was lonely, but Miguel was lucky. There were several babies and toddlers on the hacienda, so he wouldn't lack for companions. Ramón and Inocente talked about white families with children, including Luis and Faustina with their two boys, but Ana was too busy to go visiting or to have guests. She might have to do that now so that Miguel would meet other children like him. The idea of organizing her life around his needs rankled. She was resentful of his presence, as if Miguel had sprung into her life to make things harder.

With one year's experience behind them, the 1846 *zafra* was more successful than the first, although they were short of their financial projections. The new fields wouldn't be ready for another season, but more land was being cleared for planting. The wind- and animal-powered *trapiche* was in need of a major overhaul. The grinders were worn and often needed on-the-spot repair, interrupting the processing. Severo recommended steam-powered crushers, but the machinery was costly to purchase, transport, and install, in addition to the time required to train workers on the new equipment.

During the *zafra,* fifteen *macheteros* were hired to cut the cane, and a few other *campesinos* were added for the less skilled jobs like carrying, stacking, and carting the stalks. Ramón and Inocente had to agree that they needed to buy more slaves.

Severo Fuentes secured ten more, and by the time Ramón and Inocente tallied the expenses, they were showing another deficit. Had Ana not asked for specifics, they wouldn't have shared the information, unwilling to let her know just how dire the situation was. She only learned that they'd borrowed money from don Eugenio when a letter arrived confirming a bank note from San Juan to a notary in Guares, who was in turn to deliver funds to Luis Morales. It appeared that the brothers had purchased more land with a loan from the neighbor.

"You didn't tell me about this purchase," Ana said, trying to keep the bitterness from her voice.

Ramón shrugged. "We couldn't let it go."

"Borrowing from your father or spending our own money are one thing. Getting into debt to a stranger is dangerous."

"He's not a stranger. He was our uncle's good friend. Inocente and I know what we're doing. Stop worrying."

"We agreed that the three of us would work together. Now you're keeping things from me—"

"This is men's business, Ana. We don't see the other women around here involved in men's affairs."

"What women?"

"The wives. If you made the effort to meet them, you'd learn that we're not quite as isolated as you think. There are charming people around here."

"I didn't come here for amusement."

"Having some fun might do you good. Doña Faustina is a lovely woman. She could be a good friend. You should have returned her visit and—"

"I can't be chatting with the neighbors while the *trapiche* is falling down and our product can't get to market for want of cattle to haul the carts, and—"

"I'd like to have a conversation that doesn't include complaints about what we don't have," Ramón shouted. "Take a moment to notice what we *have* accomplished."

"I don't believe you're speaking to me this way."

Ramón's anger vanished. "Things are different in the middle of nowhere," he said, as if he'd just discovered something about himself. He was going to say more but changed his mind. Without another word, he ran down the stairs.

Ana was confused and hurt. It was unlike Ramón to be rude or to raise his voice in anger, but it was obvious that he was disappointed in her. Yes, she'd disregarded her wifely roles of hostess and social consort to focus on the needs of the hacienda. In the process, she might have wounded Ramón's (and Inocente's) male pride by being a more capable manager than they were. They'd used her confinement and *cuarentena* to exclude her from the everyday operations of the hacienda. Now that she had a child, they wanted her to turn her attention to female pursuits, as if being a mother reduced her ambition and drive. No, Ramón, she said to herself, what we're building here is not for our amusement; it is for him, and for future generations.

EL TIEMPO MUERTO

———◆———

The end of the sugarcane harvest was the beginning of *el tiempo muerto,* the dead time, roughly June to December. With no cane to cut, load, transport, process, and ship, free *campesinos* had to find other work to keep themselves busy and to provide for their families. Those with friends or relatives on coffee or tobacco plantations migrated there for the season, but long distances, poor roads, and cost made travel impractical for most. The peasants waited until the harvest came around again, buying on credit whatever they couldn't grow, trade, or barter, so by the time the *zafra* came with its promise of work, they were already deep in debt.

To feed themselves and their families, *jíbaros* tended meager plots and coaxed plantains and yuca, malangas and *ñames* from the soil. They fished oceans and rivers. They kept hens until they laid no more eggs, then sacrificed them into *asopaos de gallina* or fricassees. They raised goats for milk and herded them to brambled hillsides, where the animals' omnivorous appetites soon reduced the slopes to stubble in preparation for tilling. When they outlived their usefulness, or when the dead time seemed to stretch longer than in other years, the goats, too, became fricassee or stews that fed a neighborhood.

For slaves, however, there was no dead time. They were too expensive an investment to be idle during the months when no cane was cut. Their days during *el tiempo muerto* began as they always did, at dawn, with the mournful clang of the watchtower bell. Their barracks were locked overnight and were opened by the foremen at the first strike. The slaves hopped from their pallets or hammocks and lined up, men on one side, women on the other, and after a quick cup of water and a chunk of boiled *batata,* they were given their tools and led to their labors until the bell clanged the return home.

During the dead time, slaves cleared land, prepared soil, planted cane shoots for the crop that took between a year and eighteen months to mature. The long-horned bulls that pulled carts loaded with four-foot stalks during the harvest now hauled trees felled in the forests and dragged to the workshop to be cut into lumber or to the *ingenio* for the fires under the *calderas.* Slaves cleaned and improved the buildings where the cane was processed, repaired machinery, maintained the tracks from the canebrakes to the *batey,* raised the berms between fields, built and cleared ditches. They staked new fences and mended deteriorated ones, dug trenches for drainage, built canals for irrigation.

Between harvests, the *ingenio* was scrubbed and repaired. This was where the cane was crushed, its juice boiled, purified, and filtered, where the resulting crystals were pressed and formed into bricks or where pure molasses was poured into barrels. Slaves cleaned and repaired the *calderas* and *pailas,* enormous graduated copper vessels where the syrup was boiled and refined. Slaves pointed the brickwork around and under the kettles, where the fires were built and stoked.

On Hacienda los Gemelos, Ana's gardens and orchards yielded fresh fruits and vegetables, and these had to be planted, weeded, pruned, and harvested, mostly by old women and children. Horses, mules, pigs, goats, milk cows, bulls, chickens, ducks, guinea fowls, and doves had to be tended, usually by young girls. The stables, sties, mangers, and coops had to be built, repaired, and cleaned, their animals fed, and those used in the fields trained and exercised.

The dead time, for the slaves, was as arduous as the *zafra,* with the added burden of the bone-rattling thunder, sizzling lightning, and sudden downpours of hurricane season that made outdoor labor hazardous. Rain or shine, dead time or *zafra,* the slaves fulfilled their duties under the watchful foremen and supervisors who were either white men or light-skinned mulattos with short tempers and quick hands. Locked in for the night in windowless *cuarteles,* the slaves led an existence defined by the demands of others, the needs of others, the caprice of others, and by the insistent throaty call of the watchtower bell.

Ana often rode from one end of Los Gemelos to the other to find out what Ramón and Inocente were doing with the land now that they didn't include her in hacienda business. Over the last few days, she'd noticed workers heading southwest behind the pastures, so she went in that direction. The June morning air was moist following rain showers, and she breathed in the smell of wet earth and mango. The fruit was reaching its peak in this particular corner of the hacienda.

She came upon a team of workers clearing brush and stones in the woods. Severo Fuentes, who was inspecting a new irrigation trench along the fields opposite, rode up as soon as he saw her, and they talked without dismounting.

"This section seems to be coming along." She looked over the immature but healthy canebrake.

"Yes, it should be ready for the next harvest."

She turned her gaze toward the workers across the path. "Preparing new fields?" she asked, as if confirming the plan.

"Yes, don Ramón and don Inocente want five more *cuerdas* here, and another ten on the northern boundary."

"Fifteen more *cuerdas,* with the same number of workers," she said, unable to keep the disapproval from her tone.

"They're hoping for a greater yield and more profit."

"But you don't agree with this plan."

There was a pause. "I give my opinion, *señora*, but they're the *patrones.*"

She rode a few feet to the shade of an avocado tree. Three women were bent over the stubbled ground, pulling roots and weeds in the sections where two men with machetes had cut down saplings.

"Isn't it harder to find workers now? I read that the Spanish Cortes enacted a law—"

"Yes, the Law of the Abolition and Repression of Slavery," Severo said. He made a sound halfway between a chuckle and a harrumph. "They keep writing laws in Madrid to keep the liberals happy, but there are many loopholes. The Crown makes too much money on taxes from sugar to allow the industry to collapse."

"I hope you're right," Ana said.

Another of the workers, Jacobo, dug around an enormous rock and realized it was too heavy to carry, so he rolled it to the side of the field where a stone fence was being erected. A few feet away, four children collected small stones and dropped them into large cans.

"Don't worry, *señora*. I'm always on the lookout for more workers."

"Thank you."

Three older boys carried the cans full of stones and emptied them along the edge of the road. She mentally counted: six adults and seven children needed to clear a rocky, wooded five-*cuerda* parcel.

"If there's anything else you need . . ."

"I do enjoy the books and newspapers you bring. I like to be informed."

"I understand, *señora*. Happy to oblige." He lifted his hat, and she saw his eyes. They were usually shadowed by his brim during the day, and when he came to the *casona* in the evening, she could hardly see them by candlelight. Now she saw how green his irises were, deep as a forest.

"I appreciate it, Severo. *Buenos días.*"

She rode toward the *batey*, resisting the urge to see if he was watching her go. Her old mare didn't like to move faster than necessary, but Ana astonished her by spurring her into a gallop. The pounding hooves, the heated air filling her lungs, the sweet, fruity aroma as she rode past the mango tree. This was joy.

"Looks like you had a good ride."

For a moment, she wasn't sure whether it was Ramón or Inocente standing outside the barn. The first few months after they arrived at Hacienda los Gemelos, they'd grown muscular and radiated the exuberance of young men who loved the outdoors and their own strong bodies. But in the last year, and especially after Miguel was born, both Ramón and Inocente had become strangely haggard. Inocente's face, particularly, was deeply lined, his lips had thinned, and he always looked like he didn't get enough sleep. She knew the brothers were working harder than ever. They were in the fields all day long, and without her to help them, they often worked into the night at the *finca*, preparing the reports demanded by the municipal government, tax authorities, and customs officials. She seethed with anger when she imagined what her meticulous books and ledgers might look like now that they had taken them from her.

"I did have a lovely ride." He made no effort to help her dismount. The brothers knew she was capable but had always been gentlemen. That, too, had changed in the last few months.

"I need a moment with you," he said.

"Let's sit in the shade, then." She waited until he remembered to offer his elbow as they walked around the pond, toward a stump under another mango tree. Unlike the ones she'd just passed, this one, according to the workers who'd lived on the hacienda for years, had never given fruit. Almost the minute Ana and Inocente sat under its shade, he stood and paced.

"Hacienda los Gemelos has been an extraordinary adventure," he said, "and Ramón and I are grateful to you. If you hadn't urged us, we'd be cooped up in offices in Cádiz. In less than two years you've created a home for us and have added to our family."

He was so formal, so solemn. Ana sat rigid, steeling her nerves. Whatever he was about to say, she thought, couldn't be good news.

"It's time that I have my own household, Ana. I'm going to San Juan to marry Elena."

Once she grasped what he'd said, and what it meant, she breathed easier. "I'm so happy to hear that." She let his words sink in, then asked, "Will you come back here, or do you plan to live in San Juan?"

"We will settle on the *finca*. It's small but comfortable enough until we can build. We should be back before the *zafra*."

Ana counted mentally. Six months. Across the pond, Ramón rode into the yard. He saw them, waved, and disappeared inside.

"When will you sail for San Juan, then?"

"I'm planning to ride. We didn't see much of Puerto Rico by sailing around the island."

"I thought that the roads aren't good."

"I'm a cavalry officer's son, and a veteran," he said with a rueful smile. "I grew up on bad roads."

"That's true. But you're not traveling alone?"

"Of course not. I'll take one of our men, Pepe, the foreman. He has family in a town near the capital. We'll leave in a week."

"So soon?"

"Yes. Elena and I will spend a few weeks in Caguas. Papá seems to be enjoying his retirement and pays little attention to the farm. I've learned a great deal about what it takes to run a plantation," he continued, as if delivering a speech to an association of bankers, "and I can help him. I also know that Elena will be as excellent a partner as you are to Ramón." He was as distant as if already many leagues away.

She didn't trust him—or Ramón. They were too secretive and were deliberately isolating her from their financial dealings. In the past few weeks, she'd noticed that there was greater tension between the brothers. If Severo was with them, they seemed to be more relaxed, and Ana soon understood that it was she who made the twins nervous. They became testy if she asked questions about the hacienda, considering them as challenges. Their testiness offended her. How dare they forget that, from the beginning, she was to be a partner? That it was her idea to come to Puerto Rico, to create a place they could own and be proud of?

Now Inocente's plan to visit the farm in Caguas sounded like a ruse. Ramón and Inocente might be tired of the unending work at Los Gemelos and miss the amusements they enjoyed in Spain and San Juan. Her mind raced through scenarios and settled on the most likely. Once in San Juan, doña Leonor would press Inocente and Elena to live closer, perhaps on the farm in Caguas, about thirty kilometers from the capital. Soon Ramón would want to do the same because the brothers didn't want to live apart.

Before they left Spain, they'd all agreed that at least five harvests were necessary to determine whether or not they could succeed as *hacendados*. Were they, after less than two years, ready to give up? Ramón would probably tell Ana that Severo could manage Los Gemelos. Had Severo encouraged their plans? She immediately dismissed the thought. It dawned on her that she trusted Severo Fuentes more than either Ramón or Inocente. He, of the three, had not yet disappointed her.

Severo arranged for Pepe to guide Inocente, accompanied by Alejo and Curro, the two men who'd pulled their dinghy to the beach the first day they arrived almost eighteen months earlier. Inocente was borrowing them to help on the farm in Caguas. As the date for his departure neared, Inocente spent more time with Miguel, studying his features with such intensity that Ana was sure he was looking for signs that Miguel was more like him than Ramón. As with their decision to share her, the twins didn't consult her and hadn't asked whether Ramón or Inocente was Miguel's father. She couldn't tell with any certainty, but she would assure them that it was Ramón. Even if she knew that it was Inocente, she'd never admit that her child was a bastard, and the product of adultery.

An early morning mist was suspended over the trees and canebrakes on the last day of June 1846. The usual birdsong was muted by the activity in the *batey*. The tamped red earth was etched by hooves, paws, the delicate markings of hen's claws, the curves of bare feet, the square heels of boots.

Inocente held Miguel, pressed his lips to his forehead, said something into his ear, then handed him to Ana. He didn't look at her directly but kissed her lightly on both cheeks with the child between them.

"We'll celebrate his baptism when I return with Elena. We'll be devoted godparents," he said. "And someday you'll do us the honor of being godparents to our children." His cheeks were flushed, as if he was embarrassed.

"Of course we will," Ana said.

Inocente rubbed Miguel's head, and this time she was able to get him to look into her eyes. She startled at the hard expression there. Contempt? How was it possible? What had she done?

"Bring Mamá and Papá when you return," Ramón said. "They can stay in one of the cottages. They should meet their grandchild. They'll be proud of him."

"They'll be proud of what we've built here in such a short time."

Inocente and Ramón stared at each other, communicating silently, saying something, she knew, about her. But what? The tension that had flickered since Miguel's birth dissolved in one gaze, and both right hands reached for the other's simultaneously, and left hands pressed the other's shoulder into an embrace. They separated and kissed both cheeks, then hugged again. They hugged and kissed a third time, each unwilling to be the first to let the other go. Ana saw then what she'd imagined since the baby was born: that they blamed her for the rift between them. It wasn't me, she wanted to scream. It was the child. You should have known this would happen.

The sun had burned through the mist, creating long, thin shadows. Inocente took a few steps toward his horse, his eyes still on his brother's. Ana moved toward him, expecting a gesture to erase the thoughts swirling around her, but he mounted without a glance at her.

"Write as soon as you reach San Juan," Ramón said.

Before his horse disappeared, Inocente turned around, removed his hat, and waved.

"*Vayan con Dios,*" Ana called and waved back, but he didn't acknowledge her.

Ramón was having difficulty controlling his feelings. He took Miguel from Ana and held him as Inocente and his party vanished down the trail into the cane.

In the days after Inocente left, Ramón wouldn't let go of nine-month-old Miguel, who was beginning to stand on his own. He talked to the boy in a high, unnatural voice, played with him, sang him *coplas,* made faces—all the things Ana didn't do. He called him *"mi hijo,"* not Miguel, as if to make sure that everyone knew he was the father. The more affectionate he was with the child, the harder the looks he directed at Ana, but he didn't criticize or reproach her out loud. She'd once thought of Ramón as the "talking twin," but since Miguel's birth, he'd been more guarded, as if it were an effort to avoid telling her things she shouldn't know. What would his brother's absence mean for him, for her, for them?

Another change in Ramón was that he'd lost interest in sex. She was bathed, Flora let him know that she was ready, but Ramón didn't come. After a while, sleep overcame her. Sometimes she heard him leave the house, and later awoke to the groan of the *hamaca* ropes in the next room. If she called to him, Ramón didn't answer.

One night she heard him scream and ran next door.

"Did you have a nightmare?"

"*¡Déjame!*" he said, turning away and hiding his face within the hammock's folds. The single word ordering her to leave him was like a stab into her heart. She left. The next morning he rode out at dawn.

Ramón didn't return until hours after the last bell. Ana heard him undress on the other side of the wall. A few minutes later he tiptoed into her room, a lit candle aloft.

"Are you awake?"

She lifted the mosquito netting for him to crawl inside. He pinched the flame off and, with the chirp of tree frogs singing in the dark, told her the truth.

"Inocente might not be back. He plans to settle on the farm near Caguas."

"That's not what he told me."

He put his arm under her head and pulled her close. "He didn't want to upset you."

She resisted his embrace. "It's worse to say he'll return and then not do it."

"Ana, you know that things can't continue . . . the same way."

He couldn't say it. For a moment she considered asking what he was talking about. She said nothing.

He, too, was silent but agitated.

"Ramón, please talk to me."

He turned to her again. "Inocente said that the day Miguel was born, when Damita called me in, he was jealous of me for the first time in his life. And he felt hatred." His voice quavered. "When he heard me say *'mi hijo,'* he realized that Miguel could just as easily be his son as mine."

Beneath his emotion she heard the question he didn't dare ask. Whose son is Miguel? It occurred to her that every child belongs only to the mother, even if she was sure of the father.

"We should have never done . . . what we did." He couldn't even say it. Ramón wept openly now. "Inocente said that he had to leave because he didn't trust himself, what he might do with his jealousy. He's never spoken to me like that, Ana, with such resentment. Dear God, what have we done? Why didn't you stop us?"

"Me?" She lifted her head and tried to find his eyes, but all they could see of each other were dense silhouettes. "It was up to me?"

"We thought you wanted it that way."

"You never asked, Ramón. You and Inocente took advantage of my . . . of my innocence."

"You could always tell us apart."

"You tricked me, Ramón, cruelly and deliberately. By the time I figured it out, it was too late."

"But you never—"

"I thought that was the only way for us, for you and me and Inocente. You were grown men; I was just a girl. It never occurred to me that there would be this—this complication."

"I'm sorry, *mi amor,*" he said, and reached for her, tried to kiss her.

She moved away from him. "Don't touch me."

"I said we're sorry."

"Don't touch me," she repeated.

The room was so dark that she couldn't see him, but she felt him struggle with what to say, what to do. She wanted to hurt him, to humiliate him, to see him suffer, but she didn't know how. For a moment, she considered lying, telling him that Miguel was Inocente's son. The rest of his life he'd believe that the boy was his brother's son, and wouldn't ever forget what he and Inocente had done to her.

Before she spoke, Ramón sat up and lifted the mosquito netting. "You're too upset now," he said, and crept from the bed. "Please know that both Inocente and I are truly sorry—"

She wrapped her pillow around her head. "I can't bear your apologies."

"But, Ana—"

She squeezed her eyes shut to push back the tears forming in the corners of her lids. "Go away."

She was alone with her rage at Ramón and Inocente for using her, rage at herself for letting them do it. She needed air. "I've been a fool," she said as she unlatched the shutters to the night. "I was so grateful for the opportunity Ramón and Inocente provided that I've let them do as they pleased while I worked and worried in the background." Above, clouds had swallowed the moon. *"Basta,"* she whispered to the rustle of cane beyond her window. Enough.

August was oppressively hot and humid. Ana woke up almost every night to thunder and lightning flashes, the trees whistling, the canebrakes alive, like a thousand hands clapping at once. The next morning the air was still and heavy. As the sun climbed, shimmering rivulets rose from the sodden ground, as if the earth were boiling underfoot. The constant activity to, from, and through the *batey* took on a dreamy quality, and moisture clung to every living and nonliving thing.

One overcast morning, the hounds announced visitors long before three soldiers rode into the *batey*. Other than new slaves, Luis, Faustina, and occasional visits by Padre Xavier, no outsider had entered the plantation in nineteen months. From the porch of the *casona*, Ana saw Ramón and Severo riding in from opposite ends of the fields. They talked with the soldiers under the shade of the breadfruit tree. She couldn't distinguish rank, but one of the soldiers with more insignias than the others seemed to be the leader. He removed his plumed hat and spoke to Ramón. Ramón covered his face, and groaned.

From the living room threshold, Ana crossed herself, pressed a hand to her chest, and prayed silently. *Dame fuerza, Señor.* The soldiers looked everywhere but at Ramón, who would have collapsed had Severo not put Ramón's arm around his shoulders to keep him upright. Severo looked up at Ana and led Ramón across the *batey* and up the stairs.

Ana helped guide Ramón to a bench inside. She questioned Severo with a look, but he wouldn't meet her eyes. She touched Ramón's cheek, tried to turn his face toward her, but he resisted.

"*¿Qué pasó? ¿Qué ha pasado?*"

Ramón couldn't speak. He was like a sleepwalker, his eyes open but unfocused, as if whatever he was seeing was within.

Teo and Flora were against the wall, waiting for instructions. In the back room, Miguel cried, and Inés shushed him, murmuring sweet words. At a nod from Severo, Teo and Flora approached, helped Ramón up, and walked him to the bedroom. He allowed them to lead him, one unsteady step at a time, like a child just learning to walk.

Ana's heart was racing, anticipating the name, dreading the moment she'd hear it. Nothing but a death in his family would leave Ramón speechless with grief. Please, Lord, let it not be Inocente, Ana prayed as she followed Severo out to the gallery. Please, Lord. Severo's face was hard, fixed into a frown, his eyes slits beneath his brows.

"I beg your pardon, *señora*," he started, "and sorry to be the one to deliver this news."

"Tell me."

"Don Inocente and Pepe were ambushed. *Lo siento, señora.*"

"Is he dead, Severo?"

He nodded. "Both are dead."

The heavy air couldn't, somehow, fill her lungs. *"No puede ser,"* she said, dropping onto the bench. "It can't be true," she repeated fiercely, challenging Severo, as if he could, he must, change the outcome. Severo's face remained impassive as he knelt in front of her, like a lover about to declare his intentions. "Inocente is in San Juan," she said. "Getting married. There's some mistake."

"There is no mistake, *señora,*" Severo said so quietly that it sent a chill to her scalp.

He stood and took one step toward the porch railing. He looked down at the *batey,* where, in deference to the crisis in the *patrón's* house, the workers had stopped what they were doing and squatted in small groups under trees and against the buildings. Ana followed Severo's gaze, and its effect. One by one the workers, the bosses included, quietly returned to their duties, their eyes cast down, afraid to look in his direction.

Inside, Miguel wailed again. Inés will not sing to Miguel, not anymore, Ana thought; neither will Flora. This is now a house in mourning. In the bedroom, Ramón groaned. Since his brother had left, tears were never far from his eyes. Ana had not known what to say, wasn't able to console him when there was a possibility that Inocente would return. What could she do now? And who would console her? Suddenly she was shaking with fury.

"Who did it?" she asked, her throat so tight she could hardly speak.

Severo turned to her as if seeing a different person. He was always considerate and respectful around her. She sometimes had the impression that he made himself smaller when he was near her, not to frighten her with his bulk, so that he wouldn't tower over her, like Ramón and Inocente. He didn't do that now. He stood over her, brawny, solid. Nothing could move him.

"Alejo and Curro have vanished. The lieutenant assumes they are responsible."

"What else did the lieutenant say?" she asked, and Severo flinched. "Tell me!" she demanded.

His eyes went vacant. "They were stabbed and hanged by their ankles from the branch of a ceiba tree," he said flatly.

She gasped, and he moved as if to catch her, but she wasn't falling. She would not fall. "What else?" Severo didn't speak. "I want to know everything," she said. *"Todo."*

He gave her the details bit by bit, waiting until she reacted before the next one. She listened, her arms wrapped around her rib cage. Her breath came in spurts, and she fought hard to control it. "What else?" she asked once she could breathe, her eyes fixed on Severo's flinty eyes.

The crime was only recently discovered because the men were dragged far from the main trail. Their bodies were so badly decomposed that they were identified only when Inocente's pouch was found near the bodies with the letters to Elena and to her parents in Spain still inside. A soldier was sent with the news and the pouch to don Eugenio's house in San Juan.

"The lieutenant is organizing a hunting party with men and hounds."

"Find them."

"¿Señora?"

"Find them," she said again. "They're our slaves. Find them."

"Sí, señora, I'll join the search, and you can be sure that when I find those devils, they'll be punished. Now, if you will permit me?" He bowed.

She nodded and Severo went down the stairs giving orders to the bosses. Within minutes, he rode into the forest, a whip coiled around his left shoulder, his rifle and revolver holstered, his two favorite hounds alongside his horse.

Ana had not been afraid of Hacienda los Gemelos. She was curious about her new world and determined to prevail over its challenges. But as soon as Severo Fuentes rode out of the *batey* to seek Inocente's murderers, Ana felt absolute terror. The comings and goings of people she'd taken for granted took on a different significance. Why was Marta crossing the yard from the kitchen to the barn? Why was Teo standing near the coops with his wife, Paula? If Alejo and Curro could kill Inocente, were the others planning to kill her and Ramón? Where was José going with what looked like a fence post? Severo had left one of the foremen to guard her and Ramón. Did he think someone would turn on her and Ramón while he was away?

She tried to suppress the dread that they might want to harm them. But where had Inés taken Miguel? And Flora, where was Flora?

As if she'd heard her calling, Flora appeared.

"Don Ramón is calling for you, *señora*."

Ana ran to him, away from her own questions.

He was hunched on the edge of the bed, his fists against his eyes as if to press back images he didn't want to see. "I shouldn't have let him go by land. Severo arranged for a ship, but he wanted to ride."

She wrapped her arms around him. "Don't blame yourself—"

"I told him to go to San Juan and marry Elena. If he had a wife, a son, we'd both have the same."

"You couldn't have imagined what happened. No one could have."

She wouldn't speak it but couldn't silence her own thoughts, what every owner knew: that slaves challenged their masters, that they killed them, that they set fire to their homes, their land, that they escaped into the woods or to sea. Severo said that young men were the most likely to run away, and those who didn't try to escape by water hid in the dense forests of the island's central mountain range. In order to reduce the possibility of conspiracies, they were forbidden to congregate in groups larger than three. Their tools were kept under lock when not being used, and they weren't allowed to carry any implements or weapons, like knives or machetes, unrelated to the work they were doing at the time.

"If they could kill Inocente, they could come after us, too," Ramón said. "And why shouldn't they?"

"Don't say that," she said, even though he spoke aloud what she was thinking. "We can't let them frighten us," she said, more to ward off her own dread than to console her husband.

"*¡Qué horror!*" Faustina climbed the steps that afternoon, breathless, to the *casona*.

"The lieutenant stopped to let us know what happened." Luis came up behind her.

"Do accept our deepest condolences," Faustina said. "Our sweet Inocente, what a tragedy, my dears, what a terrible loss."

"We're here to help," Luis said. "You shouldn't be here alone in your sorrow. Do you own firearms?"

"We have a rifle. You don't think—"

"Just a precaution," Luis said.

Having them around relieved some of Ana's anxiety, and don Luis seemed to be a comfort to Ramón. But Faustina's chatter overwhelmed her. She pressed Ana for details about Inocente's trip. Why had Severo left them alone? When would he be back? The more she wanted to know, the less Ana wanted to tell her.

"You poor child," Faustina finally said, dissimulating her frustration at Ana's vague answers. "Clearly, you're overcome with grief and here I am, asking impertinent questions. Please forgive me."

Ana said nothing.

Faustina pulled her rosary from a pocket. "Our faith is a solace at times like these. We can pray."

They spent most of the night in prayer. Ana was sure that neither she nor Ramón would've been able to sleep in any case. The clicking beads and the rhythmic waves of the invocations soothed Ana's nerves, and allowed her to be silent with her grief but not alone in her fear. The next morning Luis talked to the foremen as they led the slaves to their chores to make sure that nothing unusual had happened overnight. He reported that Severo had left strict orders for keeping the slaves under close watch while he was away. Only Teo, Marta, Flora, and Inés were allowed to come near the *casona*.

Visitors appeared over the next three days, until the hounds went hoarse from barking at strangers. Marta, Teo, and Flora managed the waves of food and drink that had to be prepared and served. The guests were new to Ana—local farmers and nearby *hacendados* or their *mayordomos*. Padre Xavier said Mass, and some of the *campesinos* joined the *hacendados* and *mayordomos*. The *blancos* and *libertos* heard Mass under the roofed *rancho,* while the slaves were grouped in the full sun of the yard. Soldiers came and went; a few merchants from town brought their wives. Ramón knew them all, and they were warm, generous people, concerned about him and Ana.

"You're so young!" an *hacendada* exclaimed when she met Ana. "You must be so lonely out here on your own."

Yes, she was young, only twenty, but she had to correct her on the second point. "I'm not lonely. There's much to do, and I like being alone." The woman backed away, offended.

Ramón walked among the guests carrying Miguel, introducing

him to the neighbors, who didn't know that a child had been born in the hacienda. Some of the women had written when Ana first arrived at Los Gemelos, but she didn't respond to their welcome notes. They stood in groups now, and even when they sat with her to pray, they seemed to belong to one another, while she was apart, stubbornly unwilling to let them into her life or insert herself into theirs. She was relieved when, by the fourth day, the flow of visitors stopped and she and Ramón were alone again.

But the fear returned. At Luis and Faustina's suggestion, Ramón insisted that he, Ana, and Miguel lock themselves in at night, the rifle loaded and ready by the bed. Having it so close made her more nervous, and after a few sleepless nights, she told him to put it away.

She resumed her chores, but she was tense. She always carried the small knife Beba had given her years ago. It was a tool for cutting stems, for slicing branches, for grafting, for peeling fruit. She didn't want this useful tool to become a weapon, especially not against the men and women who helped her in her gardens and orchards. Arming herself against them scared her more than pretending to be confident and unafraid.

Slaves weren't allowed to look at *blancos* directly, and their sideways glances made them seem furtive and evasive. Severo had trained them to keep their hands clasped in front when talking to a *blanco,* and Ana was grateful, because whenever she approached, they dropped their tools if they were working and showed their hands. She mirrored the posture. They stood before each other, mistress and slave, no less than three paces separating them, the ground between them vast as the ocean.

Severo returned six days later as dusk was falling. His clothes were ragged and stained; his face was covered with golden stubble. He removed the whip from his shoulder and carried it, still coiled, to the porch, where Ana and Ramón waited. When Ramón pointed to the bench where he should sit, Severo placed the whip at his feet, where it lay like an expectant serpent.

"Forgive my appearance," he said. "I thought you'd want to know right away. Those *demonios* were caught and punished."

"How?" Ramón asked.

Severo looked at Ana, then at Ramón. "They were hiding in caves," he said, "with the other three *cimarrones* who ran away from here before you came."

Ramón thought that Severo wasn't about to give more details with Ana present. He stood. "You must be tired and hungry. We can talk more tomorrow."

"*Gracias, señor.*" Severo gathered his whip. "Good night, *señora.*" He bowed.

She didn't want him to leave. He was unkempt and unwashed; his face drawn, he looked exhausted. Ramón had mentioned that Severo lived with a woman on land he owned close to town, but neither brother had met her, and Ana thought that she was far from his thoughts right now. As he bowed in her direction, his eyes lowered yet seeking hers, she knew that he was waiting for a word from her. He wanted confirmation of what they both knew: he went after the runaway slaves to impress her, not to avenge Inocente.

"I'm grateful to you," she said, stretching her hand toward him, "for bringing justice to the men who did this terrible wrong to my brother-in-law and to Pepe."

He seemed startled to have her hand within reach. He wiped his palm on his trousers, then took her fingertips in his and kissed them. "It's my honor, *señora,*" he said. Following her example, Ramón, too, gave Severo his hand.

"We will not forget this," Ramón said.

The next day, Ramón went to a notary in Guares and drafted a document deeding Severo Fuentes five *cuerdas* on the new *finca* by the river.

DESESPERADO

———— ◆ ————

Severo knew the land, every curve of it, each hill and its eventual valley, the sandy patches where the river overflowed during the rainy season, the dry, rocky slopes where only brush grew, the moist hollows of black earth where life writhed unencumbered. Even on a moonless night, the seemingly impenetrable darkness that surrounded him was as familiar as a cloak, its weight tangible and humid. He mounted his horse, Burro, so named not because he bore any resemblance to a donkey but because he was dull-witted, stupid enough to have no fear. Burro hurtled into the night following the customary paths through the labyrinthine canebrakes, his gait smooth and secure on the uneven ground.

Severo kept his head down, the brimmed hat pulled tightly over his ears to block the onslaught of flying insects into his face. He'd been on these paths at night so many times that it didn't feel much different from riding them in the full brightness of day, except that, were he to look back, he'd have no sight of the windmill in the middle of the plantation.

A hundred meters from where the trail disappeared into the forest, he halted under a mango tree. Still mounted, he removed the whip from around his arm and tied it, coiled, to his saddle. He unbuttoned his shirt and flapped it back and forth to drive the sweat from his damp undershirt and armpits. He rebuttoned and tucked in the shirt, tugging at the collar until he thought it looked straight. He removed his hat, ran his fingers through his hair, and wiped the sweat off on his pants legs. Satisfied, he urged Burro around the tree, onto a path barely visible in daylight that now appeared to swallow him.

He crossed a swale and was once more in the cane, along the narrow berm between two rows of sugar. He rode at a walking pace, the cheeping frogs competing with the whispering cane on either side of him. The field opened into a meadow. On the far side, a solid wall of coconut palms grew so close together they seemed planted deliberately to keep intruders away. Burro took the path that wound around two huge palms, along an avenue of coconut and *almendros* toward the clearing where Consuelo's *bohío* rose on piles fifty feet from the placid Caribbean Sea.

"Consuelo, *mi consuelo*," he called in a low voice as he unsaddled Burro and led him into a shack where he fed and watered him. He took off his shirt and undergarment, and splashed water on his head and neck, under his arms, around his chest. He rubbed his torso and arms dry before he dressed again, tucked the garments in neatly, refastened his belt, and combed his wet fingers through his hair. He walked around to the front gate and was immersed in fragrance, as if the garden emitted smells only within the space enclosed by its reed fence.

"*Pasa, mi amor*," Consuelo called from the *hamaca* strung across the porch beams.

The end of her cigar was a beacon, her voice syrupy and languid, filled with promises. Below her on the floor was a bottle of rum. Severo reached for it, swigged, and wiped his mouth on his sleeve. He sat on the edge of the hammock. The ropes around the beams groaned, and the cotton stretched to hover a few inches from the floor. He leaned against her. She was naked, her long body all curves and mounds, fleshy until she seemed boneless, like a giant sea creature. She brought the cigar to his mouth, pressed his fingers around it. He inhaled the tobacco until it, and the rum warming his belly, made him light-headed. Her hands roamed his body, undoing the buttons he'd so recently fastened, tugging at the shirt tucked in minutes earlier, removing the belt that held up his pants, pulling off his musky undershirt. She unlaced his boots and he kicked them off. With agile toes, she rolled off his socks, pulled down his pants, and let them fall over the side of the *hamaca*. As naked as she, Severo twisted and turned, rubbed himself against her ample flesh, seeking the wet.

"*Ay, mi amor, qué desesperado*," she laughed, but didn't make him stop. Severo was not the first *desesperado* to find his way to Consuelo

Soldevida. Every man needs consoling at one time or another, and she, who took her name literally, provided it. Her mother, Consuelo, brought comfort to men. Her daughter Consuelo would, too, as would untold Consuelos after them.

Consuelo was the illegitimate daughter of Roberto Cofresí, the most daring and famous pirate in the Caribbean. Consuelo's mother was one of the pirate's mistresses, a tall and bosomy *mulata* born of a white soldier and a black free woman. From her, Consuelo inherited her tamarind skin and a long-limbed, fleshy, rounded body. Her cacao hair was the same shade and wavy texture as the pirate's. She'd never owned a mirror, but she knew her eye color changed with the light, a fascination to the men she consoled.

She had keen memories of her notorious father, who, like Severo, came to see the two Consuelos with no prior notice and stayed just long enough to be missed when he left. He established Consuelo and Consuelo in a cottage near the beach on the outskirts of Cabo Rojo, his hometown. He often brought them trinkets and coins, pewter spoons, fringed shawls, and painted china from the ships he captured. His favorite targets were the well-appointed North American cargo ships. He told Consuelo that English sounded like barking, and that the *yanquis* were arrogant and more imperious than even the *españoles*.

The Spanish government didn't actively pursue pirates so long as they didn't attack ships flying the Spanish flag. Cofresí's exploits, however, and his cruelty toward captured sailors, pressured the Spaniards to go after the infamous pirate. Cofresí was captured in 1825 and executed by firing squad in El Morro. A few days later, soldiers appeared in the two Consuelos' cottage, searching for hidden booty. They ransacked the house, took everything of value, then set the place on fire. Consuelo was ten years old. She hardly remembered the next four or five years except that they walked and walked and walked until they reached Ponce, the bustling self-important city on the Caribbean, where Consuelo the elder entered a tavern, and soon she was comforting its customers. Consuelo the younger knew her first man's hand on her body when she was eleven.

After her mother died, Consuelo left Ponce and walked west, toward the ruins of her burned house, but she didn't make it that far. She knew how to do only one thing and, weary and hungry, she found a home and employment at a crossroads, north of Guares, in a hut behind a bar, available to whoever paid with money or goods. A fat hen was as acceptable as a few coins, so even the poorest *campesino* tilling the most unforgiving soil had hope of Consuelo. One day Severo Fuentes entered the bar at the crossroads looking for laborers. He spotted Consuelo leaning on the threshold of a door that never closed. Within days, he'd taken her away to a house by the sea, and all hope of comfort for the *campesinos* went with her.

The next morning, Severo woke up alone just as dawn purpled the sky. Consuelo was in the garden, snipping herbs between her hard thumbnail and index finger.

She looked up when she saw him stand, naked, the fine golden hair that covered his body shimmering. He whooped and ran into the sea, his muscular arms dipping into and emerging from the water in even strokes.

By the time he returned, Consuelo had heated fresh water in the shack where her cooking fire was never extinguished. She rinsed the salt water off his body and hair. A clean change of clothes was folded over the railing, and he dressed himself as she made the coffee. She served them both the strong, steamy liquid in the hollow of burnished coconut shells.

They sat in silence for some minutes, watching the sky lighten and the dew slide from the long, narrow channels of palm fronds. When they finished their coffee, Consuelo returned to the kitchen shack and came back with a gourd full of warm, soapy water, a leather strop, and his shaving blade. She wrapped a clean rag around his neck and, in slow strokes, shaved six days' growth from his face and neck, finishing with a splash of jasmine-scented water on the jaw. A few minutes later she watched him mount his stupid horse and ride into the canebrakes.

Severo traversed the same path as the previous night, but when he neared Los Gemelos, he turned left toward the hills instead of right toward the *batey*. It was too early for the workers to be out but soon the bell would toll, signaling the beginning of the workday. Severo urged Burro up a steep, pebbly mesa to the top, where the land was carpeted with fine, bright green grass. The slopes were a tangle of thorny lemon and grapefruit trees, guava, passion fruit vines, *amapola* bushes, and brambles. From the valley, it was impossible to guess that this hill was so flat at its summit, and that mild, aromatic breezes blew upon it all day long. Once the taller trees were cut, the spot would afford a panoramic view of the fields, the pastures, the river, the hazy mountains, and the brilliant Caribbean Sea.

She'll like it here, Severo thought, dismounting and walking circles around the land, using his machete to chop saplings grown too tall since the last time.

Severo Fuentes chose this as the perfect spot for the new, the real, *casona* of Hacienda los Gemelos. He envisioned the house as a masonry and tile palace for Ana. He took her plans for a house with a roofed wraparound terrace and altered them to fit the site. He imagined Ana sitting in a shady corner of the *balcón* even on the hottest part of the day, the breezes playing around her shoulders. She'd be dressed in pale green, like on the first day he saw her, with her black hair pinned, revealing the fine down along the back of her neck.

The first time he saw Ana, the voice inside Severo's head, until then silent for years, said, "There's your wife." Ana would be his. She'd be his and so would Los Gemelos. The voice didn't mention Los Gemelos, but he soon learned they came together. Coming to Puerto Rico had been her idea, Severo knew; Ramón and Inocente simply followed her ambitions.

With Inocente dead, Severo had no doubt that Ramón would soon lose heart. The tropics had crushed better men. Tens of thousands had taken advantage of the Crown's Real Cédula de Gracias of 1815 encouraging white settlers to colonize and make their fortune, with the certainty that they could leave after five years, presumably enriched. Like many Europeans who dreamed of building wealth from sugar, Ramón and Inocente were speculators, not agriculturalists. A little money, optimism, and willingness to work hard weren't enough. You had to be tough, you had to be strong, and every time your eyes rested on black skin, you had to be able to silence your conscience. Neither Ramón nor Inocente could do that, but Ana could. He knew it from the first. And the afternoon that she looked him in the eye and said, "Find them," he was certain. He knew that, like him, Ana was ruthless enough for this land in a way Ramón and Inocente were not.

Severo predicted that without his brother, Ramón would soon doubt his ability to manage the plantation. Don Luis had already begun putting doubts into Ramón's head. He had his eye on the hacienda, but he was overextended, even though he'd managed to scrape together enough to give Ramón and Inocente a loan. It was part of his plan to keep the Argosos indebted to him, to let them improve the land while he strengthened his own position. Then he'd call in his loans. But don Luis had a weakness, and Severo knew that too. He was *vicioso,* a man with a taste for every imaginable vice. His lechery and abuse of his female slaves were only the beginning. He was a gambler, and over the years, his losses were Severo's gain as Luis came to him again and again for loans. To his credit, he paid if he won, but no one so reckless could win every time. If he didn't lose at cards, it would be at cockfights. If not those, horse races. Severo bided his time. He wouldn't allow don Luis to own Hacienda los Gemelos. If he had to use his own money to pay Ramón and Inocente's debts, he'd do that, too. If Ana was to be his, the hacienda must be hers, and he would protect her interests.

Severo expected that Ramón would turn to him with increasing uncertainty. One day, he'd inform Ana that they were leaving, that he could manage the business from the city, like other Europeans who'd settled on the island before them. Ramón would argue that Severo was an effective and efficient manager, and that they'd come to Los Gemelos in the summer, when San Juan was insufferably hot and humid.

Ana would refuse. Severo was certain. Ana was enthralled by the land, its mystery and romance, just as he was. Sometimes, when they all sat together on the porch after dinner, a warm breeze would ripple through the leaves and Ana would close her eyes and turn her face in its direction as if toward a lover's kiss.

Her small size made her seem delicate, but from the very first he saw her courage and determination. She rode like a man, with authority and strength, uncomplaining about her mount or the rough terrain. She displayed no squeamishness at the rustic conditions and worked as hard as any white man. Even when she was huge with child she was out in the gardens, or in the barns, or seeing to the fowl in the henhouses, the livestock in the pastures, the hogs in the sties. He chose Flora as her attendant because the maid was skilled, but more important, because she was cheerful. Severo wanted Ana to have someone to keep up her spirits.

After two meetings with the Argoso brothers, Severo concluded that their pride was too tied up in their success for them to be good companions for Ana. They were overly preoccupied with proving to don Eugenio and doña Leonor that they'd made the right decision in coming to Los Gemelos. At the same time, they took chances that more experienced men wouldn't. Encouraged by don Luis, they were buying every contiguous piece of land they could get. They didn't take into account that the more land they owned, the more *brazos* they'd require. The hacienda just wasn't producing enough for their extravagance.

The damage done by years of neglect was of more immediate concern. Grinders operated by a barely functional windmill supplemented by yoked bulls pressed the cane. Severo suggested that the windmill be replaced by a steam engine, and went so far as to show them various models that could be ordered from the United States and could be made functional before the next harvest. The brothers demurred. The boiling house was crumbling, and the barns and work buildings might easily come down the next time a hurricane blew through the island. The brothers argued that the price of sugar was down, and that planters were selling their lands and moving on. Ramón and Inocente wouldn't invest in the infrastructure of the plantation while there was land for sale. It was foolish, Severo thought but, of course, could not say aloud.

Severo whacked a sapling close to the ground with his machete and smiled. When he first met them, it hadn't occurred to him that the brothers were sharing Ana. In San Juan, and in Spain, too, he surmised, they took pains to dress alike so that it would be hard for people to tell which brother was which. At Los Gemelos, however, they weren't as careful. Sometimes one shaved and the other didn't, or one wore a blue waistcoat and the other a brown one. Severo observed Inocente's more choleric, sarcastic temperament; Ramón was more even-tempered and sentimental, easier to manipulate.

It was Flora who, just weeks after she met them, confirmed that the brothers took turns with Ana. Severo gave Flora a length of yellow cotton for this information and promised her more if she found a way to prove it. She'd receive nothing, however, if anyone else heard about what she'd told him. So Flora paid attention and reported which twin was with Ana when, and how she could tell whether it was Ramón or Inocente.

As he watched Ramón, Inocente, and Ana, Severo's suspicions became a certainty. They were too comfortable around one another. She was as familiar and open as a wife toward Inocente, not observing the affectionate-but-respectful distance due a brother-in-law.

Severo finished clearing the weeds and saplings and mounted his horse. Burro seemed confused about where the trail started downhill, so he guided him toward an opening in the brambles. In a few minutes the bell would toll, the workers would trudge to the fields, and the planting of next season's crop would resume. He was short two slaves and one foreman. The loss of Alejo and Curro was greater than the loss of Pepe, who could more easily be replaced.

Severo had joined the lieutenant and two soldiers on the search for Alejo and Curro. Severo's hounds flushed them from a cave with the other three *cimarrones* three days' ride from Los Gemelos. Severo and the soldiers flayed them, then marched them to the ceiba tree. Severo hog-tied and hanged the five men from the same branches they used for Inocente and Pepe, but lower. He let his hounds play with them until the men begged for forgiveness for their deeds. He made them say the Lord's prayer, then slit each of their throats. The lieutenant went into the bushes to vomit because, he said, he'd never seen so much blood.

I DON'T KNOW WHAT TO TELL YOU

————◆————

One morning three weeks after the news of Inocente's murder, Ramón delivered the hacienda books and two bulging portfolios to Ana. He was sheepish, as if he'd been forced to turn them over against his will.

"I can't do this. Inocente was in charge and I can't make sense of any of it." He stood like a boy expecting a scolding.

Ana frowned over the portfolios but didn't open them. She skimmed the ledgers. The figures were in a neat, clerkish hand. "This is not Inocente's handwriting," she said.

"Severo," Ramón said.

Thank goodness, Ana thought. "I see. Would you like me to take care of this from now on, as I used to?"

Ramón grimaced, then: "Please."

"Is there anything I need to know that is not here? Papers. Invoices. Loans."

"Everything should be there." He was uncomfortable, as if by relinquishing the materials, he was divulging more than the financial necessaries of the business.

"*Muy bien,*" she said.

"If you have any questions, Severo can probably explain."

She almost laughed. "I'll see him later"—she pressed the portfolios and ledgers to her bosom—"after I go through these."

She spent the better part of that Saturday comparing paid from unpaid invoices, bills of lading, balances on customs and tax demands, deeds for the purchased lands, promissory notes from don Luis and from don Eugenio. The figures showed her what her husband had been unwilling to share: that they now owned almost six hundred *cuerdas,* mostly woods and forest that at least paid lower taxes than cultivated fields. There were three farmhouses, excluding the one by the river that Ramón had given Severo. Sixteen of the seventy-one slaves in the hacienda belonged to Severo, even though they lived in the *cuarteles* and were treated the same as the de Argosos'. In the slave log the ones who belonged to Severo were entered with their first name followed by "de Fuentes." The most surprising item in the portfolios, however, was that another four hundred *cuerdas* contiguous to the southern boundary of Los Gemelos, including the cove, belonged to Severo. Ana had no idea he had the resources to own so much land and so many slaves. Contraband, she concluded, was more lucrative than agriculture.

Over the next months following Inocente's murder, Ramón's eyes lost even more of their brightness; his features slackened as joy faded from them. He was often in a doddering confusion more appropriate for someone far older than his twenty-seven years. He stumbled frequently, as if he'd lost the connection between intention and action. He carried Miguel around as if the boy shouldn't touch the ground, while Inés and Flora followed close behind. He constantly caressed and kissed Miguel, but seemed irritated if Ana touched him or stood too close when they were alone. She had the impression that her presence was painful to him. Ramón had condemned her for their sexual situation. Did he also blame her for Inocente's death? She didn't know how to broach the subject without sounding defensive or accusatory.

Doña Leonor's letters became longer and more frequent after Inocente's death, and left no doubt whom she blamed for her son's murder. "I begged Ana," she wrote to her one remaining son, "not to put romantic notions into your heads, and now look at what happened." Had Leonor forgotten that she read every piece of correspondence that came to Los Gemelos? Neither Ramón nor Inocente was fond of writing the long letters expected by their parents. It was in Ana's hand that the chatty responses to Leonor's questions were drafted; Ramón and Inocente later copied and signed them. After his brother's death, however, Ramón answered his parents in his own sprawling hand but didn't ask Ana to stop reading his mother's letters. She was sure he was speaking to her through doña Leonor.

———

One night, Ana and Ramón were having their coffee on the porch while listening to the tree frogs: *coquí-coquí-coquí.* A candle burned by the door, its flame sputtering every time an insect flew into it. When she noticed him staring at her, Ana expected him to speak. Instead, he blinked without acknowledging her, then turned his gaze to the treetops beyond the railing and took a long drag from his cigarette. The gesture was so offensive that she stood abruptly and went into the bedroom, expecting him to follow, asking what was wrong, or at least to apologize. But a while later, when her door opened, it was Flora who entered with her bowls and cloths and cheerful hum. There was a moment when Ana's mood showed enough to change Flora's smile into a worried frown.

"I do something wrong, *señora?*" she asked, instinctively stepping back.

"No, Flora." Ana let Flora bathe her, but the usually relaxing ritual was marred by anger.

Ana had experienced reactions like Ramón's in the mirrored salons of Sevilla society, in the waxed halls of the Convento de las Buenas Madres, on the streets of Cádiz and San Juan. It was a look that said, "I see you, but I deign not to speak to you." It said, "I see you but I do not share the high opinion you have of yourself." It said, "I see you but you're not who I want to see." It said, "To me, you don't exist."

After her bath, Ana sent Flora to let Ramón know she was ready for bed, but the maid returned with a sheepish expression. *"El señor no está."*

"Where did he go?"

"I don't know, *señora.*" Flora looked away.

"Is there something you're not telling me?" Ana asked, and the maid seemed to be caught between wanting to please her and wanting to protect someone else's secret.

"No le sé decir, señora," she finally said. The phrase could mean "I don't know how to tell you" or "I can't tell you because I don't know," but Ana suspected that Flora meant the former.

"I order you to tell me what you do know."

"Por favor, señora." Flora shrank away, but she couldn't leave the

room without permission and couldn't refuse to obey. *"No sé nada,"* she whimpered, but Ana knew she was lying. Before Ana even realized what she was doing, she slapped her. Flora dropped and quickly folded into a position that exposed only her back and her hands wrapped around her head.

Ana had never hit anyone before. In the orange glow of the candle, she stared at the protective lump Flora had become and she was filled with shame. Her hand smarted, and it would be Flora she'd complain to about the hurt. Flora would examine her fingers one by one, then rub something on them to stop the pain. But Flora was now whimpering at her feet, expecting another blow, protecting her face, her breasts, and her belly from the woman whose naked body she'd just washed and powdered. Ana turned and walked off with a heavy tread so that Flora could hear her moving and expect no more blows.

"¿Señora?" Flora knelt, prepared, Ana thought, to curl up again if she should strike.

Ana walked as far as the candlelight reached, to the shelf that held her brushes and hairpins. "You can go, Flora," she said, but the maid didn't budge. *"Vete,"* Ana repeated, but Flora stayed on the floor, staring in front of her and wringing her hands.

"What is it now?" Ana asked with undisguised exasperation.

"If you didn't ask," Flora said.

Ana heard a buzz in her ears, like when she stood up too quickly. A deafening ringing followed, but it couldn't silence Flora's words.

"He goes to Marta, *señora*. Like don Inocente used to."

Wide-bottomed, gossipy Marta, the bucktoothed cook who, weeks before Ana gave birth, was moved from the room on the ground floor to her own *bohío* on the path beyond the barracks. Ana thought that Severo had settled her there for himself, but it hadn't occurred to Ana that Ramón or Inocente would go to the slaves. Least of all Marta.

Flora hadn't moved from her kneeling position and kept her eyes lowered, but Ana felt that she guessed what Ana was feeling and thinking. Were some of those children Ramón's or Inocente's? It also seemed to Ana that the maid, dismissed before she spoke, released the information to get even for the slap.

"Vete," she repeated. The room was lit with just one candle, but was that a smile on Flora's face as she turned to go?

Ana tossed all night between sleep and wakefulness, jerking with every creak of the house timbers, the shrill call of night birds. She listened for Ramón's steps and the groan of the hammock ropes. Several times that night, Miguel woke up crying, and Flora shushed and hummed until the child quieted. Flora had stopped singing to Miguel after Inocente's death and didn't resume until after over a year of mourning, when Ana changed from black garments to blue. Ana didn't intend to put an end to the mourning, but her black clothes had been mended too many times. After river washings and sun dryings, the black faded to an uneven, dirty gray. On Severo's next trip to town, she instructed him to purchase black cotton for the simple skirts and blouses that were her uniform. He showed up with a length of navy blue fabric, full of apologies that he wasn't able to secure black.

"It can be dyed, I was told, if you wish," he said.

She made a skirt and blouse and wore it for the first time on an October Sunday morning when Ramón was to read a pamphlet that related the story of St. Luke that began: "Many have attempted to write in an orderly manner, the history of the absolutely true events that have taken place among us."

The slaves listened patiently and some even devoutly, but fidgeted and silently tapped their knees with their fingertips, counting the minutes until the reading would be over. They noticed her blue clothes. Within days, the women resumed their colorful head wrappings and every night there was more and louder singing and playing of instruments in the barracks.

When they first arrived at Los Gemelos, Ana had enjoyed riding to the farthest edges of the hacienda in self-satisfied ownership. After Inocente's murder, however, she never ventured beyond the property's original boundaries and never left the *casona* alone after dark. Though her days were filled with the same hard work as ever, the nights in Los Gemelos were as full of mystery as if she were still reading about them in Spain. When she sat on the porch, or when she lay at night, sleepless, she tried to identify the sounds around her. The music and singing from the barracks were easy, as was the ubiquitous *coquí*. The dogs barked sometimes. The mournful lowing of cattle at night always sent a shiver down her spine. But there were also rattlings, creaks, thuds, splats, bumps, and rustlings that made her wonder what could possibly be moving beyond the thin walls of her house. When Ramón was home, his snores were a comfort, a reminder that she wasn't alone in a wilderness. Miguel's cries, too, even when they awakened her from deepest sleep, made Ana feel accomplished, purposeful. Her work here, she told herself, was meant not just to finish what her ancestor began and to fulfill her own destiny, but also to extend her lineage and to secure Miguel's patrimony. With Inocente dead and Ramón slipping into his strange, premature old age, Ana needed a reason to justify her refusal to leave Los Gemelos, in spite of the letters from Elena, don Eugenio, and doña Leonor begging them to return to the city.

A squeak on the boards, a soft step, the slow rasping of a hinge as Ramón came back minutes before the sun broke through the gaps in the walls. Outside, Marta was cracking twigs to feed the smoldering *fogón.*

Ana jumped from bed as if the sheets were on fire and, barefoot, ran from her room and into Ramón's without knocking or even thinking about what she was doing.

"How dare you," she hissed, "deceive me with that . . . that woman?"

The room was unlit, but she could distinguish Ramón's shirtless figure near the hammock. He sighed, long and low, emptying himself of air. She could smell his warm, tobacco breath and pungent sweat.

"Have you nothing to say?" she asked.

Ramón sighed again, and she expected him to argue, to apologize, to lie about it even, but not to calmly climb into the hammock and turn his back to her.

"*Déjame tranquilo,*" he said with the same intonation as on that night months ago when she came to him not in anger but with love and compassion.

"How can you expect me to—," she started.

"*¡Déjame!*" he yelled, and sat up as if to strike her.

She froze, awestruck that Ramón, gentle, laughing Ramón, would raise his voice and a hand threateningly in her direction. She had the sudden urge to protect herself the way Flora did, but the next moment it vanished. In the room across the hall, Miguel cried and Flora murmured. Ana had the feeling that the whole plantation was alert, listening. They've all been waiting for this moment, she thought.

They've all known what was going on, and were waiting for me to realize it and to see what I'd do.

"Next time you go lie with that *perra puta*," Ana said through clenched teeth, "don't bother coming back here." She turned to go, but he pulled her by her braids. He slapped her, but she slid from his grasp and ran screaming for the door. He blocked it and pushed her down, then kicked her so hard that it sent her sprawling across the room.

"You are the bitch," he snarled. "You are the whore. You."

On the floor, Ana tried to protect her face, her belly, and the back of her head, but Ramón's blows found the parts of her that were exposed. She couldn't see, but she heard footsteps running in her direction. Severo. He was there, suddenly, tussling with Ramón and pressing him against the wall. Then Flora was beside her, helping her up and leading her back to her bedroom. Through the thin slats that separated them, she heard Ramón abusing Severo, threatening to fire him, questioning his authority to come into his house, into his room. But soon Ramón was silent and both men left.

Ana couldn't face Flora. Last night's shame was now humiliation. She kept her eyes to the ground as Flora helped her to the bed. Flora called Inés, who listened to her instructions, then disappeared. Flora rolled up the mosquito net and helped Ana change from the torn, bloodstained nightgown into a fresh one.

"Easy, *mi niña,* slow, let Flora help," she said, her strong hands moving in several directions at once, dropping the gown over Ana's head, lifting her arms, and guiding them into sleeves, stroking the hair from her face, pulling the hem over Ana's hips, tying the ribbons around the neckline.

Ana didn't resist. She closed her eyes and let Flora's competent fingers do their work. Her hands and knees were raw. She brought her right hand to her face and saw a splinter wedged into the fleshy mound beneath her right thumb. Through squinted eyes, Flora squeezed until her nails met around the splinter and, with one swift, painful jerk, pulled it out. She pressed her thumb over the hurt and held it there while with her other hand she wiped Ana's cheeks with the hem of her apron.

"It only hurt for a little, *mi niña,*" she soothed.

Flora then turned her attention to Ana's knees, which felt as if they'd been scratched against the metal *guayo* used to grate yuca and plantains. Her right knee throbbed, and when Flora tried to straighten it, Ana groaned. The maid pressed the flesh under and around the knee.

"No worry, *señora,* not broke. Big bruise, that is all."

There was a knock, and Ana tensed. Inés entered with a pitcher of cool water in one hand, a fragrant unguent in a gourd in the other, and a stack of cloths over her arm. She looked curiously toward the bed, but Flora immediately covered Ana and stood between them as Inés set the things on the bedside table and left with her head high and the air of someone who was denied but wouldn't admit to being offended.

Ana let Flora tend to her bruises, unable to curb her tears. Until last night she'd never hit anyone, until this morning she'd never been hit, not by her anxious mother or strict father, not even by the rigid, vengeful nuns of the Convento de las Buenas Madres. In her experience, the only men who hit their wives were from the lower classes, their actions fueled by alcohol. Ramón was an educated man who didn't drink much.

"You are the bitch," he spat as he'd hit her. "You are the whore. You."

"It was your idea," she cried back. "It was your idea that I wife you both."

Sunshine broke through the chinks in the walls, and the morning bell clanged the beginning of the workday. There was another knock and Flora returned with a pot of steaming coffee.

"Inés made this for you," Flora said. "Don Severo took Marta away."

She dozed and woke to Miguel's gurgling laughter. Ana closed her eyes and listened. What was Inés doing? Was she tickling him, making funny faces? Ana didn't make her son laugh. Even when she spoke endearments, Miguel's mouth remained set in the angelic pout of all handsome children, his eyes solemn and watchful, as if he didn't trust her. Ana knew it was ridiculous to believe that a baby could have such feelings, but she couldn't help it. The boy, she was certain, didn't love her. The thought made her desolate.

To her left, Flora was wrapped within the folds of her *hamaca* as if inside a shroud.

Ana tried to get up, but she ached with every move. Her left knee throbbed. A sharp pain around her ribs made her groan when she lifted an arm. Her left elbow bent only with effort and heavy breathing to ward off the pain. Her lips were swollen.

Ana's moans brought Flora to her side.

"Let me help you, *mi niña*."

At the sound of Flora's voice, Inés's and Miguel's giggles were replaced by Ramón's hurried footsteps toward her room. Flora turned her back to the opening door; over her shoulder Ana saw Ramón standing on the threshold, waiting to be invited inside. His eyes met hers and immediately turned to focus on Flora's back.

"*Déjanos,* Flora," he said. The maid held on to Ana with such force that Ana's ribs hurt. Ramón took one step into the room, leaving the door open. "Flora, you can go," he said again.

The maid didn't budge, but Ana felt her trembling. Ana loosened her grip on her. "Wait outside," she said, and Flora reluctantly let her go and backed out of the room, her arms wrapped around her middle. Ramón watched Flora leave as if she were some newly discovered creature. When she further shrank from him as she passed him, he blushed crimson.

Had she not seen that change, Ana might have cringed against her pillows. Instead she felt satisfaction at his insecure step, at the way he held on to the bedpost and couldn't bring himself to come nearer. The left side of his face had long, red scratches from her fingernails.

"Ana. Ana. I'm so sorry," he said with so much emotion that she thought he'd burst into tears.

"You're sorry," she shot back, looking at her hands, now fists. She released and flattened them against her belly. "You're sorry," she repeated, taking small breaths, each punctuated by sharp pain in her ribs.

"*Sí,*" he said, in a broken voice. "*Sí, lo siento. Perdóname, mi amor.*"

He stood at the foot of the bed, his hand around the bedpost, begging forgiveness, waiting for her to grant it before he stepped closer. Ana turned her face away to avoid his sheepish expression, his hesitancy, the way his lips moved but the only sound that came from them was the intention.

"Get away from me!" she said quietly, and Ramón jumped in place as if she'd screamed. "*Canalla. ¡Sinvergüenza!*"

Flora peeked around the half-open door and quickly moved back to the hall. Ramón seemed to be pinned to the floorboards, and his body was as rigid as the carved bedpost.

"Don't talk to me like that," he said, lips barely moving, but his voice resonated with the same steely edge from earlier that morning. He continued rooted to the floor, however. An invisible wall was between them that he couldn't cross, and she felt no fear of him.

"*Cobarde*. Only a coward would strike a woman."

Ramón seemed about to burst through the invisible wall, but instead he thrust his index finger in her direction. "I swear that if you were a man I'd kill you for your insults."

She tightened her jaw and held his gaze. He dropped his arm and the sheepish expression overtook him, and he was once again the pathetic reproduction of the elegant, handsome, cheerful man she'd met four years before.

"I'm not the same man," he said mournfully, reading her thoughts. "Who have I become?" He looked hopefully at her, as if she had an answer. When all she did was stare, he continued. "Coming here was a mistake. Let's go home."

"This is our home."

"No. No, it is not. Let's go back to Spain. There's no disgrace if we admit we were wrong. We'd be leaving the plantation better than we found it. We can be proud of what we've accomplished."

"I'm not leaving."

"There's no real society here, no culture, no comforts. We live only slightly better than the slaves. This is not how you or I were raised to spend the rest of our lives. No, Ana."

"We knew this would be a challenge. We all agreed."

"My brother is dead, Ana! Viciously murdered and buried who knows where, far from his country, his people." He sat on the edge of the bed. "My poor mother."

She was moved by his grief but disgusted by his tears, by the stench of regret that weighed him and threatened to crush her. There was a time when she would've wrapped her arms around him, sought to console him with kisses and caresses. But mention of doña Leonor, and a vision of her curls, laces, and ribbons, brought to Ana's mind a life she refused to accept as her destiny. She would not be bound by the stifling rooms of the city either here or in Spain, by the despotic rules of women without enough to do and little power over their lives. And I won't be like Elena, Ana thought, silent and distant in muslin with a perpetual, servile smile, eyes cast down humbly. I refuse to be that woman.

Ramón's shoulders heaved in silent sobs and Ana looked away, embarrassed by his weakness and sentimentality. No, Ana thought. I'm wrong about Elena. I've always been wrong about her. Elena would've been a stronger partner. She has more backbone than all of us put together. I should've encouraged Inocente to marry her from the beginning, to bring her with us. He would've done it. He would've done anything I asked then. He would be alive now.

Through the window she saw movement in the foliage. A tiny bird buzzed around a branch of the flowering breadfruit tree. It wasn't a hummingbird, nor did it seem interested in the abundant white buds. It perched on a branch, its green feathers blending into the leaves, its long beak pointed upward. In one smooth, sudden move, it flew horizontally, trapped an insect in its beak, and returned to its perch, to wait silent and still. Ana watched closely because the bird was so tiny that it was easy to lose sight of. Once, twice, three times the bird darted from its branch, beak open, to snap it closed around an unseen insect. Each time it flew back to the same spot, to stand immobile and wait for its next prey.

When she looked back at Ramón he was staring at her, his red face stained with tears, anger, and hurt. "You don't care," he said, and the revelation changed his world. "You're not even listening. You don't care about me, you don't care about my brother, that he's dead, dead, dead. You don't care about your son, our son, Miguel. You don't care about anyone but yourself. You simply do not care," he repeated talking himself into believing his own words.

"Ramón . . . ," she started, but he stood and pointed again, shaking his finger.

"You're the reason my brother is dead. You bewitched us."

"Don't be ridiculous, Ramón."

"I'll never forgive you," he said. "*Jamás.* Not so long as I live will I forgive you. Never."

The words were barbs, and for a moment they stung, but the next second she was angry because she knew that his imperious attitude would crumble with one word from her, one look, and he'd again become a weak-willed, easily crushed shell.

"I haven't asked for your forgiveness, nor do I need it," she said through gritted teeth. "I've done nothing wrong." Ramón stared, trying to recognize a new Ana, and the shell began to crack. "I'll never forgive you for raising your hand to me. Now leave."

Ramón backed away. He stood at the threshold for a moment, his unblinking eyes lizardlike, empty. She turned her gaze from his, seeking the tiny bird she'd noticed earlier, but it was gone.

EL BANDO NEGRO

After the terrible night Ramón beat her, he never again slept with Ana. José had crafted a second bed, identical to the one in the marital bedroom, intended for Inocente, and Ramón set it up in the other room. When he stayed in the *casona,* however, he seldom slept through the night. Almost as soon as they retired, Ana heard him leave and didn't see him until the next day. His shuffling gait worsened; he let his hair, beard, and nails grow and lost so much weight that he looked like an elongated figure in an El Greco painting. If she mentioned his appearance, or asked about his health, or suggested that he seemed tired, Ramón snapped that he was fine.

"You need not be concerned about me."

She didn't know what to do to help him, but she knew he was safe and where he went. Severo moved the laundress, Nena, to a *bohío* beyond the barracks. One morning, as Ana was riding by, she saw Ramón lying on the hammock inside the one-room cabin, Miguel curled on his chest, both of them fast asleep. They looked peaceful and completely in their element, like a *jíbaro* with his son, not like the *patrón* and heir of Hacienda los Gemelos. She didn't feel anger or resentment toward either Ramón or his fourteen-year-old mistress for his betrayal of her as his wife. She was, rather, angry at his indolence, as if her refusal to leave Los Gemelos absolved him from responsibility.

It took her months to disentangle the paperwork jumbled by Ramón and Inocente. There was the notarized document deeding the land by the river to Severo, but Ana had to dig to the bottom of the second folio to find the original title. How the notary could have signed a deed without the title was beyond her. She spent most afternoons trying to understand their intricate finances. For example,

Severo Fuentes was an employee, but he was also a vendor, since half the field workers were rented from him. He owned several hundred *cuerdas* along the southern shore of the hacienda, which meant that in order to get to ships, products from Los Gemelos must traverse his land or be transported to the docks in Guares. He probably carried out his contraband business along the shore, one reason, she imagined, that there were no docks or buildings. But she imagined how much faster and more cost-effective it would be to move hogsheads and puncheons from a wharf closer to the *trapiche,* perhaps even from the cove where she'd first landed. It was a tantalizing idea to have a dock and warehouses so close, but it would cost thousands of pesos and take years to build, and Ana didn't think Severo had that kind of money. What she found most fascinating was how dependent his future was on that of Hacienda los Gemelos. She gleaned all this from the ledgers and folios. Severo managed his own business, as far as she could tell, and she imagined that, while he entered the figures that he, as the *mayordomo* must report in the ledgers, his own affairs were in better shape than those of Ramón and Inocente.

An unpleasant revelation in the paperwork came from a series of legal notes signed by Ramón and Inocente to Luis Morales Font. Ramón and Inocente had borrowed 2,148 pesos at the astounding rate of 15 percent interest. She was furious, especially when, after collecting the papers, she realized that not a penny had been paid and the notes were due within the quarter.

When she was angry, she went into the gardens. Her plan to put the elders and young children to plant, weed, and maintain the orchards, herbs, and flower gardens was more successful than even she had envisioned. The soil was as giving and fertile as reported by don Hernán and the monks, travelers, and scientists, whose accounts she'd devoured before she emigrated to Puerto Rico. In the gardens there was always something to do that focused her attention away from the miserable numbers and Ramón's disregard for their financial affairs. She had to talk to him about the notes to don Luis, but Ramón avoided her as much as possible. If he sought her company, it was to argue, and the easiest way to raise her temper was to remind her that they'd assured don Eugenio that the hacienda would be profitable within five years. If the next two harvests showed losses, Eugenio would sell.

"Obviously, we'll lose money again." Ana waved the notes of credit in Ramón's face. "You've squandered our savings and indebted our future at usurious rates to that awful Luis."

"What's wrong with him?" Ramón said, more disposed toward the neighbor than to her.

"He's calling in the loans." She shuffled them in front of him. "Or did you think they were gifts?"

"Of course I knew they were loans." He didn't even look in their direction.

"He robbed us even before we came here. He cheated don Rodrigo. He's hoping that we'll founder so that he can get the hacienda at a bargain. Don't you understand anything?"

"You don't trust anyone. That's why no one will talk to you. I should've noticed that in Spain. You had no friends."

"And you have an abundance, all of them taking advantage of you."

He shook his head. "No one has taken more from me than you, Ana."

She winced and hoped he hadn't noticed. "According to you, I'm always the one at fault. You take no responsibility."

"You're wrong. I regret that Inocente and I believed you. You would have said or done anything to get us to come to Puerto Rico. Anything." He paused to let her interpret his meaning.

"You always circle back to old grievances and arguments. You wallow in regrets while I work as hard as any man on this land." She put the notes in their folios, knotted the ribbons to keep them from falling out. "I get no praise for our modest successes, but I'm condemned for whatever goes wrong."

"What we have endured in Puerto Rico is the result of your conquistador delusion."

"This is where you're wrong, Ramón. It wasn't my idea to spend all our cash on land when we had more urgent needs. It wasn't my idea to put us in debt to don Luis. That was you, not me," she said. Offended and unwilling to swallow her anger anymore, she slammed the folios on the table and vented her fury with her only weapons, words that would hurt him. "It wasn't my idea that Inocente ride to San Juan when it was safer by sea. That, Ramón, is your handiwork."

———

"There they go again." Inés pouted toward the *casona*.

Flora looked up from the pants she was hemming. She'd been listening to the rising voices while keeping an eye on two-year-old Miguel playing with two other children. "Getting worse every day." She finished the stitch, ran extra thread inside the seam, then snipped it with her teeth. "Where Efraín?" She picked up the next garment, a pair of shorts for Miguel.

"Don Severo took him with more of José's carvings for the sailors."

"How much he keep?"

"Half. He gives the rest to José. At this rate, he'll be an old man before he can buy his freedom. We have less than twenty pesos. We need hundreds."

"At least he has something to sell," Flora said.

"Did you make money before you came here?"

"Doña Benigna didn't let."

"But the law says we can work in our free hours."

"The law says if master agrees."

"Where I worked before," Inés said, "the mistress rented me to other houses. Supposed to be my free afternoon, too, but she kept the money, never gave me a penny."

"You're lucky don Severo give José half."

"You always look on the bright side."

"What else am going to do?"

Inés was about to respond, but she pouted again, this time toward the carpentry. Miguel was listening to the loud voices from the *casona,* his lower lip trembling, his big eyes scared.

"Come here, *papito,*" Flora called. "Come to Nana." He ran into her arms. She held him tight and Miguel pressed his face into the curve between her neck and her shoulder. "We go sing mother forest," she said into his ear. He nodded. "Call me if she need me," Flora said to Inés.

"Can I go, too?" Indio was at their side, tugging on Miguel's leg.

"Me, too," said Pepita, another playmate. Carmencita came out of nowhere. "I want to go!"

The children clamored around them, trying to get Miguel to lift his head from Flora's neck.

"What you say?" Flora asked Miguel.

His face still pressed against her. *"Sí."*

"Todos con nosotros," she said.

They walked down the path toward the river. Flora sang and the children repeated her words. They loved to sing with Flora, who called the forest mother, even though in Spanish the forest was male. *"Gracias, madre bosque, por la sombra bajo las ramas. Gracias, madre bosque,* for many avocados to eat. *Gracias, madre bosque,* for the mangos sweet. *Gracias, madre bosque,* for little bird with yellow beak. *Gracias, madre bosque, por la araña que no pica."* She lifted Miguel's face. "Do you see something to sing?"

Miguel looked around shyly. "Thank you, mother forest, for the rock so big," he sniffled, and the other children chorused, *"Gracias madre bosque por la piedra tan grande."*

For a place so seemingly far from a big town or city, news arrived in Hacienda los Gemelos from the outside world with surprising dispatch, due to Severo's contacts with ships. Once Severo realized that Ana was a voracious reader, he brought books, pamphlets, and newspapers that somehow had evaded the censors in San Juan. Through them she learned that Carlist reactionary forces continued to besiege the tenuous government of Queen Isabel II. War raged between Mexico and the United States. Tens of thousands of Irish peasants were dying or abandoning their country for the Americas because of widespread blight on potatoes, their main food source. War, famine, and government instability were like tales from another history.

In her remote part of the world, Ana had more than enough tragedies and their aftermaths, and her own hardships were more absorbing than anything she could read. There were moments when she compared her present life to what could have been, examined her choices, and asked, What now, what's next?

She'd turned her back on family, society, and country with the confidence and arrogance of a stubborn adolescent. She'd used every artifice to ensnare Ramón and Inocente into believing that they were as capable and entitled as conquistadores. She flattered and coaxed them even though she knew that they were irresponsible and immature, that for them life was about appearances, tricks, and games. Now she was almost twenty-two years old, had a child, had spent her fortune. Her marriage was over, and Hacienda los Gemelos might fall into Luis Morales Font's hands. If I'd followed Elena's plan, I'd have Elena for comfort and affection, but I was greedy, she thought.

She missed Spain in unexpected moments. She'd be in the garden and recall the fragrant meadows studded with wildflowers in her grandfather's farm, and the honey-scented air as she raced Fonso and Beba across the fields. A sparkle in the pond brought memories of Sevilla's yellow light and the serpentine Río Guadalquivir reflecting silver clouds. But as soon as she was aware of them, she pushed those thoughts away because she felt disloyal to herself. This is my life now, she reminded herself, the one I worked so hard to get. No one will ever know what it cost, only what I've created.

History was both personal and universal, and Ana was conscious that it swirled inexorably whether people paid attention to it or not. She was curious about other invisible lives in untraveled places, aware that her own days were unseen and unknown beyond the boundaries of Hacienda los Gemelos. She envisioned someone standing in the same spot a century after herself wondering who else had stepped upon that ground, seen that tree, the pond, the stone shaped like a pyramid. Had her conquistador ancestors asked these questions so long ago when they stood on this land, so foreign, so far from Spain?

When Ana received a letter from her mother, she begrudged Jesusa's effusive love now that she was across the ocean. But she grieved when news arrived of her grandfather's death at ninety-three. He was found sitting in his chair, his legs on his footstool, his blanket on his lap. Unlike her parents, Abuelo Cubillas had encouraged her curiosity and valued her intelligence, and after his death, he continued to have an impact on her life. Three weeks after the news that he'd passed away, Severo returned from Guares with formal and impressive documents for Ana. Her grandfather had left her fifteen thousand pesos.

She said nothing to Ramón about her inheritance, worried that if she told him about the money he'd spend it. She wrote to her father and asked him to arrange that most of the funds be kept in an account in Sevilla that she could draw upon when necessary. She didn't care that don Gustavo would know by this request that something was amiss in her marriage. When he confirmed her instructions, she knew he wouldn't interfere. He deducted the precise amount owed to Luis Morales Font—a total of 3,167 pesos, including interest—to settle the notes he held against Hacienda los Gemelos. She gave the bill of exchange to Ramón so that he'd pay don Luis.

"Where did the money come from?"

"A loan from my father," she lied.

"You'd go behind my back to ask don Gustavo for a loan? He'll think that I'm unable to take care of you and my son."

"That's precisely what he's worried about. You seem more concerned about his good opinion than mine."

"I do care more about his good opinion," he said and, narrowing his eyes as if to erase her from his sight, added, "you, I despise."

A cry escaped her lips, surprising her as much as it did Ramón. No one had ever said anything so mean-spirited to her face. She was thousands of miles from the only homes she'd ever known, where there was no love but never hatred, not hatred. She felt utterly alone in the world.

Ramón's face changed from loathing to regret to pity. "Ana, I'm sorry."

She stopped him with her hands, unable to speak because her throat was as closed as if he'd pressed his fingers around her neck and squeezed. All the angry words we've hurled at each other before this, she thought, had led here.

"Say something." Ramón stepped closer, to touch her, but she hardened her face and backed away.

"There's nothing that can ever expunge those words from my heart," she said. "You despise me."

"I didn't mean it—"

"You did, Ramón. We have nothing left to say to each other."

"What more do you want from me?"

"I want nothing from you," she said. "*Nada*. You can abandon me here, if you like. You already have, with your *putas*—"

"They mean nothing to me."

"Please don't insult me, or your women, for that matter."

"I won't abandon you, Ana, or my son," he said. "Yes, I've been unfaithful, but the pressures we've faced . . . this was supposed to be an adventure, but it's a nightmare. No, don't remind me we knew it would be challenging, but . . . I'm not made for this. I'm only still here because of you and Miguel. I promised to try it for five years. I'm an honorable man, Ana, but I'm counting the days until January 10, 1850—nineteen months. No, I will not desert you. You see, I mean to keep my promise to you and to my father. But when the five years are up, we will go. If I have to drag you by force, Ana, we'll go home. Whatever happens after that is up to God."

"In twenty-four year work for doña Benigna and don Felipe," Flora said to Inés and José, "I never hear yell so much like doña Ana and don Ramón."

"My other *patrona* would die," Inés said, "before arguing with her husband where other people could hear."

"We're not 'other people' to them," José said. "We're not people at all. If there was other *blancos* around, they'd be smiling and pretending they like each other."

"That's true. *Allá ellos que son blancos y se entienden.* Look at them now." Inés gestured with her head toward the *casona,* where Ramón and Ana were having dinner with Severo Fuentes on the porch as if the argument earlier that afternoon had never taken place.

The slaves' meals were eaten outdoors, too, but not at a carved table. They sat on the ground, on stumps along the shady side of the barracks, or on the thresholds or steps to the *bohíos.* While older girls washed and cleaned up after supper, the adults had a chance to relax and watch the children play. Because Teo served the *casona*'s meals, Flora had a couple of hours until Ana rang her bell to let her know she was ready for her bath.

Flora liked Inés and José and their two boys, Efraín and Indio. They were all born in Puerto Rico, but José's parents were both Yoruba, which explained his artistry with wood. Inés's parents were born in Puerto Rico, but she remembered her Igbo maternal grandmother and paternal Mandinka grandfather. Both José and Inés were sold as children, never again to see their parents, sisters, and brothers. When she thought about this, Flora was glad she didn't have children. She still had nightmares about her firstborn being flung over the side of the boat that stole her from Africa, and the bloody miscarriage of her second child after Mistress pushed her down the stairs. She felt lucky that, after she was sold to don Felipe, neither he nor any other *blanco* forced himself on her. Don Felipe didn't make her marry one of his male slaves, either, because doña Benigna forbade it.

"Look how small she is, how narrow her hips," she told her husband. "She's likely to die giving birth, and where will I get another Pygmy?"

By the time she overheard that conversation, Flora had long decided that if this was life, she'd never deliberately bring another human being into the world.

Miguel was playing with Pepita and Indio a few paces from her. He was the only white child on the hacienda, the only healthy one, the only one wearing clothes. Until about four years old, most boys and girls were naked, their round bellies out of proportion to their skinny limbs. They were malnourished and suffered from intestinal parasites. Flora knew that half the *negritos* chasing each other around the *batey* wouldn't live to be adolescents, their bodies unable to withstand tropical anemia, *paludismo,* measles, tuberculosis, tetanus, meningitis. Half the girls who reached puberty would die in childbirth or soon thereafter, and the boys who grew to manhood would die by their early forties from overwork, disease, and accidents in the fields. A few would be maimed or crippled, another one or two would commit suicide. And there was always the possibility that any of them, child or adult, could be sold for money or to settle debts.

"If they go back to the city," Flora said, "they'll sell us to don Luis."

"*¡Ay, no!*" Inés said. "Siña Damita's youngest son goes up to San Bernabé on errands for don Severo, and he says there isn't a more pitiful group than the ones in their barracks."

"Artemio says the *patrones* have a big house, and they're building another one. But the workers live in a barn. Men, women, and children in one building," José said. "At least we get our own *bohíos* here."

"That man is two-face," Flora said. "He smile and make *blancos* think he friend, but he cunning. He has don Ramón like this." Flora put up her pinky and twirled it around. "I hope he don't sell us to him."

"He can't," José said. "We belong to don Severo."

"If they sell the hacienda," Inés said, "Severo must not scatter us."

"He won't," José said. "He told us he wouldn't."

"You believe him?" Flora sucked her teeth. "*Blancos* will say anything."

"But he usually buys families," José said, "like Siña Damita's. And us, and Teo and Paula . . ."

"He thinks if we have our families here, we won't want to run."

"I'd never leave you and my sons."

"But what if," Flora said, "Efraín or Indio try to run away?"

"*Ay,* let's not talk about that," Inés said. "*Dios salve.*"

Including Flora, every *bozal* at Hacienda los Gemelos had attempted escape, and a couple of the *criollos,* too. Before the *patrones* arrived, don Severo had lined up the new arrivals with the slaves already in the hacienda and told them that if they tried to run away, he would find them.

"And when I do," he said. "I will not trade you away. I will not hobble or cripple you so you can't run again. The law gives me the right to whip you before I hang you in front of the others, in front of your husbands, in front of your wives, in front of your children until you die."

After Inocente's murder, they knew he meant it. When he came back from searching for Alejo and Curro, smelling of death, his hounds at his heels, they didn't need details to know that don Severo had killed the *cimarrones.* Weeks later, they heard how he did it. His vicious dogs, the efficient single slice of his machete across their necks, the blood soaking into the earth were still talked about among slaves and masters alike.

Young boys like Efraín were used by the *mayordomos* and *patrones* as messengers. They passed on what they saw, but they weren't as reliable as the hired workers who also brought stories from nearby villages and from town. But the most dependable source of information for the workers at Hacienda los Gemelos was Siña Damita.

As a free woman, she went where she was needed so long as she carried the notarized papers stating that she was a *liberta.* She traveled on a spavined mule that might collapse at any moment and that she cared for and fed as if the animal were a thoroughbred stallion. She was the best *curandera* and midwife in the area, so she needed to move quickly when called to attend women in labor, to cure children with fevers, to bandage wounds and salve bruises. The doctor in town, Dr. Vieira, preferred to treat the wealthy and left the others to *curanderas* like Siña Damita.

Most of the *campesinos* paid for her cures and treatments with a few eggs, a bunch of bananas, a length of cloth. Some of her work, however, had nothing to do with sickness. She went to Guares weekly to deliver love potions, to cleanse rooms of disturbed forces, to counteract the effects of the evil eye, to conjure restless spirits, to rinse the hands of gamblers for good luck. For this *trabajo,* she expected money, at least one Spanish real, sometimes more, depending on the work. She was often consulted to resolve family squabbles, and was the intermediary for parents who needed to place a child in the household of a wealthier relative or friend. *Hijos de crianza* were raised and educated by foster parents. Siña Damita looked in on the children to make sure they were being treated well by their new families, and reported back to the parents, who usually lived far from them. In at least one case she placed a baby whose mother didn't want her with a woman who'd just lost her own child. For that *trabajo* she received ten Spanish pesos, the most money she'd earned at one time.

Siña Damita was saving her money to free Lucho, her husband. Once she bought him his freedom, they could work together to manumit their sons, Poldo, Jorge, Artemio; their daughters-in-law, Coral and Elí; and their grandchildren. So far, in the six years she'd been saving, Siña Damita had accumulated thirty-two pesos, two reales, a small portion of the three hundred pesos don Severo wanted for Lucho, who was forty years old, strong and a trained butcher.

The opportunities to make money in Guares were increasing as what used to be a village grew into a town. The *jíbaros* squatting on unclaimed lands along the harbor were being evicted as the municipal government took over and made the plots available for homes, offices, businesses, warehouses, and stores.

The town now had a middle and a professional class. The sons of successful *hacendados* returned from their studies in Europe full of idealism and optimism. As Siña Damita moved among her customers, she heard news, rumors, gossip that she shared with her family and friends at Hacienda los Gemelos.

Blancos treated all blacks, free or enslaved, as if they were invisible. They talked, argued, wooed, and complained within sight and hearing of blacks whom they believed to be stupid and unable to understand or care. Siña Damita was both intelligent and interested, especially if these conversations had anything to do with her as a *liberta* and the wife and mother of an enslaved family. In 1847 and 1848 the new and settled inhabitants around Guares and its environs were preoccupied with wars, invasions, and revolutions in France, Mexico, the Dominican Republic, and Italy. She didn't know where those places were, but she knew that in those distant lands people were rising against oppressive governments and demanding rights that were granted only after much bloodshed.

When *blancos* talked about what was happening across the ocean, they usually ended up trying to ascertain how those events might affect Puerto Rico. Siña Damita heard *señores* venting their frustrations with the Spanish government's laws. *Hacendados* and merchants complained that the fees, duties, and taxes they paid were sent to the Spanish treasury, leaving no money for public works on the island. Thousands of soldiers, she'd heard, waited in vain for guns, ammunition, horses, and salaries that never arrived.

One night, Siña Damita was attending the death vigil of an *hacendado*. As she crossed from the bedroom to the outhouse, she heard one of the sons telling the other that after planting, harvesting, processing, and transporting sugar, their father owed fees, taxes, customs, and export duties amounting to 117 percent of his income that year.

"Our government is strangling us slowly," the younger son said.

"And not a single official is a native Puerto Rican," the older one continued. "All those jobs are reserved for *españoles* who couldn't care less about the future of this island."

"So long as we're a colony, we'll suffer these indignities. It's intolerable. Things must change."

Siña Damita knew that she could make money if she reported that conversation to the authorities. It was against the law to criticize the government, to talk openly about independence. But she also knew that independence for Puerto Rico would mean the abolition of slavery. It had happened in every other former Spanish colony.

It was unusual to hear young people talking like the *hacendado*'s sons. Something told her that the climate was changing. Maybe these young *criollos* returning from their travels in Europe and in the United States were seeing things differently from their conservative parents. It could only be good news for the slaves. Siña Damita

wasn't going to say anything that might silence those kinds of conversations in any home in the land.

As the 1848 *zafra* wound down, Siña Damita could spend more time
with her husband and sons. Severo wrote a pass so that Lucho, Jorge,
Poldo; their wives, Coral and Elí; their children; and Artemio could
spend Sunday afternoons in Damita's *bohío* once they finished their
chores. A few times they arrived to an empty cabin, because she'd
been called away. Lucho and their sons repaired and improved the
cottage while the women cooked whatever she'd left for them.

One Sunday afternoon Siña Damita rode up when it was almost
time for the family to start the walk back to the hacienda. She was
bone-tired from a long vigil in Guares, and when she reached her
bohío, she was as breathless as her wheezing mule.

"The town is upside down," she said. "Slaves on another island
killed the masters and burned the estates."

"What island? How close?" Jorge asked.

"Martinca, something like that . . . I don't know. Ay, *nena,* some
water." Coral went to the barrel while Lucho helped Damita to sit
on the threshold. *"Gracias, hija."* She drained the cup.

"Take a minute, Mamá," Jorge said. "We're not leaving until you
tell us."

Siña Damita took a few deep breaths, but she was too excited.
"This little boat sail with *blanco* families. It was miracle they not
drowned. There was men, women, and kids. When they come to
shore, one woman got on knees to kiss the sand! They didn't speak
one word of Spanish, but don Tibó translated. Ay! More water, *hija*!"

"Don Tibó? The Frenchman who owns the cantina?"

"Yes," Siña Damita said. "He said that the French government
freed the slaves on their island, but . . . I don't know why . . . There
were riots and burnings . . . people killed. The captain in Guares put
soldiers on alert. They're sending word to haciendas. I was stopped
five time before I got here. Sure you have all your papers and travel
together. Now you better go back to Los Gemelos. The soldiers
think we will rebel, too. . . . I don't want you in trouble. Go! I be fine.
I come tomorrow morning."

———

The refugees that Siña Damita saw kissing the sands in Guares had fled from widespread slave uprisings in the French colonies of Martinique and Guadeloupe in advance of official manumission. They and others brought tales of entire families slaughtered in their beds, their houses and belongings set on fire while groups of self-liberated slaves roamed the countryside.

"Our people are aware of events," Severo told Ana and Ramón. "Sometimes they hear things before we do."

"Are we in danger?" Ramón asked.

"I've ordered that the foremen be vigilant," Severo said. "I've increased the patrols around the perimeter. I don't expect trouble from them, but it's better for you to stay close to the *casona,* and for them to know we're watching them."

More refugees from the Danish colony of St. Croix arrived in San Juan with reports of violence as bands of slaves wreaked vengeance on their owners and plantations. The military governor of Puerto Rico, Field Marshal Juan Prim, Conde de Reus, ordered troops to aid the Cruzans in quelling the rebellions. He unsuccessfully tried to get the Danish government to reverse abolition in St. Croix—hastily declared during the violence—because of the adverse impact it would have on nearby Puerto Rico. The Danish government refused.

To ensure that slaves in Puerto Rico wouldn't rise against their masters following the example of the Martinicans and Cruzans, Governor Prim issued the Bando Contra la Raza Africana, or Bando Negro. The Proclamation Against the African Race stipulated a military trial with no recourse to civil law for any black or brown person *(negro o pardo)* who committed a crime against a *blanco.* The Bando Negro didn't distinguish free people from slaves; it was aimed at Africans and their descendants, and enforcement was based solely on skin color. The Bando Negro established severe punishments for even minor transgressions (like not ceding way to a *blanco* on a narrow path) and authorized owners to put to death any slave who participated in insurrectionist activities.

"We're supposed to read the contents of the Bando Negro to the workers," Severo told Ana and Ramón. "This one is the first proclamation of May 31, 1848. The second one, published on June 9 details punishments for infractions. We received both on the same day."

" '. . . *la ferocidad de la estúpida raza africana* . . .' Ferocity—the stupid African race?" Ana looked up. "This preamble is extraordinary." She passed the sheets to Ramón. "Is this serious?"

"*Sí, señora,*" Severo said. "But it does seem extreme, in my opinion."

Ramón read in a low voice, " '. . . *sentimientos que les son naturales; el incendio, el asesinato y la destrucción* . . .' " He read the same passage again, louder: " '. . . Their natural inclinations toward arson, murder, and destruction . . .' "

"Language more likely to incite violence, not curb it," Ana said.

"These proclamations are written in San Juan by soldiers and city folks," Severo said, "terrified of the few malefactors who turn on their masters. Forgive me, *señor,* if this pains you."

Ramón accepted his apology with a nod.

"Well," Ana said, "we won't read this ridiculous claptrap to our people."

"Unfortunately, it is required," Severo started.

She took the papers from Ramón's hands. "They appear to be hurried documents by a frightened aristocrat in San Juan," she said, returning them to Severo.

"Yes they do, *señora,*" he said. "And my guess is that its provisions are driven by scared absentee landowners."

"But the Conde de Reus is the representative of the queen, *que Dios guarde,*" Ramón said. "He certainly wouldn't go to such lengths if the dangers weren't real."

"We've had no trouble here or nearby—unless you've kept it from me." Ana looked at Severo.

"Of course not, *señora.*"

"If the slaves hear about the rebellions," Ramón insisted, "they—"

"I will keep things under control," Severo said. "No further travel passes. More guards at night."

"And if they've already heard about the Bando Negro," Ana said, "we'd best let them know we're aware there was trouble elsewhere."

"I agree, *señora.*"

"Don't read the preamble, only the provisions and punishments, and let them know that they will be enforced."

"Very good, *señora.*"

Ramón watched his wife and Severo speaking rapidly to each other, making decisions as if he weren't there. For an instant he saw a softening in Ana's features when she looked at Severo, and Severo's own recognition of that look, but the moment was so fleeting that Ramón doubted what he'd seen.

The *batey* bell rang four times, paused, clanged four, paused, clanged three. There was a longer pause and the series was repeated as the workers and foremen came from their duties to assemble in front of the barracks. Ramón took Miguel into his bedroom on the other side of the house. Ana closed the windows and doors facing the *batey* but left one shutter ajar. The opening was large enough for her to see through, but no one could see her.

Although they weren't lined up in any specific order, Severo's slaves huddled together in one group, while those owned by the hacienda stood in another. Siña Damita came to the threshold of the *bohío* that served as an infirmary and stood there, scowling and violently chewing the inside of her lips. Three of the foremen were mulatto freemen who lived with their families in cottages on the other side of the plantain patch. The fourth, a *liberto* married to a white *campesina,* lived in a *bohío* at the edge of the west pasture. Slaves or free, everyone looked worried. It appeared to Ana that they expected this news.

"I know that you've heard about trouble in other places," Severo said as if talking to them about the weather. "But this is Puerto Rico, and we're all subjects of Her Majesty Isabel II, may God keep her. You must obey the laws here regardless what other countries or governments do."

One by one, Severo read the nineteen articles of the Bando Negro, waiting a few moments after each so that everyone could understand what it contained. "A black or person of color who threatens a *blanco* in word or in deed, shall be put to death if a slave, and if free, will lose the right hand."

From her perch over the *batey,* Ana could see only the backs of the men and women who stood, heads bowed and still. The foremen shifted in their places. Until then, slave codes hadn't applied to free *gente de color,* but now, because the foremen were not *blanco,* they were bound by the provisions of the Bando Negro.

When at last he finished reading the proclamations, Severo dismissed everyone to their duties. Ana watched as Siña Damita crossed the *batey* to her mule tied to the post. The solid, dignified woman now slumped her shoulders as she walked.

Over the next few days, Ana felt just as she had in the days following Inocente's murder. Everyone was nervous and avoided behavior that in any way could be interpreted as aggression, a threat, or disrespect. Even the children were subdued and constantly shooed by their elders. The distrust on both sides was as palpable as the mist following a July afternoon rain shower. Flora was somber and quiet. While she bathed Ana, she was as attentive as usual, but she didn't sing, although she'd once told Ana that even in their grief her people sang. Ana knew that asking Flora to sing would be interpreted only as another order. She couldn't bring herself to demand more from her.

Travel passes were suspended, so Damita's family couldn't spend Sundays with her. Instead, Severo allowed her to spend the afternoon with them at the hacienda. She brought food for her daughters-in-law and always had more than enough to share with others. Sundays were more relaxed at the hacienda because Severo wasn't around. In the morning after chores, the workers assembled in the *rancho*. If someone had died the previous week, there were special prayers but no novenas for slaves, unlike for *blancos*. After services, everyone went to their cabins or to the barracks, but armed guards circled to make sure that no more than three adults formed into groups.

Doña Ana spent most of the afternoon scratching marks on her papers, and don Ramón floated aimlessly, sometimes taking Miguel for a walk but just as often alone. Siña Damita had never seen a man so lost in his own life. He wore nothing but white now, adding to Nena la Lavandera's work. The laundress was near due with his child, and Damita counted it to be the ninth baby born from don Inocente or don Ramón. She didn't know what doña Ana thought about the mulatto infants born on the premises. Maybe she believed they were don Severo's, but Damita knew he didn't use the women on the hacienda. He had enough with the *campesinas* and Consuelo. Sometimes doña Ana stared at one of the children, like three-year-old Pepita, but Siña Damita was sure she wouldn't ask anything about it. *Blancas* had a way of lying to themselves that Siña Damita found peculiar.

With the constant patrols on the roads and byways to and around Guares, Damita didn't go to town except for an emergency. One night, she was about to blow out her candle before wrapping herself inside her hammock when there was tapping on her door.

"Who there?"

"It's me, Mamá, Artemio. . . ."

Her heart jumped to her mouth. She'd heard the lights-out bell from the hacienda long ago, and her youngest son should be in the barracks. She let him in, bolted the door. Artemio threw himself on her as if chased by a ghost.

"*¿Qué pasó?* What you doing here?"

"Forgive me, Mamacita. . . ." He covered his face and sobbed like a child and Damita held him, caressing her youngest son as he told her the worst possible thing he could've said. Artemio and three others from San Bernabé were escaping.

He'd been to San Bernabé on errands for don Severo, and fell in love with a *muchachita* there. Belén was brown as cocoa, with big round eyes over high cheekbones on a narrow face. She was prone to high fevers and abscesses on her arms and legs because her blood was so hot that it boiled. Damita had treated her and her brother, who had the same condition.

"Don Luis bothers all the women there, and she couldn't take it anymore. She convinced us to run away. But when we met in the woods, she'd changed her mind. She tried to talk us out of it. We were confused. I should've gone back, Mamá, but then she said she was going to tell. . . . If she did, she'd be free. . . . I was so scared," he said. "I hit her. I hit her and she fell—"

"Did you—"

"I don't think . . . she was moaning and . . . I didn't mean to kill her," he said. "I didn't know what to do. The others left me and I hid in the fields until after the bell rang and then I came here."

Before she had a chance to tell Artemio which way to go, before she could find her money so he could bribe someone to help him, before she could kiss and hug him once more, hounds were growling at her door.

"*¡Abre la puerta, Damita!* Come out, now!"

Siña Damita and Artemio emerged holding on to each other. Don Severo was pointing a rifle at them. He whistled and reluctantly the dogs backed off.

"*Disculpe, señor,*" Artemio pleaded over and over again, his hands together in prayer. "Mamá had nothing to do with this. It was me, *señor,* please don't punish my *mamita, se lo ruego, mi buen señor.* I beg you."

Don Severo was about to respond, when four soldiers charged into the yard.

"*¡Por la reina!*" they called, invoking Isabel II. Upon those words, anyone within hearing must stop all movement and wait until soldiers release them.

"We're still searching for the others," the lieutenant said to Severo. "We'll take these two. . . ."

"The boy is mine, and she works for me," Severo said. "I'll take care of them."

"I'm sorry, don Severo," the soldier said, "you're within your rights for minor offenses, but not for this. Don Luis said they killed a girl. Who knows what they were planning. We have to interrogate them all. The boy was caught on her premises; she's probably an accomplice."

"She had nothing to do with it!"

"Be a man!" Severo snapped. Artemio gulped his cries. "I'll see you at the *cuartel* in Guares," Severo said, and rode off with his dogs to join the search for the others.

Their hands were bound behind their backs, nooses knotted around their necks. The other ends of the ropes were tied to different horses in such a way that if Damita or Artemio didn't keep up or if they stumbled or fell, they might hang or choke themselves to death. Swirling clouds veiled a full moon one minute, revealed it the next. The road was bright as day, but when the moon hid, everything disappeared as the world became as dark as the inside of her mouth. Damita couldn't help but wonder why Artemio and the others had chosen a full-moon night for their escape. But she knew desperation. It forced her to run away on a similar night when she was about the same age. The scars on her back now throbbed as if never healed.

As they reached the curve beyond San Bernabé, she heard the dogs, yells, and running. Damita had to keep moving in a wild dance as the rope around her neck tightened and loosened when the horse skittered.

"*¡Por la reina!*" soldiers called. "We got them."

The soldier holding Artemio handed his reins to the one holding Damita and ran into the woods with the others, his saber aloft. The other runaways could be heard screaming and begging Severo to pull the dogs back. "*¡Por amor a Dios!*"

Damita looked at Artemio. The moon hid behind a cloud so she could not see him, but the next moment he was in full light. He was her youngest son, the most obedient, she thought, until this night. He was the most affectionate, the sweetest. Their gazes locked, and she felt his fear, and hers, and her love, and his, and his remorse. The moon hid and he scuffed nearer.

"*Perdóname, Mamá,*" he said once more.

As the moon brightened, Artemio screamed and kicked the horse. The noose around Damita's neck tightened as the horse she was tied to jerked out of the way. She fell and was dragged a few feet until the soldier managed to control the beast. Another soldier grabbed her, loosened her noose, and helped her stand. Before the moon disappeared, Siña Damita saw the other horse galloping into the dark dragging Artemio's lifeless body.

II

1844–1863

NEWS FROM SAN JUAN

———————◆◆◆———————

Leonor was proud that over the thirty-two years of their marriage, she'd made a home wherever Eugenio was posted, but she had resisted the move to Puerto Rico. She swallowed her misgivings, but premonitions continued to agitate her even as she adjusted to her new life.

At first she couldn't get used to the smallness of San Juan—only eight by seven blocks for businesses and residences, the rest a fortress. But she soon found much charity work to keep her busy, and good society for leisure. Because of the many functionaries and soldiers living and working in Puerto Rico's capital, active or retired officers of the military and their families were among the elite, along with businessmen and merchants. Much to her surprise, after just a few short months, she came to love the city and its people.

San Juan was a microcosm of Spain, whose regional dialects, prejudices, partisanships, and quarrels traveled across the Atlantic Ocean but were diffused by forced intimacy in the citadel. Catalan bankers, Basque mariners, Galician priests, Andalusian ranchers, and Castilian artists lived and worked alongside French dance masters, Venezuelan coffee planters, Irish grocers, Corsican tobacco growers, and North American accountants.

It was possible to learn how long someone had lived on the island by the wearing, or absence of, regional dress. The local climate was warmer, the sun brighter than the European arrivals had experienced before. Wool ceded to cotton and linen, felt yielded to jipijapa for hats, cravats loosened their stranglehold on men's necks, and the stays on women's corsets slackened.

There was a constant flux in the population. Entire regiments came from Spain, and so did *desterrados*—political exiles serving their sentences. Refugees from civil unrest in South America and the nearby islands stayed long enough to terrify the locals with their stories. Sailors made mischief along the waterfront. Gamblers, quacks, and charlatans sought their marks, found them, swindled them, and disappeared, their exploits adding drama and color to conversations.

San Juan was a lively, gay city if Leonor didn't look too closely at the dismal infrastructure, the frequent droughts, and the nonexistent sewerage. She learned that almost everything she needed to keep a comfortable household had to be imported, including essentials like olive oil. The locals used lard or coconut oil for cooking, which weighed heavily on her palate.

Her mornings were spent at her desk, composing letters. The very morning that Ramón and Inocente left, Leonor dispatched a barrage of warnings and instructions for surviving the rigors of their endeavor based on her extensive experience as a military wife. Their responses, weeks later, were chatty and impersonal and didn't address her main concerns. Leonor knew that Ana wrote them, even if they were in Ramón's and Inocente's hand. After all, she'd composed Eugenio's letters to his family after she married him; this was a wife's chore. She resented it, however.

She was sure that her sons' lives were harsher than Ana's letters allowed. She knew that if her sons visited San Juan after living in the *campo,* they wouldn't return. She'd introduce them to the friends she'd made in the capital. They'd persuade her sons to do what they did: live in the city and visit the hacienda once or twice a year for a few weeks of riding and leisure.

Leonor's friends in San Juan were the husbands and sons of planters, some of whom had heard of Hacienda los Gemelos. When she mentioned it, however, the men's faces hardened, and their women lowered their eyes and suddenly found need of the breeze provided by their fans. They knew something she didn't know, but they wouldn't talk about it. When she mentioned it to Eugenio, he claimed not to have noticed anything out of the ordinary. Elena looked at her pityingly but would not explain.

The day Elena received a letter in Inocente's formal style, not in Ana's cheery voice, and with trembling fingers handed it to her, Leonor cried with happiness when she read of his intention to return to

San Juan, marry Elena, and help his father with the farm in Caguas. If Inocente lived near San Juan, Ramón would soon follow, no matter what Ana said or did. Her two boys, Leonor knew, couldn't live without each other.

After Inocente's murder Eugenio and Elena tiptoed around her as if she'd explode into curses and recriminations every time Los Gemelos was mentioned. But Leonor mourned her son with quiet dignity, arranging novenas, attending Mass, spending hours in prayer with Padre Juan or with the nuns at the Convento de las Carmelitas, and donating to religious charities in Inocente's name. She no longer reminded Eugenio and Elena about her premonitions. Inocente's death had vindicated her. She didn't cry if he was mentioned, nor did she tell them that she blamed Ana for Inocente's death. Now that her worst fears had come true, Leonor didn't wish to jinx her remaining son's life by constantly talking about the unease she still felt, fears that she tried to banish with prayer and with the sweet sherry she sipped to calm her nerves and help her sleep. She was glad that after Inocente's death Ana was no longer writing Ramón's letters. Each page was full of sorrow, and he answered her questions thoughtfully, although he was still unspecific about when he, Ana, and Miguel would come to San Juan.

Another year passed. Ramón reported that Miguel was a healthy little boy interested in everything around him. His letters, however, seldom mentioned Ana, and Leonor noticed that correspondence to Elena from Los Gemelos was more and more infrequent. She interpreted this as a sign that Ana's influence over her son was diminishing, but still she couldn't understand why they didn't come.

Leonor and Eugenio had often discussed a trip to Los Gemelos, but when they wrote to their sons, and later to Ramón, there was always a reason why it wasn't the right time. At first, it was because the trip via merchant ship followed by a long ride on horseback was arduous, especially for Elena, who was not as accomplished a horsewoman as Leonor. The land route required traversing a mountain range where many of the roads were little more than paths cut through the vegetation with machetes.

The specter of an ambush further advised against land travel during the spring and summer of 1848, when San Juan was in a state of high alert as news about uprisings in nearby islands poured into the capital. The Bando Negro was instituted. Volunteer militias were formed to supplement the professional soldiers in El Morro. Rumors about trouble in Puerto Rico circulated at every economic and social level.

Eugenio, who'd tried the life of the gentleman landowner with mixed results, responded when the Field Marshal, the Conde de Reus himself, asked him to lead the volunteer militia sworn to protect the capital against possible uprisings.

"But you're retired, Eugenio," Leonor protested.

"I'm only fifty-seven," he said, "still young and strong enough to protect you and Elena from arsonists and murderers. Don't be so alarmed, my dear. Trust the courage of our Spanish soldiers, and the leadership of our Field Marshal. Besides, you know by now that I can't resist the call of the bugle."

He took command of the militia and spent the next six months in training exercises and early morning musters. Leonor admitted that Eugenio seemed happier and more settled now that he again wore gold epaulets and his hands found reassurance in the ornate pommel and hilt of his sword.

Leonor's worries intensified as events in the interior of the island further unnerved the capital's residents. In July, a slave conspiracy was discovered in the southern city of Ponce—fifty kilometers from Hacienda los Gemelos. The slaves planned to ransack and burn their estates and kill their owners. The leaders were found and shot. Two others who knew about the conspiracy but didn't alert the authorities were sentenced to ten years in prison. Others known to be a part of the plot were punished by one hundred lashes each.

A month later, a slave in Vega Baja, closer to the capital, alerted his master that a group was scheming to revolt and escape to Santo Domingo. The leader was arrested and executed and two others were imprisoned.

The news and rumors magnified Leonor's disquiet. Nightmares about her sons, murdered in the jungle, broke her fitful sleep. In San Juan, surrounded by soldiers and Eugenio, she and Elena were protected. But who was watching for the safety of her remaining son? Who was protecting her grandson? They could all be dead already, and the news, like Inocente's, might arrive weeks after she could see them one last time.

In November 1848, the Conde de Reus was replaced by a new governor, Juan de la Pezuela, who abolished the Bando Negro but established other restrictions, such as forbidding the machete by slaves who weren't actively using them at work.

As unrest subsided, life returned to normal but Leonor's nightmares increased. A racing heart that she knew was caused by forebodings over her son and grandson plagued her.

"Another year, Leonor," Eugenio said when she asked for the umpteenth time when she'd see Ramón again and meet Miguel. "The commitment was for five years, remember? One more year and we can all return to Spain."

"I can't wait another year! I wish to see my surviving son and my grandson. I want to place flowers on my dead son's grave. Is that too much to ask?"

"No, my dear," he said, squeezing her shoulder. "I, too, wish to do those things. But we agreed."

"Please, Eugenio," she said. "They will not come to us. Let us go to them."

When Eugenio started to repeat the same reasons, Leonor placed a soft hand over his mouth and gently pressed his lips. "I won't hear that it can't be done."

He kissed her hand, took it from his lips, and wrapped it in his fingers.

"I've never defied you, Eugenio," she continued. "Not in thirty-four years have I challenged your decisions. I've followed you wherever you've asked me to go, and I've also waited for you. I've waited in dismal rented rooms, in cold cities in Europe, and in dusty villages in North Africa. I've not questioned your judgment about what was best for our family. But now . . . I will not give in on this, Eugenio. I will not give in."

He looked into her gray eyes. She was fifty-two, still pretty and vibrant, but he was saddened by the sorrow that dimmed her sparkle.

"I'll consult Captain de la Cruz. Perhaps he can recommend some men as escorts."

"Thank you, my love," she said, kissing him.

"But you must prepare yourself, my dear. They live humbly."

"I just want to see Ramón and our grandson. I want to hold him before he grows too big to carry in my arms."

Their journey began in late June. The ladies traveled in a battered but sturdy coach purchased from the estate of Gualterlo Lynch, Irish citizen, engineer, whose name and crest were emblazoned on the doors in vivid green edged with gold. Eugenio and the hired escort went on horseback. As soon as they learned of their plans, friends offered their country estates, and those of relatives and friends along the way, so that the Argosos need not spend a single night in rented lodgings with dubious reputations and unpredictable services.

She appreciated their friends' generosity as soon as San Juan was behind them. Wind-driven rain pounded the dry, cracked earth and turned the ruts on the road into deep puddles filled with a clay-like mud that neither coach nor horses could easily maneuver. Rain pursued them on their journey south, making it impossible to see anything through the foggy windows of the vehicle. Leonor's impatience to reach Los Gemelos was further tested as she, Eugenio, Elena, and their escorts spent more days than anticipated waiting out the rain in borrowed rooms, in a true test of the hospitality of their hosts and servants.

When they crossed the Cordillera Central and began their descent into the drier southern slope, the problem became the unforgiving sun that made the coach feel like a stove in spite of the occasional breeze that blew through its open windows. They left their lodgings at dawn and traveled until the sun was directly overhead. They then detoured into tree-lined drives leading to *estancias* where they took lunch and a siesta, followed by a light supper and conversation with their hosts, repeating the news of the night before in a different parlor to a different audience, adding what gossip their previous hosts had shared.

They were delayed twice when the coach needed repairs, and then Leonor, Elena, and their hostesses attended Mass in cool churches and walked circles around tree-lined plazas at dusk.

So far, while the journey wasn't easy, Leonor couldn't account for her sons' and daughter-in-law's insistence that they not travel to Los Gemelos because of the poor roads leading to the plantation. She, as a soldier's wife, had seen worse, had ridden over steeper terrain, had slept in less comfortable beds in structures lacking the grace and beauty of any of the homes they visited on the journey. If there was unrest, it was invisible to Leonor and Elena, perched inside the wine-colored coach, surrounded by men with swords and rifles.

The military road from north to south was well enough traveled, but when they began their drive west, the road narrowed into paths that made the horses skittish. Low-lying branches, buzzing insects, and small birds battered the coach and knocked hats off the men riding behind. Once, they stopped so that Leonor and Elena could run around beating their skirts and shaking their petticoats because a lizard had crawled under them, but neither lady was certain whose skirts had been invaded. Another time, the roof of the coach, piled with luggage and gifts, banged against a dangling hornet's nest, and while the ladies were spared, Eugenio and their escorts on horseback and on foot suffered stings. One of the men was stung around the eyes and his lids swelled shut. He had to be guided back to the nearest town.

Ramón had arranged for them to stay their last night on the road at Finca San Bernabé. The Argosos drove into the tamped dirt yard in late afternoon, followed by the escort. The residence was a long wooden house with a peaked roof known as *techo de dos aguas*. Next to it, a larger, square masonry house with a flat roof and central courtyard was under construction. When they pulled into the drive, the workers on the new building stopped and stood with their heads bowed while the ladies were helped from the carriage and up to the front porch of the original dwelling, where Luis and Faustina waited to greet them. Their boys stood next to their parents and were introduced as Luisito and Manolo. They all looked alike—Faustina a female copy of her husband, Luisito and Manolo smaller echoes of the same features and corpulent shapes.

"*Bienvenidos*, please come in, welcome, this way, please make yourselves comfortable." Faustina's voice resounded from her bosom with an undertone of jollity, as if remembering a joke she was eager to share. Luis, too, seemed to be enjoying himself enormously, and their two boys were all smiles and ingratiating gestures. Leonor accepted as a good omen that the closest neighbors to Los Gemelos had such high spirits and took obvious delight in their country life. Their size and rosy cheeks, their smiling, hospitable air were comforting, as if closeness to these happy people somehow reached over the miles of overgrown paths and stony roads to the center of Los Gemelos. Forgetting her intimate knowledge of her son's and daughter-in-law's true personalities, and contrary to every fear and concern suffered over the past four and a half years, Leonor now imagined Ramón, Ana, and Miguel as round and jolly and loquacious as every member of the Morales Moreau household.

From the outside, their home seemed a simple wooden rectangle with a broad front porch, but it proved to be airy and roomy inside, furnished simply but comfortably. It was clear from the doilies that covered the side tables, the cushions propped against the wooden and cane chairs, the valances over the shutter windows and adorning the doors leading to interior rooms that Faustina was a prolific crocheter.

"I'm sure," Faustina said, "that you'd like to freshen up." She led Leonor and Elena to the rear of the house and showed each into a different room, where maids waited to help them with their ablutions.

"What's your name?"

"Ciriaca. *A sus órdenes, señora,*" the maid answered, neither docile nor assertive, but in a combination of both. She was a striking woman, with almond eyes and high cheekbones. The bright orange turban circling her head, the ends tied into an insouciant bow at the side, enhanced the undertones of her chocolate skin. "Shall I pour for you?" she asked, and with a steady hand she tipped the clay pitcher just enough for a stream of water to fill Leonor's cupped hands over the basin. She splashed her face, her neck, and just as she was about to ask for the towel, Ciriaca presented it to her unfolded, releasing the scent of lemons. Their eyes met, and Ciriaca dropped her gaze immediately, but again, Leonor thought that the woman was not submissive so much as well-mannered. "If you permit me, *señora,*" Ciriaca said, and with the used, now damp towel, she brushed away pieces of leaves, dead insects, and twigs from Leonor's clothes and, kneeling in front of her, used what corners of the towel were still clean to wipe the dust from the hem of her dress and from her shoes.

Elena came from her room at the same time as Leonor emerged from hers, looking refreshed and happy. Luis, Faustina, and Eugenio were sitting on the porch, each holding a tall glass of fruity water. The boys were nowhere to be seen.

"I hope you like the flavor of *mamey*," Faustina said, handing Leonor and Elena glassfuls. "It took me a while to develop a taste for it, but I now find *agüita de mamey* the most refreshing drink after a long journey."

"What a pretty, tranquil place you have," Elena said, her lovely face tinged in soft pink, as if expressing an opinion were such an unaccustomed deed that it made her blush.

"*Gracias, señorita.*" Luis inclined his head in an abbreviated bow. "Faustina chose this spot for the house. As you can see, we're expanding." He waved chubby fingers toward the new construction. "When we first came here, there was nothing but a few shacks and a pigsty. But we've done better than expected."

Faustina turned to Leonor. "It's not easy to live so far from the amenities in the city, but we do our best. Your room is comfortable?" The question at the end of what began as a sentence invited a compliment.

"Charming," Leonor said, "and Ciriaca was very attentive."

Faustina smiled complacently. "Yes, she's very good. I inherited her from my brother, may he rest in peace. It's a pity we can't keep her, but we really don't need more domestics. Luis plans to trade her, and her daughter, who waited on you, *señorita* Elena, for more laborers."

"The truth is," Luis added, "that a business like ours depends on peons. We don't keep a town house, so servants like Ciriaca and Bombón, with few skills beyond the four walls of a great house, are practically useless to us."

"I hope our son and daughter-in-law have done even half as well as you have done here," Leonor said, wishing to compliment their hosts once more. Then she saw it again, the cloud that swept over the faces of people who knew something about Los Gemelos that she didn't, the flutter of the eyelids, the pressing of the lips, the sudden urge to change the subject.

"What news," Faustina asked brightly, "do you bring from San Juan?"

EL CAMINANTE

——◆——

They left San Bernabé at first light, pursued by glorious birdsong. The farm was situated in the high hills along a river, and in every direction that Leonor and Elena looked, there were cultivated groves of fruit trees, coffee, bananas, and plantains; terraced gardens where peons worked close to the ground; men, women, and children hoeing, weeding, moving earth while overseers on horseback rode from one end of the fields to the other. The coach slanted downhill; the wheels and frame groaned and screeched as if they could feel pain on the slopes as the horses picked their way down the serpentine paths. Several times Elena covered her eyes when the coach rolled close to the edge of a sheer drop, the vegetation so thick that it could be night at the bottom. Hidden among the thickets were cottages roofed with palm fronds, and smoke curling into the wind from cooking fires.

One minute they were in the forest and the next moment the landscape opened to a broad plain with canebrakes at various stages of cultivation. It was a violent shift from shadow to light, from steep to flat, from breezy coolness to a powerful oppressive heat and a pitiless sun rising to its zenith. As they entered the cane, Eugenio rode ahead, and when Leonor peeked out the window, she saw that he was talking to another man on horseback accompanied by two hounds, upon which Eugenio and his mount kept wary eyes.

"That was Severo Fuentes," Eugenio reported on his way back. "We'll be there in about an hour. He's gone ahead to let Ramón and Ana know."

Within seconds the interior of the coach hummed like a boudoir before a ball as Leonor and Elena scratched through the traveling cases at their feet for linen hand towels and flasks of water, perfumes, combs, powders, fresh gloves, clean lace collars, and cuffs. They helped each other button and fasten, tug and smooth bodices and waistlines, straighten stockings and tie laces on their shoes so that by the time the coach rolled into the *batey* the two women looked and smelled as if they were ready for the first waltz.

Severo Fuentes opened the carriage door, and as Leonor stepped down, the first person she saw was an old man dressed in loose white pants, shirt, vest, and jacket. A shapeless straw hat drooped over long, stringy hair and shadowed what could be seen of his face surrounded by an unkempt beard. Neither the hat nor the shadows could hide the most vacant eyes Leonor had ever seen. It took her a moment to realize she was looking at Ramón.

"*Hijo,*" she cried, and threw herself upon him, but softened her hold at the sharp bones beneath his too-big clothes, her once exacting, perfumed boy now stinking of sweat and defeat. She pulled away, held him by the shoulders, looked into his blank eyes, and saw tears. "What has happened to you?" she asked before she could stop herself, and Ana, who was standing near Severo Fuentes, stepped closer with an insipid smile, as if she hadn't heard the question.

"Lovely to see you again, doña Leonor." Ana kissed her cheeks, then signaled to a woman next to her to present the boy, her grandson, who bleated like a frightened lamb when Leonor opened her arms toward him. Miguel buried his face in his nurse's bosom in an attempt to be invisible.

"*Ven, Miguelito,*" Ana said. "Nana Inés has to go now. Meet your abuela and abuelo. *Ven niño, no tengas miedo,*" she cooed. The child held on to Inés, who tried to pry him away, without success.

Ramón ran his bony hands over the boy's head, and Miguel turned around, threw himself at his father, and wrapped his arms around his neck and his legs around his waist. Leonor instinctively reached out, afraid that her son would break from the violence of such passionate love. Murmuring in the child's ear, Ramón persuaded Miguel to turn his face so that his grandparents could get a good look at his features. To Leonor's disappointment, he was the spitting image of Ana.

Leonor had waited so long to see her son that she couldn't take her eyes off him the whole first afternoon and evening they were together. She barely noticed the house, its furnishings, and Ana's demeanor. She saw only how thin Ramón was, how his eyes didn't quite meet hers or his father's. She noticed his sickly yellow skin, wrinkled and furrowed where the straggly beard didn't grow. His hands had bronzed into leather, his nails were cracked, his fingertips were raw and sore, as if he'd been digging earth with bare hands. He still moved with the grace of the excellent dancer, but as if through water, deliberate and labored.

Leonor and Eugenio were installed next to Ana and Ramón's bedroom, and Elena was assigned the one across the hall. Miguel went to stay with his nurse next to the workshop.

"We're so sorry," Ana said, "that the accommodations aren't more luxurious." Her face wrinkled into a grimace that was supposed to be an apologetic smile. "I'm afraid the work on the land means that we haven't paid enough attention to our own comfort indoors."

After a short siesta and an early supper, they sat on the porch. As Eugenio and Elena related the gossip they picked up on their travels, Leonor kept eyes on her son, on his newly aquiline features, the way his head bobbed as if he was agreeing with what was said but was actually listening to an internal conversation. When the bell clanged lights out, they all retired. The plain wooden slats dividing the rooms meant that Leonor was aware of every movement on the other side of the wall. There was pacing and urgent murmuring, as if Ana was trying to convince Ramón of something and he wouldn't agree. After a few minutes, Ramón left the house. When Leonor turned to her husband, he, too, was awake, listening.

"Where could he be going at this time of night?"

"I can't imagine."

"We have to bring him back with us," she said. "He's not well."

"Yes, I know."

"Right away," she insisted. "He needs a doctor."

"I'll speak with him in the morning," Eugenio said into her ear. "Rest now, dear. We had a long journey."

Ramón wandered the paths and lanes in the dark. Following no particular route, he kept moving, even when it rained, even when mosquitoes attacked him in swarms, even when night birds and bats crashed into him in their blind flight and huge toads hopped against his shins. He needed to keep moving away, always away from Ana, away from the locked barracks, away from the *bohíos,* away from the barns, the boiling house, the warehouses. He moved up one path, down a lane, across a plowed field, along irrigation ditches.

Some nights were so bright that his shadow was a solid black figure that mimicked his movements, and he found comfort in its company. Other nights were so dark that he walked right into trees and fences. He walked into a pond once and was knee deep before he noticed, terrified that he was being sucked into the mud, where he'd drown. He clambered out, sat on the bank until his heart regained its normal pace, then kept walking. In the morning his hair and beard were caked with fine clay, his clothes filthy, and the leather of his boots stiff, pinching his feet with every step.

Neither he nor Inocente had feared the night, even in Spain, where bandits roamed the countryside, city streets, and alleys robbing and murdering. They were excellent swordsmen, especially Inocente, who was agile and tricky. While each defended the other in encounters with outlaws, neither suffered more than minor scratches and torn clothes. The same couldn't be said for their assailants, who mistook their foppish dress and light step to mean they couldn't defend themselves.

Inocente always took care of himself, but he looked out for Ramón, too. He was fearless and should have made a career, like their father, in the cavalry. The military would've suited him, but he wouldn't leave Ramón in order to pursue a soldier's life. Ramón imagined that Inocente put up a vicious fight when he was ambushed. Beyond that certainty, he refused to let his mind go into the specifics of what his brother's last moments might have been. When Severo tried to tell him how Inocente died, Ramón stopped him. He'd fought alongside his brother and had seen the fury Inocente unleashed against opponents, often out of all proportion to the offense.

Ramón didn't carry a weapon anymore. Still, the slaves were afraid of him. They didn't fear him like they feared Severo, who could whip or set the dogs upon them if he chose. No, the slaves' fear of Ramón was superstitious, because he was alive and his twin was dead. He'd heard one say to another that he was a ghost. He felt as insubstantial as a ghost, as transparent, as useless. He'd never known such loneliness. He felt phantasmal, forever wandering alone while others lived, ate, and loved.

Sometimes when he walked, he was sure that he slept as he moved.

He'd arrive someplace and wouldn't know where he was, and had no memory of how he got there. He'd spent enough time outdoors with his father and brother to know that, if lost, he should be guided by the stars, but the constellations were arranged in different configurations in this part of the world, and he soon stopped looking up for guidance and simply waited for daylight. The bell tower or the windmill always showed him where the house was.

Some nights he'd be out walking and hear a horseman and know that Severo Fuentes was looking for him. Ramón was easy to spot in his white clothes, so he just waited until one of the dogs came up sniffing. He reached up his hand, and Severo pulled him up on his horse and he rode behind him, often falling asleep with his head between Severo's shoulder blades, his arms around his waist, and next thing he'd wake up in Nena's *bohío.* Other times he'd find himself at her door with no memory of how he got there. Nena the laundress led him inside and washed him and helped him climb into his hammock.

He liked Nena la Lavandera. She was shy and quiet, brown as cacao, and smelled like river water. She was warm and soft where Ana was cold and angular. She hardly ever spoke, unlike Ana, who constantly nagged and berated him.

He'd shared La Lavandera with Inocente, like they'd shared many women before Ana, like they shared Marta, the cook, whom Severo sold to don Luis as soon as Ana found out. But Marta was brought to him sometimes, at the *finca,* and because she was the first black woman he'd been with, Ramón liked her best. Marta, like La Lavandera, had pillowy breasts and high, firm buttocks. She smelled like smoke and cooking spices.

So that Ana wouldn't know about La Lavandera, Severo moved her from the *cuarteles* to her own *bohío.* Ramón was sure that Ana knew he went to her, but no longer cared. She hadn't let him touch her since the day he struck her.

Whenever Ramón remembered that day, he felt ashamed. He'd seen Inocente slap women in brothels. He'd slapped Marta and Nena but, as far as Ramón knew, had never struck Ana. He contained his violent impulses around her out of respect because she was Ramón's wife, but Ramón had dreaded the day Inocente would forget himself.

Ana had never complained about Inocente's temper, which made it even worse for Ramón, because if Inocente had hit her at least once, he wouldn't have seen that look of terror when he dragged her by her braids. She might have defended herself instead of rolling into the infuriating, whimpering ball of fear that taunted him. Had Inocente hit Ana, she might have fought back and stopped him before he lost all sense of self and entered the strange trance that made him slap and push, kick and punch. Had Severo Fuentes not intervened, Ramón feared that he might have killed Ana, his wife, the mother of his child. His child? Or Inocente's?

Ramón reached the highest point of a knoll with an ancient ceiba tree whose roots loomed over him in the darkness. The *borinqueños* believed that the ceiba connected the underworld to the living and to the spirit world in the sky. He now leaned against one of the curved roots, at least a foot taller than him, to listen. Nights in Puerto Rico were a cacophony of insect, frog, and bird song, wind, the endless sighing of the *cañaveral*. "It's not fair." A horned moon appeared from behind a cloud, painting the world silver. Below him, the cane undulated like a tide, soughing, "It's not fair." In the distance he could barely distinguish the windmill, the bell tower, and between them, the solid shapes of the barracks, the house where his wife and his parents slept.

He couldn't bear to picture his mother's face when she first stepped from the coach in her finery. His mother hadn't mastered the art of dissimulation. One look at her and he knew that the slaves were right: he was a ghost, somewhat more substantial than his brother's shadow pursuing him day and night, whispering that it wasn't fair, it wasn't fair that only one twin, the weak twin, the sentimental twin, the twin who never stood up for himself, should be walking upon the earth.

WOMEN'S WORK

———◆———

In the week they'd been together, Leonor noticed how much Ana and Elena had changed over the last four and a half years. In the tropical sun, Elena's skin had acquired a gleam that added to her beauty, while Ana's had become tan and dry on her face, and darker still, and leathery, on her forearms and hands. Ana habitually pushed her sleeves to her elbows, preparing for manual labor. She seldom wore a hat and gloves outdoors, unlike Elena, whose broad brims, long sleeves, and white gloves left very little skin exposed. There was a roughness about Ana's movements and gestures that contrasted unfavorably with Elena's measured gentleness and femininity. It was as if Ana was battered by the elements while Elena lived in a hatbox.

Ana wasn't as graceful as Elena, or as pretty, but this is where the two women differed the most. Elena was a beauty, no doubt about it. Ana's features had lost their youthful freshness, but she was handsome in the way much older women are after years of childbearing and suffering. She looked now the way she'd look when she was fifty. Their voices had changed, too. Ana's had gained volume and depth, now that she was accustomed to giving orders. The effect was of a very small woman with a big voice, a woman who must be obeyed. The two girls Leonor remembered from their last days together in San Juan seemed to have nothing in common anymore. They circled each other uncomfortably, as if each saw in the other the opposite side of a mirror that revealed what was not.

The men mounted right after dawn, and Leonor, Ana, and Elena were left to themselves until the midday dinner. Ana was always busy, so Leonor and Elena accompanied her as she performed her duties. In her circuits with Ana, Leonor understood why the letters from Los Gemelos were always about the yield of plants and animals and the effects of weather. Ana was proud of her kitchen garden, vegetable patch, and orchards. She delighted in the pigsty and corrals, the barns, chicken coops, and dovecote, and in the animals she raised there.

She introduced each slave and free man or woman, black or white, as if they were equals. They, in turn, were humble but also with a familiarity that seemed improper, given her role as *la patrona*. Leonor guessed they thought she was a good mistress.

Ana walked them past two long, ramshackle buildings that faced each other, where the unmarried male and female slaves lived. Farther down the path squatted a few palm-thatched cottages for families, surrounded by small plots called *conucos,* where slaves grew their own tubers and plantains. Ana showed them the palm-roofed, open-walled *rancho* where Ramón read prayers every Sunday, and where a priest from the nearest town sometimes said Mass and baptized newborns.

They reached the river's edge, where the laundress and two young girls washed the slaves' and overseers' work clothes. Nearby a boy tended a *fogón* that heated water in a cauldron for boiling the finer clothes and linens of the *casona.*

At the other plantations visited on their trek to Los Gemelos, the women spent most of their days indoors sewing, tatting, crocheting, painting pottery or china, reading religious tracts, or practicing music on pianofortes chipped and battered by their trip across the Atlantic. Not one of the women they met was as active in the everyday operations of her plantation as Ana. There was something inappropriate about it, Leonor thought, but she admitted there was also something admirable about Ana's confidence and her surprising skills and knowledge.

Ana took little interest in Miguel, however. The boy practically lived with his nana Inés, her husband, José, and their two sons, Indio and Efraín, who were slightly older. The three boys played well together and liked to build elaborate towers with the scraps from the workshop where José made the furniture that was beginning to choke the *casona*'s small rooms.

"José is a gifted craftsman, as you can see. It all looks a bit too ornate in our simple house, but we plan to build a *casa grande,*" Ana explained as they walked back toward the *casona*. "This house isn't really appropriate for us, but there's so much work needed on the outbuildings, and we could use more *brazos*. . . ."

They sat in the shade of the breadfruit tree, where the maids set up chairs and a table. Ana didn't just sit, however; by her chair was a basket full of clothes to be mended.

A swing dangled from the branch of another tree, where Elena and Inés took turns pushing a laughing Miguel back and forth.

"You're certainly more involved in the day-to-day operations than I would've guessed," Leonor said, unable to disguise the edge in her voice.

"I didn't come this far to sit indoors embroidering," Ana said tartly. "I've always had an active life, different from my mother's and her friends'. You understand, doña Leonor. You traveled and had many adventures following don Eugenio—"

"But I did none of the fighting. That would've been . . . wrong."

"I'm lucky that way. There's no society here. No one to impress or be judged by."

"Oh, but you can't escape gossip. Even if you never leave, some of what happens here gets abroad."

"Is that so? Have you heard something I should know?"

"No. No, I haven't. But if I mention Los Gemelos, people change the subject."

"You were overly sensitive, Tía Leonor," Elena said, "because for so long you've wanted to see firsthand."

"And now that you've been here for a week," Ana asked, "have you seen anything that merits gossip?"

Leonor thought for a moment. There was no use criticizing Ana; she'd be herself no matter what. But Leonor couldn't let her off easily. "In your letters, you didn't mention that Ramón was unwell."

"I didn't know how to tell you. We were all horrified, of course, by Inocente's murder. But Ramón naturally took it the hardest."

"How many times did I ask about him, and you never wrote back that he was sick?"

"He's not sick, doña Leonor. He's grieving. We all are, as a matter of fact. As far as we can tell Ramón isn't ill, he's . . . well, he's tired. He doesn't sleep well. You might've heard him leave our bedroom at night," she added, knowing that no movement in the small, creaky house could pass undetected. "He walks around the *batey* until he's tired enough to sleep. The guards know to keep an eye on him. Severo has come after him a few times, and has brought him to rest in the *finca,* where we keep an office. People grieve in their own way, doña Leonor, and in their own time. He lost the person closest to him in the whole world. That's not something one gets over easily."

"You forget who you're speaking to." Leonor puffed her chest indignantly. "I lost a son!"

"Yes. Yes, I know. And I didn't want to add to your sorrow, or to worry you needlessly."

"Needlessly? Have you seen him, Ana? Ramón is bone thin. He hasn't shaved in weeks. And he smells. Have you noticed the bags under his eyes, his yellow skin? I hardly recognized my own son when I first saw him. . . ." Leonor tried to control the tears that pushed against her lids, the rage at Ana's nonchalance that made her hands shake and her voice brittle. "It seems to me that anyone with an ounce of concern would notice that Ramón is not just in mourning, he's sick and needs a doctor, a doctor, Ana, not the slaves' *curandera.*"

"Siña Damita is very capable."

"You selfish girl! Why must you always have your way when others are clearly suffering?"

Ana sought and held Leonor's eyes, as if she could climb through them into the older woman's soul.

"You've never liked me, doña Leonor. But it was I who gave your sons ambition. They were floundering when we met, aimless. More than living up to a reputation as dandies, gamblers, and womanizers. I gave their lives a purpose, doña Leonor; I, not you, who pampered and indulged them. I gave them something to work toward. I gave them meaning, and more besides. My hard work and my fortune have gone into this plantation. Hacienda los Gemelos is our plantation, not just mine, ours."

"How dare you speak to me like this!"

Leonor realized she'd raised her voice when Inés and Elena stopped swinging Miguel and watched Ana and Leonor as if they were spectators at a performance.

"You feel perfectly free to criticize me, to call me selfish and who knows what else behind my back," Ana continued, oblivious to the stares of the others. "But you don't like it as much when I tell you the truth to your face."

Leonor stood and placed herself between the seated Ana and the rope swing. "You're an insolent little bitch," she said, loud enough for Ana, but not the others, to hear. "You take credit for my sons' industry, for their ambition. But are you also willing to take the blame for Inocente's murder?" Ana winced, and Leonor continued. "You drove him from here, why and how I don't know. But in his last letter to me, that he composed, by the way, in his own hand, he said that he couldn't bear to be here any longer. He couldn't bear it."

Ana closed her eyes for a moment, as if gathering strength, then again focused on Leonor, but this time the older woman, standing over her, didn't flinch.

"He was jealous of Ramón. He envied our lives as husband and wife, as parents. You taught them to share everything, but some things shouldn't be shared."

"What do you mean by—"

"Inocente couldn't stand it if Ramón had something he didn't." Ana took a deep breath and studied Leonor, assessing how much to say. She saw Miguel on the swing, his head turned toward her with a worried expression. Ana shook her head as if driving a thought from it and sighed. "We were fine until Miguel was born."

Leonor sat again, choked with rage and tears, but unwilling to cry in front of her daughter-in-law. Under the avocado tree, Inés resumed swinging Miguel back and forth. Elena watched Leonor and Ana, ready to intervene if necessary but unwilling to interfere.

"How can you blame a child for coming between two brothers? Inocente loved Miguel as if he were his own," Leonor insisted. "You're to blame, Ana. It wasn't enough for you to snare one son; you captured both and then drove a wedge between them. In the name of all that's holy, take some responsibility for your actions."

Ana's hands trembled. She again captured Leonor's gaze and trapped her inside it. "It wasn't me who drove Inocente away, it was your incessant questions about when we'd leave this place," she spit out. "You refused to accept that they could be happy here. You wrote them constantly to warn them what a terrible mistake they'd made. Your letters were about what could go wrong, not about what they were doing right. Your letters were about how miserable you were because they lived so far away, as if the only thing that mattered was their nearness to you, not the life they chose as grown men. And you dare call me selfish."

Hooves pounded toward them. Severo galloped into the yard and in one motion dismounted and began shouting orders at workers who dropped whatever they were doing and raced to follow his instructions. He strode to Leonor and Ana, removed his hat, and bowed, breathing hard.

"*Señoras,* I'm sorry to bring you bad news, but don Ramón has fallen from his horse and is injured."

"Oh, dear God!" Leonor ran in the direction that four men took into the woods, carrying a hammock and long poles, but as soon as the path narrowed she ran back. "Where is he? Is he badly hurt?" Elena chased after her, trying to calm her down.

"He'll be brought here," Severo said. "We need bandages. I've sent for Siña Damita," he told Ana, who stood under the breadfruit tree as Leonor and Elena ran back and forth. Severo spoke in a low voice, forcing Elena and Leonor to be still and stop crying so they could hear. "I'm afraid it was a bad fall. I've sent riders to fetch Dr. Vieira, but even if they can find him right away, it'll be hours before he gets here."

"Would it make more sense to bring Ramón to the doctor? Is he too injured to travel?" Leonor asked.

Severo turned to her. "He fell down an embankment. His leg is broken and he's badly bruised. He must have hit his head because he lost consciousness for a few minutes. Moving him further might be worse than trying to treat him here."

"But it might be better to go toward where the doctor is," Leonor said, near hysterical.

Severo looked from Leonor to Ana. "San Bernabé is halfway to town. We can stop there if the doctor is already headed this way."

"Do whatever is necessary," Ana said, her voice brittle.

"*Sí, señora,* I've ordered a cart. We can decide once you and Siña Damita evaluate the wounds. . . ."

"If it's as bad as you say, doña Leonor is right. We should get him to town as soon as possible," Ana said. Severo tipped his hat and was off again.

Within moments the raised dust from comings and goings by people and animals clouded the *batey*. Ana fetched a stack of linens for Leonor and Elena to tear into bandages. She told Paula to boil water in the kitchen as Teo readied basins. Benicio and Juancho hitched the cart to two mules while Ana, Flora, and Damita smoothed and flattened straw on its surface, and covered it with a sheet to make a bed as José rigged an awning over it. Miguel clung to Inés's skirts, frightened by the sudden rushed activity.

"Indio! Efraín! Take him to play somewhere."

With much cajoling, Indio and Efraín lured Miguel away so that the adults could continue their preparations.

An hour later, Eugenio and Severo galloped in, followed by the men running into the yard carrying the hammock, its right side bloody. Leonor threw herself in its direction as her grim-faced husband tried to keep her away so that the men could load Ramón onto the cart.

"Let me see him, let me hold him, please!" she cried, and Eugenio loosened his grip.

The men stood so that Leonor could peel back the hammock folds and look inside. She recoiled. Eugenio grabbed her before she collapsed, and half carried her to the chair under the breadfruit tree, where Elena and Flora tended to her. Once Ramón was transferred to the cart bed, Damita and Ana assessed and bandaged the wounds. Ramón moaned pitifully, and his voice brought Miguel from where his playmates had taken him.

"Papá! Papá, why do you cry?" He tried to scrabble up to his father, but Indio and Efraín dragged him to Inés, who carried him off, all of them crying uncontrollably.

More composed now, Leonor climbed onto the cart. Through her tears, she wiped blood and grime from Ramón's face as Damita and Ana took care of his right leg. The splintered bone poked through the skin below the knee, and his ankle was turned at an unnatural angle. A belt tourniquet had been applied, but there was much blood. Ramón's face was scraped, his nose raw. Tiny pebbles and gravel pocked the skin on his hands and arms. Damita gave her a clean rag to cool his forehead. Ana was stabilizing the leg between two boards secured with strips of cloth. She looked angry, but Leonor had seen that expression on field doctors and nurses working on difficult breaks. Her quick, efficient movements were devoid of emotion.

"Be gentle, please," Leonor said.

Ana looked up quickly, then returned to her work. "I'm doing the best I can."

Leonor pressed the cool cloth on Ramón's forehead, and in that moment, he screamed and fainted. Damita seemed startled and looked from Ana to the leg, which was now straighter than before, fastening it to the board. Damita retrieved a vial from her apron and passed its contents under Ramón's nose until he revived.

"We should go," Severo said. "It's a long way to town." Ana squinted in the direction of the path away from the *batey* and her hands trembled. "It's better if you stay, *señora,*" Severo suggested. "Siña Damita can tend to him."

"I'm going," Leonor said. No one dared contradict her. She looked defiantly at Ana, who shrank under her gaze as Severo helped her down from the cart.

"Someone . . . must . . . stay here." Elena put her arms around Ana's shoulders and held on to her as the cart rolled away.

Severo rode ahead, but Eugenio followed alongside, keeping an eye on his son and another on his wife, who held on to Ramón's hand with the ferocity of someone extending a short rope to a drowning man.

Ramón's breath was labored, and several times Leonor thought that life had left his body as his hand went limp and his eyes fluttered uncontrollably. But just as she thought he was dying, he shuddered and moaned and resumed his shallow breathing. Once, he opened his eyes fully and looked into hers. His face softened into the trusting expression of the helpless infant she had nursed at her breast.

"*Aquí estoy, hijo.*" He smiled and she summoned all her strength to remain calm. She held his hand and prayed. Every once in a while Damita handed Leonor a wet cloth to put to Ramón's lips, and he sucked at it thirstily. Damita applied compresses to his forehead, and with impressive dexterity, given the pitching and bouncing of the cart in the uneven terrain, she used her fingernails to pick out every tiny stone and shard from the broken skin on Ramón's face, arms, and hands, and cleaned around them with a rag moistened with a fragrant liquid.

The doctor and his assistant met them less than one hundred meters from the turnoff to San Bernabé. Eugenio, Leonor, and Siña Damita sat under a tree while Dr. Vieira examined Ramón. The doctor clicked his tongue and slumped his shoulders in apparent defeat as he examined the improvised splint. With every poke and prod Ramón screamed, and Leonor assumed the pain as if it were being inflicted on her own body. Eugenio helped her stand when the doctor approached.

"I'm sorry, Colonel." Dr. Vieira spoke with a Portuguese accent whose hard consonants added extra syllables to his Spanish. It annoyed Leonor that he addressed Eugenio while completely ignoring her. "I've done what I can to make him comfortable, but please understand that these are not optimal conditions." He waved his left hand toward the cart, and she noticed that he was missing the pinky and ring fingers.

"Fuentes went to ask don Luis if we can bring him there for treatment."

Dr. Vieira spun around and looked skeptically at the steep terrain leading to San Bernabé, then turned to the rocky dirt road curving and disappearing into the green.

"We thought it would save time to bring him toward you," Leonor said.

"Moving him was probably not the best decision," Dr. Vieira answered, speaking to Eugenio. "He's lost much blood. His breathing is shallow from broken ribs. He also has serious fractures made worse by the jostling in the cart. I can stabilize the leg, but there's always the danger of infection."

Leonor collapsed and Siña Damita drew her away. Once she was out of hearing, Eugenio took the doctor's elbow and walked a few paces.

"I've been a soldier all my life and have seen men with worse injuries who recovered. You make sure that my son comes out of this alive."

"But, Colonel, I can't guarantee—"

"Do you see my wife? That woman has more backbone than most men, but she has already lost one son. If she loses Ramón because of her own poor judgment—" Eugenio's voice broke, and he pulled himself up straighter, wiped his hand from his forehead to the tip of his beard, and took a deep breath. "Whatever it takes, Dr. Vieira, to save him."

Luis and Faustina received them in their *batey,* their normal cheer suppressed.

"Our boys are visiting relatives in Mayagüez," Faustina explained. "We've put Ramón in Luisito's room, where he'll be most comfortable. Ciriaca and Bombón can nurse him once the doctor and his assistant fix the leg."

Leonor felt comfort in Faustina's gentility and in her confidence in Dr. Vieira and in Ramón's recovery.

"The doctor has earned the esteem of everyone around here," Faustina assured her. "I've ordered that dinner be served under the trees by the pond," she said as she left Leonor. "As soon as you've freshened up, Ciriaca will bring you there."

An open tent was raised near a stream far enough from the house that as Dr. Vieira worked on Ramón, his screams were masked, if not entirely silenced, by a gurgling cascade.

Luis, Eugenio, Faustina, and Leonor sat uneasily at the linen-draped table, unable to eat but trying to be polite for one another's sake. How could she possibly eat, Leonor thought, while her son's broken leg was being painfully manipulated in a bedroom decorated with the toys, books, and drawings of a schoolboy? Did the doctor have the right equipment? How could he operate with two fingers missing? Was Luis's homemade rum strong enough to dull Ramón's pain? The Moraleses tried their best to make conversation, but none of them could take their eyes off the path to the house and the comings and goings of the servants, who looked at Leonor pityingly, the only ones, it seemed, who didn't pretend they couldn't hear the screams coming from Luisito's room.

Leonor sat by her son's bed, counting Ave Marias on her rosary's silver beads. Ramón slept—if sleep could be possible through so much whimpering and groaning. There was certainly no rest in it.

He smelled like the drunks that she avoided in the streets of the city, a stench of liquor and urine and sweat and, in her son's case, the bitter scent of blood. Ciriaca and Bombón had wiped away much of the blood, but each fresh bandage around Ramón's leg quickly became red. Leonor had volunteered in enough military hospitals to know just how bad a sign this was. Dr. Vieira set the leg in a fashion similar to what Ana and Damita had managed, but tighter and straighter. He hoped, he said, that he wouldn't have to amputate.

Leonor wondered if Dr. Vieira was a trained surgeon, or if his missing fingers made him reluctant to inflict a similar injury on his patients. She didn't dare question him because, whatever the answer, Ramón's life was in his hands and he was trying his utmost, Leonor was sure, to save him.

Dr. Vieira asked Bombón to shave Ramón so that he could treat the scrapes and cuts on his cheeks and jaw. Leonor was grateful for this, because she could now see her son clean-shaven, as she'd always known him. His features were etched with deep creases around his eyes and from his nose to his lips. His forehead had drooped over his eyebrows. Two of his front teeth had been chipped long before his fall from the horse, judging from their yellowed edges.

"Mamá." Leonor was unsure if she'd really heard the word, or if the sound was another variant of the croaks that from time to time escaped her son's lips. "Mamá, take him with you," Ramón said with such vehemence that Leonor was afraid the effort was too much for him.

"Who, *mi amor*? Take who?"

His eyes opened, and just as quickly, closed. "Miguel." He fell silent again.

She pressed a cool cloth to his face. He was feverish, and since she'd taken over the watch, before dawn, his lips moved in an interminable garble punctuated by the moans that had kept everyone in the house unable to sleep through the night. In this case, however, his voice was clear. She was certain what she'd heard. Ramón wished her to take Miguel away from Los Gemelos, from Ana.

After that lucid moment, Ramón's fever rose and he became delirious, carrying on a conversation with Inocente, mostly unintelligible to her except for a few phrases. "*Mira,* Inocente," Ramón said, as if he'd discovered something extraordinarily beautiful that his brother must see. *"No te vayas,* Ino," he called, as if his brother had strayed too far. *"No fui yo,"* he contended another time, as if Inocente had accused Ramón of doing something that made him angry. In the hour since telling her she should take Miguel away, he'd not recognized or spoken directly to her.

Just as the sky lightened, the door creaked and a maid entered carrying a tray with a steaming pot and a dainty china cup and saucer.

"Disculpe, señora. I took the liberty. I thought you might like something to drink. It's chocolate."

"That's kind of you," Leonor said.

The maid set the tray on the bedside table, but her eyes fixed on Ramón, taking in every aspect of his appearance. *"Pobrecito señor,"* she said. "He was a good man."

"Is a good man."

"Sí, señora, is a good man," she amended, flattening her upper lip over her protruding teeth as if to control a smile.

"What's your name?"

"I'm Marta, *señora,* at your service. I was the cook at Los Gemelos before I came here."

Leonor took a good look at her. She was big boned, brown, and flat nosed, with teeth too big for her mouth. She had broad shoulders, large breasts, a round belly, and masculine hands.

Ramón moaned and both women turned to him. "Inocente," he called in a frightened, childish voice that tore through her. "Inocente, *no me dejes."*

"Aquí estoy, hijo. Mamá is with you, son." She took his hand, and with her other hand caressed his forehead and pushed strands of sweaty hair from his temples. Marta stood on the other side of the bed, avid, as if willing Ramón to recognize her. Her expression was strangely gleeful, the look of someone who delights in bearing witness, preferably if it puts her superiors in a bad light, so that she can later relate every detail, exaggerated for maximum effect.

Leonor frowned and Marta looked for something to do. "That's all," Leonor said tersely. "You can go." Marta stood a moment, and a look of disdain crossed her features. She pressed her hands over her belly, and Leonor saw that she was not fat but pregnant. Holding her belly, Marta curtsied deeply, mockingly, before leaving the room.

"Mamá," Ramón called again. "Inocente is going."

His eyes darted from side to side, up and down, as if following the erratic movements of a hummingbird. His body tensed as his breathing grew shallow. With strength she didn't know he had, Ramón half lifted off the bed and let out one piercing scream, then fell back gasping for air.

Eugenio ran into the room, followed by Luis, Faustina, Ciriaca, Bombón, and lastly, Dr. Vieira, who had been sleeping in Manolo's room next door. The doctor took Ramón's pulse, lifted his eyelids, and peered into his pupils. He examined the bandages and pressed his ear to Ramón's chest.

None of what he did, Leonor knew, could save her son. Doctor Vieira could not reverse the wheezing of lungs that couldn't take in enough air. Ramón gasped, released a long exhalation; his hand in hers relaxed and his features slackened. Somewhere outside a rooster crowed and dogs barked. Leonor wrapped her arms around her son, pressed her face to his chest, and sobbed. Her husband embraced her from behind, and his tears burned into her shoulder.

Dr. Vieira asked that Leonor leave while he prepared the body, but she wouldn't move from Ramón's side.

"There's nothing more you can do for him, Dr. Vieira," she said with more aplomb than she felt. "This is now women's work." Ciriaca and Bombón stood by her, and the doctor, faced with their determination, withdrew, and moments later he and his assistant rode out of the *batey* as the morning began to warm.

The three women rocked Ramón from one side of the bed to the other as they washed the blood, dirt, and grime that pain made impossible to wipe when he was alive. They washed his hair and trimmed it neatly around his face, shaved him again so that his cheeks were smooth, even if bruises and scratches marred his features. They clipped his nails and rubbed *manteca de cacao* over his body. They changed the soiled bedcovers and wrapped him in a linen shroud from a sheet that Faustina brought them. She thoughtfully removed the festive tatting along the borders but could do nothing about the embroidered initials under the Morales crest.

"Luis sent a messenger to Los Gemelos, to notify your daughter-in-law," she said. "We sent for Padre Xavier last night, but he's attending another family on the other side of town. He'll be here later today."

Leonor had no idea when Ramón last confessed or took the Eucharist, but imagined it was the day before they set sail from San Juan, over four years earlier. He'd be buried far from his brother, from his homeland, from the family plot in the churchyard of their hometown of Villamartín in northwestern Cádiz province. Eugenio's and Leonor's ancestors were buried there, a hundred yards from one another on the same side of a tree-lined path. Ramón and Inocente would be the first of their clans to be scattered across the sea. Bombón covered Ramón's head with the shroud. And as Ciriaca held her, Leonor let the full weight of her grief moisten the maid's solid bosom, and her strong arms support her as Ciriaca led her away from the room decorated with the hopes and dreams of the Moraleses' little boy, even as her own boy, aged before his time and broken, lay still and cold on the narrow bed.

For the second time in just over a week, Leonor was on her way down the mountain from Finca San Bernabé to the flatlands spiked with cane. She was too small for both Faustina's mare and her riding skirt. On horseback, the slopes to the unseen bottoms were even more frightening than they looked from the closed coach. The sure-footed mare stepped over the pebbled paths, away from the slippery edges. Leonor tried not to, but she couldn't help looking, imagining Ramón tumbling down an embankment like the ones they passed, his body bouncing against sharp rocks and boulders into the depths.

Two men from Hacienda los Gemelos carried Ramón inside a hammock down the hill. They could maneuver more easily and quickly than riders, so they waited at the bottom of the hill.

Eugenio had gone ahead to make sure everyone was ready to receive them at Los Gemelos, but Severo Fuentes rode nearby. Once he'd ascertained that Leonor was a good rider, he left space between them, often riding ahead to cut low-hanging branches with one swift whack of his machete. Faustina insisted that Ciriaca accompany Leonor to Los Gemelos. The maid rode a mule uneasily. Raised as a domestic servant, she wasn't used to being in the uncontrollable environment of the *campo*. Were the occasion not so solemn, Leonor would've smiled at Ciriaca's flapping the air ineffectually when insects flew into her face, and her fear of the movement and screeches of unseen birds and other creatures.

Leonor was moved by how many people were waiting for them when they reached Los Gemelos just before dusk. The slaves, the foremen, the *libertos* and *campesinos* stood to form a path toward the open *rancho,* their heads bowed. Their labor had transformed the *rancho* in just over a day. Benches formed a center aisle leading to an altar featuring Ana's antique crucifix. There were flowers everywhere, and vines crept around the legs of sawhorses for the coffin. Next to the *rancho* was a closed tent, and in front of it, Ana, Eugenio, and Elena waited with Padre Xavier. The women were dressed in simple black dresses that were obviously hastily made and didn't quite fit. Elena and Ciriaca helped Leonor upstairs, to the room next to Ana's, where, on the bed, a black dress like the ones Ana and Elena wore was waiting for her.

THE TRADE

———◆———

In her room, the windows half shut, Ana cried until her eyes were swollen. She was twenty-three years old, a mother, and the wealth she'd brought into her marriage was invested in the hacienda. She'd sacrificed her fortune, youth, and looks to be a pioneer in a wilderness, had committed the sins of adultery and fornication without seeking penance. With Ramón's death, it would all have been in vain. Hacienda los Gemelos belonged to don Eugenio, who, with both sons dead, was likely to sell it. She might be forced to return to San Juan or even to Spain—and worst of all, to be dependent on her in-laws or her parents, floating aimlessly through stifling rooms and indolent years of mourning as her son grew up.

When she saw the shrouded body, Ana couldn't believe that Ramón was within the folds of the linen. Eugenio and Severo shouldered the poles holding the hammock and brought Ramón into the tent, followed by Padre Xavier. Ana was left under the sun, faced with the solemn hum of prayers. Flora took her elbow.

"Venga, mi señora," she said. "They ready now. You will see him one more time." Damita took her other elbow, and Ana was grateful to have them there because she was scared.

The ground was littered with wood chips and sawdust. José had built the mahogany coffin in just a few hours but couldn't control his decorative impulses. Compared with his furniture, however, the vines and flowers around a crucifix on the top of the box were beautiful and subdued. The men had placed Ramón inside, still wrapped in linen. His clean face looked so much younger than twenty-nine that it erased her last image of him, bearded, aged, and tormented. Ana ran her fingertips across his smooth cheeks, his lips that once smiled so brightly, his eyelids. He was cold. *Te perdono,* she said silently, but the words sounded meaningless. *Perdóname,* she mouthed as she bent to kiss his forehead, and the smell of chocolate from the *manteca de cacao* was repugnant. She jerked back, and Flora and Siña Damita carried her away because she could no longer stand on her own.

Over the next days Ana moved as if within someone else's life. She managed to get through the wake in the *rancho,* the prayers, and the condolences. The same mourners who'd come after Inocente's death drove up in carriages or on horseback. These were the "charming people" Ramón liked so much, don so-and-so and doña *fulana de tal* wearing years-out-of-date European clothes and speaking in a babble of regional and national accents. They were subdued by the circumstances, but happy to break the isolation in their haciendas, even for a funeral. Men and women alike peered at her with unabashed interest. Ana felt less like a grieving widow and more like an exhibit in a museum. Faustina greeted every arrival with kisses on both cheeks for the women and squeezes of the hands for the men, then led them to the front of the *rancho,* where Ana sat with Eugenio, Leonor, and Elena before the coffin.

Padre Xavier lingered around the family. He tried to talk Ana into burying Ramón in the Catholic cemetery, but in one of the few decisions she made during the hours right after his death, she refused to allow it.

"This place meant more to Ramón than a town he seldom visited," she said, wiping away tears. "I'd prefer it if you'd consecrate the ground, because when my time comes, I, too, wish to be buried here."

Severo picked a spot on a knoll for Ramón and had men build a stone fence around it for a burial ground. Even Leonor and Eugenio agreed that it was a peaceful site, shaded by an ancient ceiba tree. Ramón was interred at the highest point, the *cañaveral* an enormous rippling carpet below. After the funeral, the *rancho* was rearranged, under Severo's direction, into an open dining room where a meal was served to the mourners before they returned to their plantations. The novenas were also conducted in the *rancho,* but the visitors dwindled over the nine days, so by the end, only the family, the slaves, and a few *campesinos* recited the prayers that Ana, Leonor, and Elena took turns leading.

Ana tried to make the Argosos feel welcome, even though Ramón had announced they were coming after they were already halfway to Los Gemelos. She'd have preferred to house them at the *finca,* which would have given everyone more privacy. But Ramón insisted that the *finca* was too far from the house.

Leonor had brought a slave with her from San Bernabé, a loan, she said, from Faustina. Ciriaca slept in a hammock in Miguel's room, now Elena's, and waited on the two women with refined solicitude and surprising devotion. Ciriaca and Elena walked doña Leonor to Ramón's grave every morning and afternoon to pray. Leonor gave Ana hateful looks when she wouldn't go with them.

Flora was jealous of Ciriaca. "She orders me and Inés like she the mistress."

Damita, too, said that Ciriaca's polished manners and commanding airs had the slaves gossiping and complaining. The smooth functioning of her household, which Ana worked so hard to achieve and maintain, evolved within days into resentful infighting among her servants.

Even though she was in mourning, Ana wouldn't neglect her chores. Every time she went by Leonor, Ana saw her disapproving eyes, because she should be sitting in a corner, like Leonor and Elena, praying and reading devotional texts. Eugenio was in the *campo* with Severo from dawn to dusk. His wife didn't make him sit with her and pray all day. Even in his grief he could work, but she couldn't because she was a woman and could express her grief only by suspending her life. She spent most of her day in the gardens, brooding about her future.

One afternoon, Leonor and Elena walked Miguel to the river for a picnic. Ana was working on the ledgers when she heard Eugenio coming up the outside stairs.

"Ah! There you are. No picnic for you?"

"No, don Eugenio. It's the end of the month, and I must go over the accounts and prepare the pay packets for the overseers and the paid laborers."

"Perhaps I can help?"

"I'm almost finished, but if you'd like to review what I've done—"

Eugenio sat beside her as she explained each item, each expense, every purchase and sale over almost five years at Los Gemelos. He leaned back as if the blue, green, and red lines across the pages made him dizzy. He wasn't for credits and debits but had spent enough time on the plantation to know that it was better run than he'd expected.

"It all looks very good," he said, nodding.

"Another couple of years of good harvests"—Ana closed the books and stacked them by her side—"and Los Gemelos will be self-sufficient. Within another two to five years we'll be making a profit."

"It's tragic that neither of my boys lived long enough to see it."

"Yes." She lowered her head, but from the corner of her eye she saw him looking around, as if taking inventory of the house and its belongings. "That's why," she said softly, "I'd like to continue the work here, don Eugenio. In their memory."

"Surely, Ana, you know that's impossible. You, alone here? No, my dear, I appreciate your sentiments, but . . . No, I couldn't possibly allow it."

Her bile rose. He, the head of the family, was compelled, was in fact bound by family ties and culture to make decisions for her. Ana tried to stay calm. She reminded herself that Eugenio was better disposed toward her than Leonor.

"It's your plantation, of course, and you can do as you please with it. But Ramón and Inocente thought of Los Gemelos as their legacy to Miguel. He was born here. This is all he's known."

"He's four years old, Ana. What does Miguel know about legacies and the future?"

"Nothing yet, but someday he'll ask what his father and his uncle stood and died for."

"And you'd have him believe they stood and died for a piece of land with rotting buildings on it? You'd have him believe that his father and uncle stood and died for a few pigs and chickens, some mules, a couple of old mares?"

"Is that all you see here?"

Eugenio strode to the window and kept his back to her for so long that she thought their conversation was over. "Luis Morales has made me a generous offer, one I'm disposed to accept."

"Whatever it is, it's not enough. Your sons and I put everything into Los Gemelos, and now that it's on the verge of being a profitable business—"

"Having looked at your ledgers, and considering Luis's offer, the sale will be a very profitable business indeed."

Ana shook her head, remembering fat don Luis strutting around the *batey* as if he already owned it.

"You need not worry, my dear. You and Miguel will be well looked after. I promise you'll want for nothing."

"But what I want, don Eugenio, is to finish what Ramón, Inocente, and I started. I owe it to them, and to Miguel."

Eugenio walked to the window again, clearly exasperated, but didn't turn his back this time. "Ana, think for a moment. How do you propose to raise a child on your own, in the middle of nowhere, far from the only other family he has? Where will he go to school? What society will he be a part of? If he's injured, will it take hours for the doctor to get to him, as it did with Ramón? What if there is another insurrection? Aren't you afraid?"

She thought a moment before answering. "Yes, of course there are times . . . at the beginning, after Inocente's murder, and last year, during the uprisings I was afraid, but I knew that if I gave in to it, I couldn't live with myself."

Eugenio chuckled. "You talk like a soldier." She smiled back. "But, Ana, a plantation needs a man to handle the workforce, slave or free, a man to negotiate with vendors and customers, a man, Ana, not a young woman with a child."

"Severo Fuentes has been an excellent *mayordomo*. I'm confident that he can—"

"And how do you think it will look for you to stay here, alone, with Severo Fuentes?"

She hoped that her blush didn't show. "He's been nothing but respectful."

"I'm sure he has, when your husband was here. But I've seen how he looks at you."

She blushed deeper, angry now. "Don Eugenio! What are you implying?"

"Nothing, my dear. Forgive me. I'm merely pointing out the reality of your situation. You're young and unprotected. He's a young man, and ambitious. How long, do you think, before he figures out that, if he married *la patrona,* he could be the *patrón?*" He sat again and leaned toward her. "Leonor and I have made the ultimate sacrifice, Ana. Two sons, dead. And, no, don't defend yourself. I don't blame you. I do not blame you," he repeated, to make sure she understood. "You're young, and someday you might wish to marry again and perhaps you'll have more children. And that's your prerogative. But Miguel is the last Argoso, and I intend to raise him under my roof, with my values and, yes, even my prejudices and perhaps some of my vices. That's my prerogative, you see, as the patriarch of this family."

Ana stood as if to leave but instead sat again, her gaze on the floor, weighing what to say next. "What if you sold Los Gemelos to me?"

"My dear, I've looked at your books. You can't afford—"

"Perhaps you could extend a mortgage."

"A mortgage? Secured by?"

"Secured by Miguel."

Eugenio stammered, unable to form the words.

Ana continued speaking quickly, to make certain she said it all before she changed her mind. "If I fail here, you get the child, and I will legally renounce all rights to him."

Eugenio stared at Ana as if she'd sprouted snakes around her head. "Do I understand you correctly? Are you offering to trade Miguel for Los Gemelos?"

"I didn't say that, don Eugenio. What kind of a mother do you think I am?"

"But you said—"

"I'm suggesting an arrangement to benefit everyone. I stay here building what your sons and I began. If I fail, I'll return to Spain, but Miguel will be yours. That way, you and doña Leonor will not be the only ones to have sacrificed sons."

"I find it hard to believe what I'm hearing." Eugenio leaned against the wall, needing the support of the sturdy beams. "In any case, Leonor will never agree to leave Miguel here. She has already made that clear to me."

"Ah, yes, doña Leonor," Ana said with a rueful smile. "She, I think, would prefer a cleaner arrangement." There was no sarcasm in her voice, but she seemed to be talking to herself. "Perhaps when you misunderstood me earlier, we were closer to what would make the most sense to her. Yes, a straight barter would make more sense."

She sighed then, lowering her voice so that he would come closer, she continued, "What if I get Los Gemelos, you get Miguel? You raise him in a more . . . suitable . . . environment."

"Ana, do you mean this? You'd give up your child?"

She looked him in the eye. "Don Eugenio, I'm not giving Miguel up; I'm sending him to be raised by his loving grandparents, who are better equipped to educate and care for him than I am."

"If that were the case, why do you need to own Los Gemelos?"

"Because I'm a poor defenseless widow whose entire fortune has gone into this place, to which I have no legal claim. And it's true, I'm still young, strong, and healthy. I don't wish to live the remainder of my life as your dependent, like Elena does. But I'm willing to live as . . . as your business partner, for lack of a better word."

"There's something wrong with this."

Ana continued, as if she hadn't heard him. "Los Gemelos should remain in your name with Miguel as the only heir. And you must agree not to sell it without offering it to me first. That seems only fair, doesn't it?"

"Yes, that seems right."

"If, as you predict, I get married again, Miguel's inheritance will be protected."

"You seem to have thought this out thoroughly."

"We're having a necessary discussion about my future and Miguel's. I appreciate your help in trying to determine what's best for me and my son, but you do understand that if I don't have my own home, I'll be forced to return to my parent's house in Sevilla, and I'll take my son with me."

"Now you're threatening me."

"I'm merely discussing my options with you, sir."

"I see." Eugenio's lips twisted, as if tasting something sour. From the yard rose the sound of Miguel's laughter, and the women's light steps coming up the stairs. "Let's continue our discussion later. They're back from their picnic."

Eugenio was preoccupied the rest of the day. He circled the pond, his hands clasped behind his back, mulling over Ana's offer and how it would affect his life.

He'd already sold the farm in Caguas because after Inocente's death his wife was afraid to live in the *campo*. Divesting himself of Marítima Argoso Marín was next. With both sons dead, there was no one left to manage the shipping business—an enterprise Eugenio didn't, and didn't want to, understand. He was heartened by Luis Morales Font's offer for Hacienda los Gemelos because he couldn't imagine himself—or Leonor—ever wanting to live there. He had trouble accepting that the black men and women on the hacienda were his property even though he'd sent money to his sons for buying slaves. Like every *hacendado,* he was convinced that slaves were necessary to the operations and better suited to the work than white laborers.

Both his and Leonor's family in Spain had owned slaves who remained with their parents after abolition. In San Juan, their friends kept slaves for their households, but Eugenio had been less exposed to the conditions of agricultural workers. He was appalled by how the—his—slaves lived, how hard they worked, how every aspect of their lives was regulated and controlled by foremen, bosses, Severo, Ana. What did it take for his sons, living and working alongside them, to accept their roles as slave owners? They never wrote about that side of the experience, but if Ana had qualms, she'd stepped into the position of *patrona* as if she'd lived that way from birth. She was kind to them, yes, he could see that, but she didn't see them as human beings, Eugenio thought. They were tools.

After the turbulence of the Carlist war in Spain and the last five years in Puerto Rico, Eugenio longed for a tranquil existence alongside his beloved wife. After selling the shipping business, he planned to return to Spain, perhaps even to Villamartín, the ancestral village where he and Leonor grew up. They'd raise Miguel alongside his people with no pedigrees or dreams of glory beyond that due to queen and nation. He also planned to find a husband for Elena. She'd been in mourning with them for two years, had worn *traje de luto* for Inocente, and would continue to wear it for Ramón for another two. At twenty-one Elena should already be married and settled. She was like a daughter, he wanted to do the right thing for her, and he knew that Leonor would want her nearby. Eugenio was certain that his wife would agree to his plans. But he'd worried what to do about Ana. Technically, even though she had a mother and father, she now belonged in his household because she was the mother of the Argoso heir. Eugenio couldn't envision her at his table for the rest of his, her, or especially Leonor's life. Ana's obsession with the hacienda solved the problem of what to do with her, and how to keep his wife happy.

Before supper that evening, Eugenio related to Leonor an edited version of his conversation with Ana.

Leonor was adamant. "Let her rot here if that's what she wants, but I'm not leaving without Miguel."

"The truth is that what she's offering is not unreasonable. We already have a substantial investment, and she's willing to continue the work while we raise the child. Luis will buy Los Gemelos any time we wish to sell."

"I don't care what sort of arrangement you reach with her, Eugenio, I don't want that woman in my house."

"I've not heard you speak so unkindly of anyone in all our years together."

"I despise her. She's mad. Our sons are dead because of her, and I won't let her destroy Miguel, too. Give her whatever she wants, but let's leave here as soon as possible."

"And do you wish me to make an offer on Ciriaca?"

"I can use her and her daughter, too."

"I'll have Fuentes handle it."

"Let's go as soon as possible, Eugenio, before Ana changes her mind. That woman is a viper."

At the *finca* a few days later, Eugenio met with Severo Fuentes and asked him to keep an eye on Ana.

"She'll be communicating directly with Mr. Worthy, my lawyer," he said, "who will expect a strict accounting. I trust she'll be scrupulous in facts and figures, but I need to know if anything else is amiss. Don Luis is interested in Los Gemelos, but at the moment, I'm not ready to sell. I'm counting on you to ensure the value of the property doesn't decrease."

"Are you concerned, *señor,* that doña Ana is not capable of managing the plantation as well as don Ramón and don Inocente, may they rest in peace?"

"I'm aware that a great part of their success was due to your able management."

"You're very kind, *señor,* but—"

"You underestimate me, Fuentes. I may be a foolish old soldier but I'm not stupid."

"I'd never think you were either of those things, *señor.*"

"We understand each other, then. It's in my interest that Los Gemelos succeed, and that Ana believe she's responsible for the triumph of man over nature or whatever she thinks she's doing here."

"She's uncomfortable traveling too far from the *batey* since don Inocente's death," Severo said. "She refuses to go to Guares even for the Holy Days, but with don Ramón, may he rest in peace, also gone, she might change her mind about living here."

"Let me make myself clear, Fuentes. She's never to forget what dangers lie beyond the boundaries of Los Gemelos, and she's to have whatever she needs so that she doesn't want to leave."

"I see," Severo said.

"You'll write to me regularly and let me know how she's doing. *Las mujeres son caprichosas.*"

"*Sí, señor.*"

"I want no surprises from her, do you understand?"

"I believe I do, don Eugenio."

"I hope so," the older man said. "But she might need some coaxing. I know you won't disappoint me. . . ."

"No, Colonel, I'm your servant."

"And you can be sure that you'll be well rewarded."

"I know you to be a generous man, Colonel," Severo said with a bow that Eugenio later thought was too ceremonious and studied to have been sincere.

CONCIENCIA LA JOROBÁ

Elena had been unable to spend time alone with Ana since their arrival. It was partly her own fault: doña Leonor needed her. Since Ramón's death, Leonor had expressed only two emotions, sorrow and anger at Ana. When doña Leonor was sad, Elena listened, consoled her, prayed with her. When she was angry, Elena placed herself between the two women, interpreting for or defending one to the other.

Earlier that morning, don Eugenio had told them they were leaving in two days, and Miguel would go with them.

"And Ana?"

"She stays."

Elena couldn't believe it. She'd assumed that they would all return to Spain, and she'd dared to imagine that she and Ana would now live together.

Later, when doña Leonor and Miguel went to feed the ducks in the pond, Elena found Ana in the garden, talking to Severo Fuentes.

"*Sí, señora.* I'll accompany them as far as Guares and pick up the supplies." He touched his hat brim when he passed. "*Buenos días, señorita.*"

She barely acknowledged him. "Do you have a moment, Ana?"

"Walk with me." Ana closed her eyes and breathed deeply. "Have you ever smelled anything so sweet?"

"Lavender?"

"A particularly fragrant variety. The honeybees love it. It's not native to Puerto Rico."

"But here it grows wild?"

"Some of these herbs can be found nowhere else on the island, but

Severo has brought me the most extraordinary seeds." She walked further into the garden. "I've put in every plant here, and every one is useful. This is aloe, to treat burns and scratches." Ana picked a needlelike leaf from a shrub. "Smell this. Delicious, isn't it? Rosemary, a cooking herb, but I make a liniment to relieve aches and pains."

"So all these plants are medicinal?"

"Medicinal and, well, they heal ailments in the body but also in the spirit."

"Ana! That sounds like witchcraft." Elena crossed herself.

"I used to think that, but I soon learned that Flora and Damita and the others could teach me many things. You'd be surprised how much *nuestra gente* know."

Elena raised her eyebrows. Our people?

"Look at the rosemary," Ana continued. "Its leaves look like fingers reaching for the sky."

"One could describe it that way," Elena said.

"Its fragrance lifts your spirits, invigorates the body and mind. It makes you happy and clears negative thoughts."

"That's a lot to ask of one plant," Elena said.

"I suppose, but so far every remedy I've learned from our people has been effective. The slaves and the *campesinos* who live nearby come to me with questions that have nothing to do with aches, pain, or injuries. They ask for love potions—"

"Ana, we're Catholic. The church forbids—"

"God gave us nature's bounty to make our lives bearable." She twirled a flower under Elena's nose. "If I believe that a bath with rose and geranium petals will make a man love me, I'm not discounting the power of prayer. The truth is that such a bath will make me smell good, and others will notice. I will truly be more attractive."

"That's different from claiming that rosemary can make you happy."

"How is it different? A scent is a sensual experience that awakens other senses."

As they walked, Ana pointed to this or that herb or flower, delighting in the colors, the fragrances, the infinite shapes of leaves, the butterflies and moths skidding in erratic patterns around them.

"I can't reconcile your upbringing in Spain," Elena ventured, "with your life here."

"Yes, sometimes I have the same trouble." Ana smiled. "But remember that I spent much of my childhood on Abuelo Cubillas's farm, even if his only involvement was to look out the window and wonder whether or not it would rain." She laughed. "Other people did the work."

"You have people, too," Elena said. *"Nuestra gente."*

"Sí, they work hard. So does Severo Fuentes. We all do. Maybe it's wrong that I've come to love a place so far from where I was born, but now it's impossible for me to imagine myself anywhere else."

"But Ana, you and I—"

"I'm not leaving Hacienda los Gemelos, Elena."

"Let me stay with you, then."

Ana took Elena's hand and removed her right glove. "Look how soft your hand is, how clean and unblemished. Now look at mine." It was tanned, wrinkled; the nails were sturdy and ragged. "You don't belong here, *mi cielo,* and I don't want to belong out there." She replaced her glove, tugged the lace frills tight over Elena's wrist, and fastened the tiny pearl button. "Take care of Miguel so that doña Leonor doesn't turn him against me."

"She won't do that."

"She'll try. I haven't been a very good mother. You've noticed, and so has she. I'm not a bad person, Elena, but doña Leonor hates me. Miguel needs to know that someone loves me."

"Ana, you're tearing my heart in two—"

"And mine." She stepped back and looked at Elena as if she were about to sketch her. "This is how I will remember you, *mi amor,* in my garden, surrounded by flowers."

"We will see each other again, Ana, please say we will."

"We will, but until then, write often. Let me know how Miguel is doing. Someday Hacienda los Gemelos will be his. Don't let him forget it, or me."

The rickety coach was loaded in the Los Gemelos *batey* before dawn exactly one month from the day it arrived. Inés carried the half-asleep Miguel and nestled him among the pillows and blankets she'd arranged on the seat.

"Adiós, papito." She kissed his forehead. "God bless you."

Eugenio and Severo tugged on the ropes that tied the luggage to the roof, while Leonor and Elena counted parcels and checked that their valises didn't go under the tarp. When everything was ready, Leonor kissed the air near Ana's cheeks and climbed into the coach as if she couldn't wait to leave. Elena hugged Ana.

"I'll write, but don't worry about responding. I now see how busy you always are."

Eugenio also embraced her, then stepped back and held her shoulders. "You let me know if there's anything you need," he said, "or anything we can do for you. Will you promise?"

"Yes, don Eugenio, thank you," she said humbly. The retinue moved out of the *batey,* led by Severo.

Ana waved until the coach was out of sight before she climbed to the house. She blew out the candles on the wall sconces and opened the wooden shutters to the dawn. She could still faintly hear the creaking wheels, the horses and snorting mules that were taking the Argosos away.

As she opened the door to the back stairs, she stumbled on a parcel on the top step. In the soft light it appeared to be a small bundle of laundry inside a dirty cloth. She picked it up by the knot and almost dropped it when it moved.

"It can't be," Ana said aloud, but her hunch was confirmed when she untied the cloth and found a tightly swaddled baby inside. "Flora!" she called, and the maid ran from the kitchen. "Look! Someone left it on the steps."

"Ugly baby."

"Get some clean rags; these are filthy. Bring warm water."

Ana knelt just inside the threshold and undid the swaddling. It was a girl with a pinched and narrow face. Her legs were bowed, too short for a torso that was twisted into an unnatural curve because of the already obvious hump over her right shoulder. Scratches around her upper back, neck, and cheeks showed that whoever delivered her struggled with an umbilical cord tightly wound around her short neck.

"Is miracle she's alive," Flora said when she looked closer. "She dead by the last bell," she predicted, shaking her head. "Maybe better that way, *señora.*" Still, she rubbed the tiny hump for good luck.

"Who's her mother?" Ana asked, ignoring Flora's prognosis as she wiped the infant and changed her dirty rags for clean ones.

"No one I know. No, *señora,* no pregnant women here."

"There are several pregnant women, Flora. Nena is pregnant; so is Damita's daughter-in-law."

"Nobody ready," Flora said, "is what I mean."

Other than the cry that let Ana know she was alive, the infant was quiet and strangely composed as she was changed.

"Poor little thing," Ana said, stroking her head. "What pretty hair you have," she cooed at the infant. "Oh, look, she's vain." She grinned at Flora, who watched her intently.

"Don Severo will be angry, *señora,*" Flora said.

Ana nestled the baby in her arms. "Go find Inés; she's still nursing. This poor child probably has had nothing—"

"Is not my place, I know, *señora,* but maybe we wait for don Severo."

"Flora, I asked you to get Inés." Ana straightened to her full height, at least half a foot taller than her maid. "And burn those rags."

Flora picked up the dirty scraps and went to fetch Inés, grumbling all the way.

The baby was not African and not Caucasian, but a creamy-skinned mixture of both races. Ana imagined she must belong to one of the families eking out a living on the periphery of the hacienda. In Spain, Ana had heard about women who, unable to take care of their children, left them on the steps of churches or on the thresholds of wealthy couples better able to raise them. Sor Magdalena, a nun at the Convento de las Buenas Madres, had been abandoned in the chapel as an infant and was taken in by the sisters to be raised among them. Almost always the abandoned children were girls.

Because of her size and handicaps, Ana thought this baby would probably survive only a few hours, as Flora predicted. She found her bottle of holy water and sprinkled some drops over the infant. As she made the sign of the cross over her forehead, she discarded the traditional names of saints and virgins.

"It is not a coincidence that you were left on my door the day I traded my son away. I have that, and much more besides, to answer for, *mamacita.* So long as you live, you'll remind me, even when I try to forget, what I have done. For that reason, I name you Conciencia," she whispered. "In the name of the Father, the Son, and of the Holy Spirit." She caressed the narrow, birdlike face with its too-close-together eyes. Conciencia's face twisted into what Ana took to be a smile.

Siña Damita claimed to have no idea who would've left the child on Ana's doorstep. "I deliver most babies around here," she said. "This one not mine." She unswaddled Conciencia and examined her thoroughly. "Umbilical cord cut with teeth," she said. "Tied tight. The mother birthed before." She turned Conciencia over and traced the tiny bones of her spine. She kissed her index finger, then gently poked the tiny hump. She bent and straightened the infant's limbs and found that her joints moved freely. As she tugged on Conciencia's leg, the child let go a stream of urine into Damita's hand. "Everything work." Damita laughed. She set Conciencia down and wiped the baby's urine over her face and neck. "Born on a night with no moon," she explained. "Her piss bring luck."

Later there was a commotion in front of Inés's *bohío* because everyone wanted to touch Conciencia's hump for good luck. Afraid that so much handling would further weaken her, Ana had her returned to the *casona*. Conciencia, who slept through most of the day, opened her eyes, black and hard as onyx. She stared at Ana as if she were trying to communicate wordlessly, the way Ramón and Inocente did with each other.

"You must live," Ana said vehemently. "I'll help you." She stroked the baby's forehead. "You'll be my conscience, but also my lucky charm."

On their way back from Guares that evening, Severo's dogs raced into the woods. There, leaning under a tree as if she'd just sat to rest, was Marta, her ears, eyes, nose, and mouth humming with flies. Her skirt and apron were stiff with dried blood. It was obvious she'd bled to death after delivering a baby. The child technically belonged to Luis, as did Marta, but Severo saw no sign of the infant.

The next morning, Severo climbed the stairs of the *casona* two at a time, as if he had urgent news. "They tell me a child was left at your door, *señora*."

"Yes, a girl." Ana looked into the basket by her side, where Conciencia slept, wrapped in Miguel's old swaddling clothes.

Severo peered inside. Don Luis would have told the midwife to smother the infant after noticing her handicaps. Marta had walked through cane and orchards on a moonless night to save her baby. Ana had no idea that the child was Marta's, fathered by Ramón, who continued to see her in the *finca* with Luis's permission. In spite of his frail appearance, Ramón had enough energy to impregnate several women in the months before he died and had orphaned at least eight light-skinned mulattoes, cousins to the ones fathered by Inocente.

"I can take her away, *señora*."

"No, don't. Obviously her family doesn't want her."

"Do you mean to keep her?"

"She might not live long. I'll make her as comfortable as possible until then."

During the following week Conciencia clung to life as if her will and Ana's were one. She slept most of the time and rarely cried, not even when Inés was late to nurse. Damita prepared herbal *guarapos* to strengthen her, and showed Ana how to dip her finger into the bowl and drop the tea into the infant's mouth.

Besides her creamy skin, Conciencia's only other beautiful feature was the luxurious black hair that covered her head and formed a fine down over the rest of her twisted body. As her birth bruises healed and her features settled, one thing was certain: Conciencia would not be beautiful, and might never be able to walk, but she was determined to live.

After the first precarious week, she thrived. Everyone noticed that as Conciencia grew stronger, Los Gemelos prospered. The hens, for example, laid more eggs than before Conciencia was left at Ana's door. The sows had huge litters, every piglet healthy and promising plenty of ham. The work in the fields went smoother for those who had touched her hump, and their rows of cane germinated and grew faster.

The orchards, too, were more fruitful. Branches bent low with round, juicy lemons, oranges, and grapefruits. Mango trees blossomed and were soon studded with nipple-size fruit that grew faster than could be consumed. The humid hollow near the creek was overrun by tall palms with purple flowers that stretched into shoots that sprouted large bunches of bananas and plantains. Sweet potatoes under the ground, stately avocado trees, taro root beneath umbrella leaves—all seemed to respond to a silent command to propagate.

Several women became pregnant, some past childbearing age. As the vegetation, animals, and people multiplied, Conciencia flourished under Ana's care, the newfound affection of Flora and Inés, and the respect her lucky hump brought from everyone else.

Despite Ana's earliest fears, Conciencia did learn to crawl and walk, even as her hump became more pronounced. Soon everyone called her Conciencia la Jorobá, and for the rest of her life no one ever asked her last name.

WHAT TO DO ABOUT THE *CAMPESINOS*

———◆———

A few weeks after the Argosos left, Ana received the terms she'd agreed to in order to stay at the hacienda. Eugenio was more generous than she'd expected. As *la patrona,* she'd receive the manager's salary of one thousand pesos a year. In addition, he provided for an allowance of five hundred pesos per annum for her personal expenses. No loans or large purchases of land or inventory could be effected without prior arrangement. Financial dealings were to go through Mr. Vicente Worthy, Eugenio's agent in San Juan.

Ana studied the ledgers for the last four harvests. Yields at Hacienda los Gemelos had increased at least 15 percent per annum, but sugar production had cost more than the income generated each year. Mr. Worthy's reports indicated that sugar prices around the world had fallen over the 1840s as India, with a huge, inexpensive labor force, had become an important producer. In Europe, beets—better suited to the European soil and climate—were less expensive to process into sugar and to transport within the continent. Spanish government regulations, duties, taxes, and customs further undercut profits for Puerto Rican planters like her.

Ana couldn't, however, stop cultivation. Cane required twelve to eighteen months to mature, and by the time it was ready for harvest, prices might be higher. In the meantime, she needed more cattle, equipment, and tools for clearing and tilling new fields. The scarcity of workers, however, was the biggest challenge facing her.

She was aware that forces beyond the borders of Los Gemelos were changing the way *hacendados* operated. A growing Creole professional and liberal elite in Puerto Rico was pressuring for greater autonomy from Spain and the abolition of slavery, both opposed by sugar *hacendados* and conservative agriculturalists. Many of those were refugees who'd lost much during the wars for independence in South America and now depended on a stable, controllable labor force. On the other side of the Atlantic, the Peninsular authorities were also concerned about the *campesinos*—a growing, self-reliant, racially mixed, unsettled, underemployed population who managed to evade taxes, customs, and fees through the barter system and contraband.

Governor de la Pezuela, who'd repealed the Bando Negro in 1848, instituted a new law, ostensibly to eradicate vagrancy in Puerto Rico, but whose object was to create a labor source for the sugar industry and to control the movement of *campesinos.* The Reglamento de Jornaleros obliged every *hombre libre,* any white or black who'd never been a slave, and every *liberto,* or freed slave, to prove that they were gainfully employed. To monitor whether they complied, the Régimen de la Libreta was designed. Every free person aged sixteen to sixty must carry a workbook—*la libreta*—specifying when and where they worked. If they couldn't prove they had a job, or that they were exempt from *la libreta* because they owned and cultivated at least four *cuerdas* of land, they could be reported to the authorities, fined, jailed, and/or forced to labor in the nearest plantations. If not needed there, they could be assigned to the government's public works, sometimes far from their hometowns.

But even with these measures, the scarcity of workers was a constant headache for *hacendados* like Ana. *Jíbaros,* unwilling to work in sugar, fled to coffee estates in the mountains. Without enough workers, the slaves were forced to toil beyond exhaustion.

Hacendados also struggled with the need for credit to keep their haciendas viable. Ana was in a better position than others. She had her grandfather's legacy, kept from Ramón and, except for the payments to don Luis, unspent.

She wrote to her parents to notify them that she was now a widow, and that her father-in-law had made generous provision for her and for Miguel. She felt no need to give them more details and was certain they wanted none. Her mother's infrequent letters were filled with the stock phrases of ladies' correspondence and novelistic sentiments that Ana abhorred. And her father sent his regards through Jesusa's messages. Ana was alone in the world and knew it. She took pride in never having asked for anything from her father, mother, or anyone else. The challenges ahead energized her. She rose with the sun, just as ever, tied up her long, black hair, and was confident that no man could claim to be smarter, braver, or more hardworking than she was. She was, she was sure, on the brink of great things.

Two months before the 1850 harvest, Ana projected that Hacienda los Gemelos would show another loss. In preparation for the *zafra,* she met with Severo in early December 1849.

"If all our workers stay healthy," she said, "we will be short twenty *macheteros* for the three hundred *cuerdas* ready to be harvested, *¿no es así?*"

"*Sí, señora,* that's my estimate, too."

"Do you think we can find twenty more men before the *zafra?*"

"Difficult," he said, "not impossible. I'll do my best."

"It might be better to pay them by the job, rather than by the day. They won't get paid until they finish."

Severo thought a moment. "Well, yes, I suppose that makes sense."

"And they can bring as many others to help them as they want."

"It's a good idea. The more they cut, the more they earn."

"We'll offer them five cents more than the going rate, four pesos per *cuerda.*"

"*Sí.* And another peso for every three full cartloads?"

"Minus the cost of their meals."

"That's right."

"And the facilities?"

"The *trapiche,* as you know, is in bad shape. A steam engine would be more efficient to operate the grinders, and press more liquid than we're able with wind and animal power."

"You've suggested this for years," Ana said. Severo nodded. "It's probably too late to get the machinery here before the *zafra,* but please look into what it will cost."

"I will, but this might interest you, *señora.* Ingenio Diana, on our eastern boundary, might be for sale."

"Please, Severo, I don't need more land. What I need is a higher yield with what we have. Most of our lands aren't cultivated for lack of workers."

"Yes, I know, *señora,* but the Diana has a steam engine. It's not the latest model, but far more efficient than our configuration. Fewer but more-skilled workers running the machinery means I can redirect others to the fields."

"I haven't seen smoke coming from that chimney."

"Don Rodrigo bought much land from the owners of the Diana," Severo explained. "They kept the fields closest to their *ingenio,* about thirty *cuerdas,* probably hoping they'd recover the land someday. But after the owner died, his sons moved away. If the land were planted as cane, a *cuerda* would fetch about three hundred pesos each, but most of it has reverted to brush. You can probably get it for about fifty to seventy-five pesos per *cuerda.* It should also be taxed at a lower rate."

"How far is the *ingenio* from our fields?"

"Manageable," Severo said. "The hacienda borders San Bernabé to the south, along the road to Guares."

"Don Luis isn't interested?"

"He will be, if he hears about it."

"And you have no interest?"

"I prefer lands along the littoral."

"I see. What will it take to have the *ingenio* operational?"

"Hard to tell. It has wooden pressers, and there are better ones now, made from iron. An engineer should evaluate it, fix whatever is broken."

"So it won't be ready for our harvest?"

"I can't say until it's checked."

"But maybe?"

"I'll do my best, *señora.*"

Severo kept his meetings with Ana brief because he wanted her so much that he sometimes avoided the *casona,* afraid he'd forget himself and take her right there on the porch, where they conducted their business because it was improper for him to be inside where there was no husband.

Dressed in mourning black, Ana stood out against the lush greenery and colorful flowers that surrounded her as she worked in the gardens or walked to and from the coops and dovecotes, clutching two baskets, a small one for the eggs she collected, a larger one with the humpbacked infant inside. As the child grew, Ana carried Conciencia in a sling that Flora showed her how to wear like the ones African women used to carry their children. Ana hadn't been that maternal with her son, and ignored the hacienda children until they were old enough to work. Severo wondered why she'd attached herself so thoroughly to this peculiar child and why she didn't question where she came from. Would she treat her differently if she knew that Conciencia was Ramón's daughter?

When he was alive, the slaves called Ramón El Caminante, because he wandered the paths at night, dressed in ghostly white, with no regard for weather, no concern for fences, no fear of the creatures of the night. He still walked in death, they claimed, and terror of encountering him along the paths and byways of the land was a powerful deterrent. They dreaded being caught outdoors after dark, and the overseers had no trouble accounting for every man, woman, and child before locking them inside the barracks and *bohíos* after the last bell. Severo encouraged their fear by spreading the rumor that El Caminante killed Marta when she tried to run away.

He sensed that Ana, too, was afraid, but not of the supernatural; she feared what lay beyond Los Gemelos. She'd crossed an ocean, sailed around an island, ridden for hours through forest and cane to come here, but she now confined her activities to a circle no larger than a couple of kilometers in any direction, its center firmly set on the *casona*. Severo wanted to expand her world, to give her a bird's-eye view of Los Gemelos and its perimeter, bounded on the north by the gentle mounds of the Cordillera Central and on the south by the placid waters of the Caribbean Sea.

Soon after Inocente's murder, he'd begun construction of the house on the hill, built from blocks made on-site from a mixture of cement, lime, and the orange clay harvested on the riverbank. The thick walls would keep it cool against the harsh sun, the rooms refreshed by the breezes coming from the ocean or dipping toward the valley from the mountains. Severo imagined the house as an aerie for Ana, whom he compared to a *pitirre,* the solemn gray kingbird common in Puerto Rico. There was a saying among Puerto Ricans—"*cada guaraguao tiene su pitirre*"—that alluded to how the much smaller *pitirre* was unafraid of, and sometimes even attacked, the larger, aggressive *guaraguao,* the red-tailed hawk. Like the *pitirre,* Ana was patient and dared to challenge authority, even though she was small in stature and a woman. Severo didn't know how she convinced don Eugenio not to sell Los Gemelos, but he admired that she stood up to him and led him to believe that he was in control of her actions.

As soon as don Eugenio left, Ana set up Miguel's old room as her study. She spent mornings making notes, entering numbers into ledgers, and writing letters, the humpbacked child at her feet. She sent a monthly report to Mr. Worthy, don Eugenio's *norteamericano* representing matters concerning Los Gemelos.

Following Ramón's death, Severo worried that what he'd worked so hard to build would crash down with the sweep of a pen across a document. Luis had his eye on Los Gemelos from the beginning, and had encouraged Ramón's and Inocente's vices to accelerate their dissolution. However, he hadn't counted on Ana's attachment to the plantation. He hadn't known, or understood, that it was Ana who brought Ramón and Inocente here, not the other way around.

When he told Ana about Ingenio Diana, Severo had been considering it for her for some time. The owners hired him to keep an eye on their property, so he was the first to learn that they might sell. Severo would have bought it, but he wanted to know whether Ana had any resources other than what don Eugenio provided. He now understood that she wasn't completely at her father-in-law's mercy. She was crafty and smarter than don Eugenio and his two sons combined.

While Ana showed no desire to go anywhere, Severo would do whatever it took to keep her at Hacienda los Gemelos, not only because don Eugenio had charged him to do so but also because he needed her near. In Spain, he couldn't have aspired to marry a lady with her education, pedigree, and money. Here she was within reach.

He negotiated the purchase of Ingenio Diana for a fair price. It helped that the owners lived in Spain. A flurry of correspondence between Ana and her father resulted in a smooth financial transaction, while Severo made sure that the *ingenio*, abandoned for six years, was ready to press cane on February 2, 1850, Día de la Candelaria—Candlemas.

A POET AND HIS MUSE—SAN JUAN

From the first days of their arrival in San Juan in September 1844, Eugenio had trouble getting used to the within-doors world of business management. He disliked paperwork, regular hours, and the collaborative nature of running a business after a lifetime in the unchallenged command of men and beasts on terra firma. He couldn't imagine ever being the capable manager that his brother Rodrigo had been, and with his sons dead, there was no one else to take over the business.

"I'm not good at this," he despaired to his wife. "You were right all along. Let's sell Marítima Argoso Marín and go back to Spain. Why should we stay and—"

"My sons are buried here," she reminded him.

"But it would be better to raise Miguel near our family, in our village."

"I won't leave our sons alone on this island," she replied with such sadness that Eugenio didn't have the heart to argue further. He requested an appointment with Vicente Worthy, the sober, Boston-born lawyer/banker whom Rodrigo trusted and upon whom Eugenio had come to depend.

Newly minted from Harvard Law School, Vincent Worthy was working for Richardson, Bodwell, Cabot, a prestigious firm in Boston, when he met María del Carmen y la Providencia Paniagua Stevens, nicknamed Provi. She was visiting her aunt Sally and would be in Boston only six weeks—or as she so charmingly pronounced it "seeks wicks." Everything Provi said and did was charming to the love-struck young man. When he shook her hand as they were introduced, her warm fingers melted twenty-five Boston winters from his heart. Her father agreed to their marriage, but only if the couple lived in Puerto Rico. The Paniaguas and Stevenses were well-respected merchants and businessmen on the island. They expected their adult children, who'd inherit their fortunes, to live near their money.

Vincent married the delightful Provi and established his practice in San Juan. He soon learned that he had to overcome the mistrust of the families who owned most of the businesses in the city. Spain and its royalists were uneasy about the United States' expansionist strategies. The War of 1812 had proven that the *estadounidenses* were determined to seize as much territory as possible, obliterating the native populations as they trekked toward the Pacific. The phrase "Manifest Destiny"—coined in 1845—defended the relentless movement west as inevitable, obvious, and ordained by God. While the government appeared to be focused toward the west, the elites of the Greater Antilles, particularly Cubans, knew the archipelago to the east was in the peripheral vision of the United States. *Estadounidenses* already owned major stakes in vast Cuban sugar and tobacco plantations, and were investing in the burgeoning Puerto Rican sugar and coffee industries.

As soon as he arrived, Vincent noticed that most industrial heavy machinery in Puerto Rico and the islands was imported from Britain, including grinders and steam engines for sugar processing. The engineers who ran and maintained them, mostly Scots, had become, over time, *hacendados* themselves and continued to trade with Great Britain. Shrewd local businessmen, even those distrustful of the *estadounidenses'* motives, however, began to look toward markets in the United States and to the technological advances coming from its foundries and factories. Vincent saw an opportunity as an intermediary.

Upon Provi's suggestion, he Hispanicized his first name to make himself less foreign. With dogged diligence, he learned Spanish quickly, so by the time his father-in-law introduced him to don Rodrigo and his varied enterprises under the aegis of Marítima Argoso Marín, Vicente could speak to the canny businessman in his own language. His discretion, acumen, and commitment to his clients earned Vicente the esteem of even the most skeptical anti-*yanqui*. In thirteen years he'd become one of San Juan's most influential citizens.

Eugenio walked to Mr. Worthy's offices in a new building over-looking San Juan harbor. Rain had slicked the cobblestones and cleansed the narrow sidewalks, but had also washed the open sewers in the streets closer to the docks down to the sea. Mr. Worthy had offered to come to the Argoso house, but Eugenio preferred to meet him in his offices. He admired the diligence of the clerks toiling on high stools pulled up to long-legged tables in the center of the main room, and the serenity inside Mr. Worthy's office overlooking the ships, docks, and warehouses that made San Juan—at least to all appearances—as wealthy and busy as any major port city in Europe.

One of the things Eugenio most liked about Mr. Worthy was his ability to understand, in few words, what his clients were asking from him even if they didn't know exactly themselves. After he ex-plained his doubts about his abilities and desires as a businessman, Mr. Worthy went through the folios in a cabinet against the wall. Eugenio had the feeling that Mr. Worthy had read these documents many times, but he scanned the ones Eugenio was least likely to study, the ones with many figures on them, double lines at the bot-toms of pages, black ink, red ink, abbreviations, symbols, seals, and customs stamps.

After showing him some of the entries on the parchments, Mr. Worthy recommended that Eugenio liquidate Marítima Argoso Marín's seagoing assets and spend the income on real estate and on local businesses whose owners and directors had a good history of making money for their investors.

"You might also consider," Mr. Worthy said, "that it's time to sell Hacienda los Gemelos. Sugar prices have dropped steadily over the past six years, and I don't see them going up in the near future. The land, however, is valuable, and you could get a good return."

"No changes to Hacienda los Gemelos," Eugenio said.

"I see."

"I promised to let my daughter-in-law manage it, and intend to keep my word, unless there's something amiss. . . ."

"No, sir. In spite of the constant losses, she's punctilious about her figures."

"Yes, I'm sure she is."

"As your adviser in these matters, however, please forgive me, Colonel, I must be clear—"

"It's in my interest that she live there. I'm willing to absorb small losses so long as the property continues to improve. Is that clear enough?"

"Of course," Mr. Worthy said. "And I'll consult with you if anything is alarming."

"That's what I expect."

"Very well. Now that we have that settled, Colonel, there are other possibilities to make money," Mr. Worthy continued, "that don't require your everyday attention."

"Go on."

By Miguel's sixth birthday in September 1851, Eugenio had divested the movable parts of the shipping business—the vessels, sails, machinery, crates, barrels, ropes, and he knew not what else—but held on to the docks, warehouses, and office buildings on the waterfront, rented at a premium. Mr. Worthy advised him on investments that he monitored in Puerto Rico and via the New York Stock & Exchange Board. He also sent an auditor to Los Gemelos every year to review the books and to make sure that everything there was in order.

Now that he no longer sat in an office listening to the droning of bookkeepers, managers, supervisors, and expediters, Eugenio became what his wife insisted a man of his age and race should be—a gentleman of means and leisure. Had he retired to Villamartín, he'd be just another old soldier living out his last years in ease and comfort, his exploits forgotten by everyone but his family. In San Juan, however, he was admired for his wealth, life's work, and accomplishments. Everywhere he went, soldiers saluted, civilian men bowed, and ladies curtsied.

He owned shares of fighting cocks and racehorses. He enjoyed their exploits without having to do any of the work of raising or training them, or of keeping them in fighting and racing health. He joined La Asociación de Caballeros Españoles, a club devoted to cards, fine wines, and aromatic cigars. Like his sons, he was a good dancer, and took pleasure in leading Leonor around the polished dance floors in private homes and ballrooms, certain that even young *señoritas* admired his form.

Because they spent most evenings out, Miguel ate his supper with Elena, who didn't like leaving him alone even if it meant missing an elegant dinner or a performance at the theater. It was Elena who listened to his prayers, who reminded him to include Queen Isabel II, Ana, Severo, the unfortunate slaves, the lepers, orphans, and everyone on the prayer list at the Catedral de San Juan Bautista. It was Elena who walked him to catechism classes, and who made sure he observed the holy days. And it was she who released Eugenio from his biggest preoccupation.

"Please don't worry about me," she said. "I don't plan to marry while Miguel is so young."

It didn't take Miguel long to get used to life in San Juan. He was young enough to revel in the love and attention of his grandparents and Elena. They were strict but kind, especially Abuelo, whose whiskers bristled when he was angry, but who seldom raised his voice and didn't spank him. Abuela took advantage of every opportunity to hug and kiss Miguel, to squeeze his hand or press his shoulder. He soon learned that Abuela's need to touch was not confined to him.

When she was not knitting, embroidering, or sewing, she massaged Abuelo's shoulders, or moved knickknacks around, or straightened Miguel's vest, or tightened the sash that held Siña Ciriaca's apron around her waist. Abuela wore curls that bounced around her face with every move and required constant tugging and pinning into place. Her black garments had ruffles, lace, and ribbons that she fussed with if there was nothing else nearby to occupy her fingers.

Miguel thought Abuela's hands were nervous because they were so quiet when she played the harp. During the period of mourning, the instrument, covered with a linen cloth, took up a corner of the parlor for months before he knew what it was. It was like a huge headless ghost, and he avoided looking in its direction. Evenings after supper Abuela uncovered it, leaned her right shoulder into it, and prepared to make music. When she played, her whole body grew still, her eyes seemed to be looking at something far away, and her hands rested gently on the strings before she began plucking, as if she had to subdue the strings before she could strum them.

In Los Gemelos the only instruments Miguel had ever heard were the sticks José clicked to keep rhythm, or the dried gourds that

Samuel scratched with a wire to make a raspy sound, or the mara-
cas and rattlers that Inés and Flora shook, or the drums that Jacobo
and Benicio fashioned from the hides of goats and cattle, then beat
with their hands. Those instruments sounded very different from
Abuela's harp. She stroked its long strings gently or plucked them
with her fingertips, eliciting a sweet sound. At Hacienda los Gemelos, José, Inés, Jacobo, and Benicio rubbed, scratched, or banged
their instruments, and the sounds they produced made Miguel's
heart race. Abuela's playing was soothing and brought to mind images of butterflies and wispy clouds. The music in Los Gemelos was
fast, and when Flora and the other women sang, their voices rose up
and down in throaty wails that gave Miguel goose bumps.

When they made music, everything around the barracks came to
vibrant, unforgiving life. The women laughed and clapped, the men
stomped their feet, and their bodies swayed, then jerked into dances
that, even when the occasion was a solemn one, became a celebration
of movement and sound. But when Abuela played, the world slowed
and quieted as she rippled the strings. Abuelo and Elena's faces, like
Abuela's, softened, and if Miguel moved or fidgeted, Abuelo scowled
and Elena waggled her fingers to let him know to sit still. When
Abuela played, Miguel wished that she'd bang on the strings. He
wished that Elena and Abuelo would clap their hands, and that Siña
Ciriaca and Nana Bombón would come from the kitchen thumping
their pots with wooden spoons and that he could swirl and stamp his
feet in the middle of the room the way he used to do in the *batey,* the
drums beating through him into the night.

One Sunday after Mass, Elena walked Miguel up the hill to the for-
tified wall surrounding San Juan so that he could look at the sea.
Soldiers tipped their plumed hats and bowed as Miguel and Elena
passed. "Friends of don Eugenio's," she explained when Miguel
looked at her inquiringly. He could tell that the soldiers admired
how pretty she was in her brimmed hat and lace gloves and black
dress with a satin black sash at her waist, but she paid no attention
to them.

When they turned a corner, a gust slapped their faces, as if the
houses kept the wind on the other side of the city. They crested the

hill and Miguel found himself before an enormous expanse of blue-green water stung with whitecaps. The sun reflected off the waves, making him squint. He brought his hand to his brow as if he were saluting, and turned his back to the sea. When his eyes stopped tearing, he saw misty mountains. He pivoted from the mountains to the sea, from the gentle green curves of the land to the endless flat ocean as if he needed to believe in one before he could apprehend the existence of the other.

"Spain is over there." Elena pointed to the horizon, as if she expected something to come from that direction. She looked sad, and when she noticed that he could tell, she turned him slowly toward the horseshoe harbor and brightened her tone. "We came on a ship like that one." A tall-masted schooner floated toward port, its square sails puffed like huge pillows.

"Spain is far away," Miguel said, but Elena knew this was a question.

"It took us a month to get here."

"Nana Inés says that there are pirates in the ocean."

Elena raised her eyebrows. "There used to be pirates in these waters, but not anymore."

"Mamá said that there were horses on her ship."

"Ay, your *mamá* was so funny!"

"What did she do?"

Elena sounded as if she wanted to laugh but shouldn't do so in public. "She and your *papá* were on the same ship with horses for the soldiers. She teased him that she'd ride one of the horses over the waves like Perseus rode Pegasus."

"Who is Per . . . ?"

"Perseus was a hero in ancient stories and Pegasus was a horse with wings."

Miguel looked at the harbor studded with tall masts like giant pins stuck into the shimmering water. He tried to imagine his mother upon a winged horse skimming over the ships and the smaller boats bobbing in the sun.

"What else did Mamá do?"

Elena's V-shaped lips narrowed and smiled, even though her eyes were serious. "You miss her, don't you?"

He lowered his head and breathed hard to keep from crying. He missed Nana Inés, and how she rubbed his back to help him sleep.

He missed playing with Efraín and Indio, and the high towers they built from the blocks José made for them. He missed Nana Flora's laughter, her songs to the trees, and her stories about where she lived when she was a girl in the forest. He missed José's workshop, the smell of wood, the sawdust on the ground, the way shavings curled when José planed a board. He missed his father. Mamá told him that Papá was in heaven, and Miguel knew that meant he'd never see him again. He missed Papá's long fingers through his hair, the way he held his hand when they walked, his tight embraces. He missed his soft voice and tender eyes. But in San Juan, every time his father's name came up, Abuela's eyes filled with tears and Abuelo cleared his throat.

"We can talk about your *mamá* anytime you like," Elena continued. "I've known her since we were girls."

Miguel furrowed his brow. It was hard to imagine either Mamá or Elena as anything but grown women.

"Did you know my *papá,* too? When he was a boy I mean."

"Yes, of course. Doña Leonor is my *madre de crianza.* I grew up with your *papá* and your uncle. They were a little older. Your *mamá* and *papá* met at my birthday party." She stopped, and her eyes again looked toward Spain. She moved her head side to side as if she both liked and didn't like the thought. "Goodness, listen to the church bells. It's fifteen minutes to twelve. Let's go back."

They hurried through the narrow streets, avoiding people on foot, soldiers on horses, wagons pulled by oxen or donkeys, vendors carrying baskets or sacks. "*¡Carbonero! ¡Carbonero aquí!*" called the coal seller. "*¡Tengo yuca y malanga!*" called the vegetable man; "*¡Tengo ñame y yautía!*" The kindling man carried a tall stack on his head, and his reedy voice soared over the whinnying horses: "*¡Leña para la doña!*"

As they walked, Miguel felt the difference between the fresh wind whirling around the seawall and the air down the hill. He could smell the lower city, the stench of animal droppings, the open sewers, smoke, meat grilling, sweat.

"When I have a house, I want it to look to the sea."

"It would be lovely," Elena said, "but sad."

"Why?"

"Because you'd always look toward where you came from."

"But I didn't come from the sea like you did."

"You're right, *mi amor*. I'm being silly. We turn here."

"Will you tell me stories about the horse with wings?"

"Yes, of course. Tonight I'll read you the story of Perseus and Pegasus."

That night she sat on the rocker by his bed and read to him from a thick book of stories about heroes and magical creatures. She stopped at the section where Perseus cuts off the Gorgon's head and Pegasus rises from her blood. "This might give you nightmares."

"It won't. I watched Lucho slaughter pigs and goats. It doesn't scare me."

She seemed surprised but continued the marvelous tale to the end. When he had no questions, she listened to his prayers, tucked him in, kissed his forehead, and left the room.

He felt heavy and at the same time light, as if he were floating over the streets of San Juan. The air was clean, the sky bright blue and clear. Below, El Morro fortress with its parapets and cannons faced the vast ocean. He gamboled in the wind, sometimes racing toward the soft green mountains, sometimes dipping to tease a ship with sails like pillows. He dreamed he was Perseus, riding upon Pegasus, battling monsters, saving princesses chained to rocks battered by the sea. But when he woke up he was just a little boy who'd spent the night chasing a dream.

On a bright, cool morning a month before his sixth birthday, Bombón and Elena walked Miguel to don Simón Fernández Leal's school. Bombón waited outside while Elena brought Miguel inside.

"Ah, here's young Argoso," don Simón said. *"Buenos días, señorita Elena."* They were the first to arrive. "You sit here," the teacher said, leading Miguel to a desk in front. "That way I can keep an eye on you."

It was supposed to be a joke, Miguel thought, because Elena smiled and blushed. Just then chimes struck the hour.

Don Simón grabbed a large bell from his desk. "Thank you for bringing him to my school." He bowed to Elena, which elicited more blushes on their faces.

"Don Eugenio wouldn't think of sending him anywhere else," she said. She stopped before Miguel's desk and took his face in her fingers. "I'll come later to take you home." She kissed him and floated from the room. Bombón waved from the street as she followed Elena. Knowing they'd return made him feel better about being alone while don Simón stepped to the door to ring the bell.

The classroom was once the living room of a private home. Two floor-to-ceiling shutters opened to the street, the lower half barred in ornate wrought iron. Double doors led from the street into a hall leading to a gallery around a courtyard lush with potted plants. Several birdcages dangled from the branches of a ficus tree in the middle of the courtyard, the canaries' song drowning out some of the sounds coming from the street, chief among them children's laughter.

The scholars trampled in, some boys a little younger, a few older, but all dressed in crisp cottons, their hair neat, the backs of their necks and ears and their fingernails, like Miguel's, scrubbed. The older boys took desks in the rear while the younger ones scattered in what looked to Miguel like a predetermined order, which he later learned was by age. They joked, teased, and playfully punched one another as if they were the best of friends. Three of them were brothers, and two of the older boys were cousins. They looked at him curiously.

"I'm Luis José Castañeda Urbina," the boy who sat next to him said importantly. "And you?"

"Ramón Miguel Inocente Argoso Larragoity Mendoza Cubillas," he said, nearly running out of breath by the time he reached the final *s*.

"*¡Mi madre!*" Luis José said. "I don't want to be you when *el profesor* teaches us to write our names."

There was a tap on his shoulder. Miguel turned around to a pair of hazel eyes, luxurious lashes, and shaggy brows that seemed to belong to a different face from the one they were a part of, whose lower half showed a delicate nose and finely shaped lips.

"Don Simón is in love with your nana, but they can't get married because he's poor."

"But Siña Ciriaca is so old!" Miguel argued.

"Not her." Luis José laughed. "Señorita Elena!"

"She's not my nana," he protested, but before he could continue, don Simón walked in with the last straggler and rapped his knuckles on the desk.

"Buenos días, jóvenes." Before him was a class of fifteen mostly well-behaved boys sent to him for their elementary education. He would have each for six years until they graduated to the Catholic boys' academy or were sent to finish their education in Europe. "It's good to have you back." He nodded to the familiar faces. "Welcome," he said to Miguel, the only new student. "Andrés," he said to the bushy eyebrows, "please lead us in the Lord's prayer."

Everyone stood. Miguel watched don Simón. He was so thin that his clothes moved on their own. His hair was the color of a dry palm frond, and large, sad, light brown eyes bulged from under curved brows. The end of his long nose dipped over a thick mustache that curled up at the ends, separated from a golden, short beard that covered his chin. His voice was deep and silvery, and he didn't have to raise it for it to carry to the back of the room.

Miguel wondered if don Simón was handsome, and if it was true that he was in love with Elena. The way they blushed and smiled convinced him that Andrés was probably right. Still, Miguel couldn't understand why being poor should keep them from marrying. Many people were poor. Even the slaves, who didn't have much, married one another.

He remembered when Coral married Poldo, Siña Damita's son. Coral wore a blue turban and decorated it with *flamboyán* blossoms. Poldo wore a white shirt over his washed and pressed work pants. He walked to the women's *cuartel* and sang to her while Coral stood on the threshold surrounded by the other women, smiling and poking each other with their elbows. Poldo and Coral walked hand in hand to the *rancho,* with the others behind them clapping, singing, and dancing. The celebration lasted until the bell rang for everyone to go to sleep. Surely, thought Miguel, if slaves could get married and have a party afterward, Elena and don Simón should be able to do the same.

Simón taught reading, writing, and arithmetic in what was once the parlor of his home, but rudimentary science took place in the courtyard, with its potted shrubs and flowering plants. Presiding over the science lessons was a bad-tempered parrot who terrorized the chirping birds (and the scholars) with human-sounding screeches.

Along one wall, jars held the preserved remains of a piglet, a couple of frogs, three snakes, and a monkey, which were the source of curious dread for the boys. At least a couple of times a day, Kiki, his dog, escaped from the upper floor to visit his master and to be petted by the boys' eager hands.

The Fernández Leales were a family of means when they first arrived in Puerto Rico, but their fortune was swiftly lost by the dissolute habits of its patriarch, murdered over a gaming table. Upon his father's death, Simón abandoned his medical studies in Madrid and turned his home into a school to support himself and his ailing mother.

He was pleased to have Miguel as his student because it gave him an opportunity to see Elena every day, at least until the boy was allowed to walk to and from school by himself. Being near her was one of the few pleasures in his lonely and unhappy life. Besides his pupils and his mother, his society consisted of other young men of high minds who congregated in the back room of don Benito's drugstore for hours of political discussions. Night after night they argued and wrote broadsheets calling for the emancipation of slaves and greater autonomy for Puerto Rico that they read to one another because it was illegal to post them for public viewing. The struggles for independence by Haiti from France, Santo Domingo from Spain, and, in 1844, Santo Domingo from Haiti to create the Dominican Republic had made Puerto Rican liberals determined to free Puerto Rico's slaves without the bloodshed and civil war that had devastated Hispaniola and forced thousands of people to flee with their assets.

When he first appeared at the druggist's, Simón worried that the discussions were seditious, the rumblings of island-born men who, like him, had nothing but their intellect to make them feel superior to the *españoles* who ruled over them. He soon learned there were people at the highest levels of society who shared the same views, even if the official position was more conservative.

His poverty, somewhat relieved during the school year by the modest dues he charged, made it impossible for Simón to frequent the salons modeled on the ones he'd haunted in Madrid. Elena's refinement, her serenity, her fair complexion and melodious voice were what he'd sought in the woman he would have married had his father not squandered his inheritance.

The first time he saw her, she was walking across the plaza with doña Leonor. On that day, she wore a yellow dress and a straw bonnet that shaded her face. A green ribbon banded the crown, with a length that dangled behind her, playing in the breeze. When he passed the two ladies, he saw her face, the serious eyes, and the V-shaped lips that seemed to smile at him, although he knew that was impossible. They hadn't formally met and wouldn't be introduced for another year, by don Eugenio, when the whole family was in mourning. He saw her subsequently at church, at holy day festivities, or in the audience when the military orchestra performed in the plaza.

Elena was his muse, the first person he thought about upon waking, the last face he envisioned before sleep. Knowing that he'd see her again gave him something to look forward to every day.

Some nights the discussions in don Benito's drugstore didn't offer anything new, or he didn't have the few coins it took to pay for the homemade *aguardiente* the druggist dispensed. Simón walked the city then, from the slippery alleys around the docks where sailors and prostitutes drank and dickered, to the fragrant park around the governor's mansion, to the iron gates of Fort San Cristóbal, to the seawall beaten by relentless waves. Regardless of where his peregrinations took him, they always ended in front of Colonel Eugenio Argoso Marín's house with its tiled threshold and massive double doors. Upstairs and to the right of that door were Elena's window and the tremulous light of her candle bleeding through the seams of drawn curtains.

Many nights, while he waited in the shadows for her to blow out her candle, he heard don Eugenio and doña Leonor returning from some amusement whose delights were evoked by the rustle of her dress or by the clicking of his heels on the cobblestones. Simón backed into a doorway and watched them enter their home, Eugenio's hand on her elbow as the fringe of her shawl hushed the night. They'd been married so long that they moved as one, and Simón envied their closeness, the familiar way she turned as he helped her up the steps.

The streets of San Juan seemed more dismal on the way home, his loneliness greater. He entered the silent house and tiptoed past his mother's door, which she left ajar so that she could hear him come in. Sleep always overcame her. Her snores and dreamed conversations punctuated his light step as he walked down the hall to his own room, where he composed love poems to Elena.

Every night, after Miguel said his prayers, Elena read to him from the book of heroes and monsters. "It's poetry," she said, "written a long time ago."

"I like it better than the poems don Simón reads to us." Miguel made a face.

"What kind of poems?"

"About ladies and birds and flowers."

"Don Simón likes the romantic poets," she said, coloring.

Miguel stared at her. When she looked at him, he averted his gaze. "Is something bothering you?"

"No," he said, but after a moment, he worked up his courage. "Yes."

"What is it, *mi amor*?"

"If Abuelo gave don Simón some money, would he marry you?"

"Miguel, what kind of question is that?"

"The boys in school say that don Simón is in love with you, but that he can't marry you because he's poor. But if Abuelo gave him some money . . ."

She didn't know what to say. No beautiful woman was ever completely ignorant of her beauty or of a man's affection. If she denied that Simón loved her, she'd be lying. She wasn't above flirting with him, but she wasn't in love with him.

It touched her that Miguel knew that a young woman ought to be married. On the other hand, she had to put a stop to gossip.

"Miguel, *querido*," she said. "These matters are inappropriate for boys to discuss in the street or the school yard. It's disrespectful to don Simón, to me, and to you, too. They're private, adult concerns. Don't trouble yourself with them. Promise me you will not discuss this with anyone else."

"I promise," he said.

She pushed his hair back, tucked the sheets around his shoulders. "You can talk to me about anything, Miguel, you know that."

"*Sí.*"

"But sometimes I will not be able to explain everything you ask." She smiled as if guarding a secret. "As you grow up you'll begin to see things differently."

He nodded. As usual before she left the room, Elena kissed his forehead and snuffed out the candle on his bed table. He was left in the dark, wishing he were already a man and could answer his own questions.

Siña Ciriaca unbuttoned Elena's black dress. Beneath it, her undergarments were dyed black as well. Siña Ciriaca helped her step out of her three petticoats, then unfastened and helped her remove the corset until Elena wore only her chemise, stockings, and indoor slippers. She stepped behind the screen to change into her nightclothes. Her white nightgown and robe were cooler than her daywear, but even these were trimmed with black ribbons along the neckline and wrists.

Siña Ciriaca made sure that there was enough water in the pitcher and a glass by the bedside, and that there were extra candles for the sconces because she knew that Elena often stayed up into the early hours. *"Buenas noches, senorita,"* she said, closing the door.

Elena unfastened her hair, which was twisted and confined all day in tortoiseshell pins capped with a small ebony comb. She bent over and brushed her chestnut waves back to front, then side to side, then front to back, and finished with a braid over her left shoulder. The water in the basin was cool, and she inhaled the sharp scent of the lemon slices floating on the surface. She washed her face, her neck, behind her ears and patted them dry with a linen towel. From her top drawer, she withdrew the velvet pouch. Ana's pearl necklace and earrings slid onto her palm, light but substantial, warm, glimmering from within. She put them on reverentially, each movement a prayer. She smiled into the mirror, admiring her smooth neck adorned with pearls, the twinkling diamonds on her earlobes. She'd been in mourning for five years, but every night of those 1,825 days she put on Ana's pearls and diamonds and gazed into her own beautiful reflection.

A month earlier, she'd observed her twenty-third birthday with no husband, without her own household or a nursery buzzing with children. Over the years, don Eugenio had brought eligible young men for her to meet. They made overtures and looked for her to show some sign of interest, but she responded with polite formality. Several tried to convince her to love them, but others, like don Simón, withdrew into distant worship. A beautiful young woman who did nothing to make a man fall in love with her was saintly, and Elena, La Madona, was admired for her restraint and self-possession. She knew she was a romantic figure. The death of her fiancé created an aura of tragedy around her that she did nothing to discourage.

Had Inocente lived, she would have married him, even though she felt toward him like a sister. She'd added to the trousseau folded inside the cedar bridal chest that doña Leonor gave her for her fifteenth birthday. The white linen napkins were edged with fine crochet, fashioned with pineapple motifs. Each pillowcase and hand towel was embroidered with an *A* for her and Inocente's last names, Argoso and Alegría. She had two fine cotton nightgowns, the collars and cuffs trimmed with lace. She'd filled the chest with bedclothes, linen, hopes, and prayers. After Inocente's death, she locked it.

She'd probably never marry. She'd be the devoted daughter the Argosos didn't have, the only one left to take care of them in their last years. They'd been generous, had educated her and provided her a comfortable life. What could a man give her that she didn't have? Well, her own child. But now she had Miguel, and she loved him as if he'd come from her womb. Sometimes an expression or a gesture recalled Ramón and Inocente, but mostly it was Ana she saw in him. She couldn't have Ana, but she had Miguel safe and secure nearby.

She smiled into her mirror again, and happiness flushed her cheeks and brightened her eyes. Every time she confessed, she admitted to vanity and to the pleasure she derived from her own image.

She dropped a black shawl over her shoulders and walked down the hall to the narrow stairs to the roof. The Argosos were at the novena for a neighbor, and the rhythmic prayers of the mourners rose from the courtyard three doors down the street. A slivered moon hung in a velvet sky dotted with diamonds. She listened to the city murmur and sing, talk, pray, and cry as the surf crashed against the rocky shore. From the roof, San Juan harbor was a darkness as deep and vast as the sky above. Lights on docked ships twinkled orange and yellow, the only way to distinguish the shore from the thick vegetation rising into the mountains that cut across the island like a spine. What would Ana be doing right now in that humble house surrounded by cane in the middle of nowhere? Almost every night Elena stood on this roof and faced southwest, sending her thoughts toward Hacienda los Gemelos, as if they could reach her lover.

She said her prayers under the sparkling heaven. The humming city was alive, its sounds a lullaby. When she heard familiar footfalls coming down the street, she hurried to her bedroom. The sound stopped below her window. Two years ago, she'd extinguished her candle and peeked through a chink in the shutters. Simón's slight figure crept down the street, his hands in his pockets, his shoulders hunched as if she'd rejected him. But he didn't declare himself, and she was certain that he wouldn't. He loved her like the troubadours of olden days, for whom sighs and poetry and repressed emotion were enough.

She put away Ana's jewelry, then blew out her candle. A few minutes later she heard Simón walk away. Before she fell asleep, she roamed her lovely body, remembering other fingers, other tongues, reveling in the violent release.

HURACÁN

—◆—

Two years, it seemed to Severo Fuentes, was an appropriate mourning period before a widow could receive the attentions of a suitor. Even though he wasn't as highborn or as well educated as Ana, he was the only unmarried, rich white man within a day's ride remotely appropriate for a *señora de buena familia*. Not that there was any competition for her hand. No one came to Hacienda los Gemelos without some legitimate business.

Ramón and Inocente had excused Ana's reticence by telling the neighbors that she was an aristocratic lady from Sevilla who was used to greater comforts and embarrassed that they now lived so humbly. The visits after the two brothers' deaths gave the *vecinos* enough information to keep them curious and interested about Ana, but Severo made sure that no one came to the hacienda unannounced. Only Padre Xavier and occasional traveling salesmen dared ride into the Los Gemelos *batey* with no warning, except for the lieutenant and his men, which always meant bad news.

It impressed Severo that Ana didn't mind her isolation. She welcomed it. She had no interest in local gossip, no curiosity about how her neighbors lived, didn't require the stimulation of the closest town nor the attentions of women of her own class. She still walked with the entitled air of an aristocrat, but she'd discarded most of the conventions of the well-bred *señorita*. The parasols she'd brought from Spain were swaddled in waxed canvas and stored in the shed where she also kept a chest with silk dresses, lace mantillas, gloves, kid shoes, fine silk fans, and fringed shawls. Forgoing the black curls that once framed her small face, she now pulled her hair back into a severe bun at the nape of her neck held with a plain tortoiseshell *peineta*. By the end of the day, loose strands fluttered along her neck. Severo had heard Leonor complaining to Elena that it was indecent for a woman to be seen without a corset, regardless of how far she lived from civilization. But Severo liked Ana's softer silhouette, compact and girlish.

Doña Leonor berated Ana for only occasionally wearing a hat outdoors, and for rolling up her sleeves and exposing her arms and hands to the sun.

"I have work to do," Ana answered. "I don't think about my appearance as much as I worry about what needs to get done by the end of each day."

Leonor was offended by Ana's response, and later told Elena that Ana worked harder than usual when they were there because she didn't want to spend time with them.

There was some truth to that, Severo thought. Ana shared little with her mother-in-law and Elena. The years on the plantation had hardened her, although no one would mistake her for a *campesina*. She was still imperious when necessary and spoke the refined Castilian of her convent education, but compared with the proper Leonor and the ethereal Elena, she'd lost polish in her years at Los Gemelos. Six years ago, when he heard the voice that told him she'd be his wife, Severo couldn't have so much as looked at a woman like Ana was then. But he'd risen in status, and she seemed determined to descend from hers. It was only natural that they should be reaching toward each other.

Ana was on her new rocking chair, built by José, lower and with a narrower, shallower seat than one for an average-size woman so that her feet reached the ground, her spine rested comfortably against the slats, and the carved armrests and back were like a protective embrace. The late afternoon was uncharacteristically quiet as she waited for Severo Fuentes.

She had an idea what was on his mind, had felt his gaze as she moved through her days. She admired his restraint, appreciated his devotion, and wasn't averse to his attentions, but the most she admitted to herself about him was that she respected and trusted him. On the other hand, he did have a sixth sense about what she needed, whether for the plantation or her person. She also liked that he was clean, fastidious even, in his habits. He wasn't well educated but made up for it through prodigious reading. Admiration of those qualities, however commendable, still didn't add up to love.

She was twenty-five and had known physical passion from the time she was sixteen. She'd lost her self-consciousness about sex with Elena, and knew how good it felt but also how quickly the feelings dissipated. She dreaded male sexual attention like Ramón's and Inocente's, the violence of it, the deathlike languor afterward. In spite of that, she had wondered, more than once, what it would be like to be held by Severo Fuentes, whose powerful, compact body was so different from those of her long-limbed husbands.

Beyond longing, beyond the fantasies of coupling with Severo, beyond the flattering attention of a man in love with her, there was the question of who he was and who she was. In Spain, Severo wouldn't be admitted into the servant's quarters of the house in Plaza de Pilatos, let alone into her bed. For him to propose marriage to her would be an act of impressive confidence and courage, but it would put her in an awkward position. Severo was a Spaniard, and regardless of his former or current social standing, he lived by the male strict code of the *español*—pride and honor above all. If she refused him, Severo might be offended by her rejection of his proposal and the humiliation would drive him from Los Gemelos.

Some weeks earlier Ana had written to Eugenio. She'd become aware of Severo Fuentes's attachment to her, she wrote, and was convinced that it was sincere. While no one could ever take the place of Ramón in her heart, she was disposed to accept Severo's proposal if and when he spoke his intentions, but only if don Eugenio had no objections. She didn't expect such a swift response with his blessing, but he had predicted this might happen. He might also be glad to dispense with her five-hundred-peso allowance as his son's widow.

The evening Angelus bell tolled as Severo came up the stairs, slowly, as if not to appear too eager. He'd trimmed his hair, shaved, bathed in water that still gave off a slight, spicy scent of bay rum and cinnamon. He was dressed in dark brown pants and jacket, a double-breasted vest of paisley cloth, a crisp white shirt, and a carefully knotted cravat. It was an outfit she'd never seen him wear, clothes that must have been fashioned in Europe because no one in

the *campo* could tailor a man's suit that fit so wonderfully. He noticed her appraisal and his cheeks flamed. The color spread to his
forehead and to the tips of his ears, newly exposed by the haircut.
To give him time to recover, she looked into the *batey.* It was empty
except for industrious hens and chicks pecking at the brownish red
ground. He'd ordered the workers to the other side of the *batey* so
that, should she refuse him, there would be no witnesses to his humiliation. This impressed her. He didn't forget even the smallest
details.

"Please sit down," she said sweetly to let him know he had nothing to fear.

"*Señora,* over the last six years I have been your most devoted
servant. In Spain our backgrounds and lives would have made it
unlikely for us to know each other. But we are in a place where anything is possible. I dare to speak today as a simple man most sincerely
and irrevocably in love with you. In your precious fingers I place my
heart, my self, my goods, and my future, and humbly request your
hand in marriage."

He'd obviously rehearsed his words, probably thinking that a
woman like her must hear pretty speeches and poetic sentiments.
There was confidence but also quiet humility in his demeanor. For a
moment, she wanted to tell him he had overreached, that she didn't
love him, that the only reason she would marry him was because
she needed him at Hacienda los Gemelos and dared not refuse him.
Their eyes met, and she flushed head to toe. In that instant she knew
that none of it mattered to either of them.

In Spain, a suitor visited on Sunday afternoons and even a widow
with children was chaperoned by a female relative or trusted family
friend. He'd sit not touching any part of her not necessary to touch
in the course of normal conversation. After a visit that was to be
neither too short nor too long, he'd go home to do whatever men
did when they were soon to be married. The woman would return
to her rooms to fantasize about married life and to finish work on
her trousseau.

After Ana agreed to marry him, Severo came up the stairs of the
casona every evening, always impeccably dressed in a newly pressed

and starched white shirt and dark pants. He'd dispensed with the cravat, paisley vest, and jacket, which Ana wouldn't see again until their wedding day.

They sat on the porch, chaperoned by Flora, who performed her duties with alacrity when Severo was near. Also within sight of the couple was Conciencia, who even as a toddler displayed none of the behavior of normal children. She sat quietly by Ana's side on the chair José had made for her, with a back lower than on a regular chair to accommodate her hump. If she grew restless, or if Ana asked her to leave them alone because they needed to discuss adult things, Conciencia went into the house, dragging her little chair behind her.

This second engagement had none of the romance or excitement of the first, none of the expectation of love thwarted and reclaimed. Most evenings, Ana and Severo sat on the porch discussing what brought them together and interested them most—Hacienda los Gemelos. But sometimes their conversation took an unintended path, when they exchanged versions of their lives, sanitized. These intimacies were careful forays into the past, and they each heard the other's silences as much as what was said. Ana didn't want to humble Severo because of his impoverished childhood by detailing just how privileged hers had been. He didn't want to elevate her by revealing just how much suffering he'd endured in Boca de Gato, in Madrid, and on his arduous journey across the sea to the door of Marítima Argoso Marín. She didn't say that she'd been a wife to two men nor did she reveal her relationship with Elena. He didn't mention Consuelo Soldevida, who washed and pressed his clothes and shaved his face every day. She didn't disclose that she'd traded her only child—her son—for the privilege of staying on the plantation. He didn't divulge that don Eugenio paid him three hundred pesos a year to make sure she never left Hacienda los Gemelos.

"Remember when I took you and the twins to a site on my land beyond the north fields?" Severo asked Ana one evening, a few days before their wedding.

"I remember. You were thinking of building there."

"The air is healthier. The ash from the chimney and from burning the fields won't bother you as much."

"I can see that's a good thing." She set aside the shawl she was hemming with crochet lace. "But frankly, I've accepted the ash and the dust and even the insects as unavoidable."

"You drew plans for a house," he persisted. "Ramón kept them at the *finca,* and we discussed them."

"I haven't seen those plans in years."

"Let me show you the place again."

"It's so far, Severo, and I'm so busy."

"It'll take a morning. You'll like it once we're there."

The next day, Flora unpacked Ana's old riding habit from the cedar chest in the *rancho.* Ana had forgotten how heavy the skirt was, its many pleats. Over the years she'd learned to do more with less, and her simple cotton skirts and blouses no longer had the fashionable excesses of her youth. The kid riding gloves and boots, the veil over her hat brought memories of her first ride from the sandy cove where she landed after the harrowing sea voyage from the capital. So much has happened in six years, Ana thought, as Flora fastened her boots.

They rode at first light, the air still moist, as night creatures burrowed into their diurnal rest and day-flying birds started their matins. Marigalante, her new *paso fino* mare, a gift from Severo, was thrilled to be venturing beyond the windmill, across the river that curved around the hill. Severo led the way, higher and higher up the path newly shorn of vegetation. His favorite hounds, Tres, Cuatro, and Cinco, bounded ahead, then doubled back to where they could see him when he whistled. As they took the last turn, the path widened, and as they reached the top, a line of men and women holding trowels, hoes, and rakes stood closely together across the path, so Ana couldn't see beyond them. Her heart jumped to her throat. Had they come upon a group of runaway slaves? But this was no insurrection. Each of them—Teo, Paula, José, Inés—was familiar, and each was smiling. Severo dismounted, helped Ana from Marigalante, and told her to close her eyes.

"It's a surprise," he said.

He took her elbow and reminded her to keep her eyes shut as he led her farther up the hill, across what felt like grass underfoot, up a wooden ramp until there was tile beneath her boots. He turned her so that she'd be facing where he wanted her to look when she opened her eyes.

"Now."

Below was an expanse of many shades of green, from deep olive to the chartreuse inside a lime. A purple sash divided the Caribbean Sea from a cloudless azure sky.

Ana was speechless.

Severo grinned boyishly. "Do you like it?"

She nodded.

"I knew you would," he said.

She peeked over the edge of the improvised railing of what she guessed would be a *balcón*. This part of the house was perched on high stilts over the crest of the hill. Looking down made her dizzy. In the valley below, surrounded by the cane, were the familiar structures—bell tower, windmill, chimney, barns and warehouses, *cuarteles, bohíos,* the *casona* in the center. Paths led from the house toward the pastures and fields. Curving in and out of the foliage, a sinuous clay-red stripe led to a distant huddle of buildings and a spire.

"Is that Guares?" she asked, with a sudden urge to cry, as if the sight of the town opened a wound healed long ago.

"*Sí,* that's the steeple of the Iglesia de San Cosme y San Damián. There"—he pointed to the right—"is the dock from where we ship the sugar."

"I didn't realize the town was so close."

"It only seems that way from here," he assured her. "It's a solid two hours on horseback, more in a cart. To the left, closer to us, is your *ingenio,* with the new roof on the purgery."

The rugged steam engine, the refurbished grinders, the *casa de calderas* where the syrup was boiled, the purgery where the sugar was crystallized had made it possible for Hacienda los Gemelos to turn a profit for the first time in its history.

"It's beautiful," she said.

He waited a few moments. "Up the hill to the left, those roofs over there?" Ana nodded. "Finca San Bernabé."

"Can they see my *ingenio* from their house?"

"From every window and door." He grinned.

She smiled and returned her gaze to the buildings around her *casona.*

"The *batey* looks so far away," she said wistfully. She felt lost in the open, exposed to unseen dangers in a way she didn't feel in the valley.

"Around us are eight flat *cuerdas*. Plantain and bananas grow on the slopes, breadfruit and *guanábana,* passion fruit."

"But my henhouses, my gardens?"

"You'll have enough to do managing a proper house," he said. "You'll have more servants, and will need to oversee the making of furnishings and the sewing of curtains and the other things a house needs. . . ." He trailed off, unable to conceive what else a woman like Ana was used to in a home.

She turned to the view again, to the surprisingly square *cuerdas* of cane, divided by shimmering canals, to her orchards, to the fenced pastures where miniature cattle and horses bent their heads to grass.

"I like working in the gardens."

"You'll have gardens and orchards. And even your hens and pigeons, if you like," Severo said, but his voice was dry.

"Show me the rest," she said, heading toward the open-roofed labyrinth.

The house was half finished, the walls no higher than her shoulders, but the rooms were laid out according to the rough plans she remembered drawing up weeks after arriving in Los Gemelos.

"I changed some things," Severo explained as they walked around, "to account for the slope of the land." Openings faced the expansive views, where each room would have a window and a door to the gallery that ran around three sides of the house.

"I hardly know what to say. When did you do this?"

"I can only assign workers during *el tiempo muerto.* We learned to make the bricks here. I've had poor luck finding a good mason, so it's been trial and error all along."

It had taken years, Ana realized, to get the enormous structure to its current half-finished state. The house was easily three times the size of the *casona.* José's furniture wouldn't look quite so imposing in these rooms, and Ana wondered if the carpenter knew this as he filled the *casona* with chairs, tables, and dressers.

Until this moment, Ana and Severo had hardly touched. He'd kissed her hand once, held her elbow when she walked on uneven terrain, helped her to dismount, brushed her fingers when handing her letters or the ledgers. But as she walked through the house, Ana needed to touch the man who built these rooms for her. As they turned into the gallery facing the mountains, she stood closer to Severo than ever and reached for his hand.

———

They were married on August 31, 1851, after Ana's twenty-fifth birthday. The women decorated the *rancho* with festive hibiscus and bougainvillea garlands on the eaves and posts, and vases full of pink and white *nardos*. Her antique crucifix was again the center of an altar where Padre Xavier said Mass, baptized babies, and declared Severo Fuentes Arosemeno and Ana Larragoity Cubillas man and wife. Witnesses to their marriage were the foremen, slaves, and laborers, who then enjoyed a feast with dancing until the sharp clang of the last bell.

As Flora bathed her that night, Ana heard Severo pacing impatiently in the next room, where earlier that day Teo had moved his things. For her wedding night, she'd stitched a new pale green nightgown trimmed with ivory lace on the neckline, cuffs, and hem. As Flora dropped it over her head, it emitted the faint scent of roses and geraniums.

He made love like a woman, slow and attentive to the nuances of her pleasure. His hands were weather-beaten, but he had a light touch, and his rough fingertips against her skin were particularly erotic. He pushed the bedcovers to one side and loosened the ribbons on her nightgown with one hand while with the other he stroked, patted, drummed his fingers all over, around, and into her. No one, including Elena, had made her feel so much.

Ramón and Inocente had always extinguished the lights before intercourse, but Severo kept the candles flaming. She saw his body naked, the curly golden hair, the skin normally covered by clothes the shade of buttermilk. The first time she saw his penis erect, she averted her eyes. It was so aggressive, and yet so vulnerable, defenseless.

"*No le tengas miedo,*" he said. "I'll not hurt you."

It was warm and heavy in her hand, softer than she expected. Once she lost her timidity, she loved her power over him with a touch, a secret look, a flicker of tongue across her lips.

He was a self-possessed lover, and even in his ecstasy there was control.

"Why?" she asked the first night he spilled his seed on her belly.

"I want you to myself before you have a baby."

The act felt incomplete. Certainly neither Ramón nor Inocente had ever done such a thing; she hadn't even seen what left their bodies. She only felt a warm liquid oozing between her legs while Ramón or Inocente fell away from her, more worn out than their exertions deserved.

Night after night Ana and Severo studied each other's bodies with the concentration of explorers memorizing a map.

"And this?" He kissed a healed scar along her left knee.

"I fell from a stool when helping my mother hang a curtain. And this one?" She touched a spot high under his right arm.

"A scuffle with boys."

He sucked the smooth skin on her belly, shoulders, buttocks, the inside of her thighs, forming red welts that didn't hurt but turned blue by morning. She did the same to him, and they branded each other with blue-black islands on pale skin.

In private, Severo called her *mi reina, mi tesoro.* Among the workers and *campesinos,* he treated her as before their marriage, with formal deference. It was customary that married couples use the informal *tú* when addressing each other in private but the polite *usted* in public. Severo, even after Ana told him to call her *tú,* refused.

"*Tú* is for my inferiors," he said, "not for you, *mi cielo.*"

Ana found it hard to get used to, since if he called her *usted* she had to do the same to him, and it felt awkward to do so in their most intimate moments. It was the only wall he'd placed between them, one extra syllable of distance.

She was in the garden with Conciencia one morning, gathering *manzanilla* flowers for tea, when Ana was overcome by a feeling of well-being.

"This is happiness," she heard herself think, and so was surprised when Conciencia turned to her. "*¿Disculpe, señora?*"

Ana laughed, aware that she had never caught herself laughing giddily in the middle of the day as she was now doing.

During their first years at Los Gemelos, heavy rains and strong winds had compromised the buildings, but the damage had been reparable. Ana and Severo knew that it was a matter of time before a powerful hurricane would hit the island, destroying the weaker structures, flooding the fields, leveling crops, and killing the animals raised for food and trade. Their fears were realized on the early morning of September 5, 1852, when a hurricane raced through Puerto Rico from east to west. For two days Ana and Severo huddled with their household slaves, Siña Damita, the women, and children in a large natural cave previously cleaned and equipped for just such an emergency. The men and overseers occupied *tormenteras,* shelters dug into the high ground near the *casona* and the barns.

When they first went into the cave, the workers didn't know how to behave with Ana and Severo in such close quarters. Severo kept his machete, whip, and rifle nearby, and the first few hours were tense with mistrust and fear. But as the storm ravaged the countryside, everyone adjusted to the forced intimacy. Flora laid a quilt for Ana and Severo to rest upon. The others sat or squatted on the ground until sleep overcame them. Some told stories in hushed voices, in a patois of Spanish and African tongues. Others gossiped and hummed. Ana prayed, and the women came closer and followed the clicks of her rosary.

When they emerged, two days later, the world was upside down. Were she not *la patrona,* Ana would have joined the laments of the women, children, and old men as they walked the sodden grounds. The gardens and orchards had been flattened. The *bohíos* were gone, as well as the roof on the bachelors' barracks and one wall of the unmarried women's building. One of the barns had disappeared with the animals in it, leaving only the outline of where it had stood. The windmill was gone, and Ana imagined its huge vanes whirling over the land faster than they ever did over the crushers. Half of the *casona*'s metal roof had peeled away in pieces, but the walls held, as well as the ground floor, where the furniture and household items were moved before they went into the cave.

Clearing the fallen trees, repairing the damaged buildings, and restoring the flooded fields would take weeks. After a head count, Severo reported that no one had died but there were injuries.

"The infirmary is gone," Ana said. She shook her head to clear it, set her shoulders, coughed so that her voice wouldn't sound as small and scared as she was. "Can you get some men to move the furniture upstairs? I can set up the sick room on the ground floor."

"Of course." He placed a hand on her shoulder and she reached to squeeze it.

"I'll be fine," she said. He nodded and gave orders to the men while she moved amid the debris with her head high, organizing her people—the women, the old and maimed, the children—to clear the yard of branches and rubble, and put to rights nature's fury.

The hurricane and its aftermath caused four women to go into labor. As she always did, before handing each baby to his or her mother, Siña Damita blessed it and whispered *foroyaa* in Mandingo into each infant's ears so that the first word the child heard was "freedom."

By the time she could return home, three days later, she was bone-tired. Her old mule had collapsed and died a year ago, and Siña Damita had been on foot ever since. She now walked through the mangled *cañaveral,* hoping that, magically, her cottage would still be standing so that she could take a deserved rest. She'd brought her belongings wrapped inside her hammock to the cave: three pots and pans, six gourd bowls and spoons, four tin cans used for drinking, one blouse, one skirt, two aprons, two head wraps. She now carried the bundle on her head. Each barefoot step was heavier, her toes gripping the muddy ground so that she wouldn't slip. When she reached the square of land on the edge of the woods, the only signs that someone had lived there were the three stones of the *fogón.* Damita lowered her weary body into a squat, breathing hard, and pressed her hands over her pounding heart.

She wished Lucho or one of their two surviving sons were there to bemoan with her the loss of her home, the decimated gardens that enabled her livelihood. But don Severo had forbidden free time until the work buildings in the *batey* were repaired. With a sigh, Damita sent forth the prayers of her Mandinka ancestors, praised Allah, offered thanks for every breath, and begged for strength and patience. She had much to do.

She saved her money in a tin can buried in the rear yard, three paces toward the morning sun from her *fogón.* She identified what direction that would be on this overcast Sunday morning. Even though there was no one to see her, she looked around before she removed the debris over the pointy rock marking the spot and unearthed her treasure. She didn't want her secret stash in the open now that the guava and annatto trees that shaded the spot had blown away. She walked into the woods until she reached a majestic *ausubo,* its lower branches at least three times her height above the top of her head. Its wrinkled trunk was so wide that Siña Damita was sure it was already there when this land belonged to the *borin-queños.* The ground was covered with thick, oval leaves that had turned brown and orange, covering small caves around the trunk. She found a hole under a curving root on the other side, buried the can, covered it with earth, bark, and leaves until it looked undisturbed. She prayed to Allah to protect her money and, just in case, put a curse on anyone who dared to take it. Whether it was the prayer or the curse, no one found it.

When she came from the forest, the sun had cut through the clouds and was directly overhead. Ordinarily, after their chores, her husband, two sons, and their wives and children spent Sunday afternoons like this one with her. With no help, Siña Damita would have to rebuild her *bohío,* or accept Ana's offer to stay with Flora and Conciencia under the *casona* until her husband and sons could help.

Damita was forty-six, thirty of those years lived as a slave. When her owner manumitted her a decade earlier, she swore that she'd never sleep in a slave dwelling again. She had her little piece of land, not owned, but given for her use by don Severo in return for her services in the hacienda. After Artemio's death, he questioned her and her family until he was convinced that Artemio had acted alone. He then interceded with the authorities so that she wouldn't be punished. Don Severo was pitiless if you broke his rules, but he was not spiteful like doña Ana, who held grudges. Damita believed that people who held grudges couldn't be trusted.

Damita removed the fallen branches from the same spot where she, Lucho, Poldo, and Jorge had built her *bohío* over a week of Sundays. With her bare hands now, because she had no tools or machete, she pounded thick branches into the yielding ground with a stone and used *bejuco* vines to tie walls and a roof with brush and palm leaves. The shelter came out to be a few inches shorter than she was, so she scooted inside, but it would be home until her husband and sons could build something better.

By the time she finished, the sun was setting. She was exhausted and had numerous cuts on her hands from the afternoon's work, especially a nasty one from the ragged lid of the tin can that held her money. She had no fire, no water to drink or wash with, no food. Siña Damita lined up her belongings along the sides and, on her knees, prayed for Artemio, whom she imagined a free man in a paradise very much like her village in Africa. As she did every night, she also appealed to Allah to protect her enslaved husband, her living sons, her daughters-in-law, and her grandchildren and to safeguard every child she'd delivered into slavery.

The branches that made up her shelter weren't strong enough to hold her hammock, so she wrapped herself inside it and fell asleep almost immediately on the still-moist earth. Sometime in the night, she startled awake gasping for breath; the bone between her breasts felt heavy. She was in utter darkness. The pressure on her chest spread to her shoulders, down her arms.

"*¡Me muero!*" she cried, but there was no one to hear her.

She called to Allah, closed her eyes, and never opened them again.

Three days later, nine-year-old Efraín was sent to fetch Siña Damita; another woman was in labor. The first thing he noticed was the lop-sided, leaf-covered shack. Then the smell of decay reached him as he approached. Then he saw the flies. Because he was a curious boy, he looked inside. No one who smelled like that could be alive, but Efraín knew that *el patrón* would want to know for sure, so, covering his nose and mouth, he resisted the urge to vomit and lifted the fold of the hammock from where he thought her face was— and then he did throw up, even though he tried not to. He crawled from the shelter, heaving and wiping his mouth with the back of his hand.

"Please, Siña Damita, please don't haunt me," he said aloud once he was less queasy. He was glad that it was daylight, because El Caminante walked the roads and byways of the hacienda, and he might be nearby with Siña Damita's spirit. Efraín crossed himself several times the way doña Ana taught, then said what he remembered of the Lord's prayer and the Hail Mary. He crossed himself again, then ran as fast as his legs could pump, as if Siña Damita's and El Caminante's spirits were chasing him. He found doña Ana in the infirmary and, between gasps and wheezes he told *la patrona* that Siña Damita would never return to Hacienda los Gemelos.

Siña Damita's death left Los Gemelos without a midwife and *curandera*. Dr. Vieira came from Guares to the hacienda only when there was a serious injury or illness. With help from the elders, Ana and Flora tried to take over Damita's duties. Severo delivered books and pamphlets that added to Ana's knowledge.

As news of the devastation in nearby plantations reached them, Ana realized that they were comparatively lucky. Luis reported to Severo that Faustina and their boys were visiting relatives when the hurricane hit, so they were spared the sight of their new home collapsed. Most of their belongings were crushed, while the older wooden structure used for storage was left intact. Other neighbors lost relatives and workers either during the hurricane or in its aftermath of disease, unstable structures, and the heartbreak of having to start over.

"I hoped to have the *casa grande* finished by now," Severo told Ana one night, after a long, arduous day.

"It can't be helped. In any case, I like living in the center of things."

"It's not appropriate. You're a lady."

"I've lived here for almost seven years. Why is it suddenly inappropriate?"

"This was not intended to be your permanent home. You need an elegant house and servants to look after you. You're a lady, and you should live like one."

"Now you sound like doña Leonor," she retorted. They both fell silent, and the space between them widened. After a few seconds, she turned to him. *"Lo siento, mi amor."* She stroked his chest. "What I mean is I don't assume I must behave a certain way because I was born in this family as opposed to that one. You should know that by now."

"There's a difference between flouting convention and deliberately lowering yourself below your station."

"Severo, you surprise me with this talk."

"We're not *campesinos*. We're *hacendados*."

So that's it, she thought. Now that he's rich, he has to prove he's no longer a peasant.

"I thought you'd like the new house," he said after a while. "I'm building it the way you designed it, on the most beautiful spot."

"I know."

"You haven't asked to go there, don't ask how the work is going or when the house will be ready. You take no interest."

"Am I supposed to ride down the hill every time I want to snip a few herbs or flowers? I'm rebuilding my gardens in the wake of this disaster. The orchards I've worked so hard to establish, the animals we grow for food. The workers who help me are all down here."

"You don't need to do any of that. That's why we have them."

"I like working in the gardens."

"All of that can happen up there." He relented after a few moments, his voice growing tighter with each word.

"You're being unrealistic," Ana said, measuring her words. "That would be like setting up another plantation. The workers won't be able to go from one job to the other easily, like they do now. It takes too long to get up there."

"Remember, Ana, think back: the first thing you did when you came here was to design a proper house."

Ana felt as if she were pushing a mountain. "I was a girl then, missing home. It was a fantasy, Severo, not an order."

They fell silent again, but she could practically hear him thinking, could feel his muscles jerking, as if he were controlling the urge to move. He'd been in love with her for seven years, and over that time, she'd shed a part of herself that he valued—*the señora de buena familia* who could elevate his status. She'd forgotten who she was, but he hadn't.

She tried to rouse him again, her fingers playing with the coarse hair on his belly. "Right now, it's more important to put our resources into Los Gemelos, *mi amor*. A new *casona* is a distraction when we have so much to do. You have made me so happy in every way possible. You anticipate my every need. And the house is beautiful. But really, it's not as important to me as—"

He took her without words, forcefully, and for the first time in the year they'd been married, he climaxed inside her.

The next morning, a Sunday, Severo awoke earlier than usual. The boards creaked with every step and made him feel heavy, ungainly.

He took pride in being the first person awake at Los Gemelos. He was usually on horseback before dawn, regardless of weather.

By the time the foremen led the workers to their stations, he would have done a circuit of the fields so that at the end of the day he could gauge how much was accomplished.

On Sundays, however, Severo let himself be seen by his tenants. He allowed *campesinos* to build *bohíos* on the boundaries of his lands. It was an inducement for *jornaleros,* and he expected them to work for him during the *zafra.* He garnered their wages to make sure they paid their rent. During *el tiempo muerto,* it was important to visit them lest they forget whose land they occupied, and that they must make it yield enough to pay their rent in the form of labor, produce, or cash, or find another place to live, another plot to farm.

He had no patience with lazy *campesinos,* the ones who spent more time on fighting cocks and cards than on agriculture. He was sorry for their women, whose only relief from hard work and worry was an untimely death, frequently as they sent forth yet another off-spring destined for hopelessness and misery. If they were widowed and showed some grit, Severo sometimes forgave a portion of their dead husband's debts so long as the widows didn't neglect their duty to the land. That was why many of his tenants were women with children, some of them his. He kept a record of his unions and his bastards, but didn't otherwise single them out in any way lest they get it into their heads that they were entitled to anything they didn't earn.

There was one exception, however. Consuelo Soldevida was not technically a tenant. She lived on his land beyond Ana's circuit. He provided for her as well as he provided for Ana, except that Consuelo's needs were simpler, her expectations lower.

Before marrying Ana, he'd lived with Consuelo, but when Ana accepted his proposal, he moved to his house by the river. During the three months of their engagement, he appeared at Consuelo's gate on Sunday afternoons after his rounds, but he hadn't been to see her since his marriage.

Over the eight years they'd known each other, Consuelo's body had changed, its contours a frequent delight. Some days she was soft and round, other days her arms and legs felt muscular, her but-tocks and belly hard. She'd been pregnant several times but hadn't presented him a child, claiming miscarriages and stillbirths. Before he married Ana, he would've legitimized a daughter or son from

Consuelo, he told her, but she'd been unable to deliver a healthy infant.

Much of his wealth went to Spain, where he enriched the lives of his mother and father, his six sisters and brothers, and their families. His father and brothers no longer toiled over a cobbling bench. His mother wore custom-made frocks with plenty of lace and had a maid to clean her house and a cook to prepare meals. His brothers and sisters, nieces and nephews ate well every day, thanks to his industry. Even Padre Antonio, who taught him to read and write and drilled Latin into him, benefited from Severo's good fortune in the New World. A niche in the church was now the Fuentes Arosemeno chapel, its Jesus on the cross surrounded by the three Marías was paid for with the sweat from Severo's brow.

He often thought that he was a man whose every dream had come true. He'd dared to strive and rise above his class, to marry a lady, to make a fortune. He now rode a fine gray Andalusian horse named Penumbra and dressed like the well-established country gentleman he was. He also knew the price he'd paid for his dreams. His neighbors considered themselves his betters because one or two generations separated them from the manual labor that his parents endured. They resented his acumen in business. Many faltered and came to him for loans that they failed to pay for the same reasons they needed them in the first place. He'd expanded his holdings from their insolvency. Arrogance, purity of blood, and noble descent didn't guarantee an ability to manage men and a business.

He was thirty-two years old and had fulfilled his responsibilities as a son, and a year after his marriage, he was ready for the next phase in his life. He was a good husband and friend to Ana, he'd settle her in the luxury she deserved, and he expected that she'd deliver sons to carry their names. His internal voice had told him there would be a son, so he'd given her a year to get to know him, and to learn to love him, although he was sure she didn't know it—yet. Severo Fuentes was a patient man.

This Sunday morning he decided to take a look at the new house, neglected since the hurricane. As he expected, the path was overgrown, trees toppled across it, so he dismounted several times to move trunks, chop branches with his machete, and lead Penumbra up the muddy slope. When he finally reached the top, he was pleased that, while there was much debris over the grounds, the sturdy walls of the house held.

A flock of dead birds lay on their side on the porch, their bodies decomposing. As he walked around the unfinished rooms, he found more birds smashed against walls, three snakes, centipedes, and a mongoose. He fashioned a stiff broom from branches tied with *bejuco* and swept the dead creatures, the leaves and twigs that the wind blew into the corners, and the piles of rubble over the side of the hill.

Since Ana had last seen the house, the walls were within a row of where they'd eventually stop. The crossbeams were stacked behind the property. The *tejas* for the roof couldn't be made on-site, but he'd ordered them from Sevilla, and expected to receive word any day that the ship carrying them as ballast was docked in Guares. The walls were formed from Puerto Rican clay; the *azulejo* floor and the roof tiles were being fired in the city where Ana was born. It was the kind of detail he hoped she'd appreciate. She was an educated woman; she would understand the poetry of his choices.

Sweeping, cleaning, Severo thought about the conversation of the previous night, but no matter how many times he went over her words, he always reached the same conclusion. It pained him that Ana, even as she reached for him in their bed, would refuse a gift he'd been working seven years to give her.

The house was cleared now, and Severo began the journey to the valley. Instead of heading for the *batey,* however, he led Penumbra toward the familiar path leading to the line of palms along the sea. Consuelo's cottage still stood near the beach, the hammock still tied to the porch rafters. Parts of her garden were damaged, but the rest was intact. He brought Penumbra around the back, tied him up, and entered the gate.

"Consuelo, *mi consuelo,*" he called, and she emerged from the cottage, as unsurprised as if she were expecting him, even though it was over a year since he'd last visited.

"*Adelante, mi amor.*" Her throaty voice was honey, and as soon as he climbed the porch steps he felt at home.

After Severo left, Consuelo rolled up the hammock and picked up around the cottage. She knew that Severo would come back to her, just as the pirate Cofresí always returned to her mother. Severo married *la gran dama de España,* as the *jíbaras* called her, but men were men. No matter how grand their ladies, they always sought *consuelo.*

Over the months since he'd last come to see her, Severo had sent Efraín to deliver tins of sardines, a hoe, two lengths of rope, six yards of white cotton, three spools of thread, a ladle, and an enameled tin coffeepot. The boy also brought fruits in season, yams, sacks of rice, *canecas* of rum, tobacco, and, of course, sugar. These gifts were Severo's love letters, because she couldn't read. His message was "Wait for me."

Consuelo waited, but she wasn't idle. She grew vegetables and flowers, she fished, she improved her cottage. Nearby *campesinas* came to visit because even though Consuelo had been a *puta,* she was the mistress of the man who owned the land they lived on. Consuelo was also generous. Any *campesina* could come to her for a handful of rice, for a sweet papaya or a bunch of *quenepas.* Their sons caught turtles or fished for octopus and always brought her some of their catch. She sent them home with a *penca* of salted codfish or a bunch of dried *manzanilla.* Sometimes the *campesinas* brought their children to bathe at her beach.

Over the first three years Consuelo was Severo's woman, she delivered three convulsing infants gasping for breath who died within hours. Siña Damita had told her that a powerful curse had been placed on her womb.

"A jealous woman, the worst kind." Damita suggested baths and invocations to the full moon, and gave her cuttings of *vara prieta, tártago,* and *cariaquillo* to grow along her fence near the gate. "They protect from bad spirits. You mash leaves, boil in much water, mix with cool water, and pour over you every day for one week. The curse will be washed away."

Six years ago, Severo came one night, *desesperado,* smelling of blood and death, and Consuelo was sure she'd conceived again. Nine months later she delivered a baby girl the color of amber. She was tiny, and like the others, thrashing and jerking, unable to take in air.

"Give breast," Siña Damita suggested, but the child flailed and gasped and couldn't suckle.

"Take her away, Siña Damita," Consuelo said. "I can't bear to see another one die."

The midwife took the baby to a woman whose own child had died two days earlier. Magda nursed and cuddled the jaundiced girl back from near death, and when Damita came to see how she was doing, Magda gave the *partera* ten Spanish pesos so that she could keep the girl, and so that Siña Damita would keep her secret, a secret she took to the grave.

CONCIENCIA'S VISIONS

———◆———

Hurricane San Lorenzo, so named because it made landfall on that saint's day, moved east to west over the Cordillera Central and changed the landscape on either side of the mountains. At Hacienda los Gemelos, the river altered course and flooded nearly five *cuerdas* of cane. The roots drowned in spite of efforts to drain the fields. After the harvest, which began in February and ended in late April, a full month earlier than usual, Ana reported to don Eugenio that it would take two years to recover from the loss, due to the slow growth of the plants. In spite of this, she planned to increase the number of cultivated fields, from 250 to 300 *cuerdas*.

That summer of 1853, two years after she and Severo married, Ana noticed that the *campesinas* living on the boundaries of the hacienda began to deliver babies with green eyes, golden hair, compact bodies. She had no doubt that they were Severo's offspring. She was furious and hurt, but she wasn't about to repeat the scene with Ramón. She remembered her conversations with Elena, their plan that when their husbands turned to their mistresses, they'd turn to each other. But on Los Gemelos, there was no one for her to turn to but Severo.

At least he was loving and passionate in bed, and treated her courteously before others. Culture and tradition had accustomed women, even one as perceptive as Ana, that this was the most they could expect from a husband. That didn't mean that she accepted the situation without a way to retaliate for his infidelity. Severo wanted a legitimate heir, so now it was Ana's turn to take pains to avoid getting pregnant. Over years of daily contact with people who knew more about plants and herbs than the trained doctors of Europe, she'd learned remedies to keep herself infertile. Besides regular douches, she prepared strong infusions of artemisia or *ruda* sweetened with honey that she drank instead of water. Every menstrual period felt like a reprisal, and he was no wiser. He never rebuked her and she never apologized.

Before the 1854 *zafra,* Severo purchased five more men. Their inventory increased to fifty-three slaves; thirty-seven owned by the hacienda and sixteen by Severo. Of this number, forty-two were able and healthy enough to do the work. Twenty *jornaleros* were already committed to the harvest, but they hoped to get more.

In January Severo took Ana's report for Mr. Worthy to the post station in Guares, and returned with a letter from Sevilla in Jesusa's looping hand, posted a month earlier:

> Mine has been a melancholy task, *hija mía,* as I choose what to give away to whom, and prepare to leave my home of thirty-five years. I wish you were with me so that we could both cry and pray together, and find solace in each other. Perhaps you're so overcome with grief that you're unable to reply. Or maybe our letters went astray. I begin my journey day after tomorrow, and will reach the convent two days later. Pray for me in my new life of silence and contemplation and know that, while we will never see each other again, you will be in every prayer.
>
> Your loving mother,
Jesusa

"What does this mean?" Ana asked Severo. "Was there another letter?"

"No, that was all. Is something wrong?"

Ana sat down hard and read the letter again as a benumbing chill washed over her. "I can't . . . it seems . . . My father is dead and my mother is . . ."

In the nine years Severo and Ana had known each other, it had been inappropriate for him to comfort her when Inocente, her Cubillas *abuelo,* and then Ramón died. She now sat stunned, reading the letter a second time, then a third, as if more would be revealed by repetition. He lifted her by the elbows, drew her against his chest, and waited for her to reach around him, but her arms remained as limp and unresponsive as a marionette's. He raised her chin and she looked at him searchingly, as if trying to recognize him. Her black eyes were moist, but there were no tears, although her face was drawn in sorrow. It was the Ana he knew, but a different one, childlike, afraid.

"Ana," he said low against her ear. *"Mi Anita."* As if her name awakened her, she responded, her arms around his neck, her shoulders heaving.

The black-edged envelope arrived a week later, even though it had been sent a month before the other. Her father had fallen down the stairs from the second floor of their home in Plaza de Pilatos and was found broken but alive at the feet of the crusader. In spite of every effort, Jesusa wrote, he didn't regain consciousness.

Don Gustavo was sixty-one years old, and when Ana last saw him, he still looked young and vigorous, even if he almost always wore a frown. Ana was now twenty-seven, and it didn't seem possible that the girl who left Plaza de Pilatos as a bride could be the woman who now sat on a stump by the pond, mourning the death of yet another man in her life.

Over the last ten years, she'd thought little about her parents. They were as distant in memory as in miles. She hardly remembered what they looked like, and as she tried to recall them now, glimpses flickered like sparkles over the water's surface.

Don Gustavo planted his heels into the earth, knees straight, shoulders back, his chest puffed from his waist. He wore his dignity as heavily as an anchor. Had all those ancestors and their exploits been an encumbrance as much as an honor? He'd done nothing significant with his life. His arrogant but discontented gaze was that of a man who'd failed to leave a mark, who hadn't even discharged his duty to father a son to carry his own name.

Her mother, no longer a wife, was erasing her identity under a veil, her finite days given to prayer and to begging forgiveness for her failures. It angered Ana that both would die awash in regret.

Nearby, four-and-a-half-year-old Conciencia harvested watercress along the pond's shore. Ana thought about her son. She hadn't seen Miguel in nearly five years, but her letters to him were frequent, and he dutifully answered. Elena wrote with more specifics about Miguel's health and his progress in school. *Does he remember me?* Ana answered her own question; of course not. She was a darker shadow in Miguel's life than her parents were in hers. She felt a pang of remorse but waved it away like a fly that came too near. If she allowed it, she might look at her life too closely, might review her choices and decisions and perhaps even bend under repentance. No, she said, no regrets.

She looked across the pond. Severo waved as if he'd been waiting for her to acknowledge him. Over the last week, he'd made sure to be in her sight, and if she gestured, he'd come, his eyes darkened to emeralds. Since the news of her father's death, he'd been more affectionate. At first she resisted his advances, but then she felt so alone that she eventually succumbed. When he caressed and stroked her, when he called her sweet names and kissed her where she never thought to be kissed again, Ana cried as if his attentions were unwelcome and as if she didn't want him. But she did. She did.

Just before her marriage to Severo, Ana had moved Conciencia to the downstairs servants' quarters with Flora. She asked Ana's permission to train Conciencia to hold her bowls and rags while she bathed Ana at night. Conciencia learned how Flora's sure hands washed her mistress, powdered her, brushed her long hair into braids tied at the ends with ribbons. Soon Conciencia was able to bathe one side of Ana's body while Flora did the other.

While she now slept with Flora, during the day Conciencia was inseparable from Ana. The two could be seen working in the gardens, Ana shorter than most women, Conciencia smaller than most girls her age, always a step behind her mistress. Behind their backs, the slaves called them La Pulga y La Pulguita, Flea and Little Flea.

"What plant is that, *señora*?"

"That one is sage, *niña*. The leaves are used to treat sore throats, and in compresses for cuts and wounds."

As she matured, Conciencia spent hours listening to the elders who remembered Africa, asking about this or that plant or cure until she extracted from them knowledge they didn't even know they had. Gathering information as assiduously as she gathered herbs, Conciencia eventually surpassed Ana in knowledge and ability.

Conciencia had a gift for mixing the right combination of leaves, flowers, and twigs into teas that relieved symptoms from stomachaches to melancholy. For burns she made a cataplasm of ground raw potato applied directly to the skin, which healed with minimum peeling. Ana's seldom-used embroidery needles became lances for boils and infected sores that Conciencia salved with ground flower petals in coconut oil or lard. After a while, the women didn't bother to ask Ana to cure their children or examine an infected cut. Even while she was still a child, they called on Conciencia, whose body, humpbacked, bent over to one side, made her look like an old woman and gave her an authority she might not otherwise have. Her short, bowed legs were powerful. She moved with a swiftness that surprised those who saw her run from the *casona* to the barracks to the garden to the fields. She seemed to be everywhere at once and appeared out of nowhere when least expected.

As she grew older, it was Conciencia who took care of the sick and injured, who assisted in births and helped prepare the dead. By the time she entered puberty, she had greater knowledge of human suffering than could be expected from a girl who never traveled farther than the gates of Los Gemelos.

Constant exposure to the cycle of life from its beginning until its often painful and violent end showed in her behavior. The evenness of temper she displayed on her very first day of life evolved into a silent, watchful character that reassured some and frightened others. Inevitably, people said that she was a witch, a label that didn't seem to bother her.

"You're fearless, my little one," Ana often told her, and Conciencia smiled.

One morning, when Conciencia was six years old, Ana found her staring into the fire in the kitchen shack.

"What is it, *niña*? Did your food fall into the ashes?"

"The workers will get sick and die," Conciencia said in a monotone, her eyes following the smoky spirals over the *fogón*. "They will burn."

Ana looked at the fire as if it held a secret for her, but saw nothing but smoke. "You had a nightmare, *niña*, that's all." She cupped the girl's cheek in her palm.

"I see it, *señora*," Conciencia said. "They will get sick. A soldier will tell don Severo to burn them."

"Where did you hear such a thing?"

"The fire, *señora*."

Ana shuddered. Her foundling, who preferred collecting herbs to playing with other children, seemed to speak with secret knowledge. Ana knelt and took Conciencia in her arms. "You mustn't say such things, *niña*, it's heresy. Get on your knees and let's say a Lord's prayer."

"But I see it, *señora*. They will get sick and soldiers—"

"Hush, Conciencia! Fire can't speak. Now kneel and pray."

Conciencia did as told, but Ana couldn't help the dread that wrapped itself around her at the girl's intense gaze and un-childlike certainty.

She was so preoccupied with Conciencia's words that she didn't see the laundress returning from the river with a bucket of water balanced on her head. As Ana stood to brush the dust from her skirt, Nena la Lavandera passed close enough that Ana bumped into her, making the young woman lose her balance. The bucket tipped and fell, splashing both of them with the water intended for the barracks.

"*Ay, señora, disculpe, por favor, lo siento,*" the laundress begged, backing to a safe distance and bowing her head.

"It was an accident, Nena," Ana said as Conciencia used her skirt to wipe Ana's dress dry.

Flora came running from the other side of the house. "Stupid girl, look what you done," she yelled at Nena, leading Ana away from the wet circle at her feet, patting dry her arms and the front of her blouse with a kitchen rag.

"It was an accident," Nena repeated Ana's words.

"Pick up your bucket and go about your work," Flora ordered, her higher status as Ana's personal maid giving her some of the authority of her *patrona*.

La Lavandera grabbed the upended bucket and ran to refill it at the pond while Flora and Conciencia tended to Ana, who crossed herself and stared fearfully at the dark red stain blooming on the hard tamped clay of the *batey*.

Nena la Lavandera had spent her life near, on, in, and around water. Her earliest memory was of being strapped on her mother's back as Mamá washed clothes in a river. She was born near the sea, on another sugar plantation where the bosses spoke a different language.

One night, when Nena was about ten, her mother woke and then shushed her as she led her through the loosened boards on the back wall of the barracks. They crept through the woods toward the rocky cove where boys went fishing for octopus.

Mamá and Nena joined other men and women scrambling over sharp rocks toward a raft that bumped this way and that while two men tried to hold it steady against the tide. After everyone had crawled onto the log-and-bamboo surface, the men swam alongside, pushing the raft away from the rocks until the wind caught the lone sail in the center. The others helped them on board, and they watched in awe as the black mound that was land and home faded into the horizon. Once on the open sea, Mamá hugged Nena closer and she fell asleep in her mother's embrace.

She woke to Mamá's arms crushing her against her bosom, and to the sound of "no, no, no," as if one word could have an impact on what was happening. The sun was unfiltered by clouds in a sky so pale and bright that it hurt to look up, but around them the sea lifted the raft over high, rolling waves, then dropped it into deep troughs. The sail had vanished. Over Mamá's shoulder Nena saw a woman clutching the air, frantic to stay aboard. In her need, she grabbed the closest body, that of a child. Other hands stretched toward them as they both slid over the edge and disappeared into the waves.

Nena held on to her mother even tighter then, but over the screams and moans she heard wood snapping and cracking, and the ropes holding the lumber and bamboo unknotted and the floor drifted in opposite directions. People splashed into the sea, and the planks knocked their heads, and hands and feet swished and slapped the ocean as they paddled toward the flotsam that remained of the raft that had brought them so far from land and home.

Nena didn't remember when she lost her grip on Mamá, or when she found a plank to float upon, or how many others survived. She woke up inside the stinking hold of a ship, surrounded by many more terrified men, women, and children than had left with her and Mamá.

Sailors who trawled the ocean for the survivors of escape attempts found them. They could return the escapees to their owners for the reward, but they made more money selling them far away from where they plucked them from the sea.

A few days later Nena was again on the open sea, her small hands gripping the edges of a dinghy rowed by two bearded, smelly white men. She didn't recognize the six men and three women who sat terrified on the wet floor of the dinghy as it approached a beach where don Severo waited with another man and two frothy-mouthed dogs. Once they landed, don Severo and the other man tied ropes around the people's hands and necks. Because Nena was small, her wrists were bound to a woman whom she came to know as Marta.

They walked for a long time away from the sea until they reached a derelict sugar plantation too big, Nena could tell, for the paltry number of slaves in its *batey*. Behind the tumbledown barns, what were once cultivated fields and meadows had been reclaimed by quick-growing, luscious vegetation. It was not called Los Gemelos then. That happened after doña Ana, don Ramón, and don Inocente came.

Nena didn't know how don Severo could tell that she'd worked alongside her mother at a river's edge.

"You, *nena,*" he said. "Here's a pail."

In addition to washing clothes by this river, she was to keep the *barracones* and *casona* supplied with water. Several times a day Nena walked below the rapids, where the river ran clearest, and filled her pail. She sat on her haunches, lifted the pail to her head, and balanced it on a rag twisted into a cushion. She then walked the half mile to the barracks, where she added to whatever rainwater collected inside a large drum by the door.

She returned to the river and came back to the *casona*'s kitchen, where she poured water into a tall funnel-shaped terra-cotta vase inside a wooden frame. Below it a pitcher collected the water filtered through the coned bottom. Nena would like to know what that water tasted like, but she wasn't allowed to drink from the pitcher reserved for the *patrones*.

Another of her jobs was to check whether the chamber pots needed emptying in the *casona*. Everyone else pissed and shat wherever the urge struck them if they were in the *cañaveral*, or if they were closer to the *batey*, they squatted over a hole on the open platform jutting over the hill behind the barn near the pond. But the *patrones* used china pots and wiped their bottoms with perfumed linen strips that they dropped into a basket for Nena to collect and wash daily.

She also emptied the waste bucket in the male and female barracks that were locked overnight. Once she emptied the chamber pots and waste buckets behind the barn, she rinsed them in the pond until she saw no signs of shit and piss. She did observe, however, that the masters' neither looked nor smelled any better than that of the slaves.

Nena's life improved somewhat after one of the *patrones* noticed her and asked don Severo to bring her to the *finca*. Soon after her twelfth birthday, one of the *patrones*, she couldn't tell which, took her virginity. After don Inocente died, she realized he was the one who liked to slap and choke. Don Severo moved her to a *bohío* and ordered her to look after don Ramón. Don Ramón wanted her to hold him close and to run her fingers through his hair, but not all the time. Another girl was given the tasks of emptying the chamber pots and fetching water for the *casona*, while Nena spent most of her days by the river, washing the *patrones*' clothes and linens, or in her *bohío*, pressing them with the heavy iron heated on smoldering coals. Her first child, a boy, was born dead.

When don Ramón died, Nena was again charged with the chamber pots and the slaves' buckets, and had to endure the derision of the other women who'd been jealous of her easier job when don Ramón was alive. Don Severo returned her to the *barracones*, and it was there that her daughter was stillborn just two weeks after the *patrona* found Conciencia at her door.

Every day, Nena repeated this history to herself as she carried water, rinsed chamber pots, scrubbed clothes, starched and pressed don Severo's shirts and pants and doña Ana's plain skirts and blouses. Every day she added something new to it, like the hours she spent in the cave with the *patrones* during the hurricane, or the time she slipped on rocks and slashed her thigh, where she now had a long scar. She wanted to remember her story because someday she'd tell a living child from her womb that her name was not Nena, and not

La Lavandera. She'd tell her child that her name was Olivia, a name with a soft, pretty sound. She'd tell her child that she'd always lived near, on, in, and around water. She was collecting stories for her future children because her own *mamá* told her nothing. Nena didn't even know her birth name or her mother's name because the sea swallowed Mamá before Nena learned who she was and what her life was like before she was born.

"I will not be like Mamá," Nena vowed as she lifted the filled bucket of water to her head and, with a grunt, stood and began the long walk through the woods to the *casona*. "I will not die nameless."

NUESTRA GENTE

———•◆•———

Ana had forgotten Conciencia's strange prediction by the time the rains battered Los Gemelos in May, June, and July 1856, four years after the hurricane had caused so much destruction. The *batey*'s ground softened into a muddy expanse of slipping and sliding men, women, children, and beasts. Ana's gardens, which once bloomed in riotous plenty following gentle showers, drooped into soggy despair, and the herbs and medicinal plants threatened to wash away over fast-flowing gullies.

Soaked to the soul, Ana, Flora, and Conciencia worked in the mud, propping up and staking plants, hoeing trenches to divert water from the gardens that had taken years to mature.

Nena couldn't go to the dangerously swollen river to fetch water or wash clothes, so José set a hollowed trunk on sawhorses near the barracks to create a washtub that filled with rainwater. But the sun couldn't break through the persistent clouds and she had to press everything dry. She couldn't empty the chamber pots behind the barn because the hill slid into the pond in a sludge of stinking mud. The contents of the *casona*'s chamber pots and the slaves' buckets now went directly into the pond, where rain dissipated the waste until it was neither visible nor foul smelling.

The fields were waterlogged. Severo deployed all *brazos* to dig channels between rows of germinating cane so that the crop wouldn't drown. The summer was usually when the slaves were kept busy with maintenance and repairs, clearing land, cleaning or forming new irrigation ditches. The unrelenting storms disrupted the order of work, and for nearly a month every available worker battled the damage caused by the *vaguadas*.

Once the sun finally burned through the clouds, visible steam rose from the soaked earth in mirage-inducing ripples. The days and nights became unbearably still and hot. Moisture lingered over the land, without the slightest breeze to push it toward the ocean.

When Nena resumed her daily trips to the river, she found that it had changed course again. Runnels had broken through into new paths and hollows. The rock platform downstream of the waterfall where she used to wash clothes was completely submerged, and the stones of the *fogón* for boiling linens had been swept away. The river seemed angry, its waters turbid, its banks dislocated by uprooted trees, branches, and the bloated carcasses of drowned animals. It would be several more days before she could wash there. Fortunately, there was enough rainwater for drinking in the drums by the barracks, which she supplemented with water from the overflowing pond.

That night, Nena lay on her pallet in the women's *barracón* and dreamed that she was floating on a stream toward a placid ocean. She landed on an island, where her mother was pounding clothes against rocks.

"But, Mamá," Nena protested in her dream, "you said never to wash clothes in seawater."

Her mother ignored her and continued beating the fabric with a paddle. "Mamá," Nena cried, because something hit her belly, except the pain seemed to be coming from her womb. She woke in a sweat. She had to sit over the waste bucket immediately.

She stumbled over sleeping bodies and under the *hamacas* to the corner, where she squatted and emptied her bowels without relief. She was very thirsty. She wanted to reach the *jofaina* with drinking water on the other side of the door, but was afraid of soiling herself on the way or, worse, of shitting over someone sleeping on the low pallets and on the floor. She sat over the bucket pressing her forearms into her belly in a vain attempt to take the edge off the cramps that discharged her bowels without any effort on her part.

"Water," she called into the night. *"Agua, por favor."*

"Be quiet and let folk sleep," someone grumbled.

"Somebody please bring me water," Nena sobbed, but her voice sounded as if it were coming from another body.

Strong hands pulled her off the bucket and led her to her pallet. Callused hands lifted her head and tipped a coconut shell to her lips.

She must have passed out, because next thing she knew it was day and everyone had gone to work, but old Fela was with her. Fela removed Nena's dress and washed her bottom because she'd soiled herself.

She was feverish, and mortified that she couldn't control her body. But mostly she was thirsty, so thirsty. *"Agua,"* she begged, and wrinkled hands brought the coconut shell to her lips. Water dribbled down her chin to her chest, but it didn't cool her. The few sips she swallowed renewed the cramps and diarrhea but didn't slake her thirst.

The door to the *barracón* opened, and the rectangle of sun on the floor darkened with a woman's silhouette.

"Es la lavandera," Fela said to doña Ana. "She's been sick all night."

She knew she was dying when doña Ana's face peered down at her and Nena saw fear.

"My name is Olivia," she whispered to the *patrona,* then closed her eyes.

Seventy-year-old Fela and sixty-four-year-old Pabla washed Nena's soiled body, finger-combed and plaited her hair. Nena didn't have another dress, so the women wrapped her inside a tattered blanket that they didn't have time to wash and dry in the sun. The girl who wanted to be called Olivia, who was always clean and smelled of fresh water, was swaddled in a sweaty, torn blanket that someone else was willing to give up because *la patrona* would now replace it with a new one.

José kept royal palm boards cut in two lengths, adult and child, to quickly assemble coffins for the slaves. They were simple narrow rectangles, and as Fela and Pabla washed and prepared Nena, José cut the boards, not as long as an adult male's nor as small as a child's. He found a scrap of laurel and whittled hands holding a pitcher, just like the one Nena used to capture water for the *patrones* under the filtering pot. He always tried to decorate the lids of the rough palm coffins he made. Inés nagged that he should use his time for the little animals that don Severo could sell for him in town.

"Who cares about adorning a coffin?" she said. "The box will be buried and no one will ever see it."

"I care," he said, "even if no one sees it again."

By that evening, when the workers came from their jobs, Fela and Pabla had put Nena inside the box on sawhorses in the *rancho* and Ana prayed over her.

That night, Ana and Severo awoke to the sounds of screaming, dogs barking, fists pounding on the barracks walls calling for help. Severo ran down with his whip and revolver while Ana stood on the porch in her nightgown, a shawl over her shoulders. She didn't have time to be scared. The voices called for water, *agua, por favor,* and others insisted that there were three sick men in the building.

Severo ordered that Luis, thirty-eight, Fernando, thirty, and Tomás, twenty-six, be carried to the infirmary *bohío* while Ana and Flora dressed quickly and brought their remedies, followed by a sleepy Conciencia. The men complained of cramps, couldn't control their bowels, and had high fevers. Ana dripped strong infusions of *sacabuche* into their mouths, which didn't relieve the diarrhea or slake their thirst. None survived the night.

By midmorning, Dina, twenty-three, and Azucena, a two-year-old orphan, were writhing in their hammocks. While Flora held her head up, Ana forced the bitter *sacabuche* infusion into Dina, then saw it almost immediately discharge from her. Next to her, the little girl bawled until her throat was hoarse. Conciencia took the baby into her childish arms, rocked her, and pressed her close, unable to do anything except keep her clean. The baby's cries affected every woman within hearing, their breasts tingling with the need to suckle and comfort the dying child. Even Ana couldn't loosen the lump in her throat and was enraged by her inability to ease the girl's torment or that of any of her people.

Fela and Pabla, who stoically washed, combed, and shrouded Nena, Luis, Fernando, Tomás, and Dina, couldn't stop crying through the washing, combing, and shrouding of tiny Azucena.

José hurriedly hammered together five more coffins, but he still found time to whittle a hoe for Fernando's box, because the man was a *talero,* who dug and formed the rows where the sugar ratoons would be planted. For Luis, who was a cutter, José formed a machete. For Tomás, who was a smith, José fashioned a horseshoe. On Dina's lid José carved a mortar and pestle because she roasted and ground the coffee beans and maize, and crushed, mashed and formed cocoa beans into a paste for chocolate. For Azucena's coffin, José whittled a lily because the child was as sweet as the flower she was named for. All five carvings were rushed and not at all as intricate as José would have liked.

By the end of the third day, there had been six deaths in thirty-two hours. They didn't know what was causing their symptoms. From one moment to the next, sufferers developed a high fever, stomach cramps, and explosive diarrhea, then died within hours, begging for water, their bodies shriveled and their eyes sunk into their heads. The worst part for Ana was that in spite of their suffering, they all seemed to be aware that they were dying, soiled and in excruciating pain.

"Help me, *señora*," they cried. "*Agua, señora, por favor.* Don't let me die, *patrona*," they begged. But when given water, they had worse cramps, and the liquid leaked from their bodies.

Ana tried other remedies: *guaco, yerbabuena, anamú,* but none had the effect she hoped for and *nuestra gente* kept dying. The cries, stench, and anguish kept her sleepless over the first three days of disease and death. Finally, Severo insisted that she get some rest.

"Let Fela and Pabla take care of them," he said.

"How can I sleep? If I close my eyes I still see them, in torment."

She had not seen anyone die of cholera, but she knew enough about the disease to suspect that it was causing the deaths at Hacienda los Gemelos. She'd read that it was caused by miasma, foul-smelling, poisoned air. She ordered that the walls and floors of the barracks and the *bohíos* be thoroughly scrubbed with lavender and *yerbabuena*.

"And burn sage and juniper twigs in every corner."

She hoped that these measures would cleanse the stuffy air produced by sweaty bodies in crowded spaces, with the added indignity of open buckets for necessities.

These precautions, however, had no effect. By the morning of the fourth day, Lula, twenty, Coral, twenty-four, Benicio, forty-six, and Félix, seventy-one, showed symptoms, and two infants, Sarita and Ruti, died heaving in their mother's arms.

"Twelve of *nuestra gente* are dead," Ana said. "Not counting the children, eight were strong and healthy." She couldn't say it, but Severo understood—eight fewer for the cane.

Severo sent Efraín to track Dr. Vieira, but the doctor had traveled to Portugal to visit relatives. Other than the apothecary in Guares, there was no medical professional within a day's ride of Los Gemelos, so Ana, Flora, Fela, Pabla, and even Conciencia took care of the sick or those who showed symptoms.

Ana rushed from the barracks to the *bohíos* to the infirmary, feeling more helpless with each sign of illness, each death. Sixty-two-year-old Oscar, twenty-nine-year-old Poldo, twenty-three-year-old Carmina, and five-year-old Sandro. Sixteen of seventy-eight slaves died in seven days.

She lived meters from them, delivered their babies, baptized them, taught them the Lord's prayer and how to follow and respond to the decades of her rosary. She stitched their clothes, distributed their rations, salved their wounds and injuries. She was closer to them than to the servants who raised, dressed, and fed her in Spain. She was even closer physically and emotionally to them than to her parents. Now they were dying in agony, and the only thing she could do was to drip bitter liquid into their mouths and tell the survivors that the dead were going to the heaven she promised them in Sunday services. She prayed, but as her people continued to die, the empty prayers formed a ball of rage in her chest, hardening until she felt its pressure. You have abandoned me, she said to God, unafraid that it was humility he expected from his people.

As Conciencia predicted, the lieutenant rode up, escorted by soldiers who looked warily around, eager to get away as soon as their business was over. Severo galloped in from a near field, and still mounted, the men stood under the breadfruit tree to talk in low voices. After the soldiers left, Severo joined Ana on the porch, where she stood waiting, her face pinched by anxiety.

"Cholera, as you suspected," Severo said. "It's also in San Bernabé, Guares, and the hamlets around us."

"What can we do?"

"Quarantine the sick, burn everything they've touched, avoid contact."

"How are we to take care of them?"

Severo seemed not to have considered this. He looked at Ana, then at Conciencia, who lowered her eyes. The gesture, which in the slaves was a sign of respect, irked him coming from the girl.

"I'll put the older ones in charge of the sick," he said. "Send your remedies, but don't go into the barracks, the *bohíos*, or the infirmary while there's sickness there."

"But—"

"I mean it," he warned her.

"They need me," she said to the air, because Severo was already ordering men to erect sleeping *ranchos* far from the noxious buildings. Within hours, the sick were moved to the men's barracks and Fela, Pabla, and seventy-year-old Samuel were assigned to tend the dying, whose pitiful wails for water rent the nights.

Anyone with signs of illness was banished to the barracks: thirty-seven-year-old Juancho, forty-five-year-old Hugo, six-year-old Juan, three-year-old Chuíto, thirty-year-old Jorge. Jacobo carried his thirty-two-year-old wife, Tita, in his arms and as soon as he relinquished her, went back to his *bohío* for his little girl, Rosita, and a few hours later his son, Chano. Jacobo was born in Africa and as a young man ran away from his first hacienda, was caught and whipped, then sold to Los Gemelos. A few weeks after Ana arrived there, he stole a machete because he planned to run away again and Severo whipped him. His screams reached Ana in the *casona* the same day she told Ramón and Inocente that yes, she'd punish a slave if she had to. Today, as Jacobo returned to his *bohío*, no matter what he might have done, Ana would be unable to add to the punishment already meted out by God and Severo. Jacobo walked from the barracks with his head bowed to his chest, his sinewy arms hanging alongside his torso, his knees slack, his bare feet barely lifting from the ground, a picture of grief and suffering. The phrases she'd learned for times like these were useless. *Vaya con Dios. Que Dios le bendiga. Que la Virgen le cuide.* She couldn't say them even to herself, or believe them.

She consulted her books and pamphlets, and following their recommendations, spent most of the day formulating ever stronger infusions and broths. Severo found her in the kitchen with Flora, Paula, and Conciencia on the eighth morning. A trestle table was laden with branches and leaves of herbs, twigs, and the desiccated peels of fruits and vegetables that they were tying into bundles. A cauldron bubbled on the *fogón*. Clear and greenish liquids cooled in several cans and bowls. The shack was stifling in the July heat. Ana wiped her forehead with her apron and followed Severo outside. He started toward the breadfruit tree, but she led him to the shade on the other side of the house.

"Nothing but bad news comes to me under that tree," she muttered.

"I'm sorry that my news will be no better," he said grimly.

She looked toward the barracks. Fela scooped water from the drum by the door and went inside with it.

"I've ordered that the dead be burned," Severo said.

"But that's a sin," she gasped, because even though she was losing her faith, she still thought like a Catholic.

"José can't make coffins fast enough."

She was having a hard time maintaining her composure. "They're dying faster than we can bury them."

"Yes," he said.

She covered her face with her hands; then, as if the gesture were too revealing of the horror she felt, she dropped them quickly and settled her shoulders. "Do what you must. Just do it far from here."

He ordered that the pyre be started in the meadow farthest from the *casona*. Dense smoke swirled over the burning mound, dispersing the bittersweet tang of burning flesh. Every time Ana looked in that direction, she saw years' worth of work dissolving into the clouds.

She was in her study early the ninth morning, preparing the pay packets for the *jornaleros*. Severo ran up the steps, tugging at the bandana that he wore over his face as protection against the pestilence and that made him look like a *bandido*.

"Three of the foremen ran off with their families," he said.

"But who's going to supervise—"

"Coto agreed to stay, at double salary, until I can find more men."

"In just a few months we'll have four hundred *cuerdas* to harvest."

"I know, but our biggest concern now is to keep the healthy from running away."

Failure had always been a possibility: poor harvests and financial exigencies, physical labor, the twins' deaths, storms, a hurricane. Failure had always been a cloud on her horizon, but she'd found a way to meet those trials through hard work and, yes, calculated manipulations. Maybe it was exhaustion, but she couldn't think her way out of this predicament.

"We'll be ruined," she said, as if her greatest fear had become real.

"We'll make sure that doesn't happen."

It had been years since she'd heard that hard, unemotional voice, that gathering of tenacious will fixed on a mission. He had confidence that she couldn't match, that frightened her. As it did the afternoon he pledged to punish Inocente's murderers, her scalp now tingled and she was glad that Severo Fuentes was on her side.

Neither Flora nor Conciencia was allowed to care for the sick, but the precaution didn't spare the Mbuti, who woke up the tenth morning with stomach cramps and diarrhea.

"*Agua, señora,*" Flora pleaded when, alerted by Conciencia, Ana went down to their room to the cries, to the smell, and to Flora's big eyes already dimming.

Severo ordered that she be exiled to the quarantine *barracón.*

"Not Flora. Conciencia and I can take care of her."

"She can't be saved, Ana. She's dying."

"Let me try."

"I can make no exceptions."

"I can't let her die, Severo, not my Flora."

Over the course of that day, Ana trickled her concoctions onto Flora's parched lips, the bitter and the sour, but none saved her. Ana held her long after Flora's body had gone slack. She felt beyond sorrow or anger, beyond tears, and buried her emotions. But she couldn't subdue her thoughts. Why, she asked herself, does this death hurt more than the ones of Abuelo Cubillas, my father, Ramón, and Inocente? She wiped Flora's face with the hem of her apron. Why you? She looked up at Severo, waiting at the threshold. She let go of Flora and said a silent good-bye.

"You can take her away now."

She went upstairs, where no one could see her cry. She was *la patrona,* and if she broke, the whole structure she'd so carefully built would crumble beneath her. She stayed in her room the rest of the day.

That night, Flora was thrown into the fire, but there was no one to sing her into the next world.

———

On the eleventh day, thirty-three-year-old Inés, who nursed Miguel and Conciencia, was sent into the barracks. Inés, who loved gossip. Inés, who berated her husband for spending too much time decorating coffins.

"Please, *patrón,* please let me bury her, *mi buen señor.* She was the milk mother to *la patrona*'s son, the mother of my sons, his milk brothers."

"I can make no exceptions."

This time, Ana didn't intercede. Cholera spared José and his sons twelve-year-old Efraín and eleven-year-old Indio, but it took his two youngest children, Pedrito, six, and Tati, four, who went into the fire hours after their mother. The only slave allowed to have tools without prior permission, José took refuge in his shop. While his sons toiled in the fields, and as his wife's and two youngest children's bodies smoldered, José chose and smoothed a mahogany board two heads taller than himself and two of his hands' width. He studied the grain, caressed the length of the board, wiped sawdust and soot from both sides. Then, starting at the far left, he began to carve with the first death, Nena: hands pouring water from a pitcher. Then came a hoe, a machete, a horseshoe, a mortar and pestle, a lily, a hen with her chicks, a broom, another hoe, a shovel, a ham, two hibiscus flowers, a bell, another hoe, another machete, a cooking spoon, a top with its twine, a long-handled ladle used to skim boiling sugar syrup, a bellows, a kite, a butterfly, a rake, a bowl, a gourd. When he reached the spot for Flora he thought a long time, wishing he knew how to sculpt a song. Finally he settled on a malanga leaf because she once said it reminded her of the ones her people in Africa used for building their shelters. For Inés he carved full, shapely lips. And for his own two children, a sun and a moon.

In the meadow on the other side of the barracks, seven-year-old Conciencia stood on the periphery as red, orange, and blue fingers blazed to the heavens. In the transparent heat billowing from the flames and in the thick gray smoke of the consuming fires, she saw the spirits of the dead rise, some in song and others in writhing agony. Mesmerized, Conciencia directed her thoughts toward the spiraling clouds and asked her questions. The fire hissed and cackled answers in puffs and swirls that took shape before her eyes as its sizzle whispered in a tongue only she could understand.

During the worst of the scourge, no one looked healthier than Severo Fuentes. No one moved on foot or horseback with more authority; no one else's eyes peered so closely into every nook and hollow of the plantation; no one else paid as much attention to the smallest details of the operations as Severo Fuentes. From the *casona,* Ana saw him coming and going, ordering men and beasts, his voice hardly raised but heard everywhere by everyone. If he slept, she didn't see it. He was out all night patrolling the lanes and canebrakes with his dogs. He stopped to see how she was doing, to bring news, and to remind her not to go into the barracks, to have no contact with anyone except for Conciencia, who delivered her meals and bathed her. Night was the hardest time. When Conciencia walked into the room, Ana always expected Flora with her bowls, her smile, her songs. Conciencia was serious, silent unless spoken to. Ana knew her entire history, so there were no mysteries about another life in another place. She was also a child, and Ana now realized how much it had meant to have another adult woman as her companion. Of course there were no confidences or intimate chats, but Flora, who was at least twenty years older than Ana, had been a reassuring presence.

With the other household slaves dead, and the survivors at some distance from the *casona,* Ana had less human contact. Flora was dead, Inés was dead, La Lavandera was dead, Pilar the cook was dead. Old Samuel, who was in charge of the pastures, the cattle used for hauling, and the cows raised for milk and cheesemaking, was dead. His two grandsons, Sandro and Chuíto, were also dead. Tomás, who was a smith, and Benicio, who cleaned and repaired the barns, corrals, and work buildings, were dead. Dina and her husband, Juancho, who worked with her in the gardens, orchards, coops, and dovecotes, were dead. Siña Damita's husband, Lucho, who raised and fattened the pigs, butchered them, smoked the hams, and made sausages from their blood and intestines, was dead. Their daughter-in-law, Coral, was dead, as was her daughter Sarita. Other than her granddaughter Carmencita, the disease wiped out Siña Damita's entire family.

The *batey,* once so full of life and activity, was nearly deserted most of the day. But still meals were prepared, linens were washed, cows were milked and fed. The gardens thrived, fruit was picked, pigs were slaughtered, sausages were made, eggs were collected, hams were smoked. The work Ana had overseen went on without her while she waited in the *casona* for the plague to end, accompanied only by a seven-year-old child.

One evening, Severo brought news.

"The governor has closed the gates to the capital. *Sanjuaneros* are ordered to stay indoors, and they're under curfew."

"There's cholera in San Juan, too?"

"In every town of the island. When I looked in on Luis, Faustina had just returned from Mayagüez. She saw an entire barrio burned to the ground. It appears that the cholera is worse in the poor barrios, so, on the advice of local doctors, the municipal council set them on fire. The Guares *cabildo* is doing the same thing."

Pockets under his eyes and the tense edges of his mouth made him look much older than thirty-six.

"If the city is closed and the poor barrios are burned," Ana asked, "where is the *cabildo* putting the people?"

"Neither the governor nor the councils have provided for that. All they care about is how to control the epidemic. People are sleeping in the open, under trees, in the church. Entire families are wandering along the roads."

"Dios nos salve." Ana crossed herself and was instantly aware that it had been a long time since she had appealed so directly to God.

"We must move up the hill, Ana. The house is not finished, but it's unsafe for us to live so close to the cholera."

"But we have isolated the sick."

"Flora got sick. She died, Ana. We're all at risk. It's been three weeks, and they keep dying. I'll not endanger your life or mine."

He'd never spoken harshly to her, never used less than the most courteous tones, addressing her as *usted* even in the intimacy of their bed. But his voice, which rumbled as if he were containing its power for her benefit, now carried the authority of an order and tolerated no challenge. She began to protest, but the warning in his eyes made her stop as if he'd physically restrained her. She again opened her mouth to speak, but once more his eyes said what his lips didn't and she was silenced. He nodded, accepting her surrender, and in one quick, catlike move, drew her to him, held her tight, and kissed her eyes. "I treasure you too much to let anything happen to you," he said into her ear. "So long as I breathe I'll take care of you." He left her alone to ponder whether, in her entire life, she'd ever expected, or wanted, a man to care for her.

The next morning, Severo went through every room of the new house, opening and shutting windows and doors. Each was empty except for the one that was to be his and Ana's chamber, where a camphor wood chest was pressed against the wall. He'd ordered Lola, the new laundress, to clean and press Ana's city clothes. He'd imagined that in the house he built for her, Ana would sometimes wear the elaborate dresses and kid slippers put away years earlier. He looked forward to seeing her glide across the blue tiles, even imagined she'd demonstrate the salon dances she learned as a girl.

Lola had folded each item between layers of muslin pillows stuffed with fragrant herbs. When he touched them, the garments felt as if they'd melt through his fingers.

This is what a lady should wear, he thought, silks and lace and pretty things. Other than the first time he saw Ana in San Juan, and later in her riding costume, he'd not seen her in anything but plain cotton, black, gray, navy blue. He longed to see her in finery, hair glistening. He wanted her to be different from Consuelo, from the *campesinas,* from the slave women, better dressed and more refined than the *hacendadas* and *dueñas* in Guares and its environs.

For the past three weeks, he'd been surrounded by disease and death. He now touched these lavish things, held them in his hands, caressed them. His fingers were scarred and callused, and he was afraid to damage the liquid fabric or the intricate needlework. But he needed to hold something beautiful in his hands.

He lifted the embroidered silk and lace clothes and spread them on the floor. He laid a corset underneath a bodice with short sleeves, its edges frilled with lace. He butterflied a skirt below it and placed gloves where Ana's hands would be. He arranged a mantilla to frame an invisible head, and posed delicate stockings inside dainty kid shoes with satin bows ready to dance. He bowed in her direction, smiled, offered his hand, imagining Ana standing before him, perfumed and flushed with excitement, eager to let him lead her across the polished floor.

He closed his eyes to better see himself with soft hands and smooth nails wearing smart clothes—a white silk shirt, a black velvet *chaleco* with silver buttons, black pants, kid shoes with buckles, and a vermilion sash around his waist. He softened his knees and swayed from side to side. When he opened his eyes, Severo looked around, as if there were any danger that someone might see him behaving so foolishly.

Down on the hill, Ana studied the four rooms of the *casona* and saw what she had ignored for years. It was small and crudely made. The green walls echoed the color of the fields, so there was no respite for the eye from the vegetation. She suddenly felt claustrophobic and stepped onto the porch. The whimpering of the sick was intolerable, so she fled to the other end, away from the barracks. In the workshop, José banged something or other, and a bird trilled in the breadfruit tree.

Ana felt powerless. She hated the feeling that she was inadequate to what was happening around her. They depend on me to take care of them, she thought, and I don't know what to do. I want to be a good mistress.

The morning had warmed. Conciencia was collecting more *sacabuche,* even though it had already proved ineffective against cholera. So had sweetened *higüero* pulp, crushed papaya seeds, guava root bark, and lemons. But they had to give the sick something to hope for. Clearing the miasma in the barracks did nothing either. In spite of every effort, she'd failed in her duty.

Ana felt a heavier burden than she wished to acknowledge, but wouldn't call it guilt. She'd accepted her role as a slave owner and did everything she could to fulfill her obligations. She knew it was inevitable that the slaves would be set free someday, but *jornaleros* were expensive, unreliable, and didn't work as hard. She hoped it wouldn't happen in her lifetime.

From the first she'd sensed that she should never bow before

Severo, that among the things he most valued was her strength of character. But there were moments, like now, when she wished she could allow herself the female prerogative to be weak, to cry loudly. She'd swallowed so many tears that someday she might be unable to hold more inside and they'd overflow into a torrent.

She never asked why she focused all her energy and sorrow on the fate and fortunes of Hacienda los Gemelos. She only knew that from the moment she saw it, the land and everything and every-one within its borders were essential to her existence. It couldn't be questioned, challenged, or explained. It just was. But over the past three weeks, she'd found it impossible to talk herself into the opti-mism that drove her over the past eleven years. Grueling years . . . *No, I can't think this way.* She shook her head to clear the mor-bid thoughts that simmered like bubbles over boiling oil. *I've been alone too long,* she said to herself, and went down the stairs to the *batey.*

Even though Severo forbade it, she had to look in on the sick. There was nothing more she could do for them, but she had to see them, to let them know that she hadn't forgotten them, that even though she didn't own a single human being—they were all owned by don Eugenio and Severo—they were hers, *su gente,* and she couldn't in all conscience abandon them.

Fela and Pabla were sitting in the shade by the door, each with a baby in her arms. The women were old, but they looked ancient now, their faces ashen, their eyes veiled with grief and hopelessness. Even though she was standing right in front of them, they didn't look at her, as if the only people they could see were the ones about to die. Ana could go no further. *They, too, will die,* she realized. *We could all die.*

She turned around and sprinted up the stairs to the *casona.* Severo was right. They were in danger. After years of struggle, her life could end in a few hours, just as it had for her long-ago ancestor, in an ignoble death. In filth and failure.

Leaving the *casona* now, while *su gente* died in the ramshackle barracks was not a defeat. It was a temporary surrender. To fulfill her responsibility to *nuestra gente,* she must live.

———

Early the next morning, Ana closeted herself in her study while men moved the furniture onto carts. She packed her books and pamphlets, catalogs and gazettes, Ramón's and Inocente's letters to and from their parents, her correspondence with Jesusa and Gustavo, Elena, and Miguel. In another crate, she placed communications to and from Mr. Worthy, the deeds, titles, reports, and transactions, dated and stamped.

Conciencia brought her lunch when the bell rang in the canebrakes. Ana sent it back without touching it. She ordered that her labeled crates be moved and was left alone, in the hottest part of the day, with her ledgers.

She kept the human inventory in a brown leather book, the pages divided into columns. The left column showed the date acquired, followed by the purchase/rental price or a check for babies born on the premises. In the next column she entered the name, then *h* for *hombre, m* for *mujer, n* for *niño* or *niña*. Within parentheses she entered their ages. The next column indicated particular skills. The last was another date and a note marking changes: *vendido,* and if sold, a price; *escapado,* and whether the runaway was captured; and *muerto,* dead.

On January 1, 1845, Severo set up the ledgers, entering twenty-five names, followed by de Argoso. Three of them were debits—the runaways. On January 9 he added sixteen names followed by de Fuentes, the ones he brought to the hacienda. On the same date he entered ten more de Argoso names, men purchased with her dowry in clandestine sales. On October 17 he recorded ten more de Argosos from the finca Ramón and Inocente bought during Ana's *cuarentena.* On January 13, 1846, he entered ten more de Argoso men. On August 8, 1847, he added ten de Argoso names, and on April 3, 1852, another five. In between there were births and deaths, so at the bottom of Ana's log, on July 29, 1856, at the height of the cholera epidemic, there were seventy-eight slaves on the premises, thirty belonging to Severo.

Ana dipped her silver pen into her crystal inkwell, both gifts from Abuelo Cubillas when she first learned to write cursive. The first entry she marked was next to December 14, 1844: "50 pesos / Nena de Fuentes / n / (10)? / laundress / July 11, 1856 / *muerta.*" She stared at the page, dipped her pen again, and crossed the name out. Above it she wrote "Olivia." She used her left index finger to find subsequent names, recording the dates when each slave died. By the time she'd entered everyone, her hand was cramped from clutching the pen so tightly. She counted and double-checked the number. With trembling, ink-stained fingers, in her precise, elegant hand, she deducted from the total of seventy-eight, and on the bottom of the page below the debit column she wrote "31, *muertos.*"

EYES THAT DO NOT SEE,
HEART THAT DOES NOT FEEL

While cholera raged in the *batey,* Ana settled in the new *casa grande* accompanied by Conciencia, the houseman, Teo, and his wife, Paula. From the hill, she didn't hear the wails from the barracks, didn't smell the flux, didn't see the emaciated bodies, pleading eyes. She plunged into her work. Hoe in hand, she broke into the dirt as if every seed and shoot might sprout a leaf, a bud, a flower to heal *nuestra gente.*

Still, over the two months of the epidemic, nearly half of Hacienda los Gemelos' and almost two-thirds of Severo's slaves died in successive waves of contagion relieved by days when it seemed the plague was over, only for the sickness to return in more virulent form. In the latter weeks, as more slaves survived than died, the pyres were doused and burials resumed. By the time it was over, Ana had logged forty-seven *muertos* of seventy-eight *nuestra gente* into her ledger. The last entries were for Fela and Pabla, who nursed a few slaves back to health but saw most of them die. They were put to rest in the very center of the graveyard, where José placed the largest, most elaborately carved crosses he could fashion.

No one suffered more than the *gente de color* in Puerto Rico during the months of the cholera epidemic and its aftermath. The disease hit hardest in the poorest barrios where free blacks, *mulatos,* and *libertos* lived. By February 1857, when the government declared the epidemic contained, more than twenty-seven thousand people had died—over half of them *gente de color.* Officials admitted that these figures were approximate, and that the number of deaths was probably higher.

Slaves fared no better than the free *gente de color*. Reports of nearly fifty-five hundred dead couldn't account for every loss in every hacienda, or the men, women, and children bought in clandestine sales unreported to avoid taxes. The government estimated that a minimum of 12 percent of the slave population of Puerto Rico died.

With so many dead—most of them men in their prime—and with thousands who survived but were weak or incapacitated, a large percentage of the Puerto Rican workforce vanished. At the end of 1856, Ana estimated that twenty slaves were healthy enough to bring in the harvest, the same number as when she first arrived nearly twelve years earlier. Only now they had not thirty but four hundred *cuerdas* in cane ready to process.

So that she could keep abreast of what happened on the valley, Severo set up a telescope for Ana on the corner of the *balcón*. Two or three times a day she scanned the deep green canebrakes for pale lavender *guajana* buds to signal the harvest. One evening, she and Severo were sitting on matching rockers on the *balcón*, the valley below sprinkled with the flickering lights from *bohíos*.

"I don't know how we'll manage," Ana said. "I expected this to be a good year. Sugar prices are slightly up, and the new equipment in my *ingenio* would have been paid for with this year's profits."

"It can't be helped," he said.

"I've never heard you say something is impossible."

"Did I say that?"

"You sounded discouraged."

"Not at all, and you shouldn't be either. *Al mal tiempo, buena cara,*" he said.

The tip of his cigar glowed red. Ana inhaled the earthy, sweet smoke that surrounded him. "How can you be so calm in the midst of all this?"

"You haven't fallen apart, either."

"I've thought about it, but no, I'm too stubborn. I'd hate myself if I gave in or gave up."

He laughed softly. "And because you know that *a río revuelto, ganancia de pescadores.*"

"It's hard to believe that there is opportunity here now when the workers we depend on keep dying."

"Look at it this way. There will be bankruptcies by planters and farmers unable to bring in their product. Most commit their profits to vendors and taxes before they even seed the ground."

"Everyone does that. We do."

"Yes, but we're in a better position. You can always appeal to don Eugenio. Most of our neighbors will have to sell assets in order to save themselves. Someone with a bit of capital can pick up land, equipment, and slaves at a bargain."

"I've never asked anything from don Eugenio."

"You're not asking, you're telling him about an investment opportunity. Credit is hard to get in Puerto Rico, and if he doesn't know that, Mr. Worthy is aware that *hacendados* and farmers resort to private loans."

"From people like you."

"I've been most generous to our *vecinos,* and while I don't want to take advantage of them when they're so vulnerable—"

"—they need cash and we need *brazos.*"

"But, of course, I don't have an inexhaustible wallet. . . ."

"I see. This is where don Eugenio can be helpful."

"The more distressed *vecinos* might be willing to rent or sell their slaves."

"That would help them and us."

"We'd be doing them a favor."

"Of course. I'll write to Mr. Worthy tomorrow."

She inhaled his smoke again. In the days following their move up the hill he'd been as passionate as in the first days of their marriage. It was hard to believe it had been almost six years. She desired him, his rough hands, muscular body. Most of all, his attention, the focused gaze of the lover, his alert listening to every word she uttered, his uncanny ability to guess what she was thinking.

"Would you like to try a smoke?" The tobacco was grown on his land, for his use. The cigar was thick, soft but firm, warm, and the tightly rolled leaves had a pleasing texture, especially along the delicate veins. She sucked and her lungs caught on fire. "Slow," he said. "A little puff, not a deep breath. Just kiss it."

She did so, and a delightful light-headedness made her feel as if she were melting.

"We should name the house," he said after a long silence.

It was another of his ideas about what rich people did. It wasn't enough to build a new house, to fill every room with custom-made furniture, to order glassware, china, cutlery, and bolts of fine cotton, damask, linen, and silk from the United States and Europe. The place must be named, like a newborn child.

"Did you have one in mind?" she asked, knowing perfectly well he wouldn't have brought up the subject otherwise.

"El Destino," he said, savoring the word as if it were a ripe fruit.

"El Destino," she repeated, liking the sibilance before the sharp *ti,* and the way her lips appeared to send forth another kiss, this one with the soft, final vowel.

Ana hadn't seen Miguel in seven years, although correspondence to and from San Juan was frequent. In her letters she never let Miguel forget that she was building Hacienda los Gemelos for him. But she had no idea whether Los Gemelos meant anything to him. She wondered whether he still resembled her, like he did as a boy. Or had he grown to look more like Ramón and Inocente? What she knew about Miguel was in his correspondence, and she hoped he wasn't as dull and unimaginative as the letters and sketches he enclosed. He was now almost twelve years old, and not once had he asked to return to the place where he was born. Ana hadn't forgotten Leonor's contempt, Eugenio's eagerness to raise him under his roof. If Miguel wanted to visit her, she was sure neither doña Leonor nor don Eugenio would encourage him. Still, it bothered her that there was no regret in his letters about their long separation.

She'd had no word from San Juan for six months, but in late 1856 a letter from Miguel reached Los Gemelos. The Argosos had survived the plague and things were back to normal in the capital. She wrote to his grandparents requesting that they send Miguel to spend a few weeks with her after the harvest.

Once the *zafra* at Hacienda los Gemelos began, Ana and Conciencia rode to the *batey* daily, carrying baskets of bandages and remedies. Ana had ordered the old barracks repaired and windows cut into the walls to create an infirmary. She was determined to keep the air moving and clean in every building to avoid the miasmic disaster of the previous year.

The frenetic pace of the *zafra* only slowed at the end, after every stalk had been processed. But in early 1857 there was desperation from the first as Ana and Severo tried to recoup their losses by bringing in a complete harvest with fewer workers before the rains of May began.

Severo managed to buy twelve more men, seven women, and four children from a bankrupt hacienda. He reminded four landowners that the terms of their loans were imminent but that they could repay him with slaves. In addition to land, four more men and four women erased the *hacendados'* obligations to Severo Fuentes. Neighbors unable to manage their estates were forced to liquidate assets at auction. Don Eugenio and Mr. Worthy agreed that the opportunities couldn't be passed up. With Eugenio's investment, Severo was able to buy more land and another five men for the hacienda.

One morning two weeks before the harvest began, Ana and Severo were in her study organizing the work.

"I've doubled the food rations for the survivors," Ana said. "Here's the list of those still recovering. Assign them easier jobs."

"I can't promise that. We need every *brazo,* from the youngest to the oldest, in the fields."

"Many of them are weak—"

"They'll be fine by the time the *zafra* starts. Don't be too easy on them or they'll take advantage of you."

"They're not. But some are still too sick—"

"We have four hundred *cuerdas* to harvest, Ana."

"I know how many *cuerdas* are ready," she snapped before she realized how rare it was for them to argue. "If we expect them to be alive by the end, we have to take better care of them."

"You might have noticed," he said through taut lips, "that I know how to manage a workforce."

"Of course I do—"

"Let me take care of that, then. May I see the supply lists, please?"

Chastened, she handed over the papers. The room was stifling all of a sudden, and while he read and marked up the pages, she walked to the *balcón* for some air. On the ground below, a rooster and his harem pecked at the ground. Unexpectedly, he flew up on the rail and strutted from one end to the other. He crowed three times, full throated and defiant, then dropped to the ground again. Yes, she thought, the cock has to crow.

"Did you say something?" Severo was in the same chair by her desk.

"No," she said.

He looked at her for a few moments, as if reading her mind, then returned to the lists.

In early February, Severo led the *macheteros* into the canebrakes before sunrise and kept them there until sundown. With fewer *brazos,* even artisans like José went into the fields, and children as young as five had jobs. Boys led the unyoked bulls to pasture, tied them to stakes, and moved them frequently to avoid overgrazing. Girls peeled *ñames,* plantains, and *yautías* for the workers' meals, boiled in huge vats.

After the cholera funeral pyres, Conciencia's visions came more frequently, but she was too young to interpret most of what she saw and depended on Ana to help her. Severo scoffed at the notion that Conciencia could look into the future.

"Ask her where I can find ten more *jornaleros,* then."

"It doesn't work that way. She doesn't do tricks. She has a true gift, but she's a child and doesn't understand what she sees."

A few days later, Conciencia told Ana that she'd envisioned a crazy bull butting his head against a fence until he broke through. Ana told Severo, and although skeptical, he alerted the men in charge of the cattle to be watchful. But Conciencia's visions didn't come with a specific date and time when something would happen. Three weeks passed and the vigilance over the most aggressive bulls waned, if not vanished. Sure enough, one afternoon, Coloso, the biggest and strongest of the bulls, ripped his stake from the ground, ran straight for a fence, butted until he splintered it, and, foamy mouthed, chased around the *batey* while men, women, and children jumped out of his way to avoid his horns and massive hooves. He stood in the middle of the yard bellowing triumphantly, then plunged into the pond, where the mud sucked him into the soft bottom the more he tried to extricate himself. Every effort to save him failed.

After that, Severo listened more closely whenever Ana mentioned one of Conciencia's visions.

One morning as she prepared to go down to the fields, Ana found Conciencia agitated.

"What is it, *niña*?"

"A dream, *señora*."

Ana's heart jumped. "Tell me."

"There was a man on fire—"

"Like the pyres, *niña*?"

"No, *señora*, not those *muertos*. It was a white man. It was El Caminante, *señora*."

"Ramón? You never knew him."

"I saw him, *señora*. He was on fire in the *cañaveral*." She was distraught, partly because the vision must have been terrifying, partly because she didn't really know what she'd seen.

"Calm down, little one. Your dream must have been about don Severo."

"No, *señora*—"

"Ramón is dead, Conciencia, and he didn't die in a fire. Your dream was scary, but I'm glad you told me. It was a warning, and you might have just saved *el patrón*'s life. I'll tell him to be careful when they burn the fields."

Conciencia hung her head as if she'd done something wrong.

There were moments, like now, when the girl looked less like a child and more like an ancient, wise woman whose eyes could peer into her soul. When Ana baptized her, she'd whispered that she would be her conscience, and sometimes when she looked at the girl, memories washed over Ana unbidden, and often unwelcome.

She left Conciencia in the infirmary and rode Marigalante to her *ingenio*. She crossed herself as she skirted the slave cemetery, Fela's and Pabla's crosses sentinels over the other graves. José had asked if he could add over the gate a board he'd sculpted. Severo later told Ana that it was José's monument to suffering.

Across a brook and up the hill was the ancient ceiba near Ramón's grave. Again she crossed herself, and as she did, she remembered what Conciencia had just said—El Caminante in flames. Ana broke into a cold sweat and shook her head to rattle the image from her brain. Lately she was shaking her head more often, and wondered whether Severo had noticed. I've seen too many deaths, she said to herself. Again she shook her head and ordered herself to stop thinking.

She rode across the fields, where the foremen drove the workers with curses and threats, with shoves and lashes. Ana turned away from them. Severo had made it clear that he managed the workforce and she shouldn't interfere. Over the following weeks she didn't complain to the foremen or to Severo that the slaves, particularly, were being pushed harder than ever. She was the *patrona,* and could have insisted that pregnant women be given less demanding tasks. She could have argued that they should not be forced to constantly bend over the long stalks the *macheteros* dropped as they moved into the canebrakes, to collect and carry the heavy bundles of cane to the carts. So far, three women had already miscarried. She didn't protest that children were doing work usually performed by adults. She didn't exempt elders who had toiled all their lives, who miraculously survived cholera, whom the slave codes expressly required that owners allow to sit quietly in the shade for the last years left to them.

During that *zafra* of 1857, Ana rode Marigalante from one boundary of Hacienda los Gemelos to the other, secure on the silver-studded saddle Abuelo Cubillas gave her, high over the bent backs of the men and women she called *nuestra gente,* and she didn't say or even think of words like "abuse" or "injustice." She had a job to do, so she closed her eyes, hardened her heart, and didn't say a word. Now she sensed their hostile glances, the silent curses.

The kitchen for the field workers was halfway up the hill to Ingenio Diana. Two cauldrons hung over fire pits where the plantains and tubers bubbled. Fatback sputtered in an enormous iron skillet on a third *fogón* raised from the ground. The men usually called for water the minute they sat to eat their meals, so boys and girls were huddled by the barrels, filling the long gourds dangling from ropes over their shoulders.

Severo helped Ana dismount. He could tell she was upset, but before he could ask, the bell tolled, and as the first clang echoed across the fields, the workers dropped their tools in front of their foremen and rushed to the trestle tables where two cooks were setting up the meal. Two lines formed, slaves on the left, free people on the right.

"If they were as fast in the fields as to the food line," Severo said, trying to lighten her mood, "we'd have finished the *zafra* by now."

He was interrupted by a scuffle.

"Don't touch me!" Moncho, a new day laborer, shoved Jacobo, who shoved Moncho back, and the two men wrestled to the ground. The others backed into their own groups, pushing the women behind the line while they urged the fighters with insults and curses.

"Go to the house," Severo said to Ana as he uncoiled his whip and bolted toward the men. "Efraín, the *patrona*'s horse," he called to the boy.

Ana had never seen Severo's whip fully extended. The moment it unfurled, the two lines of workers backed even farther away from Jacobo and Moncho. The whip snapped into precise arcs, once across Jacobo's legs, then Moncho's, Jacobo's again, then Moncho's, and a third time as the men scrabbled from it and each other.

"I didn't do anything, *patrón*!" Jacobo called, and another arc formed and fell across his thighs, then almost immediately, across Moncho's calves.

"That whip is for slaves," Moncho yelled. "I'm a free man and a *blanco*!"

He lunged at Severo, swinging fists, spitting threats. Ana would never forget the silence when Moncho dared to attack Severo, as every man, woman, and child held their breath. Moncho was a smallish man, thin, sinewy, and before he could strike more than a couple of ineffective punches, Severo heaved him off the ground and threw him several feet.

Moncho crashed against the raised *fogón,* toppling its contents. A sizzle. A shriek. Ana didn't think. She sprinted toward the voice behind the raised *fogón* where the skillet filled with fatback had overturned. On the ground was a little girl, one of the cholera orphans, her left side shimmering with boiling lard.

Her name was Meri. Severo had brought her and her older sister, Gloria, from a bankrupt hacienda. Ana had hardly noticed her before, her attention focused on the adults who did the brunt of the work. She ripped the child's clothes off her body and used her own skirts to absorb the hot grease from Meri's arm, shoulder, and back.

"Bring some water," Ana said.

The women surrounded Ana and Meri, holding full gourds. Ana

poured water on Meri's arm and shoulder to cool her skin. Meri's stick-thin limbs jerked with every touch. A woman appeared with aloe leaves, her hands scratched and bleeding because she'd pulled the spiky leaves from the ground with her bare fingers, and split them open with her nails. Ana scooped the gel from the leaves and slid it over the burns. Once she'd covered every burn with the aloe, she carried Meri down the aisle dividing enslaved from free laborers to where Severo held her horse.

She moved as if in a trance, detached from her actions but exquisitely aware of every step, every breath. *Another death* the engines clacked and banged. *Another death* the cattle snuffled and stomped. *Another death* the bells around their necks jangled. *Another death* bare feet dragged across the littered ground as workers backed away. Each sound was distinct from the others but dull, as if her ears were stuffed with cotton. She saw no bodies, just huge eyes following her progress toward Marigalante. *Another death* black, brown, blue pupils bored into her as sharp as needles. She walked upon dry cane leaves and stalks, carrying a burden too heavy yet much too light. *Another death*. She handed Meri to Severo while she mounted, then took the child from his arms and draped her across the saddle in front of her. Wordlessly, still in her strange daze, she galloped to the infirmary, to her unguents and leaves, her only remedies against calamity.

After so many, she couldn't let this child she hardly knew die. She rode across the paths where towering cane eradicated the horizon and didn't cross herself when she passed Ramón's grave. *Too many deaths,* as she rode beyond the slaves' cemetery. I didn't save them, but this one—she will not die.

Ana treated Meri with raw potato poultices, honey, palmarosa and helichrysum unguent, and the soothing aloe gel. She was seriously burned along her neck and left arm, on her chest and foot. No matter how tender Ana's ministrations, Meri squealed when she was touched, even in places where the hot grease hadn't reached. After her throat swelled from crying, she continued to emit gutwrenching sounds that made the hair along the back of Ana's neck stand on end.

She was sitting by Meri's pallet, forcing sweetened tisanes through her lips, when Severo appeared. "You've been at her side for three days straight. Let Conciencia watch her for a while."

"If I leave her she will die."

"What difference does it make? If she survives she'll be crippled."

She checked the dressing above Meri's elbow. "She might be."

He watched her for a few moments. "Why are you all of a sudden taking such interest in a useless child?"

"She's not useless!" She looked up fast enough to notice him flinch. "Not a single one of them is useless. You have surely noticed that nothing can be done around here without them."

He stepped closer but didn't try to touch her. "Don't talk to me like that, Ana."

He was like ice, and for a moment, he scared her. She gathered her wits and stood up, which forced him to step back.

"I'm sorry to have raised my voice," she said. He acknowledged her apology with a nod. "When she recovers I'll put her to work in the sewing room."

"You don't need to reward her," he said, "for surviving."

Meri whimpered. Ana returned to the stool by her side, dropped more liquid into the girl's mouth. When she looked up again, Severo was peering at her like a *guaraguao* at a *pitirre.*

"*Buenas noches,* then." He inclined his head again, eyes dark as a forest. He turned toward the door but stopped. "You might save her," he said before he left. "But don't believe that after all you've done she will be grateful."

After ten days of constant attention and care, Ana was confident that Meri would live, even if her arm, shoulder, and chest would be permanently scarred. She had the worst injuries but wasn't the only patient in the infirmary. Every day someone was brought in with cuts, bruises, sprains, or infections. To discourage *jornaleros* from missing work when they didn't feel well, Ana and Conciencia treated them and delivered their babies. During the harvest months, the adults, free or chattel, were kept too busy for sexual relations. The months of *el tiempo muerto,* then, were actually the beginning of life, when most children were conceived, to be born in March, April, and May, at the peak of the harvest.

Besides the women in labor and newborns in the infirmary, there were other victims of the canebrakes. Severo had trained the workers to set controlled fires that scorched the leaves but left the juice-rich stalks exposed and easier to cut. Even during these burns there were accidents. The spectacular flames often entranced the boys who managed the bullocks until the heat singed their skin and hair. A barefoot worker might step on a smoldering patch that seemed doused. A calm day could turn windy and sparks might jump over rows, starting fires in a completely different area from what was planned, causing panic and isolating workers inside walls of flames and smoke.

While Severo avoided setting fires at night, it wasn't unusual for the work to extend after sundown. This presented its own problems. Men, women, and children were in smoky darkness, swinging machetes, shovels, hoes, and pikes. It was more likely they'd be wounded by the tools used to combat the fire than by the heat and flames.

Even before Meri's accident, Ana spent much of her day in and around the infirmary, assisted by Conciencia, Teo, and Paula. This year, she noted that there were more serious injuries, miscarriages, and stillbirths than ever, all due to the brutal pace. In this, her thirteenth harvest at Hacienda los Gemelos, there was also an alarming number of workers who'd been whipped. The scars on the workers' bodies were the most conspicuous sign that as the months ground toward the end, Severo was frantic to bring in a complete harvest, as he'd promised. She didn't challenge or encourage him. She both admired and despised him for the same reason: his ability to set aside compassion in the service of a single-minded goal. But when she thought about it, she saw the same quality in herself, except that she believed she was not, like Severo, inured to the suffering of *nuestra gente*. She felt it, even if she wouldn't sacrifice her own ambitions to change their circumstances.

By the end of June, when she had to settle the accounts for the harvest, Ana could report to Mr. Worthy that in spite of the losses during the epidemic, Hacienda los Gemelos was in excellent financial health. She was fully aware of the irony. Mr. Worthy and don Eugenio had no interest in the well-being of the people of Los Gemelos so long as the columns at the bottom of the ledgers showed a positive outcome relative to losses. Her conquistador ancestors, she, Mr. Worthy, don Eugenio, Severo, and thousands like them, had come to this land to prosper from its riches—by might or fright. Their wealth and power was, and continued to be, erected upon corpses.

MIGUEL GETS ALIVIO

❖

Life for Miguel in San Juan was good. He lived in a roomy, elegant home where he was coddled and spoiled by Abuela Leonor, Elena, Siña Ciriaca, and her daughter Bombón. The city was full of soldiers and people from all over the world. His grandfather was an important man who doted on him, and don Simón was a kind and inspiring teacher. Miguel had two great friends in Andrés Cardenales Romero and Luis José Castañeda Urbina, the first two boys he met in school. Like Miguel, they were born in Puerto Rico. Andrés, who was a year older, was tall and muscular with a head that seemed too big for his body. The ladies sighed over his long lashes and copious brown hair that required frequent visits to the barber. By eleven, he already showed an incipient beard, although his parents didn't allow him to shave.

Luis José was short and chunky, blond and hazel-eyed with carob skin. He was endearingly mischievous and loquacious, a good mimic and irrepressibly cheerful. His family nickname was Querubín, to his dismay now that he was a big boy.

Miguel was thinner and shorter than Andrés, taller than Luis José. He had Ramón's and Inocente's graceful physique but Ana's stature. He had light brown hair and, as don Eugenio liked to say, his grandmother's gray eyes.

The three boys were inseparable once they discovered they lived steps from one another's doors. Andrés was four houses down from don Eugenio's, and Luis José lived directly across the street. When old enough, they were allowed to walk to and from school together and one was seldom seen without the others. They learned swordsmanship from the same masters, attended catechism classes, and received their first Communion together. They were as indulged as princes but were also expected to conform to a strict code of behavior. Around ladies they were to be chivalrous, trustworthy, charming gentlemen, and the three boys learned their lessons well; but they lived in a fortress city, surrounded by soldiers, adventurers, and exiles. They were learning that when among men, they must be patently virile, courageous, honorable, and exhibit a zest for life while at the same time be willing to die for a worthy cause.

Andrés had a reputation as a seducer, even if, at eleven, he used his allure mostly to charm his way out of trouble or to cadge favors from his parents or servants. Luis José's gift for palaver was touted as confirmation that he'd grow up to be a civil lawyer like his father, whose garrulous persona he emulated. Miguel was serious, reserved, fastidious, and dutiful. He was a bit of a dandy, but then again, don Eugenio was raising him. Part of the mystique of Spanish cavalry officers was that some were known to change their uniforms two or three times a day, even during battle.

The Argosos' friends knew the dreadful story of the identical twin brothers who came to Puerto Rico to seek their fortune but found death instead. Some of the *vecinos* had met Ramón, Inocente, and Ana during their stay in San Juan years earlier, and the young men, especially, left lasting, favorable impressions. The *vecinos* attended Mass following the death of each brother, visited and comforted the Argosos after the tragedies, and took particular interest in Miguel.

The neighbors didn't believe that his grandparents and godmother were raising Miguel just because Hacienda los Gemelos was so remote that he couldn't get a good education there. Puerto Rico was crawling with unemployed émigrés from wars and conflicts in Spain, France, Italy, Venezuela, Mexico, the United States. Hundreds of tutors and governesses competed for posts with wealthy families in San Juan and the hinterlands. Even the most remote *hacendado* could find one or two teachers until their children were twelve or thirteen, when they were sent abroad to complete their education. Obviously, there was more to the story than the Argosos were willing to disclose, and the *vecinos* asked one another the same thing: What kind of mother never came to see her son and didn't send for him during school vacations or holidays?

Miguel wondered the same thing. Whenever he mentioned Hacienda los Gemelos, Elena assumed he missed his *mamá,* and told him something about her. "She's not very tall," she once said, "but so strong! And a magnificent horsewoman. That's why you're such a good rider."

When he told Abuelo that he was a good rider because his mother was so proficient, Abuelo grunted.

"Your father and uncle were expert horsemen before they met your mother. Don't forget that I'm a colonel in the cavalry and taught them, and you, to love horses and to ride well."

As he grew up Miguel learned not to mention his mother or Hacienda los Gemelos, especially around Abuela, who squinted and pressed her lips so hard that they disappeared into her mouth.

He was not allowed to forget either his mother or the hacienda, however. Every Sunday evening Miguel had to write to Mamá while Elena knitted nearby.

"Remember to mention that you have the highest mark in drawing, and include one of your sketches," Elena prompted.

He hardly remembered Mamá, but whenever he thought about her, he felt acute anxiety.

"Why does she always write that I belong with her at Hacienda los Gemelos?" he finally asked one night as he wrote another letter when he'd rather be with Andrés and Luis José near San Juan Gate, where a new regiment from Spain was disembarking.

"Because your *mamá* misses you so much, *mi amor,*" Elena said. "She loves you very much."

"Then why doesn't she come to see me?"

"I'm sure she wants to. Of course she does. But your darling *mamá* has many responsibilities at your hacienda, and she can't be away for long. Maybe you should go for a visit."

"Maybe." The idea was not appealing, but Elena's sky-blue eyes lit up at her own suggestion.

"I'll go with you. We can go by ship. Why don't you ask permission from your grandparents, *amorcito?*"

Clearly Elena was excited about going to Hacienda los Gemelos, and Miguel liked to please her. But he was afraid to ask Abuelo or Abuela. What if asking to go to the hacienda would sound to his grandparents as if he didn't want to be with them? He was reasonably certain that neither Abuelo nor Abuela liked Mamá, and if they thought he did, then they might not like him anymore and not want him to live with them in the beautiful big house on Calle Paloma just steps from his best friends in the world.

A few days later, Miguel wanted to show Elena his sketches of the gurgling fountain in the courtyard. It had taken Miguel three days to finish them, and he was proud of the details he'd captured from every angle. He was not in the habit of listening in on adult conversations, but as he approached the *sala,* he heard his name, so he stopped just outside the half-open door.

"It's natural that Miguel would want to see his mother," Elena was saying.

"She's made no effort to come to see *him.*"

"You know that she will not leave the hacienda, Tía Leonor."

"That's her choice, isn't it?"

"I used to think so but don't believe that anymore. For whatever reasons, she can't leave. I don't think she knows why."

"It's because she's mad. I'm glad she's there with that . . . that man she's married. He's another one—"

"Please forgive me, Tía, if I speak harshly to you, whom I respect and love, but it's cruel to keep Miguel from his mother if he wants to see her."

There was a moment of silence and Miguel was about to tiptoe back to his room, but he froze in place with his grandmother's next words.

"You admire her so, but you don't know her. She doesn't care about Miguel. She traded him for Hacienda los Gemelos. Traded him, Elena, the way she trades for slaves. That's why she's there and Miguel is here. I will never allow him to go there, never."

"Please, say no more, Tía Leonor."

"That place is cursed and that woman is a witch. My two sons died because of her, and if Miguel sets foot there, he will not come out alive."

"Tía Leonor, please!"

Miguel didn't hear the rest. He ran to his room, closed the door, and pressed his pillow around his head, wishing he could erase those words from his ears.

———

The cholera epidemic did not spare San Juan. Civilians were ordered to stay home, close their shutters to the street, and avoid contact with others. Communication practically ceased. What few letters managed to get through had black stripes along one edge, indicating that an acquaintance had died. Confined indoors, Leonor practiced the harp for hours. Her melodies resounded to the street, where the few passersby stopped to listen to the sweet music and to wonder whether there were angels trapped behind the carved doors.

Elena felt the change in the city most at night, when she prayed on the roof. The evening chatter and novenas rolled in, muffled by closed windows and doors. Even the church bells tolling the hours were hushed. As soon as it was dusk, patrols increased throughout the city. *El sereno*—the night watchman established eighteen years earlier, during a slave unrest—continued his rounds. His mournful chant, *"Todo bien, gracias a Dios, salve la Reina,"* echoed through the cobblestone streets. Added to his call was the jingle of soldiers' spurs as they walked up and down the streets enforcing the curfew. Elena missed don Simón's walking down Calle Paloma to stare at her window until she blew out her candle.

In late July, no one could ignore the cries from the Urbina Castañeda house across the street. Leonor and Elena prayed constantly, but on the fourth afternoon they heard a cart pull up to the door. Through chinks in the shutters, Leonor, Elena, and Miguel watched as a priest went into the house and emerged praying and blessing doña Patricia as she carried the small body of her youngest daughter, Ednita.

"Que Dios les bendiga," Leonor and Elena called as they crossed themselves, but doña Patricia didn't respond. She went in and out of her house three more times carrying a small body while the priest's invocations lulled the afternoon. The last, the heaviest body she carried from the house, was wrapped in a blanket. Before Leonor or Elena could stop him, Miguel opened the shutter and leaned over the sill.

"Doña Pati," he cried, *"¿dónde está Luis José?"*

Her eyes were blank and her lips a solid line, as if she'd decided never to smile again. "All my children are dead," she said in a monotone. *"Mi Querubín está con Papá Dios. . . ."*

Miguel didn't care that boys, like men, should never cry, especially before women. Elena pressed the sobbing Miguel into her chest.

"Is there anything we can do for you?" Leonor called.

"Pray for my husband," doña Pati said. "He's still sick." The priest helped her climb into the cart. "Pray for their souls, Leonor. Pray for me."

"Every day, Patricia." Leonor crossed herself. *"Que Dios te bendiga. Que Dios los bendiga a todos."* She prayed at the window until the cart turned the corner.

"Come, *querido.*" Elena took Miguel away. "Let's go to your room."

"Will you all die?" he asked as she wiped his face.

She knelt before him. Miguel was a frightened little boy, with a distant mother, a dead father. Behind his question was the fear that everyone else he cared about—her, doña Leonor, don Eugenio, Siña Ciriaca, Bombón and her husband, Mateo—would die and leave him alone. He couldn't imagine himself dying, but it was possible to think that everyone he loved would.

"We're all healthy and doing everything possible to stay safe from disease," she said. "Only God knows when he wants us back in heaven. This is such a sad time, *mi amor,* that maybe Papá Dios needed Querubín by his side because he needed someone to make him smile."

In 1857 Miguel turned twelve years old, the age when boys were sent abroad to continue their education. He was closer than ever to Andrés, and especially after Querubín died, the boys were more like brothers than friends. Andrés's father had lost his wife and three other children to cholera, and was reluctant to send his son away. Leonor also wanted to keep Miguel nearby, so the adults chose to enroll both boys in the local parochial school. Don Simón would supervise and supplement their work and help them to prepare for exams and school projects. Miguel also studied at an art academy established by a recently exiled painter.

Outwardly, the boys were disappointed that they wouldn't go to Europe, but Miguel, at least, was relieved. He wasn't adventurous by nature, and were it not for the more fearless Andrés, he'd be just as happy in the big house on Calle Paloma, reading, painting, and being pampered and indulged by Abuela, Elena, Siña Ciriaca, and Bombón.

While he enjoyed sketching, he didn't like the public aspect of it, especially in a city where his every action was noticed and talked about by the *vecinos*. He eschewed landscapes and focused on still lifes and portraiture. He flattered friends and neighbors by asking them to sit for him, and their likenesses hung on their walls in a chronology of his evolving skill. He always signed his initials on the lower left side of the canvas—RMIALMC, for his official name, Ramón Miguel Inocente Argoso Larragoity Mendoza Cubillas. Three generations later, a collection of nineteenth-century Puerto Rican art and crafts was donated to the Smithsonian Institution, among them fifteen canvases with the enigmatic initials. The paintings were cataloged and stored in a warehouse near Andover, Massachusetts, where they languished alongside thousands of other paintings by dead artists no one remembered.

On the evening following Miguel's fifteenth birthday party, Eugenio invited him for a walk. They frequently strolled around the plaza after dinner, sometimes with the ladies but more often alone. Before they left, Abuelo patted a stray hair from Miguel's shoulder, buttoned his jacket, straightened his cravat, and pulled his sleeves until they showed evenly below his cuffs.

His grandfather's attention to his appearance alerted Miguel that this would be no ordinary walk. Months earlier, Andrés related his visit, escorted by his father, to a house well known to nearly every man in San Juan, but that the decent women of the city pretended didn't exist. Every young man of Miguel's race and social standing had, around his fifteenth birthday, walked through the wide door and up the staircase to fragrant rooms overlooking a garden whose beauty was lost on them. The ground-floor parlors were spacious and comfortably furnished if a bit frayed from use and the stale smell of cigar smoke and spilled liquor. Upstairs, youngish women chosen for beauty, charm, and discretion, trained in their profession by Socorro and Tranquilina Alivio, occupied eight bedrooms. The *chicas* were white *españolas* or light-skinned *mulatas* from backwater towns, all disgraced by men who'd abandoned them. They'd rather work in the Alivio house than hire themselves out as servants, to perform work done by slaves or *libertos*. Regardless of their family name, they used the surname Alivio while they lived in the house.

The Alivio house was on a narrow street halfway down the hill leading to the docks. Municipal gas lamps reached to the corner, leaving the two steps to the door in shadows. Eugenio rapped the heavy knocker and an eye appeared behind a grille. It looked at him and took in Miguel, standing nervously behind his grandfather. The iron slide bolt scraped along a groove on the cement floor as the tallest man in San Juan opened the door. He was very black, wearing a colorful robe. His ears were trimmed with gold hoops, and several bracelets were wrapped around both wrists and ankles. His enormous feet were bare save for rings on his toes. He was Apolo, Socorro's husband, and Miguel had seen him on the street many times, dressed like an elegant gentleman of leisure, but never in these colorful clothes with jewelry winking from every limb and his earlobes. Apolo led them down the corridor. Guitar music and women's laughter issued through the heavy drapes screening the rest of the house. The air smelled of cigar smoke, candle wax, and perfume.

Apolo opened another door for Eugenio and Miguel to enter Socorro Alivio's private study. Two caned rockers faced each other in front of a long table under a painting of a muscular Leda copulating with an enormous swan. Miguel wanted to study the painting, but given the circumstances, he was embarrassed to look too much in its direction.

Socorro was shorter than Tranquilina, but there was about her a settled roundness and confidence that singled her out as the elder of the sisters. Boys took pride in knowing which sister was which and speaking their names in meaningful tones. In this curtained room, Socorro seemed luminous, but on the street, she and her sister looked sickly pale, as if they never saw the sun, making the color on their cheeks and lips unnaturally bright in contrast.

She greeted Eugenio with red kisses on each cheek.

"Welcome," she said to Miguel. "I was looking forward to meeting you."

Miguel bowed, as to any lady.

Socorro smiled and touched his cheek. *"Qué dulzura,"* she said to Eugenio. "You've raised him well." She served him wine, which

Miguel downed in two big gulps. "It's not unusual for a young man to be nervous the first time he comes here."

"No need to be afraid, son. Tranquilina knows what to do." Eugenio chuckled, and Socorro giggled as if tickled. He poured more wine for Miguel. "Go on, son, fortify yourself."

A bit unsteady, Miguel followed Socorro to an upstairs room dominated by a four-poster bed covered with a colorful quilt. As soon as she closed the door behind her, another one opened and Tranquilina appeared on the threshold, her chemise and pantalets clearly visible through the lacework of a flounced robe.

"*Hola, mi amor.* Don't look so scared. I don't bite—unless you want me to."

In addition to introducing Miguel to the Alivio women, Eugenio made sure he moved comfortably in upright society, where he left lasting impressions among tittering girls and their watchful *dueñas*. Miguel dazzled fathers and brothers with his horsemanship during the festivals of San Juan and San Pedro. He endeared himself to mothers by his obvious devotion to Leonor, always the first female he led to the dance floor at the parties and balls hosted by the military governors and other officials. He was a competent swordsman, although not as aggressive as Eugenio wished, and it seemed to him that Miguel went through the motions to please him, rather than to defend himself.

Following in the footsteps of their beloved teacher, Miguel and Andrés became regulars at don Benito's drugstore, where other young men of leisure gathered to study and discuss politics. By the late 1850s and early '60s, strictly enforced censorship of all forms of public expression ensured that liberal ideals were nearly impossible to disseminate. Fines were levied on newspaper editors and publishers for infractions like the use of the words "tyranny," "despotism," or "independence." Liberals depended on contraband books, magazines, and newspapers from Europe, the United States, and Spanish America. The same private homes and businesses that hosted what might be considered seditious discussions also acted as informal lending libraries for the forbidden literature.

Benito was a fourth-generation native-born Puerto Rican. "*Cri-*

ollo to the core," he said. He was an orator and a singer, and displayed both skills in the gatherings in his *botica,* where he tried to instill *criollo* pride in another generation. Most nights, the discussions were informal and followed a meandering path determined by how much liquor he dispensed over the course of the evening. At other times, he prodded the young men to focus on issues crucial to an understanding of history and the situation on the island as a colony of Spain. On such occasions, Benito prepared a discourse, delivered in a booming voice, gesticulating passionately, taking frequent sips from a glass with rum and water by his side.

"From the day Cristobal Colón landed on our shores in 1493," Benito began, "Puerto Rico has been little more to Spain than an outpost. The military has unlimited powers to enforce laws designed by *peninsulares* to benefit them and their compatriots."

The young men voiced their agreement.

"Even the most insignificant government post is filled by *españoles.* You know what that means. We, born on this island, have no say in how we're governed."

Miguel attended these evenings out of camaraderie rather than political conviction. He'd rather spend time at an art opening or at the theater than with these men whose emotional appeals never went farther than the walls of the drugstore or one another's smoke-filled rooms.

"The high taxes collected from landowners and businessmen go directly to the Spanish treasury, with scant investment on the needs of our *vecinos.* You've addressed this before us, Félix Fonseca, with your usual erudition." Félix Fonseca nodded, and those sitting by him patted his back. Benito continued: "Those of you who've traveled to the interior know that with the exception of the roads near the capital and bigger towns, transportation *en la isla* is a disgrace. Public works, paid for with the exorbitant taxes the Crown imposes, are undertaken only if they improve the life of *españoles* and foreign colonists in San Juan and the bigger towns like Ponce and Mayagüez."

Again the men turned to one another in agreement. The druggist leaned back, enjoying the effect of his words on the young, eager minds of these *criollos,* the generation that he hoped would create the Puerto Rico for Puerto Ricans that he envisioned yet was unable to realize.

Benito acknowledged don Simón. He'd been the teacher of most of the younger men present, and they regarded him with respect and affection.

"Thank you, don Benito. As usual, you remind us of the issues we should be discussing around your generous table." Benito nodded. "We cannot forget," Simón continued in his soothing voice, "the deplorable condition of education on our island. In San Juan and the bigger towns we're fortunate to have public and parochial schools, but *en la isla*, public education is virtually nonexistent. After decades without a census, the one conducted in 1860 gives us a more dismal picture than we ever imagined. It reveals that eighty-four percent of our *compatriotas* are illiterate. How can we build a *nación* if over two-thirds of it can't even sign their name?"

Andrés raised his hand. "Our esteemed *maestro* points out that eighty-four percent of our population is enslaved by their ignorance. But twelve percent of its residents are also physically, emotionally, and legally enslaved. To overturn the tyranny of Spain we must work toward freeing them with as much passion as we seek freedom for ourselves."

Forbidden to utter their aspirations for their future openly, the younger men aired their views in private, frustrated that a large and powerful segment of the island's elite opposed them. Abolition was at the heart of the debates. The island aristocracy, many of them refugees from the wars for independence in North and Spanish America and on Hispaniola, came to Puerto Rico with their fortunes and their slaves precisely because the *vecinos* hadn't taken up arms against the colonial government.

Twelve years earlier in Guares, Siña Damita had observed political disaffection, although in the late 1840s there was no organized leadership. After the indefensible government response to the cholera epidemic—closing off the capital, burning barrios, sending thousands of homeless into the roads and byways of the island—politicized, educated, courageous, outspoken young men and women emerged as leaders. The most prominent among them was Dr. Ramón Emeterio Betances, an ophthalmologist, poet, writer, and Mason who'd already challenged the colonial government and had been threatened with exile by the authorities.

Betances reminded his followers that the Cortes in Madrid continually met requests for reforms from Puerto Rican *colonos* with indifference and disdain. He exhorted Puerto Ricans to take the future of their island into their own hands. To the horror of the more conciliatory liberals, Betances advocated armed revolt like the successful struggles that had resulted in independence for every former Spanish colony, with Cuba and Puerto Rico the only exceptions.

In the American hemisphere, Betances wrote, political independence and reform had been won only through armed struggle. He envisioned Puerto Rico not as the half-forgotten outpost of a dying empire, but as a shining jewel adorning an Antillean Confederation composed of Cuba, Hispaniola, and Puerto Rico. It was a grand idea, and Miguel and Andrés wanted to be part of its creation.

A revolution, however, needed more than young men's nationalistic ardor and dreams of glory. A revolution needed leaders, a coherent message appealing to the masses willing to fight to the death for an ideal, and money to fund rebellious activities. Miguel was too much a follower to be an effective leader, and too introverted to be an orator able to incite others to battle. But the generous allowance from don Eugenio made it possible for him to contribute his share toward the costs of recruiting, arming, and training rebels.

Miguel and Andrés were compelled by the revolutionary concepts espoused by Betances and the activities of his supporters, who depended on a network of secret societies. Unlike those who gathered in the *botica* and places like it, the truly secret societies didn't meet in the easy-to-infiltrate *tertulias* of poets, apothecaries, and known liberals. They met in small groups in members' homes, along the narrow streets of the capital and outlying towns, in the back rooms of bordellos like the Alivio house, on the *fincas* that dotted the landscape near rivers and harbors, on the *estancias* where men came together to ride and race horses, watch bullfights, enjoy a bloody cockfight, to drink, gamble, and plot.

Leaders forced from the island were kept informed through visits from their associates with freedom to travel. Correspondence was hand delivered by trusted members who carried documents sewn into their clothes.

The question at the forefront of the leaders' discussions was how to motivate the average *campo*-dwelling, poor Puerto Rican to rise against the oppression that was so obvious to the upper-class *criollos* leading the nationalist movement. The burgeoning patriots wanted to go from talking about reform to making it happen, something that would be impossible without popular support.

But pamphlets, bulletins, posters, and other written materials were useless in a population that couldn't read. Public discussion, speeches in town squares, even songs and poems with what the authorities considered subversive content were banned.

As the members argued about how to bring their message to the *jíbaros,* as ideas were batted around, plans were made, and people were assigned roles, Miguel floated along the margins, trying to find his place in the glorious mission. He was enamored of the romance of *patria, igualdad, libertad,* and believed he'd found something worth dying for. What better principles for a man to live and die for than his nation, equality, and liberty for all? He listened to the better rhetoric of his neighbors, studied the history of armed struggle, and gave money as he waited for the opportunity to prove himself worthy of the cause.

He and Andrés joined one of the secret nationalist societies that exchanged documents, money, and information in the Alivio house, in conversations in low voices in the plazas, in the *cafetines* that dispensed strong coffee and news. Miguel donated part of his allowance to a fund that purchased slave infants from their owners at the baptismal font, then turned them over to their grateful parents as *libertos.* Miguel and Andrés didn't tell their liberal parents about their involvement in the secret society, lest they forbid their activities as too dangerous. Members were encouraged not to change their habits in such a way as to provoke suspicion, so the young men continued to frequent Benito's *botica* and listened to their elders, not sure which ones were also in the society, which ones were spies, which ones were there just to drink the *aguardiente.*

Reports about the outbreak of civil war in the United States had arrived through ship's captains and periodicals smuggled onto the island. In early 1863, copies of the text of the Emancipation Proclamation arrived in Puerto Rico, but by then *sanjuaneros* knew something momentous had happened *en el norte* because large numbers of Spanish soldiers disembarked and were sent directly to the hinterlands to discourage rebellion once the nearly 42,000 slaves learned the news. Letters from business associates and family members in Cuba reported even tighter control over the nearly 370,000 slaves working in the sugar industry of that island.

One night following another debate, Andrés seemed particularly thoughtful. Miguel invited him to take his mind off his worries with a visit to the Alivio house, but in spite of the distractions with the smiling *chicas,* Andrés still seemed troubled as they walked home.

"Tell me, *amigo,* what's bothering you so much that you wouldn't sing along with La Chillona? You're not yourself."

Andrés stopped under one of the gas lamps in the plaza. Unlike Miguel, who affected poetic shoulder-length hair but was clean-shaven, Andrés cut his thick hair short but seemed unable to keep up with the luxurious growth on his face. His abundant eyebrows and thick lashes also resisted efforts to control them. They shaded his gaze so effectively that many people didn't know his eyes were hazel.

"How long have we known each other?" Andrés asked seriously, as if he truly couldn't remember.

"Let's see, I'm almost seventeen, and we met when I was almost six. Eleven years at least."

"And in all that time we've always told each other the truth, haven't we?"

"Of course."

"I've meant to say this before, but haven't spoken from respect for you."

He was so dejected that Miguel searched his mind for how he might have offended Andrés in the recent past.

Andrés continued. "You don't speak of it, yet everyone knows that don Eugenio owns a plantation and you are, presumably, his only heir." Miguel nodded. "But there never has been any discussion about the fate of your slaves, Miguel."

He spoke the last sentence with more than a tinge of resentment. The emotion behind his words surprised Miguel.

"What do you mean my slaves? They're not mine," he stammered, and was immediately sorry because, even to himself, he sounded defensive. "What I mean is—"

"There's no need to explain to me," Andrés said. "But it is a matter of conscience for you. Especially if you continue to be a part of our activities."

"I don't own any slaves, my grandfather does. Some of the others are slaveholders. Why am I singled out?"

"You're not being singled out. I speak for myself, to you. No one else is involved." He put a reassuring hand on Miguel's shoulder, then took his elbow and began walking down the street. "You see, *mi hermano,* we spend hours talking about the evils of slavery, drafting papers and resolutions that will put an end to this abominable practice. And you're right, some of our friends own slaves, yet they speak as passionately as if their workers were free. Don't you see the hypocrisy? It seems to me that if we truly believe what we say, we should set an example."

"But compensation for slaveholders is at the heart of our discussions. We can't expect people whose entire fortune is tied up in such an investment . . ." He stopped midstep and pressed his fingers to his face. "Holy Mother of God, what am I saying? Whose words are these?"

Andrés put his arm around Miguel's shoulder. "You understand, then. All our talking and debating continues to disregard the fact that they're human beings. Even we think of them as property. As humanists, *hermano,* we're failures."

Miguel didn't know much about his grandfather's business. Even though he often mentioned that Miguel was his heir, the old man made no effort to train him in more than the manly arts of riding, swordsmanship, drinking, whoring, and gambling while his grandmother and godmother drilled him in the social graces of a *señorcito de buena familia.* Years after he came to live with his grandparents, Miguel still had little idea what Eugenio did to keep them firmly ensconced on the respectable side of colonial society. His meetings with Mr. Worthy took place in the lawyer's office or behind the closed doors of the study. Not once was Miguel invited to the conferences within the amber-colored room that smelled of aged port, cigars, and men's conversations. He knew that slaves were the workforce of Los Gemelos, but like other slave-owning abolitionists, the Argosos fell on the side of indemnity upon manumission, not an unusual position for even the most liberal families.

Eugenio and Leonor raised Miguel to think of slavery as a sin. They reminded him that, while Siña Ciriaca and Bombón were purchased from Luis Morales Font, they freed both women once they arrived in San Juan. Over the years, the Argosos helped Siña Ciriaca buy the freedom of her three other children and their spouses. But they hadn't extended their moral stance to the far-off plantation that made their comfortable lives in the city possible.

Andrés's words affected Miguel, but he couldn't bring himself to challenge Abuelo. Respect for him, gratitude for the life he'd made possible, and love for both grandparents prevented him from doing anything to cause them to question his loyalty or affection. He wondered if it was a sign of weakness to avoid a discussion that would surely be interpreted by his grandparents as criticism. Miguel avoided confrontations of any kind, and did mostly as he was told, even when it meant he lay awake at night asking himself questions he might have best answered in daylight, with a frank exchange of opinion and a willingness to argue his point. His evenings at don Benito's were mostly spent half-listening to others debate while his mind wandered.

Miguel recalled a childhood filled with love and every material and intellectual exigency of a wealthy *señorcito* from whom important things were expected. Who he was to become, however, was never clearly defined, and he often felt as if he were floating in a sea of expectations with no clear destination. When he thought about it, he was grateful for the happy, comfortable childhood his grandparents and Elena made possible. The only dark cloud over his rosy life was the fading memory of a wild and distant place with an insistent female voice.

Ana wrote frequently and assured Miguel that no matter what other preoccupations filled his days, she had only one fervent wish— to have him by her side. As he grew older, Ana's letters came more often. The hand-cut pages were dense with baroque descriptions of the *campo* illustrated with amateurish drawings of people, flowers, fruits, buildings, and animals. Whenever the postman delivered one of her letters, Miguel found every excuse not to read it right away, and let it languish among less important correspondence. Days would pass until Elena gently asked what news there was from Hacienda los Gemelos before he remembered to read it. Ana's letters left him feeling as if he'd failed her in ways he didn't understand and couldn't help. And it unnerved him that over the last fourteen years every one of her single-minded, relentlessly cursive letters was signed with the same words: "Your loving mother, who waits for you."

MR. WORTHY'S SUGGESTION

Leonor was not a melancholy person. She grieved the inevitable sorrows of a long life, she mourned the untimely deaths of her two sons, the passing away of parents, brother, sisters, and friends, but she always found her way back to her natural spirit, involved in her life and that of her loved ones. One morning, however, as she turned from the mirror after pinning her hair, she was seized by an overwhelming desire to cry. She faced the mirror again, as if the reason for the tightness in her chest and the sting of tears in her eyes could be found there. "I'm old," she said aloud, surprising herself both by the sound of her voice and by the fact that she'd never uttered such an observation.

Eugenio peeked in from the alcove next door, where he slept when he came home late after evenings without her.

"Did you say something, dear?"

"No, talking to myself."

He disappeared back into his room. She finished her toilette and left her chamber, afraid to face the mirror.

It was a busy month.

The city was observing the 355th anniversary of the conquistador Juan Ponce de León's first settlement in Puerto Rico. The conquistador was exhumed from his place of rest in the Iglesia de San José, and eminent doctors from Spain in the presence of representatives of the queen examined the remains. His body was then reinterred in a new lead coffin within a cedar box in the Cathedral of San Juan Bautista. There was to be a Mass, a lecture, exhibitions, and dinners to commemorate the events. Besides attending the activities surrounding the observance, Leonor was to host a luncheon and coffees for the ladies of the Peninsular dignitaries.

She held herself together during the two weeks of ceaseless activity, but it was hard. Every word directed at her was an intrusion into a grief she couldn't name. Her throat ached and nothing relieved the pressure around her chest except locking herself in her room to cry for a few minutes. Everyone in her household noticed her red eyes and distraction, but only Elena dared say something.

"Are you unwell?" Elena asked after she noticed that Leonor counted the same napkins for the luncheon four times before she got the number right.

"A bit tired."

"It's been hectic the past few days. Why don't you lie down for a while? Bombón and I can finish with the linen."

"Yes, that's better."

Elena's and Bombón's eyes followed her, worried, she knew, because she rarely took a siesta, and never before noon. She was drawing the drapes when Siña Ciriaca appeared, doubtless alerted by Elena. The maid helped her unlace her corset, took her shoes off, and covered her with a light blanket. The moment she was alone, tears sprung and Leonor let them slide down her temples. She dozed, but woke up when she bit her tongue in her sleep.

She couldn't account for her sadness. Certainly it shouldn't have come unexpectedly that at sixty-seven she looked like an old woman. She was aware that her looks had changed years ago, when clothes didn't fit quite the same, when her hair changed color and grew sparser and less manageable. She'd adjusted her dress according to what her body accepted and seemed appropriate for her age; but until the past few weeks, she hadn't felt the years quite so much.

"It's all this activity around Ponce de León," Eugenio said. "The exhumation was macabre."

Leonor managed to get through the lectures and Masses, through the dinners with personages and the coffees with their wives, but she felt as if she was performing, while all she wanted to do was to crawl under the bedcovers.

The morning after the festivities were over and the dignitaries gone, Leonor said she was too tired to get out of bed. She closeted herself in her chamber, curtains drawn, refusing food but agreeing to the *yerbabuena* and *manzanilla* tisanes Siña Ciriaca served her.

"Shall I call the doctor?" Eugenio asked the second day.

"No, *mi amor.* I'm exhausted, that's all. I'll be fine."

"Promise to eat something, then. You can't regain your strength if you refuse food."

"I will," she said, and closed her eyes.

Eugenio found Elena in her room. "What shall we do about Leonor? I've never seen her like this."

"It's been only a day. Maybe she really is tired. We should let her rest and she'll be fine in a few days."

"I'm worried about her."

"Let's indulge her and watch for any other signs of illness. She'll probably be up and about again in a day or two."

Three days later, the doctor was called. Leonor received him and allowed him to take her pulse and listen to her heart, but when he emerged from her room, he could only report what Eugenio, Elena, Miguel, and Siña Ciriaca already knew.

"Her pulse is slow, but not alarmingly so. Let her rest as much as she needs so long as she takes liquids."

Siña Ciriaca prepared dove broths and alternated them with the tisanes with honey. Eugenio, Elena, and Miguel visited her, but only for a few minutes, because while Leonor seemed happy to see them at first, she'd soon close her eyes and fall asleep.

Ten days after she'd taken to her bed, Leonor rose, dressed, and joined them at the midday meal as she always did, except that she pushed her food around.

"It's wonderful to have you up and about again, *querida,*" Eugenio said, kissing her hand.

"I was tired, that's all."

She'd lost weight. Her round cheeks had drooped, and her face had lengthened. Deep lines crisscrossed her features, and the loose skin under her neck shook with every movement. Eugenio, Elena, and Miguel tried not to stare as Leonor listlessly chewed a piece of bread and sipped her sherry. The conversation over the meal was sparse, because they were all afraid of saying something that might upset or make her sad again. Leonor didn't notice. She nibbled bread and asked Miguel to pour another glass of sherry, which at least brought some color to her cheeks.

As they finished the *almuerzo,* Bombón announced don Simón, who was so ebullient he seemed about to float through the roof.

"*Buen provecho,*" he said upon entering.

"Siña Ciriaca, another place setting, please," asked Elena when Leonor didn't.

Simón blushed and bowed. "Very kind, *señorita* Elena, but *gracias*. I've already eaten." He turned to his star pupil. "My dear Miguel, I bring momentous news. Spain's most illustrious living painter, Maestro Pedro Campos de Laura, has agreed to let you be his student in Madrid." The schoolmaster could barely contain his joy as Miguel, Leonor, Elena, and even Siña Ciriaca, who'd just removed the meat platter, gaped.

"My goodness, you're full of surprises, don Simón," Leonor said.

"Not at all, my dear. Don Simón and I've been working on this for weeks." Eugenio avoided her eyes.

"I know nothing about it," Miguel stuttered.

"Don Eugenio and I didn't want to say anything, in case Maestro Campos de Laura didn't accept," don Simón explained with a satisfied grin. He was so happy that he was insensible to Leonor's uncharacteristically stiff posture. "He doesn't teach, Miguel. This is a great honor and a tribute to your talent."

"Getting you an apprenticeship with an artist of Maestro Campos de Laura's reputation wasn't easy," Eugenio said solemnly. "Don Simón knows him from Madrid, and I was owed some favors, and when our own governor Izquierdo was recalled to the Peninsula, he met with *el maestro* to persuade him to consider you."

Miguel looked from Eugenio to Simón to Elena to Leonor. "I don't know what to say; it's such a surprise."

"We always do what's best for you," Eugenio said.

"Yes, sir, I understand that. Still—"

"It was so good of you to go through all that trouble, dear," Leonor interrupted. Everyone except don Simón heard the acid in her voice.

"I have more news, Miguel," the schoolmaster continued. "Your good friend, Andrés, will also be in Madrid. He was accepted at the law school."

Leonor pulled a fan from the creases of her skirt and waved it around her face. "It's warm here, isn't it? Shall we move to the courtyard?"

Eugenio and Miguel jumped to help Leonor from her chair. She turned her back on her husband and smiled on her grandson. Eugenio backed up a step.

Simón finally noticed that something wasn't quite right. "Did I say something to offend her?" he murmured to Elena as he escorted her to the courtyard.

"Please don't worry. She's been unwell the past few days and we're all sensitive to her moods."

"I will let you enjoy this happy news *en familia*. Congratulations," he said, pressing Miguel's shoulder.

After the teacher left, Eugenio, Leonor, Elena, and Miguel sat around the painted wrought-iron table, each deep in thought, as Siña Ciriaca poured the coffee. As soon as she left, Leonor stood without so much as lifting her cup. "Eugenio"—she stretched her hand to her husband—"may we speak in private?" Rather sheepishly, he led her up the stairs while Elena and Miguel watched them go until the door to their room closed.

"You knew nothing about this?" Elena asked Miguel as they sat down again.

"Neither Abuelo nor don Simón ever mentioned it."

"They think it's a great honor."

"I hardly deserve it, Elena. There are much better—"

"Don't say that, *querido*. You're very talented."

Miguel knew that he was, at best, a mediocre artist. But he didn't have time to argue her assessment when they both became aware of the loud voices coming from the upstairs rooms.

"You'd send him away without consulting me?" Leonor asked her husband as soon as he closed the door. She sat on the divan by the window and beat the air with her fan.

"Of course not! I meant to tell you weeks ago, but with all the activities around Ponce de León, and then you weren't feeling well." Her skeptical look forced him to change tactics. "Besides"—he sat at the foot of the divan, slipped his fingers under her petticoats, and rubbed her leg—"it wasn't at all a sure thing. We didn't want him to get excited about it only to have Maestro Campos de Laura say no."

"Why can't he continue his studies here?" She gently but undeniably kicked his hand away.

Eugenio noticed that his waistcoat was open. "He's gone as far as he can. He needs more advanced instruction," he said, focusing on the otherwise second-nature task of fastening a button.

"Tell the truth, Eugenio. Why are you sending him away?"

He finally looked directly at her. "Leonor, I've not wanted to worry you."

"You're keeping something from me."

"Yes, my dear, I'm sorry, but I thought it was best if I took care of it. Bartolo Cardenales and I have handled the situation."

"What does Bartolo have to do with this?"

Eugenio took a deep breath. "Miguel and Andrés are involved in activities that could compromise them."

"I don't understand. Compromise them with a girl?"

"No, my dear," he said with a rueful smile. "That's easy to manage. Unfortunately, our boys admire that firebrand Betances and are involved in one of his secret societies."

"Those so-called secret meetings in the *botica* are hardly a reason to banish him to Spain." She squinted suspiciously. "Everyone knows it's just men hearing themselves talk."

He hadn't discussed his plan to send Miguel away because he wanted to avoid this conversation. "No, *mi amor,* it's more serious than that."

Her thin eyebrows crept toward each other in the familiar gesture that brooked no half-truths.

"The governor took me for a stroll around the gardens at La Fortaleza a few weeks before the Ponce de León exhumation." He paced, as if he needed to move in order to think clearly. "It appears that our boys have been meeting with men organizing an armed revolt."

"By *blancos?*"

"They're not foolish enough to try to arm the blacks. They're recruiting *campesinos,* and the plan is still in the early stages. Coded messages were intercepted and the leaders identified, but Andrés and Miguel were spotted with people on those lists. As far as we know, they're on the fringes, but they could easily be enmeshed in something that can't be untangled."

"So your solution is to send them away?"

"The governor's recommendation, Leonor."

"It didn't occur to you to talk to Miguel about this before banishing him from the island?"

"He's not being banished; he's being given a rare opportunity to do something he loves. At the same time, we're distancing him from associates who might tarnish his good name. He's seventeen years old, Leonor, and hasn't traveled beyond the walls of this city except for weekends at our friends' *fincas* and for patron saint celebrations in nearby towns. He's never had to fend for himself."

"Why is that wrong? What else would we do with our wealth but to make his life easy?"

"I'm not talking about material things; of course we'd give him every advantage. What I mean is that Miguel is easily influenced. He lacks . . . a sense of adventure, I suppose."

"Look what a sense of adventure did for our sons."

Eugenio grimaced. He pulled a handkerchief from his pocket and wiped his forehead. "We can't protect him so much that he doesn't know when he's moving on his own, or is being pushed by others."

"He's a boy!"

"He's a man, Leonor, young, but a man nevertheless. The problem is he's incomplete. He lacks the confidence of a man who knows his own power. He's too passive, has never challenged us—"

"So you're sending him away because he's too respectful?"

"I'm sending him away so that he can learn to stand on his own convictions and not be so easily swayed by anyone, including me, and especially not by a charismatic man whose activities could land him in trouble. We can't give him a sense of his own strength without sending him into the world to be knocked about a bit."

"You resent him for his easy life."

Eugenio had had enough. "You've resisted every suggestion I've ever made about what I believe to be best for him." She started to protest, but he didn't give her a chance. "I didn't argue when you and Elena took over his education." His voice rose, but he didn't care. He was in the right, and even Leonor's recent delicate health didn't keep him from trying to get her to acknowledge it. "I didn't insist when you refused to send him to military training. I haven't forced him to learn the intricacies of business. I haven't interfered in his upbringing except to teach him what I know about how to be a man and to be a positive example for him."

"Please lower your voice; they can hear you."

Eugenio wiped his forehead, behind his ears, around his mutton-chop whiskers. The handkerchief was soaked. "Sometimes I look at him, and I'm disturbed by his passivity." He paced up and down the chamber, his arms behind his back. "We've raised a man, Leonor, who doesn't know who he is, a man with no goals or ambitions. I feel as if I've failed him."

"So you want him where you're not reminded you're a failure?"

Eugenio stopped pacing and looked at his wife's haggard face. They'd been married almost fifty years, and as she aged, she'd always seemed beautiful, worthy of his love and admiration. They'd argued often, even before they were married, sometimes in loud voices, but he almost always came around to her point of view. There was no one whose good opinion mattered more to him. In their lifetime, however, in none of hundreds of arguments, had she ever said anything so cruel. "You haven't known me, then, our whole lives, if you think I'm a failure."

"Forgive me." She stood to run into his arms, but fell against the divan as if struck. "Oh!" she said, and a look of panic crossed her face as she brought her hands to her chest. He reached her just as her body went slack and she slumped to the floor.

"Miguel! Elena! Come, please, hurry!" He crouched over her, tried to sit her up, patted her cheeks to bring the color to them, but he knew there was nothing to be done.

Eugenio had been to so many funerals that except for Ramón's, he couldn't remember most of them. He'd been a pallbearer for soldiers cut down in battle, had attended courtiers felled by lechery and gluttony, had dug graves for villagers silenced by war, famine, and exertion. He worried about his own death so often that his papers were always up to date so that his family would be provided for after his inevitable death. But he never imagined he'd be widowed. He never contemplated a life without Leonor Mendoza Sánchez de Argoso at the beginning and end of each day.

She was the friend of his childhood, the flirtatious *señorita* of his adolescence, the loving and valiant wife who followed him wherever fate led in his pursuit of glory on the battlefield. She was such a part of him that he could not envision life without her.

During her wake, he kept his eyes on her face, now devoid of expression. He'd watched her sleep so often that he expected her nostrils to flare, her lips to purse as if kissing the air, her lashes to flutter. He wanted her to live. He wanted her to sit up from the satin-lined coffin and organize every aspect of his civilian life. He wanted to feel her lovingly pinning the ribbons and medals on his uniform. He wanted to feel her palms pressing down on the lapels of his jacket until they lay flat. He wanted to feel her fingers quietly flicking a mote of dust, invisible to everyone else, from his shoulder. He wanted to hear her laughter when he said something funny, to hear her singing when she watered the plants in the courtyard, to hear her playing the harp. He wanted her to walk across a room, her step firm and determined yet feminine. He wanted her to dance again, her skirts swinging back and forth like a bell. He wanted her powdering her round shoulders and applying scented cream to her arms. He wanted to touch her hair, soft as cobwebs, to touch her lips and feel her kissing his index finger, to press back the lace around her nightcap and loosen the ribbons on her nightgown. He wanted to touch the parts of her no other man had ever seen or touched. He'd loved her since he was five and she was a few months old, and he didn't want to live without her.

He wandered through their house, the first real home he'd given her, expecting to see her arranging a curtain or placing cut flowers in a vase. He tried to sleep on their bed only to awaken reaching for her in the night. He sat at the head of the table, Miguel and Elena on either side of him, as always, but when he looked across, he faced an empty space that seemed more desolate than a cloudless sky.

After the wake, after the funeral, after the Masses and the novenas, after reading the letters of condolence and choosing the words to be carved on her tombstone, after choosing the words to be carved on his, and after making sure that Mr. Worthy had everything in order, Eugenio went to bed one night two months after he'd buried Leonor and repeated her last words over and over in a litany of sorrow and despair.

"Forgive me."

He held the rosary she'd given him so many years ago that he couldn't remember the occasion and prayed to her for forgiveness, and prayed to God to forgive him for praying to her as if she were a goddess. He couldn't forgive himself for scheming behind her back to send Miguel to Spain, even though it was for his own good. Miguel needed independence and experience, the company of men, the uncertainties of living on his own.

In the weeks of plotting with Simón, Eugenio had avoided telling Leonor, hoping that the great honor bestowed upon Miguel would convince her that it was the right thing to do for her boy. But she'd lost two sons, and he should have known that if the queen herself summoned Miguel to Spain, Leonor would have resisted sending him far from her watchful care, from her fears and premonitions.

"Forgive me," he said over and over again, expecting to hear her voice absolving him, knowing he'd never hear her voice again. She'd never wanted to come to Puerto Rico, had suffered what no mother should ever experience in her lifetime. Her heart, broken twice, could not go on beating if she lost her only grandson. "I should have never allowed our sons to convince me to come here when you were so opposed to it."

He tossed and turned most of the night in anguish, begging God to take him, too. "I can't live," he prayed, "without her. I don't exist without her."

As the sun climbed over the distant mountains, he finally fell, the rosary clamped around his fingers. His chest rose and dropped in deep, smooth breaths that became shallow and uneven, until at last, and with a grateful sigh, he was released.

During his grandmother's wake and funeral, and two months later, at his grandfather's, Miguel was overcome by memories he didn't know he had. He kept revisiting his father's death nearly fourteen years earlier. He vividly remembered crimson stains on the hammock where Papá was carried from the accident. He heard again his father's screams as he was lifted onto the cart, and he remembered Nana Damita's surprising agility climbing in after him, and Mamá's face pinched into an angry frown, as if she didn't approve of the fuss being made over his father. He remembered dust from people running here and there, and Severo's big horse and his dogs. The bright midday sun, he now remembered, made the shadows round.

So many memories! Nana Inés carried him from the *batey* to the rocks by the river where Nena washed clothes, and Indio and Efraín followed, and they cried inconsolably, even Nena, and no one told them to stop. When they returned to the *batey,* everything was quiet. Nana Inés took him to her *bohío,* and she cooked while he and Indio and Efraín built houses with scraps from the workshop. The next morning, José was making a long box, and when Miguel asked what it was for, José's eyes watered and Miguel knew his father was dead. He wailed, and Nana Inés left her *fogón* and took him in her arms, and Indio and Efraín stood next to her, and José rubbed his head, and they hugged and kissed him, which felt good, but not like when Papá caressed and kissed him.

"You have to be a good boy," Nana Inés told him. "You have to be brave, *mi hombrecito,* because now you're the man of the house."

He didn't know what she meant then but understood it now, in front of his grandfather's coffin. He was the last Argoso of his clan. Even though he'd felt like a man the night he lost his virginity to Tranquilina Alivio, he knew for certain that his life as a man was only just beginning. And yet, all he could think about was how tenderly Nana Inés held him when he was just a boy, and how sweetly she kissed his forehead and murmured, "It will be all right, *mi hombrecito.* Everything will be all right."

Elena and Siña Ciriaca had always known what to do for Miguel. After his grandparents died, the two women walked the rooms of the house aimlessly, looking after things that would never be used again, like Abuela's harp and Abuelo's saber and plumed hat. Miguel sensed that Elena and Siña Ciriaca needed something from him, but he didn't know what that might be. He couldn't bring himself to tell them what to do, which seemed to disappoint them, but he had no idea what they could do for him other than the usual. He was just as lost as they. If he left the house for a *cafecito,* to visit don Simón, or simply to stroll around the plaza for some air, the two women stood together at the top of the stairs watching him go until he'd closed the street door behind him. With their black garments and somber faces, they looked like twin crows with no potential for flight.

Because he was in mourning, Miguel couldn't pursue the usual amusements that filled his hours. He gave up evenings at the Alivio house, playing cards with friends, and accompanying Andrés on the guitar while they sang love songs under the balconies of deserving *señoritas.* There were no more visits to Benito's drugstore for discussions into the late hours, and the few men he knew to be part of the secret society had suddenly vanished from the city. A few days after Abuelo's funeral, Andrés embarked for Spain, so even his closest friend deserted him at the moment when he most needed him.

During the first weeks of mourning after the novenas, the only regular visitor to the Argoso home was Mr. Worthy. In his will, Eugenio had provided generously for Elena and left money and instructions for the purchase of Siña Ciriaca's remaining two nephews and their wives. To Miguel's and Elena's shock, Eugenio left nothing to Ana. Miguel was now sole owner of Hacienda los Gemelos and his mother, technically, his employee.

Ever since the night of his discussion with Andrés about the fate of the slaves at Los Gemelos, Miguel had thought about them but did nothing. Andrés never mentioned it again. His father sold his farm with the workers on it, which wasn't exactly the same as setting them free, since what he did was to free himself of them. Miguel expected that Eugenio's testament would manumit the Hacienda los Gemelos workers, a not uncommon last wish from slave owners with guilty consciences, but there was no mention of them in the will.

Miguel spent a sleepless night mentally rehearsing the first real decision he'd ever made, while thunder, lightning, and rain pounded the city. It was painful for him to think of this, but no, his grandfather hadn't done the right thing, and Miguel intended to right that wrong. He felt noble, principled, and generous. On the blazingly clear morning after, he walked to Mr. Worthy's offices on the second floor of a new building across the street from the docks and warehouses. Mr. Worthy and his two partners occupied private rooms fronting the harbor, while the clerks and secretaries worked at facing desks along the length of the windowed corridor overlooking a side street.

After the preliminaries, Miguel cleared his throat to deepen his voice. "I'd appreciate it, Mr. Worthy, if you could begin the necessary paperwork to free the slaves at Hacienda los Gemelos."

Mr. Worthy nodded soberly. "I see," he said, and whirled in his chair toward the view of the harbor. Miguel followed his gaze. The bay was cluttered with merchant ships, their gold-and-red flags in garish contrast to the cerulean sky. Mr. Worthy returned his eyes to Miguel. "I'm sorry, young man, that your request, while laudable, cannot be fulfilled."

"Why not?" Miguel said, sounding even to himself like a child denied.

"Because don Eugenio's will stipulates that major decisions affecting business operations are the purview of the trust established until your twenty-fifth birthday. You do remember my explaining this to you the day we read the will?"

"It was a very confusing time," Miguel mumbled. "Can you remind me of the terms?"

"Of course." Mr. Worthy strode to a cabinet by the wall and riffled until he found a thick brown folio tied with red ribbon. "Here it is," he said, spreading before Miguel parchments with seals and signatures and dangling ribbons that looked ominously official. "My two partners and I administer your trust until you come of age. These are the documents that set forth the terms; you will recognize don Eugenio's signature here and here, and on these documents, duly witnessed and notarized. These are the certificates of ownership of the businesses we manage on your behalf. These are for the stocks, here are the titles to the wharves and warehouses that you own, these are the leases of your tenants, here the deeds to your house in San Juan and to Hacienda los Gemelos. You can examine these documents whenever you wish so that you can familiarize yourself with your holdings. This is an inventory of the furnishings and jewelry that your grandparents identified as heirlooms that cannot be sold or given away until after you reach majority, should it be necessary. Obviously, your grandparents hoped that you would not do such a thing and wished that those items remain in the family in perpetuity. This is the receipt for the box where your grandmother's jewelry is stored. The key will be given to you upon your twenty-fifth birthday."

Miguel was glad when Mr. Worthy finished explaining what all the papers represented. He was certain that it would be some time before he could distinguish one from the other. But the man was not done. He pulled out more parchments from under the folio.

"Here are the pedigrees for your horses, and lastly"—he removed a stack from inside an envelope and fanned the pages on the desk— "the most recent chart of accounts for Los Gemelos indicating that, contrary to all expectations in these difficult times, the plantation is doing rather well."

Miguel stared at the documents, unable to make sense of any of them but feeling like he must say something. "It all looks very . . . complete."

Mr. Worthy collected the papers into a neat pile. "Freeing the slaves now would be financially devastating for your mother and the hacienda. It must disappoint you to be unable to handle your own business affairs, but you see, don Eugenio thought that you should be more experienced before making decisions that would affect your future financial well-being."

Miguel stared at the stack of papers representing who he was in the world to men like Mr. Worthy. It was clear that, if only these papers were consulted, he was a man of consequence, even power, but he felt neither important nor commanding. He'd entered this office with one idea in mind—to free the slaves. He now realized that don Eugenio hadn't trusted him. Who better to control his impulses than this gloomy *norteamericano* whose every word led only in the direction of the acquisition, expansion, and protection of wealth?

"If I may"—Mr. Worthy interrupted his reverie—"there's something I'd like to ask, if you allow."

"Yes, of course."

"You remember that in his will don Eugenio made no provision for your mother?"

"I'm aware of that."

"It is, of course, not up to me to question the colonel's reasons or motives," Mr. Worthy said while doing just that. "But other than what would come to her in the event of her husband's death—and I'm not privy to his financial health, since he seems to manage those affairs himself—doña Ana has been left unprotected . . . financially, that is."

Miguel said nothing.

"She receives a salary, of course, and as the *mayordomo,* don Severo is paid rather handsomely," Mr. Worthy continued. "The colonel might have thought that with her income from him and her marriage to señor Fuentes, doña Ana didn't need a separate legacy. But she had a considerable investment in the hacienda when she first came to Puerto Rico that has never been recognized—and again, I'm speaking strictly of the financial realities. It could be an oversight," Mr. Worthy concluded, "that perhaps you'd care to remedy."

"A few moments ago, sir, you said I could make no decisions until I'm twenty-five—"

"You're only eighteen, and it might seem like a ridiculous concern now to be preparing for your eventual demise. It's wise, however, now that you're a man of property, for you to have a will. You might eventually marry and have heirs, at which time we'll discuss those provisions. For now, however, you might wish to ensure that, in the unlikely event that you predecease doña Ana, she need not rely on the auspices of either her husband or your future survivors. I only met her once, but I know her to be a proud and tenacious woman. What she has accomplished at Los Gemelos is impressive, and should be rewarded."

"Thank you, Mr. Worthy," Miguel said. "You're right. What should I do?"

"We can draft the necessary language, based on your current position, for you to review. Once you're comfortable with the distribution, the document need only be signed and dated before witnesses."

"Please get it under way then. . . ."

Mr. Worthy scratched a note on a pad before him.

Now it was Miguel's turn to look toward the harbor, and beyond it, to the sinuous line of the Cordillera Central. "I've not seen my mother in years," he said. "I'd like to protect her interests, of course, as much as possible. She has protected mine."

"She has indeed," said Mr. Worthy. "It is unfortunate that you'll have no time for a visit to Los Gemelos before your trip to Europe."

Miguel blanched. All talk about Madrid had ended the day it started.

"I know that your grandfather and don Simón went to great lengths for you to get an apprenticeship with Maestro de Laura."

"They mentioned something like that," Miguel said, "but after Abuela died, and he—"

"I understand." Mr. Worthy allowed a silent moment to pass before he continued. "A few days before his untimely death, don Eugenio came to make sure that I'd prepared your paperwork for the trip. By then I'd already arranged for your crossing and lodgings according to his instructions." He removed an envelope from a drawer on his desk. "Here are all the particulars. You're leaving in ten days."

"Mr. Worthy, I—"

"Don Eugenio was most insistent that you go to Spain for an extended period," Mr. Worthy said, "most insistent."

"He said that to you?"

Mr. Worthy walked to his door, checked that no one was listening, clicked the door closed again, and returned to the middle of the room. "I believe that if people are given the information they need, they can make the best decisions," he said. "From our discussions and my own observation, it appears to me that your grandparents, may they rest in peace, might have protected you too much—"

"I've had a very happy childhood, but I'll be the first to admit that much was kept from me."

"And you have kept secrets from them, haven't you?"

Miguel startled. "What do you mean?"

"Don Eugenio was worried about your . . . affinity with certain persons."

Did Mr. Worthy know about the secret society? Miguel said nothing.

"Your grandfather had it on good authority that it was best for you and Andrés Cardenales to be away from the island for a while. Of course, with your recent bereavement, that was impossible. As your trustee, however, it behooves me now to strongly advise you to do as don Eugenio wished."

"Am I in danger, sir?" Miguel's heart pounded so hard against his chest that he was certain Mr. Worthy could see it palpitating even through his shirt, vest, and jacket.

"You've committed yourself to activities that could place you in danger. The governor appreciated don Eugenio's work with the militias and his illustrious service to the nation. When your name was mentioned among others in illegal ventures, your grandfather assured him that if you were involved, it was due to your youth and impressionable nature. He was promised that if you left the island for a while, concerns about your association with men considered dangerous to the authorities would be overlooked."

"Abuelo never said anything to me," Miguel said.

"It was a delicate business, young man. I'm sure he didn't wish to worry you or your grandmother, may she rest in peace."

Miguel remembered the angry voices from the bedroom the afternoon don Simón brought the news about Maestro de Laura. He was suddenly overwhelmed by guilt.

Mr. Worthy gave him a few moments, then continued. "It appears that Dr. Betances, several of his associates, and others are soon to be exiled again. It would be better for you to leave voluntarily than to be *desterrado.* Let me be clear: if the authorities act against you, the government can seize your property and assets—all of it—and make it difficult for you to ever live on the island with the same freedom you now enjoy."

Miguel's head throbbed with fear, anger, and guilt. "What you're saying is that either the slaves or I can be free, but not both."

Mr. Worthy sat in his swiveling chair again, placed his hands on the desk as if in prayer, and looked at Miguel. "My work prevents me from public displays of my private views, but that doesn't mean I share the prevailing opinion of how this island should be governed."

Miguel didn't know what to say. Mr. Worthy was an *estadounidense,* and criticizing the Spanish government could get him deported. He didn't understand why Mr. Worthy would expose himself to him. Members of the society were never supposed to either admit their membership or ask anyone else if they were involved, but he now wondered whether Mr. Worthy was one of them.

Miguel again turned to the window with the sense that men discussing important things must allow weighty pauses between them. His eyes were focused on the scene before him, but he was more aware of the clopping hooves on the cobbles, squealing carriage wheels, flags and sails flapping on the breeze, the grunts of stevedores as they carried loads upon their backs along the docks.

"I came here with the goal of freeing the slaves at Hacienda los Gemelos," Miguel said quietly, "but you've given me much more to think about than I expected."

Mr. Worthy also turned to face the window and the busy harbor. After a moment, he spoke again. "While I'm not at liberty to contravene your grandfather's will, I can help you look for ways to fulfill your humanitarian aims," he continued. "For example, your will can specify that the slaves be freed upon your death. It's standard practice among slave owners."

Miguel flinched; he hated the sound of those words applied to him. "I understand. Please include it in the document you're drafting."

"Of course," Mr. Worthy said, noting it again on the pad before him. "And upon your twenty-fifth birthday, you can dispose of all your property as you like. The trust can't interfere, although I hope you will allow me to advise you."

"Of course. Thank you, Mr. Worthy." Miguel stood and extended his hand. "I appreciate your help."

"If I can be of further assistance arranging your journey—"

"I'll let you know."

Miguel drifted down the hallway, pushed by a wave of pen scratches against parchment, of fluttering papers, of secretaries and clerks in muted garments, of their hushed voices, of the smell of ink, of the floating motes inside a triangulated sunny shaft on the painted cement wall, of the stillness and heat of the approaching equinox as he stepped into the cobblestone street.

The slamming of doors as merchants shuttered their businesses for the *almuerzo* and siesta fractured the sense that he was in a dream. Pedestrians hastened indoors, the street cleared, and Miguel faced the stark reality that he was about to leave Puerto Rico for the first time in his life. There'd be no time to visit Hacienda los Gemelos, an idea that hadn't occurred to him until Mr. Worthy said he couldn't go there. He was strangely elated, as if having an excuse not to visit his mother had weighed on him. I'll go there first thing after I return from Europe, he thought.

He knew that the Miguel who walked into Mr. Worthy's office didn't leave it. The Miguel who went inside had dissolved among bills of lading, notarized documents, leases, contracts, and brown folios knotted with ribbon. He had all the right instincts, but not the strength of character to stand on his principles. Betances had already been exiled once, returned to Puerto Rico, and it appeared that he was about to be *desterrado* again. How much had the patriot lost in his struggle to free men and women whom he didn't even know? Miguel was a different man. The minute his easy life was endangered, his integrity crumbled. He had another long-forgotten memory: his mother under a tree, still as a post, while everyone and everything in the *batey* whirled and circled around her. It could not be a real memory, it could not have happened that way, but that was what he remembered, her stillness and her black eyes staring at him.

It was probably a good thing for his growing sense of self that he wasn't going to face his mother's shrewd, penetrating gaze at Hacienda los Gemelos.

III

1860-1865

EL QUE VIVE DE ILUSIONES MUERE DE DESENGAÑOS.

———◆———

He who lives on illusion dies of disappointment.

VISIONS AND ILLUSIONS

———◆———

During the *zafra,* Severo Fuentes had no time for society. While he had daily interactions with men, he could rarely be with them as equals. His power over their lives prevented him from befriending the day laborers and small farmers. He felt comfortable among military officers and ship captains, but as a landowner he belonged to the settled establishment, not to the transient hierarchical society of soldiers and sailors. The business and professional men in town were not disposed toward greater intimacy with him than civility demanded because many of them were indebted to him.

From time to time Severo called on Luis Morales Font, the only planter in the environs who always seemed happy to see him. Severo came away from those visits with a particular repugnance for the older man. Don Luis was obsessed with his vigorous youth, and Severo endured hours of the old man's gleeful recollections of his priapic feats with the female slaves. His only surviving son, Manolo, had no interest in agriculture. In 1860 he married an *española* who refused to live in the *campo,* and they were building a house in what was becoming the elegant part of Guares. Every now and then, Severo Fuentes saw Manolo and his haughty wife, Angustias, strolling around the Guares plaza and wondered what the pompous young man would think if he heard his father reminiscing about his escapades.

Don Luis was no longer the threat to Hacienda los Gemelos that so worried Ana in their first years. Then he was younger and mostly sober, all smiles and ingratiating charm. After Faustina and his older son died in the last days of cholera, Luis sank into liquor. Over the years he'd become a violent drunk who mistreated his remaining slaves more now that his wife wasn't there to curb his temper. Severo only called on him so that San Bernabé didn't dissolve into ruin like its owner. Luis was heavily mortgaged to him, and Severo expected that the farm and its slaves would fall into his hands. This certainty became greater when, in December 1860, don Luis suffered a stroke that paralyzed him from the waist down. He recovered his faculties but, in spite of Manolo's entreaties, refused to leave San Bernabé. He hired an overseer and his sister to take care of him, both as abusive and vulgar as their employer.

After calling on don Luis, but before his Sunday nights with Consuelo, Severo rode through La Palanca, a hamlet of twenty shacks and *bohíos* that he'd allowed to develop on his less productive lands between Hacienda los Gemelos and Guares. During the *zafra,* the residents worked in the fields, and during *el tiempo muerto* they cultivated minor crops. A portion of their harvest belonged to Severo. The arrangement worked well. He'd created a reliable, more or less permanent community of indebted *jornaleros* who lived on land that would otherwise be fallow. What cash they earned during the *zafra* was spent on a *colmado* he provisioned, operated by a *campesina* and his illegitimate son, now eighteen years old.

The voice in his head had promised Severo that he'd ride the fields of Hacienda los Gemelos with his son, but since the cholera, Ana had lost interest in their lovemaking, and he wouldn't force her. It appeared that, like Consuelo, she'd become barren. He loved them both, Ana because she was ambitious and a lady, Consuelo because she was neither. He wouldn't give either woman up because she was unable to carry a live child of his seed. Instead, after ten years of marriage to Ana with no heir, he began to single out some of his illegitimate sons for the better jobs on the hacienda. The voice in his head hadn't specified which of the thirty boys, by his last count from *campesinas,* so he kept an eye on them all, and kept them hopeful as he trained skilled laborers he could depend on. The boys lived on the expectation that if they did a good job Severo would increase their opportunities. A few dared imagine that he'd make one of them his heir and imagined themselves upon his fine Andalusian stallion, looking down on the valley from El Destino. Severo had once been a hungry young man, so he let them dream and compete against one another for his favor. But until he was sure which one of them would succeed him, he wouldn't allow any of them to call him Father.

Like Severo, Conciencia had visions of the future. As she matured, her visions increased, although she didn't report anything as dramatic or disturbing as cholera. She foresaw the arrival in Guares of two new doctors, who appeared a month later to introduce themselves to Ana. A year after that, Conciencia saw men running from the *trapiche* in a cloud of steam. When Severo and the engineer inspected the machinery, they noted that one of the spanners was improperly fitted and would have injured workers and disabled the engine in the midst of operations.

Conciencia told Ana that her visions were flashes or shadows in the smoke, and she didn't understand everything she saw.

"I wish you could see them, too, *señora*." She finished patting Ana dry, then powdered her underarms, back, and inner thighs before dropping a fresh nightgown over her head.

"Do they frighten you?" Ana sat on a stool for Conciencia to braid her hair.

The girl stopped a moment, and Ana watched her eyes focus on a spot across the room, the brush in midair. Still with that faraway stare, Conciencia nodded as if conversing with a ghost. Ana shuddered.

"Are you cold, *señora*?" Conciencia returned from where she'd mentally retreated.

"It was like you flew away."

"*Disculpe, señora,* but you asked if I'm scared." She dropped to her knees and covered her face. "Sometimes the fire shows me things I don't want to see."

"What sorts of things?"

"If someone appears in the smoke dead, he or she will die no matter how many herbs I give them." Her eyes were moist. "I do everything I can to save them, in case the fire is wrong, but if they're dead in the smoke, they die, no matter what I do."

"You poor child." Ana gathered her in her arms.

"I wish the fire didn't show a thing."

"Maybe instead of wasting your effort trying to save those who are supposed to die, you can help them to die well."

"*Sí, señora.*"

"You can help them to go *tranquilos.*" Ana held Conciencia for a few minutes, then let her go. The girl resumed brushing her hair as if their conversation never took place.

Ana thought for a few moments. "Conciencia, remember when Meri was burned? Was she supposed to die?"

"The fire doesn't tell me about everyone." She braided the right side of Ana's head.

"Have you seen how I will die?"

"*Ay, señora,* I don't want to think about that!"

"You've seen it? Is it so soon?"

"*No, señora mía, no.* You will be a very old woman!"

Conciencia was eleven, and to her, old could be thirty-four, Ana's age. "How old, Conciencia?"

"I don't know how to count so high." In spite of Ana's efforts to teach her to read, write, and figure, Conciencia was as illiterate as on the day she was born. Again she thought a moment before answering. "The fire says many things I don't understand. Most of the time I only know what it was saying after things happen."

"What's the use of a vision of the future if we can't do anything about it?"

"Maybe we're supposed to prepare, not change what will happen."

"Is there something you're not telling me?"

"I saw a big fire, *señora,* on San Bernabé."

"When, Conciencia? When will it burn?"

"*No le sé decir, señora.*"

She hated that infuriating phrase. "Next week, next month?"

"I don't know, but—"

"What else?"

"I saw him again, *señora.* El Caminante. Burning in the fields."

Ana's visions didn't come from internal voices, nor did they appear as swirls of smoke. They were plans in her journals, lists on ledgers, practical goals to be compared with previous targets, weighed, and measured. She was in her study one morning when she looked down at her fingers, stained to the knuckles from the entries she'd been inking onto her pages. When did my life become an endless line of figures and numbers? She turned to the stacks on her desk, the ledgers on her shelf, the catalogs for machinery and parts, brochures for chandlery and agricultural implements. What happened to the girl bent over don Hernán's journals, imagining the romantic land he wrote about and sketched? She remembered believing that Puerto Rico meant freedom, but it now seemed like the long-ago dream of a naive girl.

She had to get away from her desk. Being outdoors always calmed and soothed the anxiety that niggled at her conscience.

Paula, who was snipping herbs near the kitchen, looked up when she heard Ana talking to herself.

"*¿Señora?*"

"*Nada,* Paula."

She plunged into the flower-lined path to the newly finished open-air chapel, the whitewashed niche featuring her antique crucifix. It was a quiet spot, well shaded by mango and avocado trees. With the small knife Beba had given her two decades earlier on Abuelo's farm, Ana now clipped newly sprouting wayward branches from the hibiscus hedge. Within minutes her bad mood had vanished.

Severo's dogs announced his arrival from the valley.

"There's a letter for you," he said as soon as he saw her.

Soon after the 1858 *zafra* ended, Ana had written to don Eugenio requesting that he send Miguel for a visit to Los Gemelos. There was no response. She wrote again, and the letter went unanswered. After the third letter, nearly a year later, she'd finally received one from Leonor. "Miguel will not be coming to Hacienda los Gemelos. This is his home. If you would like to see him, we cordially invite you to visit him here."

"The old harpy!"

"Not good news?"

"She refuses to send Miguel. I should shock them all by appearing at their door."

"It can be arranged," he said with a bemused smile.

She didn't laugh but returned to the house, mentally drafting a response to doña Leonor. In Ana's mind, the capital might be as far away as Sevilla, or the Convento de las Buenas Madres in Huelva, and a return to any of those places conjured memories of a life that might have happened to someone else. After discarding several attempts, she didn't answer Leonor's letter. Instead she wrote to Miguel, and over the next few months, did so more often, hoping that he'd ask to visit the hacienda. He never did.

Even though the boy showed no interest, Ana told herself that her work at Hacienda los Gemelos was for Miguel. He was far away, under the control of people who hated her, but he'd eventually inherit his grandfather's assets, including the hacienda and Ingenio Diana. She imagined that, as Severo's wife, she'd inherit his fortune, too, if he died before her. With no legitimate heir, Severo's wealth would also go to Miguel through her. Her animosity toward the Argosos didn't extend to the child. He was still young, under the influence of his grandparents, but someday Miguel would come home to claim his legacy, the world she'd created for him.

During the short-handed *zafra* following the cholera epidemic, Severo had become a different man in Ana's eyes. She'd seen him at his worst, as a cruel, unfeeling, violent man, and it was hard for her to envision him in any other way. She still talked to him, shared meals, even allowed him to make love to her, although when he noticed her reluctance, weeks passed and he didn't press her. He spent more nights away than usual. She didn't reproach him, didn't argue, didn't challenge him because nothing she could say or do would change him or their situation. There was no one else to turn to, as she'd realized years ago. She had to learn how to be with him every day without allowing her increasing antipathy show.

Either he didn't notice her coldness or didn't care, but every month more children she took to be his were born to white *campesinas.* By now she'd figured out that Severo didn't take black women as mistresses. The mulatto children she'd always believed to have been fathered by Severo were possibly—no, probably—Ramón's and Inocente's. How soon after their arrival at Hacienda los Gemelos did they begin to deceive her? She thought the eldest, Pepita, now married to Efraín, was the first product of their betrayals. Sixteen years later, Ana still held a grudge against the twins. At the same time, she'd pretended not to know about Severo's infidelities for nearly a decade.

One morning she awoke on the marital bed alone. She'd avoided imagining Severo with other women, even when they came to the infirmary, almost apologetically, to bring forth another of his bastards. Now she was angry at herself for allowing him to parade his lovers and his illegitimate children before her, as if to prove something. But what? As she dressed, she knew one thing. She'd had enough.

She rode to the valley when a swirling morning fog still hung below El Destino. Halfway down the hill, the mist turned to a fine drizzle, so by the time she reached the *batey* she was soaked through. The *casona* was now used as an office and supply room. She kept fresh clothes there, and changed into a dry blouse and skirt. By the time she'd done so, the sun had broken through, promising a hot, dry morning.

Severo came up the stairs of the *casona* about an hour later, when he saw her horse tied to the post below. He hung his sombrero on its peg and coiled his whip on the floor. She'd ordered coffee and bread, guava jelly, cheese, and smoked ham, set on the homely, hacienda-made crockery. As they ate, he reported on the work that had been accomplished over the past two days. She could tell that he knew something was on her mind, but he didn't ask, and his lack of concern made her angry. After a while, she couldn't keep silent anymore.

"Last night another of your *cueros* delivered a baby."

"Don't be vulgar, Ana. It demeans you."

"Not as much as the spectacle of your mistresses and their cursed offspring."

"You've never complained about them before." He sipped his coffee, watching her over the cup's rim.

His admission was infuriating. "First Ramón, then you, betray me."

"I thought you didn't care."

"Why wouldn't I care, Severo? I'm your wife."

She'd rarely seen him lose control, but she now saw that below the exterior calm, he was seething. "Ramón was your husband, but it didn't keep you from sleeping with his brother."

They both knew that he'd overstepped a boundary that should have never been breached. Ana paled. Severo raised an eyebrow, then smiled.

"Let us not play games, Ana. I knew from the beginning, and yet it made no difference at all to me."

"Yes, it has. You've been punishing me for all these years. I didn't know why, but I do now."

"Don't act the victim. I know you too well—"

"You do not."

"More than you imagine. You married me just to keep me here, helping you. I was sincere when I proposed to you. I've loved you, and have tried to make you love me." He stood and paced away from her, then came closer, looming over her. "But admit it, Ana. You've never seen me as anything but your *mayordomo.*"

"No, no, Severo, that's simply not true, and—"

He stepped away. "This is the kind of conversation neither of us likes or wants to have. I've already said things that I'm sorry for." He fetched his sombrero from the peg by the wall. "Don't worry. Nothing will change. Over the last couple of years, we've become more business partners than husband and wife in any case." He retrieved his whip from the floor and adjusted it on his shoulder. "I'm glad we've cleared the air. You'll no longer have to pretend you love me. And I don't have to pretend it doesn't matter."

He kept his word. Nothing changed in their work interactions, but a chasm had opened between them. He lived in El Destino but slept in a separate bedroom. He exaggerated his always respectful manner, reverting to his more formal, premarriage demeanor. She mirrored his behavior until they circled each other, their work the focus of their everyday lives. He had dinner with her several times a week, but their companionable hours on the *balcón,* smoking and sipping rum, ended. After supper he went into his room or rode off she didn't know where.

She missed his company. She had no other friends, but her stubborn pride told her that it had always been that way, except for the years at the convent with Elena. She was sometimes afraid in El Destino. Teo and Paula, Conciencia, Gloria, Meri, and the others lived in *bohíos* nearby, but when Severo wasn't home, the house felt enormous and unwelcoming. She was afraid of the male slaves, many of them new to the hacienda after the cholera, most of them with a history of running away. What if they knew she was alone, and . . . No, she couldn't think about it, had to banish the frightening scenarios. She also refused to feel sorry for herself, or to let Severo know that, in spite of herself, the sound of Penumbra's hooves on the path up the hill made her heart race with anticipation.

She still consulted him on anything to do with the hacienda, and one evening she told him what she'd been thinking.

"Last year the *norteamericanos* raised the sugar tariffs, and now our prices are down to four cents per pound."

"We'll take a big loss on this harvest, then."

"If we sell it. I think we should warehouse our products until prices go up."

"We don't know how long the war will last. The prices might go even lower."

"That's true, but their plantations are in disarray. Sugar and molasses from the Southern states are not making it to the distilleries and markets in the North. Even if the war ended tomorrow, it would be a while before they could. Whenever the war ends, there will be an even greater demand."

He grinned. "Ana, I never imagined you as a speculator."

She was caught between pride and the uncomfortable feeling that she'd descended to another level. "I'm just trying to keep our business healthy."

Within days, Severo had workers building another warehouse behind the mill at Ingenio Diana. Ana wanted to plant another fifty *cuerdas,* but insufficient *brazos* continued to be a major obstacle. *Campesinos* were moving to the hills, where coffee was a major product, and enslaved workers were almost impossible to find. If Severo found any, they were costly. The last time contraband human cargo arrived in the hidden cove was in 1860, when a captain delivered five strong men, two women, and four children.

"I'm bringing two more men from San Bernabé tomorrow," he told her at the height of the 1862 *zafra.*

"Are we renting them from don Luis?"

"No, they're mine now."

Severo was swallowing San Bernabé one *cuerda* at a time, one slave at a time, especially after don Luis had his stroke. Ana had never let go of her rancor toward don Luis, and felt particular satisfaction that he was losing his property to Severo and, by extension, to her.

She rode to the valley every morning, looked in on the infirmary, then went to Ingenio Diana. Since she'd owned it, the mill had been enlarged. The new iron crushers from the United States now produced twenty times more cane juice than the animal-powered *trapiche* had pressed and probably fifty times what the original windmill had squeezed. The purgery, where the sugar bricks were formed and where the molasses dripped into barrels, had also been expanded, as well as the warehouses. Her mill was so efficient that the time to harvest had been halved even as the number of fields increased. With the profits from Ingenio Diana, she'd bought 243 woodland *cuerdas,* now being turned to cane.

She was toying with a new, possibly even more lucrative idea. Nearby haciendas couldn't produce as much as Hacienda los Gemelos and Ingenio Diana. Ana could continue to buy fields, but cultivated land was expensive and taxed at a high rate. Why couldn't she buy the cane from their neighbors? If she could get it at a reasonable price, she wouldn't have to worry about the chronic scarcity of workers because the stalks would be delivered cut and ready to press. The smaller *hacendados* could focus on growing the product without the expense of building, maintaining, and operating a mill.

When she rode from and to El Destino, or when she galloped on the now familiar paths surrounded by cane, Ana felt pride that she'd rescued Hacienda los Gemelos and Ingenio Diana from decades of neglect. Those moments of joy she'd told Elena about, the sparks of happiness that she didn't expect but was grateful for, came more often as these, her creations, flourished.

It felt to Ana that after the cholera the world outside the gates of Hacienda los Gemelos shrank, while within its borders her world grew. The flatlands in the valley, once covered by woods, brush, fruit trees, and coconut palms were now a ripple of cane in every direction. Even the forested slopes she'd seen from the *casona* in 1845 were being cleared and planted with the majestic stalks. This world, narrow outside her borders, expansive and beautiful beyond imagining within, was hers in deed if not in fact, and as the hacienda prospered, her feelings toward Severo Fuentes began to change again.

In late October 1862 she was riding from the *casona* to the *ingenio* when she crested a knoll between two newly planted fields. The midafternoon sun created long shadows, and water sparkled on puddles and on the irrigation canal. A team of workers was clearing the trench between the fields, some knee-deep in the water, others along its shores. Severo was on the far end, his back to her, inspecting the work from his saddle. From the ground, the foreman listened intently to whatever Severo was saying, and the workers had stopped as they waited for instructions. Every eye was on Severo Fuentes, his gestures economical but unambiguous.

During almost two years of near estrangement, he'd continued to treat her as politely as always, considered her ideas and suggestions, performed his duties assiduously. He'd never wavered in his commitment. Hacienda los Gemelos could not have prospered without Severo Fuentes. He was not a perfect man, but he'd always placed her interests first and never asked for anything in return. She'd assumed that the financial rewards were enough, but she now remembered that he'd always hoped for more than money.

Someone must have told him she was on the knoll, for just then he turned and, with a word to the foreman, rode toward her. As he approached, she saw a powerful, wealthy gentleman on a fine horse, the indisputable master over the land and all within it. He's mine, she said aloud before formulating the thought. It flustered her. This was the man everyone else saw, the one he'd strived to become. The next moment she knew that Severo Fuentes must be rewarded. He was hers, and she'd get him back. No *campesina* could ever give him the one thing he most craved, and she could provide.

That evening, Severo came to El Destino, as Ana had requested. She heard him walk past the dining room, where the exquisite crystal, china, and silver she never used was artfully arranged over an embroidered cloth on the dining room table. A sterling candelabrum was alight with six candles. From the porch, she heard him go into his room and emerge half an hour later, showered and shaved. She'd always appreciated that he didn't present himself sweaty and dirty from the fields, but this evening she was impatient to see him, and for him to see her. When he came to the *balcón*, she was gratified by the expression on his face, the darkening of the green eyes, the alert movements.

"Ana."

He touched her face, stroked her hair freed from its tight bun at the nape of her neck and falling like black ripples down her back. The pale green frock that had been stored and now years out of fashion, fit her, at thirty-six, as if she were still a girl, even around the narrow waistband. He held her for a long time without moving while the intoxicating scent of roses and geraniums wafted around them. "Ana."

The way he said her name made her feel as if she'd come home after a long journey.

"*Mi amor,*" she said. He kissed her and as she responded to his lips, she knew that, for the first time in her life, she'd meant it.

News about the 1863 Emancipation Proclamation in the United States sent a ripple of hope through the barracks and fields, and there was a flurry of reports of unrest in haciendas closer to the capital. Severo increased the patrols, and the dogs that accompanied him on his rounds were more suspicious and nervous than ever.

One afternoon he found Ana in the old *casona*. When things were quiet, she often sat on the porch, absorbed in newspapers.

"Two men from San Bernabé were captured hiding in the hold of a cargo ship in Guares," he told her. "I'm gathering the workers to remind them that Spain and the United States are different countries and that whatever happens in one doesn't mean it will happen here."

"Are we in danger?"

"Be alert. When you ride alone, carry a firearm."

She blanched. "I haven't touched one in nearly twenty years."

"I'll set up some targets behind the barn. It will be good for them to see you."

"I can't imagine any of them would—"

"This is a precaution."

"What's happened to the runaways?"

"Luis had the overseer deal with them. They won't run away again."

She didn't ask for details and he didn't offer any. She poured him fresh water from the pitcher.

"Abolition in the North has given momentum to the liberals here," she said, pushing the newspapers aside. "Betances is calling for open rebellion."

"Unlike in the United States, the troublemakers here don't have enough support within the government and can't organize the slaves. They're isolated on the haciendas."

"They don't need to be organized to make trouble," she said.

"That's true. Anything can happen." He finished his drink and wiped his mouth with the back of his hand. "That's why we have to remind them that we don't tolerate disorder here."

In the barracks, in the fields, in the *bohíos* and shacks in La Palanca, in the elegant homes of the newest streets in Guares, and in the offices of notaries and bankers, in don Tibó's cantina, in the *colmados* and *cafetines,* on the steps to the new church, around the shaded plaza, on the anchored ships docked in Guares and on the ones circling the island, in the most recondite corners of Puerto Rico, slaves, *jornaleros, hacendados,* merchants, soldiers, farmers, sailors, and captains were paying attention to the war in *el norte*. Everyone knew that with emancipation in the United States, centuries of government-sanctioned exploitation of Africans and their descendants had ended everywhere in the Americas—everywhere that is, except for Puerto Rico, Cuba, and Brazil. No one was more aware of this than the men and women toiling under the sun of endless cane fields in those three countries.

A man is a man, even when forced to work like a beast, made to live like a beast, expected to become one. Jacobo de Argoso, born Idowe, Yoruba, was captured as a child; thrown into the dark, filthy hold of a ship; starved, chained, whipped, sold, pushed, prodded, and cursed into the canebrakes; locked inside airless barracks; chased by dogs when he ran into the woods; whipped again; sold again; sent into other fields; locked inside again. He stole a machete to use against Severo Fuentes, who'd keep him from running, but Jacobo was caught, received twenty-five lashes, and when the wounds were not quite healed, was dragged back into the waving cane. Jacobo stopped running and bent into the cane while he had a wife and children who needed him. He worked like a beast, because a man did what he must to survive and provide for his wife, his children. But when the plague killed his wife, his children, he began to think again about escape.

Jacobo still remembered his village along a broad and fast-flowing river and knew he'd never see it again, or the long-legged women walking to their plots, or the knobby-kneed boys leading goats to the hills, or the sinewy men prowling the forest to hunt. In his mind, they continued to walk, lead, and prowl because if they didn't, he'd never existed, had never been but a slave with a machete in a foreign land. He had not forgotten his name, Idowe, had not forgotten the other four boys captured with him, none of whom made it alive across the big water from freedom to slavery. By 1863 he'd lived and worked through thirty-six harvests, his spine curved over the moist earth, the towering stalks rustling and cackling overhead and around him, his right arm rising, falling, slicing, the left arm throwing the stalks behind for someone else to pick up and carry. Thirty-six harvests of dark to dark days and, in between, implacable sun, thirst, hunger, snakes, the long, sharp cane leaves slicing into his skin, and insects, always insects, pricking and biting his punished flesh. The whip, too, engraved more scars upon his legs when a *blanco* accused him of touching him, something he'd never do even if he could. White skin like the belly of a lizard's was repulsive to Jacobo.

So much had been taken from Jacobo de Argoso, born Idowe, by his thirtieth *zafra,* during the cholera, that for six more years he bent ever closer to the ground, as if he might find some of his life again between the endless rows of the *cañaveral.*

One day, as Jacobo was helping Efraín de Fuentes carry a load of lumber to the workshop, he heard the news.

"The slaves are free in *el norte,*" Efraín said. "Maybe *el libertador* Abrámlincon will come here to free us."

Efraín was twenty and, like his father, José, his brother, Indio, his stepmother, Lola, and his wife, Pepita, Efraín would rather crawl on hands and knees over ankle-deep shit before giving don Severo cause to unfurl the terrible whip. It surprised Jacobo, then, that Efraín would speak so openly.

"We have a *libertador* right here on this island," Jacobo said. "Dr. Betances, and he's not across an ocean."

"I heard you say a name you're not supposed to mention," called Meri, who was walking behind with her sister Gloria, both of them carrying baskets full of mangoes. Meri's left arm, scarred from the burns, had healed bent at the elbow.

"You're not supposed to be listening to adult conversations," Efraín called back.

Jacobo and Efraín stopped under a tree to change the load from their right to their left shoulders.

"When I was brought to these islands," Jacobo said, "I heard about the first *libertador,* Simón Bolívar, who fought the *españoles* and won independence for his people in countries to the south. He sailed here to invade Puerto Rico to free the slaves."

"I've heard about him," Efraín said.

"The *españoles* found out about it before he could start a rebellion," Jacobo said.

"You're not supposed to say those words, either," Meri said.

"If we get in trouble," Efraín warned her, "we know it was you who told."

"She's not saying anything," Gloria said, "but you shouldn't be talking like that. You never know who's listening around here."

Jacobo shifted his load again and fell silent; he didn't have to tell the story. Everyone had heard it. After news reached them that Bolívar was trying to land on Vieques in 1816, east of Puerto Rico, many took to the sea. Slaves directed flimsy rafts that slammed against angry waves, or were eaten by sharks, or drowned, or were caught by pirates and sold in other lands.

Now, forty-seven years later, another *libertador,* from the north this time, Abraham Lincoln, had freed the slaves in his country, and the men and women locked in the barracks and *bohíos* of every hacienda and farm in Puerto Rico were fantasizing about imminent liberty. Jacobo wouldn't race into the sea in a makeshift raft to be eaten by sharks, and in any case, he was too old to believe he could brave an ocean. But he would run into the mountains, even if chased with hounds at his heels, and would hide and live in bat-infested caves if he had to. He would fight on this land that had swallowed his name, had soaked his sweat and blood, had consumed his beloved wife, his adored children. He'd fight to the death if he had to, because there was nothing left for him but what he had when he started so many harvests ago. Freedom.

SEGUNDO

From her perch in El Destino, Ana had learned the landscape below as intimately as the curves and hollows of her own body. Over the seven years since they'd moved up the hill, the canebrakes, meadows, roads, paths, the treetops in the groves and forested slopes had become so familiar that she marked the growth of the plantation, the activity in the *ingenio,* the hamlets sprouting up along the boundaries, the expansion of the town around the harbor, and the passing of the seasons by the changes in the colors and shapes of the countryside.

Severo had moved the workshop, the pottery, the dovecotes, and ordered new barracks and *bohíos* for the old, crippled, and maimed who made up the labor force in Ana's gardens and orchards at El Destino. The path was widened to make it easier to move up and down the hill to the fields of Hacienda los Gemelos and Ingenio Diana.

Ana now focused the lens of her telescope and saw Efraín and Jacobo climbing toward the workshop, their backs bent under lengths of lumber. They disappeared under the trees and emerged farther up, having transferred their loads to their opposite shoulders. Behind them came Gloria and Meri carrying baskets. Even from here, Ana could tell Meri was chattering. The girl was so talkative that the others called her La Lorita, Little Parrot. She was in constant pain from her scars and held a particular animosity toward Jacobo, whom she blamed for her accident. Now twelve years old, she was a housemaid but was becoming a skillful seamstress, while Gloria was being trained by Paula to be the cook.

Ana pushed her telescope aside and went into her study. There was a letter from Miguel, who was now in Paris with Maestro de

Laura. She had expected that, after his grandparents' death, Miguel would come to Hacienda los Gemelos. He was then not quite eighteen, still technically a minor, and should have come to his mother, but Mr. Worthy explained:

> You can, of course, insist that Miguel live with you, but I strongly advise that he be allowed to go away for a time. His youth and idealistic nature have brought him close to individuals under too much scrutiny by the authorities. Before his untimely death, don Eugenio, may he rest in peace, was advised at the highest levels to send Miguel from the island. Maestro de Laura and his wife will treat him as a son, and Miguel's familiarity with someone of his stature will certainly benefit him in the future.

Ana knew Eugenio and Leonor were liberals, so it was to be expected that Miguel would come under the influence of abolitionists like Betances, the person under scrutiny Mr. Worthy was alluding to. Rather than going to live with artists, bohemians, and anarchists in Europe, he should have come to Hacienda los Gemelos. Here he could witness the other side of slavery. She'd show him how well she cared for her people, how they were housed, clothed, and fed, given important work, and provided for in every respect. The living conditions of *libertos* and freed slaves, like the ones she saw in San Juan, hadn't improved in the eighteen years she'd lived in the *campo*. In fact, from all she'd read, they were much worse, with *libertos* and freed slaves settling in ever larger shantytowns around cities where they could find work. Her people ate well, dressed well, were housed better than *libertos* or *gente libre*. Her workers, she believed, were better off under the protection and guidance of good masters like herself and Severo. She brushed aside that they were locked in barracks at night, that they worked to exhaustion, that they could be whipped, that family members could be sold away from one another.

She filed Miguel's letter in the folio where she kept his correspondence, planning to answer it later. In the middle of her desk were stacks of business letters to write, bills to pay, reports to be filed with the *cabildo* and customs. The paperwork for the business was more onerous every day, especially the correspondence to and from the United States, which was in English. She answered queries and concerns in Spanish, then sent the drafts to Mr. Worthy, where the correspondence was translated and posted. It took longer to get anything done, as the civil war in *el norte* seemed to have no end and communication was harder.

Ana rested her head on her hands. Lately she'd felt tired. Conciencia had formulated strengthening teas, and Paula and Gloria offered her broths made from organ meats to increase her strength, but nothing helped.

"Some cool tea for you, *señora,*" Conciencia interrupted Ana's musings. "Mint and lavender to soothe your nerves."

"Do I seem nervous to you?"

"You do, *señora,*" Conciencia said, not at all intimidated. "You'll have news for *el patrón.*"

"What news?"

"You've been so weak, *señora,* and irritable."

Ana frowned. "No impudence."

"*Disculpe, señora.* I meant no offense."

"What am I to tell *el patrón*?"

"I should've noticed sooner," Conciencia said. "Your moods, your fatigue, the thickness around your waist."

"No. Don't say it."

"*Sí, señora,* you're pregnant. A boy."

Years of herbs and douches had come to this, a child born around her thirty-eighth birthday. It was indecent.

When she saw Ana's horrified expression, Conciencia blamed herself.

"A woman's body wants to conceive," she explained. "I should have changed the balance of the herbs as you entered *la edad crítica.*"

That she was at a crucial stage was as unexpected as her pregnancy. Well versed in animal husbandry, she nevertheless hadn't transferred that knowledge to the processes in her own body. With no women of her class to consult about intimate matters, she ignored them, as if the natural laws that troubled other females didn't apply to her.

Ana sent Conciencia away and sat in her study, trying to make sense of the latest crisis. Whether through neglect, or *la edad crítica,* or the female's need to conceive, everything would now change.

Over the last eighteen years she and Severo had built Hacienda los Gemelos, but half of its canebrakes, pastures, and forests belonged to Severo Fuentes. She knew that, as with her conquistador ancestors, much of his wealth went to Spain. On the other hand, he'd also assured her that he had no intention of ever going back. She guessed that he was a more important man in Boca de Gato by his absence and largesse than if he walked among them, in their eyes still the cobbler's son in fancier clothes.

He appeared to be content to be whom he'd set out to be so many years ago: a man of fame and fortune. Married to her, an illustrious *española,* he was also the stepfather of a Spanish military hero's grandson. By all accounts he'd risen in a way impossible to do on the Peninsula. The only thing he hadn't achieved was producing a legitimate son to carry his name into the future. The name Fuentes was officially linked only to the slaves he owned.

Now he'd have an *hijo de sangre pura.* If the boy also inherited his father's ability and intelligence, it might be this child, not Miguel, who'd continue their work and carry their names into generations.

Ana hadn't thought about her father in years. What would the arrogant don Gustavo think if his illustrious line devolved into this: the son of his unwanted daughter and the son of a village cobbler?

Ana would be watching the sun go down, as usual, from her rocker. Conciencia was fanning her, but as soon as she heard his step, she disappeared into the house.

"*Buenas tardes, mi reina.*"

There was a sadness about her that wasn't there before. Teo brought the sherry, and they waited until they were alone.

"I'm pregnant, Severo," she said with no preamble.

He wasn't sure he'd heard right. "I beg your pardon?"

"Pregnant."

He knelt at her feet and looked into her face. She was doing everything possible to avoid his gaze.

"Ana, is it true? You're carrying my child?" He placed his hand over her belly, which through the layers of cloth felt no different today than two days ago, two weeks ago, two years.

"I know this news makes you happy."

"Of course."

"It complicates everything!"

He sought her eyes and she didn't look away.

"You're worried about two heirs fighting over our inheritance."

"It's inevitable."

Hard, hard, hard Ana, he thought. Even the poorest, most miserable *campesina* allowed herself a moment of joy upon learning she was pregnant, but not Ana.

"We've faced greater complications," he said.

"I'm too old!"

He pulled her off the rocker into his arms. "No, *mi cielo,* you're not. You're just the right age. Our early years were so difficult. You were wise to send Miguel away to ensure his survival. But our child will grow up in our beautiful home and will have the best of everything. We'll be able to enjoy being parents. Do you not see that, *mi amor?*"

She held on to him as if she'd fall if he let her go. He kissed her hair, waited for her to agree that, yes, a baby at this stage in their lives was a gift. But she just buried her face in his chest. Ana might never be the mother their son deserved, but with this child, he'd be the father he'd never been.

"Let me see," he said, walking her inside the house.

"See what?"

"Where the baby is growing. Show me."

"There's nothing to see," she said, horrified and aroused at the same time. "It all happens inside."

He picked her up and carried her through the *sala,* past the study and the dining room where Teo and Gloria were setting up for supper, beyond the guest rooms, to their suite at the end of the hall.

"Set me down," she laughed loud enough for him to hear but not so loud that the servants would. But she didn't fight him as he carried her into the room and placed her on the bed. She didn't complain as he unbuttoned her dress, unlaced her camisole and *naguas,* untied the muslin pantalets, removed her shoes, and unrolled her stockings until she was naked.

She was angular, with small rounded breasts and pointed nipples. He was so moved by the sight of her, bare and vulnerable against the white sheets, that he couldn't speak. Severo Fuentes kissed the hollow between her breasts, then pressed his ear to her chest and listened to the heart that beat within, the hard heart their child would have to conquer.

Ana didn't want to let her condition change her routines, but her body wouldn't ignore that almost nineteen years had passed since her last pregnancy. With Miguel she'd been strong and vigorous, resolved to work as hard as the men she'd lured to Puerto Rico. She hardly remembered being pregnant. This time, aches she'd never experienced disturbed her sleep and forced her to move more slowly than she liked. It was difficult to concentrate on the paperwork that consumed most of her mornings, and she lacked the stamina to manage her day-to-day activities.

"Conciencia," Ana said one night as the girl was helping her get ready for bed. "Why didn't the fire show me there would be another child?"

"No le sé decir, señora."

"Because you didn't know, or because you didn't want to tell me?"

Conciencia finished braiding Ana's hair and deftly tied ribbons into bows at the ends. "When I see something, I tell you, *señora,* but the fire never shows what people want to know. It shows what they need to know."

"I need to know everything about Hacienda los Gemelos, about *el patrón,* about the future of this baby."

"Maybe, *señora,* they don't need as much of your attention right now."

"Is that what you think?"

"*Señora,* it's not my place to advise you about these things. I can only tell you what I see, and you decide."

"I'm asking for your opinion."

"*Ay, señora.*" Conciencia thought a moment, seemed about to say something, changed her mind, then spoke. "You need to pray for your other son, the one across the ocean."

"You're humoring me, Conciencia."

"No! You asked for my opinion, just like everyone who comes to me. But my answer doesn't satisfy you."

"Because it disturbs me"—Ana climbed into bed—"that slaves and *campesinos* get more from their consultations with you than I do."

"I'm very sorry about that, *señora.*"

"Why do you think that is?"

Conciencia assumed unexpected power when seen in lamplight through the haze of mosquito netting. Ana had the impression that what separated them was not sheer fabric but shifting ripples of smoke. Leaning to one side, her too-close eyes peering into Ana, Conciencia seemed to be reading her. Although they'd been looking at each other, Ana was startled when Conciencia spoke.

"Slaves and *campesinos* need me more, *señora*. But they ask for less."

The statement was insolent and deserved a reprimand, but rather than affronted, Ana felt ashamed. Conciencia's crooked figure, the hump that became more pronounced as she grew older, was a rebuke. "You can go," she said, and the girl backed away as if Ana were a potentate on a jeweled throne.

Conciencia was the only slave Ana owned. She'd claimed her, raised her as if she were a daughter, not a servant, but Conciencia was neither of those things. Ana had assumed that the baby who appeared on her door the day Miguel was taken to San Juan belonged to her, not like a child belongs to a mother but like an object to be used. Conciencia had not been, in her mind, a distinct being with her own will and intelligence. She'd been her shadow, her maid, her assistant, her prescient, if unreliable, companion. Now Ana saw a young woman, gifted beyond her age and experience, dependent on her, yes, but old enough and smart enough to pass judgment on her behavior and actions.

Ana recalled herself at that age, seeing her parents through her own resentment and prejudices, implacable, unwilling, unable to forgive them for real or imaginary transgressions. Conciencia, named so that she'd remind Ana of the compromises in her life, was becoming the conscience Ana had imagined she would be. But now Ana didn't want to examine her scruples. No, it was too late; a conscience at this stage in her life was too great a burden.

On the early morning of April 7, 1864, after a twelve-hour labor, Ana awoke to the hush of women. She kept her eyes closed, mentally surveying the soreness in her body. She had a vague memory of Conciencia placing the squirming, slippery infant on her throbbing belly, and of Paula wiping the child clean once Conciencia cut and tied the umbilical cord.

"A son, *señora*."

Gloria helped Paula wash and swaddle the baby, and then the old woman brought him to Ana and pressed his face to her chest. Paula pinched Ana's nipple and guided the baby's mouth to it. Ana lay back and closed her eyes, enjoying the warmth of his hungry mouth and the release that came as the milk dropped.

She must have fallen asleep because, next thing, Severo was kissing her on the forehead, the baby in his arms.

"He'll be named after your great ancestor," he said, "to honor you."

He presented the swaddled child as if the infant were another of the packages with rare goods he brought her from time to time. The next moment, Paula was at her side, squeezing her nipple into the baby's mouth, and Ana had the sensation that everything she was or would ever be was flowing through her breast into her child's body. Again she fell asleep as he nursed.

"You're awake, *mi señora*."

"*Sí*, Conciencia." Ana opened her eyes to daylight. The shutters were half closed to keep the room shadowed and cool.

"*El niño* needs to suck again." Conciencia helped Ana to sit. Behind her, Paula held the baby, her wrinkled face alight with the miracle of an infant in her arms.

"I just fed him," Ana said.

"No, *mi señora*, that was some hours ago. You've been sleeping."

Again his hot mouth released the milk, but this time, Ana didn't sleep. She looked at her son.

Around the bed the women of her house—Conciencia, Paula, and Gloria—were smiling proudly, as if Ana were the first mother and he the first child ever born and nursed.

"Can he see me?" she asked Conciencia.

"He knows you're his mother," she said.

"His eyes are like mine, but otherwise, he looks just like his father," Ana observed. The women nodded.

"*El patrón* went to Guares to register the birth," Paula said before Ana asked.

Ana looked at her child again. His hair was golden, like Severo's, and his little body was compact but heavy. "Severo Hernán Fuentes Larragoity Arosemeno y Cubillas. Such a big name for such a little boy," Ana said into her child's ear. "Can you live up to it?"

As Padre Xavier formed the characters for the two names and four surnames on the top line of a fresh page of the parish register, he marveled at the habit of the rich to keep adding names to their offspring, climbing the family tree as high as they could until they reached the most illustrious ancestor they could claim.

"There it is." Padre Xavier turned the book so that Severo could see that he'd used his best handwriting. Everyone knew that Severo Fuentes had enough offspring in the environs to fill several pages of the records if he chose to recognize any of them, but except for Severo Hernán, his other children were officially listed under other men's names, or those of their mothers.

"And which of these illustrious names will you use in everyday life for your son?"

"Segundo," Severo said.

"Ah! After his father and—?"

"My wife's ancestor."

"I see. Bless him," Padre Xavier said, forming a cross in the air. None of the child's official names referred to saints.

"We will celebrate a baptism Mass when my stepson, Miguel, returns from Europe. He's agreed to be his godfather." Severo pulled a pouch from his pocket and handed it to the priest. "In celebration of our son's birth, my wife and I wish to make a donation to your church."

Padre Xavier resisted the urge to look inside but felt the solidity of many coins. "God bless you and your family, señor Fuentes," he said humbly. "Your generosity will be rewarded."

Padre Xavier often prayed for the equanimity necessary to keep from judging his parishioners, but every day presented a new challenge. The men and women who chose to leave their towns and villages in Europe to settle in America were not easily led. Even the faithful sought ways around church doctrine when it tested their circumstances. But people like Severo Fuentes and Ana Larragoity de Fuentes baffled him.

Ana baptized newborns and every so often invited him to say Mass for the workers at Los Gemelos, but she never confessed or asked for the sacrament of Communion. Until this day, Severo Fuentes had not set foot inside his church and was not present at services in the hacienda.

In his twenty-five years in the colony, Padre Xavier had become accustomed to a church for women. Their men fulfilled their financial obligations to the parish but whenever possible avoided church and consistently ignored at least five of the Ten Commandments. Their faith, if they could be said to have one, was in salvation by proxy.

Severo Fuentes Arosemeno and Ana Larragoity de Fuentes treated him as someone who provided a necessary service, but could be and was ignored when not needed. What troubled Padre Xavier most, however, and what now caused him to fall to his knees in fervent prayer, was that Ana and Severo appeared to have no concept of or any concern whatsoever about the precarious state of their eternal souls.

Ana didn't want to observe the *cuarentena,* resting and getting to know her baby. For three days Paula and Gloria fed her insipid broths and Conciencia offered her sweetened teas, but Ana refused to be confined in the middle of the *zafra.*

On the fourth day after Segundo was born, she walked to her study and was appalled by how much she'd neglected during the last weeks of her pregnancy, when she had barely enough energy to walk from one end of the house to the other. Merely looking at the stacks discouraged her. At the top of one, she caught the familiar handwriting on fine paper.

> My darling Ana,
>
> Your intrepid spirit took you into the forests of Puerto Rico, but over those same years, I humbly submitted to a conventional life. Now my beloved protectors are in heaven, and you, my dearest, continue to follow the footsteps of your distinguished ancestor. I have tried to be a patient and devoted friend to your son, as you requested. Now that he's a man and exploring his own world, he does not need me anymore.

One morning some weeks ago I woke up and counted how many years were behind me, and envisioned what might lie before me. You are well settled with your husband and by the time you receive this letter, with a new baby. Miguel is enjoying Europe with no plans to return for some months. After much silence and prayer, examining my life as it has been, is, and could be, I concluded that I do not want to spend the rest of my life alone. I've agreed to marry Miguel's esteemed teacher, don Simón. We have known each other for fifteen years, but we only turn toward each other now, in the absence of our darling Miguel, who brought us together.

My fondest wish was that Miguel would walk me down the aisle, but I will not interrupt his travels on my behalf. Our good friend Mr. Worthy will do the honors. With Miguel's frequent moves between Madrid, Paris, Rome, and London, it's entirely possible that he hasn't received all my letters. What a surprise it will be to find one from señora Elena Alegría de Fernández! When he was a child, he wondered why Simón and I didn't marry. He will be happy to learn that we have finally done so. I hope you will be happy for me, too, my darling Ana.

Your devoted, loving friend,

Elena

Elena, married! Ana felt a twinge. Until now, Elena had only known one lover—Ana. She wondered if Elena ever thought about the timeless movement and sway of their flushed adolescent bodies. Would she compare their lovemaking with that of her new husband? Might she already have made love to him? Many times in her own life Ana had awakened from the middle of a dream next to Ramón, or Inocente, or even Severo and reached with desirous hands, only to be disappointed by the body next to her, bulkier, hairier than the lithe Elena's. And now some other hands, other lips . . . She stopped herself. Memories, she knew, were the seeds of regret.

"*¿Cómo están mis tesoros?*"

Ana looked up at Severo. "Your little treasure is always hungry," she said, feeling, and even to her ears sounding, petulant. "Your big treasure seems unable to satisfy him."

Severo kissed her, then the baby, who was latched on to her breast but making disappointed faces.

"I've tried, but he needs a wet nurse." She switched Segundo to her other breast and settled into the pillows with an exhausted sigh. "Pepita is still nursing and has a mild temperament." She didn't realize she'd dozed until she opened her eyes and met Severo's, gazing with such intense desire that a blush rose to her scalp. "Severo, you know we can't."

"I've never seen you like this," he said, nuzzling her neck, her shoulder, Segundo's head, kissing it, stroking his son's face, then kissing her lips, but she pulled away.

"Your attention is most flattering," she said coyly. "And will be welcome later."

"*Está bien.*" He took a few steps around the room, gathering himself before he left.

Jealousy pounded against Ana's temples, and she was aware that even now, during the first days of his newborn child, it was possible that he'd consume his passion with another woman, but she didn't speak a word. It didn't make it right, but she'd accepted many things she might have challenged in other circumstances. "So long as he comes home to me," she said to herself—the same phrase that women had whispered to themselves for centuries to excuse the same betrayal.

"Consuelo, *mi consuelo,*" Severo Fuentes called, and she emerged, smelling of smoke, ash, and cigar. He took her with a ferocity that astonished them both and afterward slept with his head upon her soft, fleshy bosom as she rubbed circles around his scalp.

JACOBO, YAYO, AND QUIQUE

The two men Severo had brought from San Bernabé slept in hammocks on either side of Jacobo in the men's barracks. Their women still lived on the farm, and Yayo and Quique were anxious about them and their daughters, now at the mercy of don Luis and Santos, the overseer. Both Yayo and Quique had children and grandchildren conceived in the rapes don Luis inflicted on their women. Over the years, both men's anger had been stifled but not smothered. Locked in barracks after lights out in Hacienda los Gemelos, they could express their anxiety over their families only in low-voiced outrage that mushroomed into frustration and finally to rebellion. At first Jacobo pretended he didn't hear them, but pretty soon he was listening to their plans. They agreed that the best time to run away would be during the *zafra,* when they'd be outdoors with machetes and other tools that could be used as weapons.

Folly grows from desperation. Yayo and Quique conspired, and their passion convinced Jacobo to join them. In late 1864, the three men were not in their first youth but did have experience of the rhythm of the *zafra.* The coming harvest would begin on the east, northeast, and southeast fields, closest to the border with San Bernabé and the main road to Guares. Between them and the town was La Palanca, the hamlet of *campesinos.* Only women and children would be in the village, since the men would be working in the *ingenio.* They expected no challenge when going through; they might even be able to steal a couple of horses or mules for their getaway into the mountains. They didn't think what might happen if their plan was discovered. They didn't think of the consequences of failure. They didn't think that the two young men who'd tried to run away from San Bernabé soon after news of the Emancipation Proclamation were whipped to death after they were caught. They didn't think that if they were successful they'd have to hide for the rest of their lives, moving from cave to cave through the rough terrain of the central mountain range of the island, pursued by hounds, soldiers, and a death sentence. Jacobo knew that if he informed on the other two and it was proved they were conspirators, he would be freed. But he didn't say a word to anyone and, along with Yayo and Quique, began to count moons to make their getaway on a dark night. They settled on the third new moon after the beginning of the harvest the following spring.

AN EVENING IN GUARES

On April 25, 1865, a merchant ship trimmed a forested cove with a stretch of glistening white sand at the far curve. Miguel Argoso Larragoity rocked and bounced on tiptoe, trying to see beyond the windswept beach that the captain identified as the southern edge of Hacienda los Gemelos. The vessel would arrive in Guares just before dusk, but it was over a week later than expected. Miguel's first ship had been delayed arriving in Liverpool, and he had to wait as it was prepared for the Atlantic crossing. The captain now suggested that if there was no one to receive him, Miguel should spend the night in the Frenchman's inn.

"It's not the most elegant place, but don Tibó will provide a horse and directions to Hacienda los Gemelos. I recommend you set out early in the morning."

Miguel was both excited and nervous. He'd spent eighteen months in Europe traveling with Maestro de Laura, who insisted on painting *en plein air* to break Miguel's habits of dreary formal portraits and even more lackluster still lifes. After hours in the outdoors, they returned to their hotels long enough to change into evening clothes. Nights, they haunted theaters, music halls, and brothels, where Miguel indulged enough to require a series of painful treatments for an unpleasant and most uncomfortable affliction. Now cured, he was more cautious. He'd lived a lifetime in a year and a half and was determined to return to Europe as soon as possible. Before he even set foot on it again, the island already seemed too small for him.

He hadn't seen his mother in almost sixteen years. His murky memories were of a bigger-than-life woman with black, implacable eyes. Her letters had followed him to every city in his travels. Her reminders that she expected him to stand as godfather to his infant brother marred the last few months of Miguel's sojourn. Only filial duty broke through his resistance, further propelled by Mr. Worthy's insistence that he come back to Puerto Rico. Perhaps he'd heard about Miguel's activities in Europe or, more likely, was concerned by the frequent requests for funds from every city he visited with Maestro de Laura. It was proving expensive to keep his tutor-mentor in good spirits.

Behind and above him, sails puffed and swelled, the high masts capped by snapping banners. Miguel's clothes fluttered against his limbs and he pushed his jipijapa over his ears to keep it on, its brim bothering his cheeks, the back of his neck. To the east, a gray cloud hovered above the verdure. As they sailed closer to land, he was struck by the lilac and purple undulations like silk scarves beckoning sinuous mountains. Chimneys sputtered pearly smoke over the *cañaverales*.

Another beach sparkled beyond the jungled east leg of the cove, protected by a wall of palms on the landward side and by a narrow coral reef along the sea. High above the tide line, smoke drifted over the shed behind a porched house surrounded by a garden. Another building was on the far end, probably a barn. Enchanted by the view, Miguel quickly captured the outlines in his sketchbook. As the vessel passed beyond the beach, a woman emerged from the house and waved. She wore a flowing dress with no crinolines, so the cloth accentuated her comely figure. Her dark hair was loose to her waist. Miguel couldn't see her features, but he sensed her smile and waved back. He kept his eyes on her as the vessel passed the cove, spellbound as she swayed along the beach. He hadn't seen a sight quite like this in Europe.

The Guares harbor was clogged and there would be no anchorage for them until morning. Miguel was rowed ashore, between and around the towering, pulsing hulls above the dinghy. Harried foremen cursed the ragtag workers who rolled, carried, and lifted the endless line of casks filled with molasses and crates with sugar bricks being loaded onto ships. With his white linen clothes, fine straw hat, and leather valise, Miguel was an incongruous sight on the pier aswarm with flies. The foremen and workers nodded or lifted their sombreros when he passed.

As he touched land in his native country, his throat swelled with emotion. During his months away, he'd often felt gusts of nostalgia.

Puerto Rico, amado mío, tierra donde nací, he'd thought, feeling the passion of a separated lover yearning for his beloved. In countless rooms, over groaning tables, he'd embellished the wonders of his birthplace—the beauty of its countryside, its tranquil oceans, clear breezes, beautiful, clever women, and brave, dapper *caballeros.* He disregarded that slaves sustained Puerto Rico's economy, and that his own wealth was dependent on their labor. As he looked around him now, he recalled that in the months he'd been away enjoying his intemperate adventures, men, women, and children were in bondage so that he could travel, paint uninspired landscapes, eat, drink, and whore. He was ashamed. His first instinct was to wonder when another ship was going back to the world where Puerto Rico was a mere speck on a map, unknown and forgotten by others. He wanted to be where Puerto Rico was what he wanted it to be: a source of pride for its children on other shores. In all the months he'd been gone it had been less painful to suffer homesickness than to see this reality and accept his part in it.

In the cities and towns he'd visited in Europe, Puerto Rico was a concept, an ideal, a place that lived in his imagination, not the actual debased humanity around him and his role in its degradation. I tried to free them, he told himself, but he well knew how feeble were his attempts. He now hoped that he'd learned more than dissipation in eighteen months. He remembered the men in don Benito's *botica,* and Dr. Betances as an example of a man measured by his actions. As Miguel stepped on the precious soil—*amada tierra donde nací*—he swore to continue the struggle he had so easily abandoned, and with such cowardice.

There were more soldiers than he expected around the Guares port, their wary eyes darting from man to woman to man to child, rifles at the ready, index fingers crooked on triggers, and on their hips, incongruous swords and sabers. He remembered that soldiers came out in force whenever the local government was threatened by events outside the island. News had reached England that the Confederacy had collapsed in *el norte,* and that surrender was imminent. Slavery was a thing of the past in that vast country to the north, and Miguel had a moment of hope for the Antillean Confederation that Dr. Betances proposed. In Spain and France he'd met Puerto Ricans who continued to discuss, plan, and write about the same concerns he'd shared in Benito's drugstore and in the secret society. But as on the island, Miguel lurked along the fringes there, too, neither opposing independence and abolition nor entirely committing to them.

Beyond the pier, humans and beasts, their bodies glistening and emitting the sharp stench and sounds of exertion under the sun, congested the streets. Before he could avoid it, Miguel stepped into dung. Within seconds a boy appeared out of nowhere to wipe his cordovans.

He gripped Miguel's coin in one filthy hand. *"Que Dios lo bendiga,"* he croaked, giving one last swipe to the shoes and disappearing into the throng before Miguel could ask him where to find don Tibó's inn.

He walked more cautiously now, around the piles of manure, over the puddles formed by a recent rain shower, past the stacks of tiles from Sevilla on an unharnessed cart. He stepped gingerly around a sleeping dog, his ribs bulging along blistered skin, what was left of his hair matted and knotted.

Guares was a small city. The skeleton of a second wharf stretched, like the first, beyond the rocky shallows. Nearly every building along the shoreline seemed to be under construction. The work, postponed until after the *zafra,* gave the impression of a haphazard, unfinished town. Wooden buildings were framed but not closed in, their beams crossed in sharp angles against the dusky sky. Stone treads rose to untiled porches; iron rods sprouted over half-finished concrete walls like ferrous grass. Bright signs dangled over the sidewalks advertising a tailor, a milliner, two bars, a barber, a telegraph office, a hardware store, two *colmados.* A bank and an apothecary were open for business a few doors from a house with a discreet plaque: JOHAN VAN ACKART, M.D., MAXIMUS DIEFENDORF, M.D. That Guares could boast of two doctors was impressive. That the men had not Hispanicized their names meant they were recent arrivals.

Miguel stopped an urchin sitting on the curb.

"Can you tell me where to find don Tibó's inn?"

"The cantina is over there." The boy pointed listlessly in a direction that could have been ahead or to the left.

"May I help you, sir?" a voice came from behind.

The corpulent young man removed his hat with the air of someone who recognized a specimen of the same breed. He was as well dressed and elegant as Miguel, except that he was taller, wider, and with the ingratiating air of a native facing a lost tourist.

"You're very kind." Miguel asked about don Tibó's.

"I can guide you part of the way." The young man stretched his hand out. "Manuel Morales Moreau, at your service, but everyone calls me Manolo."

"How do you do. Miguel Argoso Larragoity."

Manolo's eyebrows rose. "Hacienda los Gemelos?"

"Yes." He explained why there was no one to meet him and the captain's suggestion.

"No, my friend, you can't go to don Tibó's. Out of the question," he said. "Your uncle and late father, may they rest in peace, were great friends of my family. My father is Luis Morales Font, owner of San Bernabé, Los Gemelos's closest neighbor. Your stepfather has been most attentive since Papá had his stroke. No, you're absolutely forbidden from spending the night anywhere but in my home, where the food and accommodations will be superior to what our French *vecino* can provide."

"I couldn't possibly impose. . . ."

"It's our pleasure, and you can make Angustias happy by sharing the latest from the Continent. Ladies place much stock on news from Europe, much more so than us men, whose concerns are more focused on local affairs."

Miguel was somewhat embarrassed by Manolo's ebullience, his familiarity, the way he tugged Miguel's elbow to keep him from stepping on puddles of questionable origin.

"I'm not surprised you were lost. Guares is growing fast in every direction, thanks to King Sugar," Manolo said. "Until the expansion of our port three years ago, we couldn't accommodate the larger merchant and passenger vessels like the one that brought you back home."

They entered a plaza where the church faced official buildings of stately construction decorated with impressive coats of arms and a very large Spanish flag. Commercial buildings lined the other two sides of the plaza, and Manolo explained that local landowners and businessmen were raising homes along the thoroughfares radiating from it toward the countryside.

The Moraleses' street stretched for three blocks behind the government buildings. Beyond the newest homes, muddy alleys connected a warren of helter-skelter shacks and tumbledown barns. The squatters, *campesinos,* and *libertos* who'd settled on the sites before the town began to grow were being displaced to the outskirts, along the military road, in the swampy marshlands, or up the steep hills.

"These barrios are an eyesore," Manolo said when he noticed Miguel's interest. "The municipal government is doing everything possible to move them and make way for decent people."

"Wealthy people, you mean," Miguel said.

"I beg your pardon?"

"The people in the barrios are poor. It's their poverty that's indecent," Miguel said.

"Yes, of course." Manolo coughed. "It's terrible that they choose to live in such conditions. Ah, look—here we are."

"Allow me to introduce you to my wife and her mother." Manolo led Miguel into a parlor that might have been lifted and transported from a well-appointed home in Madrid. Two aggressively fashionable ladies stood to greet them, and at first, Miguel had trouble distinguishing between mother and daughter, because they looked about the same age. Their extravagant tiered skirts took up most of the floor space.

Doña Almudena and Angustias began to order the servants while Miguel and Manolo had a tall cool glass of *mamey*-water spiced with rum.

"I'm glad you didn't try to get to Hacienda los Gemelos tonight. I didn't want to say anything at first, but we've had disturbing news. Presidente Lincoln was assassinated ten days ago. We learned about it earlier today, and the *cabildo* has alerted everyone to be especially vigilant."

"Now I understand why there are so many soldiers," Miguel noted.

"You can't be too careful. Betances and his ilk are likely to make a martyr out of Lincoln. The slaves already worship them both."

Miguel nodded but said nothing. Another pang of guilt made him adjust the tightness of his cravat.

"Please, Manolo," Angustias said, with an indulgent smile, "the authorities have the situation under control. Let's enjoy our evening without such anxieties." She turned to Miguel. "Mamá and I are beside ourselves with curiosity. Won't you share some stories about your travels?"

THE FIRE CALLS

———◆◆◆———

Earlier that evening, at around the same time as Miguel was sketching the woman waving to him from the beach, Ana found her usual spot on the *balcón* to watch the sun go down. A strong wind rustled leaves and creaked branches, but an afternoon rain had emptied the sky. As the sun dropped into the sea, frogs chirped, toads croaked, insects buzzed, owls hooted. Thrilling life pressed its evening cacophony around her. Sparks whirled over the boiling-house chimney toward a shrouded, attenuated moon. Other than the lights around the mill, the valley was an expanse of impenetrable darkness. The landscape was black and flat as a tabletop, but from Ana's perch at El Destino, with the forested mountains to the north and east, the valley appeared like the bottom of a dark bowl about to spill its contents into the Caribbean Sea.

"*Disculpe*, doña Ana." Meri came to the *balcón*. "Shall we serve your dinner?"

"No, I'll wait until my husband comes home."

"That's just it, *señora*. A boy came to let you know that *el patrón* is not coming. He sent this message." Meri handed Ana a scrap torn from the ledgers where the foremen kept track of the laborers' hours. It was folded several times, and inside, the writing was scribbled in a hurry.

"American president murdered. Guards will be out all night."

Ana had to sit down.

"Is something wrong, *señora*?"

Ana shook her head, but her mind was racing. News traveled quickly through the barracks. Certainly, Lincoln's assassination had probably reached El Destino's workers before Severo's message reached her. Ana was suddenly aware that the vast house behind her was strangely empty.

"Where is everybody?"

"They're all eating in the back, *señora*."

Just then, an enormous tongue of flame rose into the sky over Finca San Bernabé. Ana jumped from her rocker and leaned over the railing as if to fly over it.

"What is it?" Meri instinctively reached to keep Ana from falling.

"Fire in San Bernabé."

"They set fire to the cane all the time, *señora*."

"I know the difference between a controlled burn and that." Ana pointed to the flames, growing and spreading quickly. "San Bernabé is a farm, not *cañaveral*."

Conciencia appeared. "*¡Señora!*"

"I see it, Conciencia."

The three women stood on the *balcón* watching the flames weave and dance in sparkling bursts of yellow, red, orange, blue.

"It won't burn for long," Meri said. "It rained this afternoon."

"Not there," Conciencia said.

They watched for some time as the blaze spread. Ana pointed her telescope in its direction. "It's completely out of control."

"No bell," Conciencia noted, and it was true. Even from here, they should have heard a warning to the neighbors about the fire and calls for help.

Ana scanned the night. On the boundary of Los Gemelos and San Bernabé, erratic lights moved like fireflies in the evening. Torches. "Someone is setting fire to our cane." As if her words were action, flames peaked over the valley in tall red and yellow flashes. The torches went in several directions at once, regrouped, and another fire started farther east.

There was nothing she could do except turn her telescope toward the mill, as if finding Severo among the movement of beasts, men, and equipment would warn him that several fields away the cane was on fire. When she first looked, there was nothing out of the ordinary near the beast-powered *trapiche chico* nor by the larger, steam-powered *trapiche grande*. But suddenly the bell clanged its insistent, unmistakable warning. Someone had seen the fire. The sound changed everything.

"Have them saddle my horse," Ana ordered, and Conciencia flew inside, calling for Teo.

"You're not going down there, *señora*?" Meri was shaking.

"Of course I must," Ana said. "There will be injuries, burns, I have to take care of them—"

"Ay, *señora,* I should have told you!"

Ana stopped in her tracks. "Told me what?"

"Jacobo was talking about . . . *¿lo puedo decir?* Rebellion. I heard him, *señora*. And he also said the words . . . the words 'independence,' 'war' against the *españoles*. I told him not to—"

"Our Jacobo?"

"Yes, that Jacobo, the man who fought the *blanco* when I was burned—"

Ana looked toward San Bernabé, then at the burning canebrakes. She hadn't considered that whoever was setting the cane on fire could be one of her people. Her knees felt slack, but she wouldn't show it, not especially to this girl whom she'd grasped from death's fingers, whom she felt owed her, yes, owed her her life.

"Are you telling the truth, Meri? Do you know of others—"

"I only heard Jacobo say those words."

"When?"

"A long time ago. Before Segundo was born. I should have told you then, but—"

"Yes, you should have."

"Do I get my freedom, *señora*? The law says that if I tell, I get my papers—"

"You're a de Fuentes, Meri," Ana snapped. "You'll have to ask *el patrón*."

Conciencia returned to fasten Ana's riding boots, followed by Gloria with the medicine chest. Teo and Paula appeared with a basket full of clean rags for dressings.

"Teo, you and Paula stay with Meri and Pepita," Ana said. "Everyone else, down to the *batey*."

The guard dogs in their pens were barking as if they understood there was a crisis. She ran into the bedroom and unlocked the cabinet where Severo kept the arms. She chose the rifle and made sure the action was clean and smooth. She'd practiced on the targets Severo had set up for her, and now appreciated how skill was a comfort in emergencies.

Pepita was startled to see Ana armed.

"*¡Señora!*"

"Don't leave the house, and don't leave Segundo alone."

"A sus órdenes, señora," Pepita said in a tiny voice.

Ana strode to the yard, loosed the dogs. They stayed near her, as Severo had trained them to do. The old men and women of El Destino had assembled near the path, shivering in the night air. She didn't think they'd hurt her. Young men were the most likely to rebel, and they'd be in the fields. The elders waited for instructions. If any of them were part of a rebellion, they would have done something already.

"We need you all." Ana spoke with as much authority as she could manage; she would not allow herself to panic. "From here it looks like there will be burns and injuries. Those of you who can't fight the fire will transport victims and help in the infirmary." They must believe it was an accidental fire. None but Ana, Conciencia, and Meri had seen the torches in different directions. The others shouldn't suspect that one or more of them had rebelled. But she was more than aware of the eyes fixed on the rifle in her hands. She pretended it wasn't there.

Conciencia led the way on her mule. Ana took one last look at the fire below, still spreading, but still, thankfully, mercifully, far from the mill and warehouses. She nosed Marigalante toward the path. A few men held lamps on notched sticks, the tenuous flames dancing gaily, just enough to brighten a few yards ahead of them.

Suddenly, Ana was afraid to ride into the path. Her mare felt her anxiety and skittered. If she weren't an expert rider, Marigalante would've sent Ana down. She managed to control her and swallowed the lump in her throat.

She'd never been on the paths at night without Severo. She was now being led down the hill by a forlorn procession of the old, the crippled, the maimed. She had a weapon if she needed to defend herself, but couldn't imagine firing at any of them. She was struck by the familiar dread whenever she remembered that she was the mistress and these were her slaves; their lives were in her hands, but now they held hers. She should have locked herself behind the safety of her door, but she'd gone too far, had been decisive without remembering the dangers that kept her under her roof once the sun dropped into the sea.

The *campo* that soothed the music of her nights from the *balcón* now sounded different when she was in the jungled, dark terrain. Her entourage stamped their feet along the rocky path to scare off the slithering creatures of the night. Branches creaked and thwacked against her. Marigalante trod suspiciously, as if she'd not gone up and down this path a thousand times. Ana kept track of the hounds as they ran ahead, returned, barked, and howled. Ana wasn't as adept as Severo at managing the dogs, but if anyone attempted to hurt her, she knew they'd protect her.

A gust of wind smacked her face, and Ana slapped it back as if she could punish it. She felt like crying but refused to give in to fear and to the rage that accosted her whenever she felt weak or helpless. She tightened her jaw and ordered the procession to move faster, even though her eyes were watering from the smoke now billowing up the hill into the night sky, the air sticky and cloying with burning sugar.

When Ana and the others from El Destino arrived at the infirmary, Zena and Toño had already opened cots and were tying up hammocks. Four workers were recovering from illnesses, so Ana looked in on them. Afterward, she and Conciencia set up their bowls, unguents, and bandages, and with nothing more to do, waited for more patients.

Ana climbed to the *casona* porch to have a better view of the fields. To her left, the fire over San Bernabé appeared to be smoldering, but along the road to Guares, flames sparked and danced like a target.

Efraín and Indio appeared on the path, and for a moment, the two young men she'd known since they were infants, coming out of nowhere, startled her.

"Why aren't you at your jobs?"

"*El patrón* sent us to see after you, *señora*."

"We're all fine here," Ana said, coming down the stairs. "Bring some hammocks for the injured, and let's go to Ingenio Diana."

"No, *señora*!" Conciencia said.

"Is there any reason to keep me here?"

"No, but, it's dangerous. We don't know what—"

"You take care of things here until I come back."

Efraín and Indio rode mules bareback, no match for Marigalante, but she let them go ahead. The path between the lower *batey* and Ingenio Diana was a labyrinth defined by the canebrakes on either side, in front, behind her. She could taste fear; every creak and rustle could have been someone waiting to jump in front of her with a machete. No, not someone, a man she knew, Jacobo, whose wounds she'd salved. Wounds inflicted by Severo.

"Ahead to the left," Efraín called. The night was so dark that they were going in the correct direction from sheer habit.

Of course Jacobo wouldn't be hiding in the cane to hurt her. He'd be running in the other direction from where she was going, running as far as he could from Hacienda los Gemelos. And why wouldn't he? What was there for him but toil and suffering? She shook her head, her usual gesture to stop thinking that didn't lead to answers, only more questions.

"Across the bridge," Indio called, and in a few moments she saw the irrigation trench to either side and the planks across it from one field to the other. There was light ahead as they neared Ingenio Diana. There was activity, movement, and purpose ahead. No time to think, no time to reflect or question, no time to look within. She had a job to do.

Severo saw the flames at San Bernabé almost as soon as they peaked over the trees. He let the *ingenio* foreman know that he was going to help with the fire, took Efraín and Indio with him, and rode toward the farm. But when they entered the path, Efraín pointed to the southeast.

"Look, *patrón!*"

A field was ablaze. Severo sent Indio to alert the foremen, and he and Efraín surveyed the burning canebrakes along the road to Guares from the *ingenio.* Dry cane leaves produced spectacular flames because they burned first, but the stalks, being mostly liquid, were consumed more slowly. That was the theory behind the controlled burns that cleared the sharp, prickly leaves for a more efficient harvest of the sucrose-rich stalks. But Severo knew this fire had been set intentionally to damage the crop; he hadn't ordered the work, as the field was not quite ready.

He organized the foremen and as many workers as could be spared from the *trapiche,* where the cane juice extraction could not be stopped. The bosses formed squads. One of them ran to Severo.

"Three from the same team are missing," he said. "Yayo, Quique, and Jacobo."

Severo looked toward San Bernabé. Yayo, Quique, and possibly Jacobo might have gone up there first to round up others and alert their women. That they set the farm on fire did not bode well for don Luis.

"Get the squads working."

Everyone knew what to do in case of fire. Picks, shovels, and hoes, plenty of water and sand were always available, especially near the steam engine, boiling house, and warehouses. Men, women, and children rushed in the direction the foremen led.

Severo ran from one end of the *batey* to the other giving instructions to the foremen, who in turn mobilized the workers, distributed tools, formed bucket brigades. The gentle evening breeze had turned into a full-blown wind, whirring and moaning like the giant bellows that fanned the first tentative coals that boiled the water that generated the steam that drove the engine that moved the crushers that pulped the cane.

As the workers ran toward the Guares road, another fire started in a field behind the animal-powered *trapiche chico* and spread quickly, jumping over berms and across paths. Severo called the squads back to contain the flames where they threatened the *trapiche* and purgery on one side and the warehouses on the other. Because the steam generator for the crushers of the *trapiche grande* was fueled by wood and the highly flammable bagasse, it was crucial not to let the fire come anywhere near where they were dried and stored, or the building and surrounding structures would be consumed in minutes.

The beasts in the work yard had spooked. Those that could, escaped to safe ground. Two long-horned bullocks still tethered to their cart bellowed, stomped, and dragged their half-full cart in a mad race across the *batey*. A worker who wasn't fast enough to get out of their way was gored, flew head over heels, crumpled to the ground, and was trampled. A spark set the cane in the cart ablaze, further terrifying the bulls, already crazed with fear. They ran straight toward the warehouses. Seeing what was about to happen, Severo shot one of the beasts to the ground as the other bull kept running. He fired again but missed. To his astonishment he saw

Ana, still on Marigalante, shoot the second bull and order workers to douse the flames with sand and water just yards from the building.

Flushed, Ana dismounted and ran toward him. "It's Jacobo," she said. "Meri heard him talk."

"Yes. We realized this as well. They can't be too far."

"They?"

He explained as they inspected the damage behind the purgery. "They chose the wrong night to run away. The civilian militia and regular soldiers are on alert because of the news earlier today."

"You're sure it was just those three?"

"Maybe some in San Bernabé. If there were more of ours, we'd know by now."

Ana examined the man from the bulls' rampage. "Gone," she sighed, mentally counting: this man, and three runaways who would probably be executed. "Four workers lost in one day. And we don't know how many *cuerdas* burned."

"We're doing the best we can," Severo said. "Keep a squad here to finish up," he ordered a foreman. "Send the rest to the east fields."

"Will you be able to save some of the crop?"

"We'll try. Those fires are smaller and seem to have been a diversion. Still, there might be injuries. I'd feel better if you were in the lower *batey*. Things are under control here." He walked with her toward Marigalante. "That was excellent marksmanship, by the way."

"I can't believe I did that," she said, looking where the bull fell.

"Very impressive," he said with a tight smile. "Now I'd better see what's happened in San Bernabé." He checked the holstered revolver and cinched the strapped rifle on his back. "Efraín, you come with me, and Indio, take *la patrona* back to the *batey* and stay with her."

"He needn't stay. He's more needed in the fire squads."

He nodded and ordered a boy to bring a machete for Efraín.

"Severo," Ana said so that only he could hear. "Be careful. Remember that Conciencia has seen a man on fire. Twice."

He touched her cheek. "I'll be careful. Don't forget that *mala hierba no muere.*"

"If bad weeds don't die, we'll both live forever," she said grimly.

He lifted Ana onto her saddle and watched her go until Marigalante disappeared.

He reckoned it was well past midnight, and the fire in San Bernabé had been blazing for at least five hours. He turned Penumbra toward the shortcut along the edge of the forest and up the slope that approached the farm from the back. Seis, Siete, and Ocho led the way. The dogs were familiar with this approach because that was how Severo went to call on Luis from Los Gemelos. It was slow and treacherous on the narrow uphill path in the dark. For most of the way, he had to rely on the dogs' superior night vision to lead them. There were times when Severo had to stop to let his eyes get accustomed to the darkness. He kept one hand on the reins and the other by his revolver. Efraín rode behind him, and even though he'd never given him trouble, Severo knew that a slave at your back with a machete in hand wasn't to be trusted, no matter how obedient he'd always been. Severo now wondered how long it had been since he'd allowed a man to walk behind him.

They crossed an orchard, and just as they were about to enter the yard, the dogs raced into the bushes, barking wildly. Severo pointed his rifle at a woman carrying a child and dragging another by the hand who ran out of the shadows, screaming as Seis nipped at her heels.

At his signal, the dog backed away, but Siete and Ocho were yapping at more figures emerging from the shadows.

"Where are the others?" Severo demanded, sweeping the dark.

"Gone," one woman said.

Severo scanned the shrubbery as the dogs flushed out more people. He counted with his rifle barrel as they emerged—five women, seven children, three infants, two bent and slow-moving elders, one of them missing an arm. A tall man with a peg leg almost as thin as his real one led a blind woman. All the able-bodied men were gone. Six men, Severo remembered, not counting Yayo and Quique.

Severo ordered Efraín to dismount and lead the group to the *batey,* the dogs circling them, biting when they lagged or appeared to want to run. He rode ahead.

The farm was in ruins. The barracks were ashes, the warehouses and barns smoldering heaps of lumber. The air was thick with the smell of burned hair and flesh; animals had been left to perish in their stalls. Santos, the overseer, and his sister sat in perpetual watchfulness on the cement steps of the house, their necks slashed. The fire was still blazing inside, and it was obvious that no one could have survived. Luis, fat and ungainly, had been unable to walk on his own since his stroke several years earlier. His wheelchair was tipped on its side in the yard.

"Severo!"

Luis was cowering behind the cement cistern across from the house. What was left of his torn nightshirt was bunched around his privates, his exposed thighs and legs scratched and bleeding. He was barefoot, but he still wore his nightcap. Since his stroke, his face had frozen into a lopsided, wanton grin that even in his dire state made him look like a huge-bellied satyr. He moaned and held on to Severo, sobbing into his shoulder that they beat him with sticks and left him for dead in a burning house. He dragged himself on his elbows, past the bodies of his caretakers, heaving his useless lower body along the *batey* until he found refuge.

Efraín led the slaves into the *batey*. When they saw the ruins, the women wailed, pulled off their head rags, and flapped their shoulders and torso, as if insects had swarmed them. Their children screeched around them, grabbing for the rags, fearing that all that flapping would cause their mothers to float up into the sky. Their cries nearly drowned out the sound of approaching horses, the jingling of spurs, and the curses of men unsheathing sabers. The lieutenant led four soldiers, and three members of the local militia flanked the sheriff. Behind them, a disheveled Manolo Morales Moreau, who was more used to riding in his pretty calash than on a horse, bobbed and jerked, making Severo Fuentes feel sorry for the stressed animal. When Manolo saw Severo with his father, he dropped ungracefully from his mount and waddled to Luis, who wouldn't let go of Severo until he recognized that the immense, blubbering man grabbing at him was his son.

"They tried to kill me," Luis wept as Manolo hugged and kissed him and tried to drag him upright, forgetting that his father's legs were paralyzed.

A soldier rounded up the slaves and made them sit on the ground with their hands on their heads.

"We caught two men," the sheriff said to Severo and the lieutenant. "One called Yayo, the other Alfonso."

"Yayo belongs to Los Gemelos. I'm still missing two more, Jacobo and Quique. Alfonso and as many as another five ran from here."

"We'll find them," the sheriff said.

Another soldier rode up and talked to the lieutenant. "Don Miguel is waiting for someone to escort him—"

"Miguel?" Severo turned to Efraín, who was holding their mounts. "Didn't you go check on his arrival this morning?"

"The ship wasn't there, *patrón,*" Efraín said. "I asked, and the harbormaster said no ships would dock today, and to come back tomorrow."

"There is a mistake. Don Miguel was with don Manolo," the lieutenant said.

Manolo and a militiaman were trying to lift Luis into his wheelchair. Severo helped them settle the still-distraught old man before questioning his son.

Manolo was breathless from the exertion but between wheezes was able to tell Severo about the ship's arrival, and finding Miguel on the street, and bringing him home. "When the alarm came, he didn't hesitate," Manolo said. "He was riding with us, but next thing I knew, he wasn't there."

"He stopped when he saw your fields were on fire," the soldier said. "He said he was going down there. He was worried about doña Ana."

Before his last words were uttered, Severo was on horseback, ordering Efraín to follow him down the hill to Los Gemelos.

Teo, Paula, and Pepita, carrying Segundo in a sling, settled in the kitchen with Meri after Ana and the rest left.

"I told her," Meri said, "about Jacobo. I heard him say—"

"Hush, child," said Paula. "Don't talk such nonsense."

"But I heard—"

"You heard nothing, and you could get a lot of people in trouble with your loose tongue," Teo said. "No one has said anything about anything. Understand?"

"But I already—"

"Don't talk anymore," Paula said. "Get your work and I'll help you with the hemming. Can you light another lamp, Teo?"

Meri was annoyed. Who did old Paula think she was, telling her what to do? Just as soon as *el patrón* gave her her freedom papers,

Meri was going to tell Paula a thing or two. Always telling her to hush! She should be quiet, the old goat.

Freedom! She'd be free, and as soon as she could, she'd leave El Destino and Hacienda los Gemelos and go away, maybe as far as San Juan. She'd open a dress shop for fine ladies, the patterns taken from the magazines doña Ana hardly looked at but that Meri couldn't get enough of. She'd make dresses with many tiers on the skirts, and ruffles on the sleeves and collars, like in the pictures. She wished she could take the Singer. Don Severo had brought it a month ago and after doña Ana learned how to operate the sewing machine, she taught Meri, who could now make a simple skirt, blouse, and apron in a day, not counting hand finishing.

Before returning to the kitchen, she decided to see what was happening in the valley so that she could report to the others. The fire in San Bernabé was out. The blaze in the southeast cane fields, however, seemed to be snaking toward the lower *batey.*

She'd never seen anyone else use Ana's telescope, but she now crouched at the eyepiece, not daring to change the height so that doña Ana would never know. She probed the darkness until she found the lower *batey.* Torches and lamps lit some of the buildings well enough to make out the infirmary and the *casona.* Meri aimed toward the burning fields but passed over them. As she repointed toward the fire, something caught her eye. She focused the lens toward the movement and saw a man dressed in white upon a pale horse. Goose bumps rose up and down her spine.

"El Caminante!"

She looked away, because watching the apparition might curse her. But she had to look again to make sure it wasn't a vision, remembering that she'd never heard anyone say that El Caminante had a horse. She surveyed the valley once more and saw the man in white again. "How can it be?" she said aloud, as if he could hear her, but just as she said it, El Caminante disappeared into the burning cane.

Ana looked in on the infirmary again, but no injured workers had been brought while she was at the *ingenio.* She returned to the *casona* porch, from where she had a good view over the fields. To her left, the fire over San Bernabé appeared to be out, but along the road to Guares, a small fire sparked like a target in the night. She nodded, recognizing that Severo had ordered the workers to trench and douse the boundaries of the farthest field to keep the fire from jumping rows, letting the inside burn.

As she watched, a cold wind swirled around her that nearly knocked her down. It whooshed like human hands, pushing her out of the way, and continued through the dusty yard into the cane, clacking and sizzling as it spun toward the burning field. Her ears rang with the sound of unintelligible voices. The hair on her arms, behind her neck, and along her scalp bristled. She heard a neigh, galloping, and yelling as a fiery crown boiled over the cane, hissed, and disappeared.

Suddenly, she was in total darkness. She palmed the porch railing toward the stairs to the yard. Every candle, lamp, and torch was extinguished in and around the infirmary. Below her, someone ran toward the cane, chased by a dog, but she couldn't tell who it was. Ana was frozen on the top tread, afraid to go down into the yard. She now heard wails and scuffling in her direction. She'd left the rifle inside the house, leaning against the wall, and now backed toward it.

The hounds skulked closer. Two came upstairs to her side. Someone managed to light a torch, and in a few moments candles and lamps were again flashing on the ends of poles. Her next thought was that she was trapped upstairs in the old, splintery *casona*. Did they mean to set the house on fire, like the runaways apparently had done to the canebrakes?

A huddle was forming at the bottom steps of the *casona,* but no one dared come closer, afraid of the dogs.

"Conciencia!" Ana called from the porch.

"The fire called her," Toño shouted, followed by shrieks.

"A spirit entered her," Zena said, and began the Lord's prayer over the weeping.

Ana realized that they were gathering in the yard not in anger but because they wanted to be near her and were seeking her protection. She thought their terror had something to do with the figure that ran into the canebrakes being chased by a dog. And she now knew it must have been Conciencia.

Ana ran to the front porch. She peered toward the road to Guares and was horrified as a column of fire rose from the farthest field.

Her breath left her, and she held on to the porch railing, watching the whirling flames licking the black sky. Over the clapping of the cane, she heard screams, voices, barking, footsteps running away, then finally toward her, with the fateful certainty that disaster had touched her again.

EYES IN THE SKY

————◆————

Earlier, just as they sat down to dinner, word had come that slaves had set fire to San Bernabé. Manolo and Miguel rushed to the stables, saddled, and rode out without a thought or a weapon. In the city or *campo,* when the fire bell rang, every man must answer, and by the time they reached the main road there were other men like themselves, dressed for a quiet evening at home but ready to do their duty. They followed the soldiers, whose mission was to quell a possible uprising, while the neighbors and volunteers were charged with putting out the blaze.

By the time they left behind the outskirts of Guares, the moon was a tenuous ember in a muddy sky. Miguel trailed the riders. At the turnoff to San Bernabé a heavy canopy of branches obscured the path, so it was nearly impossible to see where they were going. The soldiers led the way uphill, but Miguel stopped at an overlook when he saw fire in the valley. A soldier stopped alongside him. It was too dark to make out his features clearly, but he had the voice of a younger man still excited about his work.

The stars cast a gray light over a landscape punctuated by the orange and yellow flickers of torches and candlelight, but below in front of Miguel were blue, angry flames.

"The Los Gemelos fields are on fire," the soldier said. "That's unusual at night. I don't see any men down there, but who knows—it's dark as a wolf's mouth tonight."

Miguel's attention was drawn to lights and barely discernible buildings beyond the burning canebrakes. "Is that the house?"

"No. The house is El Destino, up there." The soldier pointed to a yellow flicker in the upper distance. "What you're seeing, where you see lights? That's what they call the lower *batey,* with the old *casona* and doña Ana's infirmary."

"Do you think she has any idea that the *cañaveral* is on fire?"

"She's sure to have seen the flames from El Destino but . . . I'm guessing . . . in an emergency she'd be in the infirmary." He sensed that he might have said too much. "But don't worry, *señor,* don Severo probably has men on the fires already. He doesn't miss much."

Miguel held up his hand to quiet him. "Voices."

The soldier listened. "You're right. As I said, don Severo doesn't miss much." He slapped a mosquito from his neck and adjusted his hat. He squinted into the darkness and decided he needed more orders. "Maybe I better let the lieutenant know."

"I'm going down there," Miguel said. "Is it to the right, when I get to the bottom of the hill?"

"Yes, but if you wait, someone will accompany you."

"All right," Miguel said.

"It will take a few minutes."

Miguel was alone on the overlook, mesmerized by the colors, by the constantly changing patterns of blue, red, yellow, and orange flames against the velvety countryside. Men's voices rose above the clatter and snap of cane and fire. Every once in a while smoke floated toward him that smelled of burned sweetness. He watched, dazzled by the shapes and fluctuating edges as fire crept in different directions. *"Thank you, Mother Forest, for orange and red. . . ."* An immense sadness tightened his chest. He couldn't understand why, when he looked at the glimmering lights, he had the sense that Nana Flora was there, that Nana Inés was there, that Siña Damita was there, and Nena, and his father, dressed in white, just like he was now, waiting for him in the *batey.* His mother was down there, too, but Miguel couldn't conjure an image of her as he could with the others. She was an elusive phantom. What he knew about her were thousands of words inked upon fine paper, steadfast majuscules curled at the ends, resolute crossbars on *t*'s, adamant tildes over *n*'s, uncompromising dots over *i*'s. She has no idea who I am. His chest felt tighter, and he knew it was the sorrow he'd carried for years. Was it true that she'd traded him for this vast darkness before him? An advancing line of fire danced and crackled in the cane as if in celebration of his return. He had to see her. He had to ask the question he'd never dared ask in the hundreds of letters he'd so grudgingly written over the last sixteen years.

He could no longer wait for the others. He guided the horse down the slope toward the valley. He wasn't thinking about the fire now, only that he wanted to reach the *batey,* to see Ana's expression when she saw him. Would she recognize him? He knew that if he saw her eyes, he'd know the truth.

At the bottom of the path were the flatlands. He went right, as the soldier had indicated. He'd never been in the *cañaveral,* not even as a boy. The horse sensed his uncertainty, but Miguel urged him along the hard-packed dirt, reassuring them both that they were on a well-traveled road. He couldn't see beyond a few yards, but in a field to his far left, flames rose into the sky and he smelled and felt the sweet, itchy smoke of burning cane. So long as he stayed on the road, he'd avoid the fields.

Soon he heard grunting, urging, pounding, cutting, calling and answering, men cursing. The soldier was right: people were trying to control the spread of the flames. He reined the horse to a halt in the middle of the road to hear better. The workers were closer than he first thought. To his right, the cane sighed and rustled, and Miguel listened, expecting secrets. The unfamiliar horse nickered, resisting the bit, and Miguel shortened the reins. He swept the darkness. A sliver of moon broke through streaks of clouds, and Miguel saw three distinct sources of light. To his right on a low hill was the glow around the mill with its chimney. High over the horizon before him, lights flickered in what he thought was El Destino. To his left, the road stretched between rows of cane, and if he sat up on the horse, he could make out lights in the *casona* where he was born. He spurred the horse toward the lower *batey,* galloping upon the hard earth toward his mother.

As a child he'd tried to avoid reading her letters. As a young man, he rarely answered them. He'd come across the ocean reluctantly, resentfully, to see her, and even before he reached her, he had plans to leave as soon and gracefully as he could. His memory of her was of a stern woman in black clothes who, for reasons he didn't understand, scared him. Now self-reproach galvanized him. She was his mother, his last blood relative, and he had to see her.

He turned left at the next turn and came upon two men carrying torches. One of them seemed to recognize him, but the moment Miguel opened his mouth to speak, the men dropped the torches and ran back into the cane.

"Wait," Miguel called.

Just then a huge cloud of gray smoke enveloped him. The horse whinnied, turned, sprinted into the cane, turned again, bucked, indignantly threw Miguel head over heels, and jounced into the *cañaveral*.

When he regained consciousness, he wasn't sure where he was. His ears buzzed, and his head felt heavy. He had no memory. No future. He was floating in darkness and space. He didn't want to awaken, but as he rested on the ground, his senses returned, and he discovered anew that he could feel. The earth beneath him was moist and he clutched handfuls of the sandy soil. He was in the rustling cane.

Miguel recalled falling hard, the sudden puff of smoke and ash that made it impossible to breathe. His eyes hurt, as if needles were prickling him, so he closed them tight. Who were those men, and why did one of them know him? He had to see. When he opened his eyes again, the purple night was speckled with ten thousand blinking, aggrieved eyes. If I die, the slaves will be free. He felt peaceful, noble; the ten thousand eyes blinked. As he watched them watching him, a veil drew across the sky. Creatures scurried past him, and he jerked with a start and a groan. He was now fully awake and aware, the canebrakes towering over him. He ached all over, but every limb, finger, and toe moved and wiggled. There were voices nearby calling his name, dogs barking. He stood but couldn't see over the cane.

"*¡Auxilio!*"

He was buffeted by a hot swirl and sparks that enveloped him and struck him down. He crawled upright then stumbled, unable to breathe, to see through the oppressive smoke. He pushed himself up again, called again. Flames surrounded him. The heat was intolerable. He smelled molasses and singeing hair. My own? His mouth filled with sugary burning ash that seared his throat, constricted his lungs. Hot pressure scorched his face. He squeezed his eyes against the smoke and fire, flailed, and cried, and knew he was dying in the *cañaveral*.

But no, I must get out. I don't want to die.

Coughing, tugging at his burning clothes, his hair, he crawled in circles trying to find a way from the flames.

"¡Auxilio!"

I want to live. I can't die now, not here. Not even if my death means freedom—

"¡Mamá! ¡Mamá, ayúdame!"

Above the sizzle, the snapping flames, he heard his name. He pushed himself to his knees, "Help me." He struggled to open eyes boiling in their sockets. Dogs were howling around him, and he was sure he'd arrived at the gates of Hades. I don't deserve to die. I wanted to free them, but they wouldn't let me. He heard his name again, turned toward the voice, and forced his scalded eyes to open. The last thing he saw was a golden-haired man running toward him, as if the flames of hell itself couldn't touch him.

Ana waited on the *casona* porch, gripping the stair rail. Below, the slaves chorused the Lord's prayer and the Ave Maria she'd taught them. She repeated the familiar words mechanically as she peered into the night and resisted her greatest fear. In the intervals between breaths, she begged a God she rarely appealed to.

"Please, Lord. Please spare Severo Fuentes."

Fulfilling her request, he hurtled from the cane carrying a pile of rags, followed by Conciencia, Efraín, Indio, horses, dogs. Severo raced past the huddle at the bottom of the stairs toward the infirmary. The bundle in his arms didn't seem real, but Ana discerned the contours of a body. A foreman, Ana thought, a *jornalero*. She followed them. Severo laid the man on a pallet, and Conciencia hurriedly scissored his clothes. He was so limp and still that Ana was certain he was dead.

"I'm so sorry," Severo said, putting his arm around her. His face was smeared, and he smelled of embers and charred hair. "He got lost in the cane."

"Who?"

Efraín hooked an oil lamp on a beam above the pallet so that Conciencia could see better. And although she hadn't seen her son in nearly sixteen years, Ana recognized Miguel.

"No! No! No! No!"

Severo held her as she looked over his shoulder at her son, his face charred, his hands bleeding. In his dirty white clothes, with his long hair and gaunt face, Miguel looked like Ramón in his last days.

"He's alive, Ana." Severo pressed her into his chest, as if to give her some of his strength. Then he let her go. She ran to her son.

"Hijo," she said so tenderly that she surprised herself.

He tried to open his eyes. A breathy croak came through swollen lips, unrecognizable as a word.

"No, *hijo,* don't speak. Let me help you."

She splashed water over his face, his shoulders, arms, legs. He was a small man, she saw, only a few inches taller than she, which made him look younger than nineteen. He was on a pallet where many slaves had lain, where many had died. She should move him. But where?

"What was he doing in the *cañaveral?"*

Severo shook his head. "Apparently, he thought you were in danger."

She looked at Severo's exhausted face, stained with ash, smoke, and dirt. There had never been anyone she could depend on more than Severo Fuentes. He loved her, and she loved him to the roots of her being. As if he'd heard her, he placed his hand on her shoulder.

"Thank you for finding him. And bringing him to me—alive." Her voice cracked.

"I've sent Efraín to Guares for the doctor."

She nodded and gently poured more water over Miguel's arms, legs.

"If you don't need me here, I'll check on the fields."

She didn't want him to leave. "The runaways? Are we—"

"They've all been accounted for. Miguel ran into Jacobo and Yayo on the road and spooked them. The lieutenant found them cowering in a ditch. He left a couple of soldiers here for the night."

She looked at Miguel. With soothing waters, she'd pour everything she'd learned about medicine and healing in two decades over her son's scalded, torn, and broken skin, and through his cracked lips. She remembered how Meri had fought her, as if she didn't want Ana to touch her. Unlike her, Miguel lay terrifyingly still even as she and Conciencia poured liquids and daubed unguents over him. She covered the worst burns on his face, ears, neck, arms, and right leg with shredded-potato poultices. With her pocketknife, she snipped the spines along the edges of the largest aloe leaves, sliced them open, and placed them facedown on his limbs until he looked like a bizarre half-man, half-plant creature.

"I'm washing your hands now," she said. He lay immobile, hardly complaining even though she was sure he was in terrible pain, but at last he responded to her voice. She'd keep talking to him until he was healed, if she needed to. "The aloe will feel cool," she said as she adjusted the leaves on his leg, his foot.

He moaned as if in the midst of an anxious dream. His lashes and brows had been singed to the skin. "Don't try to open your eyes now, *mi niño,*" she said. "I'm covering them with this cloth to keep them moist."

Conciencia brought a tisane with lavender and cane juice. It had been effective when Meri's throat swelled from crying. Ana now had to insert a finger into Miguel's mouth to separate his lips enough to dribble in the liquid drop by drop.

Conciencia hung a curtain to isolate Miguel from the other patients. Lamplight quivered along the outer reaches of the wall. Ana dropped more tisane into Miguel's mouth and spoke to her son. If she was silent, he dropped into lifelessness. Only her voice roused him.

"Drink, *hijo.*" He swallowed the sweet potion. "You're home, *hijo mío.* Drink the *guarapo, te lo ruego, por amor a Dios.*"

She wanted to keep her voice strong and confident but heard her desperation, the fear that all her skill with brews and concoctions might be useless. "Help me, Lord," she said. "Help him, sweet Virgin. Help us, dear Jesus."

Until earlier that night, she hadn't spoken to God with such conviction in a long time. She couldn't count how many sins she'd committed over her lifetime. Of one thing she was sure, though. Twenty years on Hacienda los Gemelos had whittled away her faith until she didn't trust God.

"I'm washing your feet now," she said to Miguel.

Just as she'd stripped her body of frills and fripperies in two decades in Puerto Rico, she'd shed religious belief in much the same way the conquistadores did, for expedience. They arrived in the New World with priests and incantations, but the history of the conquest was strewn with their atrocities, their false promises, rape, their bastards, plunder, and murder. They lost their moral center, compromised their faith in the New World. They then erected gold-encrusted cathedrals in the Old World to turn humanity's eyes toward beauty and away from their sins.

She dropped more liquid into Miguel's mouth. He gurgled, swallowed. She recalled her last moments with Ramón as she and Siña Damita worked on him on the cart that drove him toward his death. Ana had never forgotten his expression whenever his eyes rested on her—hatred, even through his pain, the same look as Inocente's the last time she saw him. Ramón's cries pierced through her like accusations. He knew that he wouldn't survive. He'd been dead a long time, had become a ghost, El Caminante, caught in the snare of her ambition, unable to free himself.

Miguel wheezed, groaned. Ana blotted his lips, adjusted the bandages and aloe leaves. "I have not been a very good mother to you," she said. Just as she was not a good wife to Ramón. She was glad that she was alone and no one could see her with her broken son. No other eyes would blame her for this calamity, but she knew, deep in her bones she knew, that she was responsible. Miguel had gone into the *cañaveral* because of her. Like his father, he was trapped in her life.

If he died, as his last survivor, she'd inherit Los Gemelos. The thought stunned her. That she'd even think this now was appalling. She banished the thought. He wouldn't die. She'd do everything in her power to save him, to pray for him even. She hadn't loved her son as she should have, but she wouldn't let him die. This boy whose body trembled under her competent fingers, this boy whom she had ignored, bartered, manipulated was her son, her legacy. Miguel and his children and his children's children would be her cathedral.

MR. WORTHY'S JOURNEY

Vicente Worthy gathered the papers he'd need for his journey and, one by one, slid them into his briefcase. There were several contracts with suppliers, two letters of credit, three purchase orders for two hundred puncheons of molasses each, plus one for five and another for seven tons of sugar bricks. There were copies of titles for real property, lists of assets, pedigrees for horses. The final folio was the last will and testament of Miguel Argoso Larragoity. Mr. Worthy wasn't used to such crisp paper for wills. Often the pages were wrinkled or torn from much handling by their owners, from additions, amendments, and codicils. Most were limp from years of being stored in cabinets, the pages yellowing, the ink fading, the folds permanently creased, which made it difficult to keep the pages open. A will from the young was heartbreaking. On the other hand, it made his job easier.

Mr. Worthy snapped his briefcase closed and made sure the clasp was tightly fastened. He'd walk to the pier, where he'd board a ship, once owned by Marítima Argoso Marín, that would bring him to Guares. By the time he reached Hacienda los Gemelos, the harvest would have ended, shortened by the unfortunate occurrences a week earlier. Mr. Worthy arranged for his trip the same morning he'd received the news by telegraph. Another telegram arrived for doña Elena the same afternoon, and within hours, the whole city knew that young Miguel Argoso Larragoity had died in his mother's arms. Those who remembered the deaths of Ramón and Inocente observed that the Argoso family had met with nothing but misfortune in Puerto Rico and rallied around the bereft doña Elena. Today, as Mr. Worthy began his journey to Hacienda los Gemelos, Miguel Argoso Larragoity was being buried.

Just as he was about to leave his office, his secretary announced that don Simón was waiting to see him. Mr. Worthy looked at his pocket watch—eleven fifteen. He was a punctual man on his way to a ship whose sailing was dependent on the winds and the tides, already ebbing.

"Don Simón, I apologize that I can't attend you as I would like to—"

"Of course, Mr. Worthy. I'm aware that you're on your way to the *Dafne,* but my wife is most adamant. We hope to visit Hacienda los Gemelos in the near future to pay our respects to our dear Miguel, may he live in glory. Elena, however, is too distraught to travel now."

"I understand. How may I help?"

Don Simón handed him a black velvet pouch. "My wife cannot trust this to anyone else, Mr. Worthy. These jewels belong to doña Ana, who left them with Elena for safekeeping. She imagined that Ana would want Miguel to give them to his future wife, but of course—" He paused. "The jewels should probably go to her other son's . . . Please forgive me, Mr. Worthy. We're still overcome—"

"Thank you for trusting me with this errand. I'll deliver the contents into doña Ana's hands."

"We are most grateful, Mr. Worthy. For this, and for your many courtesies to this family. May God bless you on your journey, *señor. Vaya con Dios.*"

Mr. Worthy placed the pouch inside his briefcase. He wasn't comfortable in the role of courier. When should he deliver the pouch, before or after the reading of the will? The delight that his cherished Provi derived from gems had convinced him that ladies were enchanted by jewels. But in these circumstances?

His valise had been sent ahead, and his cabin prepared with as much comfort as the merchant vessel could afford. At the end of the journey, someone would be waiting with a horse to lead him to El Destino. In spite of his sad mission, Mr. Worthy was looking forward to seeing Ana in person after two decades of correspondence, reports, accounts, and records. What an extraordinary woman! He'd met her only once, in the Argoso home on Calle Paloma. She was just a girl, but even then she conveyed spirit and energy. She'd endured the subsequent tragedies with admirable grace and unswerving vision. He wished that all his clients were like Ana Larragoity de Fuentes.

Mr. Worthy settled in front of the tiny desk in his cabin. He'd brought much work on this trip. His clients did not pay him to be idle. When he reached into his briefcase, his fingers brushed past the crisp envelope, notarized and sealed. He gave himself a moment to feel the heartache of his melancholy task. He'd known Miguel since he was a small child whose drawings and paintings he'd praised because he had to, not because he wanted to, and he wondered if anyone else who'd admired them felt the same way. He scratched a note to make sure an inventory was prepared of what might be left in the house on Calle Paloma and in the crates Miguel had sent ahead from Europe.

If the winds were favorable and the seas calm, Mr. Worthy would be in El Destino in less than a week, reading a will that would change Hacienda los Gemelos forever. All the de Argoso slaves, which now numbered 127, including elders and children, would be freed. Of that number, and according to doña Ana's meticulous annual reports, those old enough to work made up two-thirds of the workforce; the rest were rented from Severo Fuentes.

Mr. Worthy was pleased that the reading of the will would come toward the end of the harvest. They might not be able to plant the additional fifty *cuerdas* doña Ana planned, but the upcoming *tiempo muerto* might give them some time to organize the work for the already on-the-ground 1866 *zafra*. This was surely the biggest challenge doña Ana and don Severo had faced so far: five hundred *cuerdas* of cane to be cut and processed with a nearly nonexistent workforce. How would they do it? Mr. Worthy couldn't imagine, but if it was possible, he knew, those two would do it.

AMEN

———◆———

The ancient *ceiba* tree near Ramón's grave was massive. Its root system had formed cavelike spaces around its trunk, and it was possible to believe, like the *taínos* did, that there was an underworld in the hollows where the souls of the dead were confined during the day and released in the dark of night to walk in the living world. Even though she rode past the site almost every day, Ana hadn't visited the grave since the day Eugenio, Severo, and Luis had dropped shovelfuls of earth over the carved lid of Ramón's coffin. It was a lovely spot, and she imagined that someday she'd be buried here. By then, if Conciencia was right, she'd be an old woman, and the people around her now might have preceded her. Who would carve flowers and leaves, hummingbirds and butterflies, a crucifix with perfectly straight edges and a halo over it like the one José had created for Miguel? Who would stand by her tomb, the moist earth fragrant of humus, promising life? There was Segundo, now but a year old, too young to know about death and sorrow. Would he pray for her?

It was midmorning, too hot for late April. Her black garments drew the sun and heat; the mantilla she'd unfolded from her bride's chest still smelled of cedar and memories. She'd adjusted it to veil her face, like the *sevillanas* of her childhood, a barrier between herself and the men and women, most of them strangers, who'd come to bid Miguel good-bye. Through the fine lace she could see them, but they could not see her dry eyes.

Earlier, as she was dressing, she'd looked in a mirror for the first time in months. She was startled by how time had cast her features into sharp angles. She was thirty-nine years old, the same age at which her long-ago ancestor, don Hernán, had died in Puerto Rico. Where was he buried?

Padre Xavier's incantations rose and fell in waves that drowned the clatter through the cane.

"Requiem aeternam dona eis, Domine."

The Latin prayers were automatic. How many thousands of times had she repeated these phrases, starting with her innocent belief as a child that there was a God who heard every word, saw every action?

Manolo Morales Moreau, his wife, Angustias, and his mother-in-law, Almudena, stood in the shade of the tent Severo had erected for the mourners. Ana had just met them that day and was surprised by their grief, considering that Miguel had spent only a few hours with them. The doctor, who'd arrived with the dawn, too late, was there, as were the lieutenant and two soldiers. One of the men from the militia had also come. Luis Morales Font sat on a specially fixed seat on a cart, his frozen, debauched face in shadows beneath an umbrella held by a boy pulled from the fields.

"Viejo apestoso," Ana couldn't help insulting him mentally, even as the prayers to usher her son toward God's arms dropped from her lips.

Behind her was Conciencia, holding a parasol over her head, and a few steps farther back, José and his two sons, Efraín and Indio, who'd been Miguel's milk brothers, nursed from the same breast, and Teo and Paula, her oldest living house servants, who remembered Miguel as a child. She'd left Segundo at home with Pepita. The rest were at their jobs. The stalks had to be cut, pressed; the juice had to be boiled, limed, and stirred; the sugar granules had to be spread on the purgery tables; the syrup had to be poured into the barrels. The *zafra* could not be postponed, even for the funeral of the young owner of Hacienda los Gemelos.

Below the knoll, the valley stretched vast and open, the purple *guajana* and less mature green fields stained by large brown swatches. Smoke still billowed from the middle of one of the fields, twenty *cuerdas* lost at a cost of tens of thousands of pesos in product and hundreds of hours to restore the land.

"Et lux perpetua luceat eis. Requiescat in pace."

"Amen," repeated the mourners.

Ana gripped Severo's arm as if he were her anchor. There was nothing else, no one else in the world but the two of them, clinging to each other on this land they had claimed and held, that claimed and held them. Don't let go, she said voicelessly, and his green gaze peered through the black veil. He squeezed her hand to let her know it was time to lower Miguel's casket. He led her closer, and she caressed the smooth mahogany as she'd never caressed the living child. I loved you the best way I knew how, but I was far too late, she thought. Not enough, not enough . . . Severo stepped back and Conciencia was at her elbow.

"*Anima eius, et animae omnium fidelium defunctorum . . .*"

The ropes stretched as Severo, Manolo, the lieutenant, and the militiaman lowered the coffin and settled Miguel into the ground.

"*. . . per misericordiam Dei requiescant in pace.*"

The first thud of earth on the lid made her flinch. My son. My poor, dead son. You came, but you did not even have a chance to see what I created. Created on your behalf. A sudden breeze fluttered the mantilla against her cheeks and she turned her face toward the cane. The voices of men and women, of children, of creatures and trees and every living thing whispered a protest. "You did not do it for him; he made this possible for you." But Ana didn't hear.

"*Amen.*"

The immense waving stalks beckoned, drew her from her husband's grave, her son's, from the hollows where the spirits that haunt the living sleep beneath the ceiba tree. There was life beyond the gate where Ramón and Miguel rested. There was life outside the fenced cemetery where Pabla and Fela watched over the slaves who'd toiled for her, beyond José's monument to suffering. There was life in the rich soil she'd nurtured, in the canebrakes, yes, but also in the orchards and gardens, in the vegetable patches and flower beds. There was life in El Destino, where Segundo, her young son, was now only just beginning to stand on his own upon the land he'd inherit. We're all walking on corpses, she thought, but this, too, is life. And she walked beneath the morning sun toward another planting season.

ACKNOWLEDGMENTS

Thank you.

Frank Cantor, my husband, has kept me safe and loved over the three decades plus of our marriage and has designed and built spaces for me and my work.

Lucas and Ila, our children, have filled my life with love, music, conversation, interesting friends, and hope for the future.

Pablo and Ramona Santiago, my parents, grew up in and near sugar haciendas and shared their memories, which helped me envision Hacienda los Gemelos and El Destino.

Molly Friedrich, my agent and friend, has encouraged, supported, protected, and nourished me over two decades and has built my confidence at the same time as she's spoken the hard truths few dare to utter.

Robin Desser, my editor, has asked pointed questions, sent incisive comments and enthusiastic messages, made time for long meetings, made encouraging phone calls, and exchanged many conversations that always left me excited and eager about the work ahead.

Her assistant Sarah Rothbard has been calm, helpful, and professional.

The diligent librarians at the Katonah Public Library have secured every book, essay, catalogue, academic paper, journal, and diary that I requested and needed during the research phase.

Joie Davidow, my good friend, gave me pep talks when the work wasn't going well, read and critiqued several drafts, and gave me a place and time during the final stages.

Silvia Matute, my Spanish editor, *por su apoyo y amistad.*

Members of my writing group—Ben Cheever, Kate Buford,

Marilyn Johnson, Larkin Warren, and Terry Bazes—have heard passages from various drafts during our inspiring meetings. Marilyn has generously postponed her own work to read drafts and to offer discerning suggestions.

John and Susan Scofield have held my hand during difficult times, have made me meals, have understood, valued, and respected the rhythms of my life and work.

Alan and Janis Menken whisked me away to their beautiful *Serena* when I needed a break, space, and time to polish the last draft.

Jaime Manrique, Nina Torres Vidal, and Carmen Dolores Hernández found ways for me to improve, clarify, correct, and enhance the novel. Their close reads have been invaluable.

My sister Norma and her husband, Mario Zapata, lent me their beachfront apartment during the final stages of the writing. Norma died before she could read the pages created on her porch, but her love, laughter, opinions, and sisterly kindnesses continue to enrich my life.

Esmeralda Santiago is the author of the memoirs *When I Was Puerto Rican, Almost a Woman,* which she adapted into a Peabody Award–winning film for PBS's Masterpiece Theatre, and *The Turkish Lover;* the novel *América's Dream;* and a children's book, *A Doll for Navidades.* Her work has appeared in *The New York Times, The Boston Globe,* and *House & Garden,* among other publications, and on NPR's *All Things Considered* and *Morning Edition.* Born in San Juan, Puerto Rico, she currently lives in New York.

A NOTE ON THE TYPE

This book was set in Granjon, a type named in compliment to Robert Granjon, a type cutter and printer active in Antwerp, Lyons, Rome, and Paris from 1523 to 1590.

This version of Granjon was designed by George W. Jones, who based his drawings on a face used by Claude Garamond (ca. 1480–1561) in his beautiful French books. Granjon more closely resembles Garamond's own type than do any of the various modern faces that bear his name.

Composed by
North Market Street Graphics
Lancaster, Pennsylvania

Printed and bound by
Berryville Graphics
Berryville, Virginia

Designed by
Claudia Martinez

ML   7/11